Tri

~ book two ~

KING'S CITY

JESSICA MARINOS

D.I.C.E. Publications

King's City
© 2019 by Jessica Marinos

Published by D.I.C.E. Publications

Printed in the United States of America

ISBN 978-0-9964661-2-7

JessicaMarinos.com

CHARACTER GUIDE

Characters from the Valley of Traiven's Pass

Trimont Family

Royston Trimont—Galen's late great grandfather and ender of the Multa Wars

Amond Trimont—Galen's late grandfather and Lady Vala's late husband

Rhoswen Trimont—Amond's younger sister and Danek's late mother

Lady Vala—Amond's wife and Galen's grandmother

Cloven Trimont (Amos)—Lady Vala's oldest son, Galen's father, and the rightful Steward King of Calderon

Thomas Trimont—Lady Vala's late youngest son and Cloven's late brother

Galen Trimont—Cloven's son (Main Character)

Trimont Castle Servants

Meklon—Sword master and gardener

Netty—Children's maid

Auden—Stable master and Netty's father

Trimont Orphans

Hazel, Haxel (Hazel's twin brother), Badrick, Hollis, Emmy, Cadby, and seven others

Tavish Family

Frederic Tavish — Searcher of the missing King Cordell and Lydia's late father
Ophelia Tavish — Frederic's wife and Lydia's mother
Creighson Tavish — Lydia's eldest brother
Garret Tavish — Lydia's second eldest brother
Lydia Tavish — Frederic and Ophelia's third child (Main Character)
Rose Tavish — Lydia's younger sister

Crevilon Castle

Sir Danek Crevilon — Lord of Crevilon Castle
Faye — Danek's childhood nursemaid
Emerson and Levinia — Elder castle gatekeepers
Alfred — Castle guard

Characters from Dresden

Amos Lukemar (Cloven Trimont) — Galen's father and rightful Steward King of Calderon
Grenfell — Carpenter and Galen's close friend
Helena — Galen's childhood nurse mother
Barley — Grenfell's apprentice

Characters from King's City

King's Castle

King Cordell — Rightful King of Calderon (missing for over twenty-five years)
Lord Breemore — Steward King of Calderon
Captain Rhys — Second-in-command

Remus — Lord Breemore's secret agent
Sir Cantley — King City's master sword teacher
Lady Laila — Sir Cantley's daughter
Sir Langston — Knight
Eldon — Knight
Alene — Children's maid and Lammy's niece
Groana — Children's maid
Destra — Castle guest

Ruins of Lenrow

Sedgwick — Preserver of the Book of Truth

Braun Hendry — Cobbler

Hildie Hendry — Braun's wife

Cote Hendry — Braun and Hildie's only son

Middle Quarters

Crankford and Cranka — Innkeepers

Corsey — Crankford and Cranka's youngest son

Lammy — Poor widow and Alene's aunt

Riggan — Free-spirited roamer and friend to Lammy

Jackson — Responsible for sending out spies to Multa

Characters from the Kingdom of Multa

Seeris — Current ruler of Multa

Lord Marcus — Late ruler of Multa during the Multa Wars

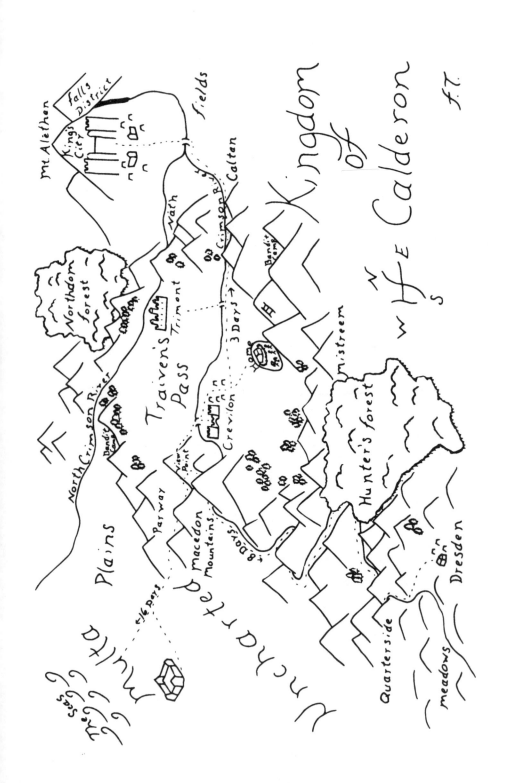

"Through his cunning he shall cause deceit to prosper under his rule."

Daniel 8:25a

Prologue

One lone rock, in one lone hand etched markings into a stone wall. The callous of the hand was unmatched, yet so was its tenderness. In such tenderness, the man sometimes paused, placed his hand upon what he had carved, smiled, and then gravely looked upward. Then the hand and rock would slowly continue on. The man's face sometimes smiled, and, at times, streamed with tears. The sound of his rock scraping against rock became to him a companion. Gravelly, harsh sound it may have been, yet to him, it dispelled the darkness and silence, reminded his eyes of people, and filled his ears with their voices.

Chapter One
~ *Lydia* ~

Trimont Castle

Willing to face my future as a stricken outcast, my bare feet bore my determination as I continued through the Hall of Tapestries. The morning sunlight blessed and kissed my feet each step I took through its bowing rays. I felt shabby for such a triumphant scene. The borrowed, oversized nightgown hung limply on my shoulders, my face was heavy from grief and sleeplessness, and my hair had been trodden down by torrents of rain. Yet my soul was more aglow than when I had walked down Crevilon's aisle as an adorned bride.

Unexpectedly, I shivered as the sunlight vanished. The hall instantly became dull and cold. Where the dust had danced in the beams of light and the huge tapestries displayed their lore, now the flecks disappeared, and the vast row of tapestries loomed in obscurity.

I peered out a window and came face to face with the scouring forehead of a dense cloud.

"Oh, Miss Lydia, you are still here!" Netty exclaimed, suddenly appearing at the end of the hall. Her head tipped in relief, causing her loosely pinned hair to flop to one side as she hastened toward me.

"Forgive me if I disturbed you, miss," she said breathlessly. "When I awoke, you were not there. It frightened me to think I was alone again. I rushed to find you because I couldn't bear the thought that you might have left or might have been taken."

"I would never leave without telling you," I assured her.

Netty lightly gripped my arm. "Please don't leave me at all. I can't be in this castle without the children and Lady Vala. At every corner, I feel as if I'm going to be snatched."

"We will stay together," I promised, and then added as the hall began to brighten once again, "Look, the sun has returned."

"I wish the children had returned," Netty said dolefully.

I opened the window to the softly knocking air, which, having been washed in the night's storm, was ready to revive the earth. The storm's flooding had burrowed scars of erosion, but in the sun, thousands of brilliant droplets nourished the fallen world.

"Are you in hiding?" Netty asked slowly.

"No, I suppose I am free."

"You didn't run away?"

"I was cast away." Able to speak of it now, I explained, "As part of my wedding vows to Danek, I was asked to renounce the Book of Truth, my father, and the rightful King Cordell." My voice wavered. "I could not. At the wedding, I refused him in front of the audience of hundreds. Danek was outraged and took my family as prisoners while rejecting my desperate pleas for the exchange of my life for theirs. He threw me out of Crevilon into the storm. I think he must have known Vala wasn't here. No doubt, he wanted to prove I would gain nothing by standing for truth."

"Oh, Miss Lydia! I am sorry."

"Knowing my family is suffering is the greatest torture.

My mother was frail from her severe illness. Garret's worst fear was being locked up and forgotten. And Rose, so young, will have no life before her. I also worry that Danek separated them in prison like he did when we were his castle servants. Rose will be terrified and Mother vastly worried." My gaze longed for my family far beyond the view out the window.

In the distance, I suddenly realized that a wagon plodded toward Trimont. The memories from the sight of the wagon brought me no kindness, yet I fixedly watched the distant image.

Netty anxiously tugged my arm. "Shouldn't we move away, so we won't be seen?"

I hid myself to the side, but remained peering out. Netty backed behind me, prepared to flee.

"Emerson and Levinia!" I cried. Turning to Netty, I assured, "We are in no danger. Come and meet them. They will have news of my family and be of great comfort. Do you have any proper attire I could wear?"

"Yes, upstairs," she said, already beginning her quick patter toward the stairs. I followed her.

"You can have my best dress," she offered, pulling out a gown from a wardrobe.

"Please save your best dress for yourself."

"I want to give it to you," she persisted.

Seeing it was a greater kindness to accept the gown, I thanked her for such a selfless gift.

Netty smiled and, for my sake, gladly relinquished her hold on the gown.

Having donned the dress, it was far less than the exquisite gowns I'd worn in Crevilon, but I liked the simple elegance as it reminded me of my own clothes. However, the hem dragged on the floor.

When Netty observed me, she voiced disappointedly, "I'm sorry the dress doesn't fit. I will hem it later. For now, I can pull up at the waist and tie it with a wide ribbon."

While she tied the ribbon around my waist, I braided my hair. The motion was embedded into my fingertips, but now I found the motion also had embedded a memory—the memory of Mother nearly dying. This was the first time I had braided my hair since then. The memory was so poignant with the current distress that my hands feebly dropped before the end of my braid was tied. It was likely that Mother would die in prison without me ever seeing her again.

Netty gently took the task upon herself to finish my hair, and then we hastened downstairs. We peered out a window before opening the door to ensure that our visitors were indeed whom I had claimed. The wagon, wet and mud sprayed, was vacant. However, my heart was steadied as I saw Emerson and Levinia crossing over the mudded lane to the castle steps. Netty and I each pulled open one of the front double doors to eagerly receive them.

"Lydia, dear Lydia!" Levinia gasped, "I'm so glad we found you here." Her voice was raspy and capped at a soft volume as if it had worn itself out from worry and deep considerations through a long night. Emerson looked upward in thankful relief. I rushed into their embrace. They also reached their arms to Netty, who timidly stepped within the intimate circle of our desperate greeting.

"I should have thought to come to you this morning," I said, "but my mind has been chained to all that has happened. I have not been able to think of what I ought to do next. But please, do you have news of my family?"

I perceived a grave answer within Emerson and looked up at him until it was spoken. His wispy whitened eyebrows were hard pressed, and his dry cheeks sagged. "No child," he answered. "Danek has secured the castle against entry and will allow no one to appeal to him or visit the prisoners. I think he intends the matter never to be spoken of again. He has acted worse than we thought him capable. I am sorry."

Despair came instantaneously with his answer, but in the same moment, Levinia took my hands within her own and led my focus into her aged, grey-blue eyes. "Lydia," she reassured me. "How you and your family responded at your wedding was beautiful. Truth radiated out of each of you so powerfully that the people of the valley will not be able to ignore what they saw. Your public decision to choose truth over a privileged marriage to a man as wealthy and esteemed as Sir Danek was more effective than you may realize. The people of Traiven's Pass now know that you value truth over all fears of suffering and over all temptations of wealth and position. Once you were gone, I witnessed the light come into so many faces of those who had watched your defense and love of the truth. There will be people turned to the truth because of your family's sacrifice."

I looked down as the swell of my heart gently swept over the shore of my lashes. "Thank you," I whispered, for emotion had weakened my voice. "I..." I could not go on because her encouraging words had so swept through me that I was overwhelmed. At length, I expressed, "I wish my family could also know their suffering is not in vain."

Emerson set his hand on my shoulder. "We have not come without hope for your family. Nonetheless, the fount of this hope is not certain. It will take time and will lay another great burden upon your shoulders."

My eyes sprang up into his. "Whatever the burden, I will bear it, for I will do anything for my family."

"Lydia, the task is greater than for your family alone. You would be bearing a burden for the entire kingdom and that of a fallen man. Will you go to Galen's father?"

Immediately, I understood that he was asking me to go to Dresden to convince Galen's father to reclaim the throne. My body pulsed, yet I could not answer. I had at one time such exalted hopes of this happening, but Galen had forged in my mind a very hard picture of his father.

When I did not answer, Emerson asked, "You do know that Galen's father was discovered to be Cloven Trimont, our true steward king?"

I nodded. "Galen told me."

"This is a shocking request, I know, for Levinia and I felt the same weight when Meklon told us someone must go to Cloven. Allow me to explain how we came to ask you.

"A little after the discovery that Cloven Trimont was indeed alive, Meklon talked with us about the implications. We knew then that someone must go to Dresden to convince Cloven to reclaim the throne as the rightful steward king, but we could come to no conclusion on who should be sent. Thus, we decided not to press an answer but agreed to wait.

"However, when Meklon told us that Breemore had taken the children and that he and Lady Vala were going to King's City to rescue the children, he commissioned us to send someone to Cloven immediately. We were quite at a loss and considered going ourselves, but since your freedom from Danek, it has become evident that you must go, dear Lydia."

My heart beat wildly toward the task. If Cloven returned, it would prove all of Breemore's lies — that he had staged Cloven's death and had stolen the throne. This was the answer to everything: freedom for my family, the return of the children, reinstatement of the Book of Truth, and a continued search for King Cordell. Still, I did not answer. Doubt was as rampant as the hope.

Was Cloven's defiance so strong that I could feel it from here, warning me away? The negative force came from the harsh words Galen had used to describe his father and from fear of my own incapableness to succeed.

I knew I could not refuse to go, but my doubt rather than my willingness was voiced. "How shall I find him and convince him? He hasn't been convinced to return in twenty-five years. How could I ever persuade him otherwise? Galen has described his father as a hard and unapproachable man, not fit to be a king."

Levinia answered softly, "That is why we have not chosen you lightly and have pondered our choice all night. Your very questions prove why it is going to take a special person before Cloven will allow someone near him. Because Meklon and Lady Vala are known to Cloven, he might never give them a chance to speak with him. You are a stranger to him, so he will not know to avoid you, yet you are equipped with all the necessary information to tell him, and you have the connection with his son. You also have a nature that can be a balm to his soul. These are advantages only you possess. You might be the only one he will listen to."

There was nothing more to be spoken. The mission was clear; I was to go. And so I nodded. After a deep breath, I asked, "How am I to travel to Dresden?"

"My father," Netty unexpectedly supplied from her

perch a few steps up.

"Your father?" I questioned.

"Yes, Auden. He has charge of Trimont stables. I will bring him." She suddenly lunged from the steps and dashed to the stables.

"Auden is a good man," Emerson assured. "I would entrust you to his care."

"Shall I leave tomorrow?" I asked as my mind now eagerly took hold of the goal.

Levinia answered, "We intend to stay and help you prepare so that by tomorrow morning we may send you off."

"I am glad of your help and of a hasty departure, for I do not wish to wait a day longer now that I am aware of how I may aid our kingdom."

Netty came back followed by her father, a shy, sincere looking man. "This is my father," she announced. "I explained the situation to him. Says he is willing to take you to Dresden."

Removing his hat and bowing his head, Auden said, "I offer my services in any way which may be useful to you."

Emerson smiled. "That means much to us, Auden."

"Please, may I come as your traveling companion?" Netty asked.

"I would be glad of your companionship," I answered.

Netty exclaimed, "I hadn't known about the discovery of Lady Vala's son being alive! This gives me such hope!"

I discovered through her exclamation that my soul too was lifting. The small taste of hope was warm and sustaining.

"You will take a carriage, of course?" Emerson inquired. Auden nodded.

"Can you have all arranged by tomorrow morning?"

"I shall." Auden slightly bowed and returned to the stables.

"I will help you," Emerson called after him, as he followed.

Levinia asked, "Are there still baking supplies in the castle?"

"The basics," Netty answered, "nothing for a feast."

"That will be sufficient. It is best that we cook simple foods which will last."

As we entered Trimont, Netty said, "I must hem your dress, Miss Lydia, and a second one." She veered to go upstairs but hesitated.

Knowing she would not want to work alone, I suggested, "You could bring your sewing to the kitchen where we can work together."

Netty smiled thankfully and scurried upstairs, not wanting to be out of our company long.

Levinia commented, "It was an awful affliction when Meklon told us of the children, but I feel it more terribly walking through these childless halls."

"Did Meklon tell you of his plans?" I asked.

"He only mentioned that he and Lady Vala must go to King's City, while another goes to Dresden to speak with Cloven."

"What about Galen? Did Meklon say anything of him? If Cloven won't return, Galen is still the rightful heir."

A shadow passed over her thin face, yet she patted my hand. "I'm sure Galen will help."

"But something worries you."

"We all love Galen dearly and store great hope in him, but Meklon is exceedingly worried about him."

"In what way?"

"He believes Galen has been strongly convinced to

11

believe Lord Breemore, and that is why he left suddenly."

I revolted against the suggestion, declaring, "Since the discovery, there could be no possible way Galen could be convinced to trust Breemore again. It is more than evident that Breemore stole the throne from Galen's father and lied about his death. And when Galen learns Breemore took the children, he will clearly see Breemore has evil intent."

"If these facts appear to be that clear then, yes, Galen will see. But as Meklon says, Lord Breemore's power lies in deception."

My body sickened. I didn't want to think Galen possible of being deceived again. He was a Trimont. He knew the truth. There had to be another reason he left so suddenly.

In scrambling to justify Galen's departure, I could only think of the time I had met Breemore not long before the wedding. He had passed Rose and me upon our return from picking strawberries. Unaware of whom he was, I had taken him for a very pleasant man. When his identity was presented, I could not deny how kind he had been. He had so seamlessly explained away the hardships which had been thrust upon my family, that even I had begun to feel swayed to believe him. The only knowledge which kept me assured not to trust him was that he had taken away the Book of Truth, and that was enough to prove that everything he spoke was a lie.

Had Galen so undoubtedly believed in the Book of Truth? I was not certain. If he did not, no matter his good intentions, he would be deceived.

"Don't be disheartened, dear," Levinia encouraged as we entered the kitchen. "When I think of how Galen helped you and your family, he will no doubt do all he can for the children."

That, however, was not my worry concerning him. I gathered flour, oil, and water for baking bread, but I could not break my mind from Galen. It was soothing when Levinia began to hum as she rummaged through the hanging herbs, picking the ones which would be useful. Netty soon joined us. Her arms were full of dresses while a sewing basket swung on her elbow.

She opened her fist to reveal a necklace. "Do you want your necklace?" she asked, handing me the pearl necklace Danek had given me. "It is so beautiful." Then she sat on a low stool and sorted her projects.

Knowing the necklace had belonged to Danek's mother and how much he loved her, I handed it to Levinia and asked, "Will you return this to him? This necklace was his mother's."

She nodded understandingly and gently wrapped the necklace in a handkerchief which she pulled from her apron pocket.

Netty asked, "Now that you don't have to marry Danek, will you marry Galen?"

Surprised by the question and restrained since hearing of Meklon's worry, my answer could not be hopeful. I said slowly, "We may be on different paths."

"You do know that before Galen left, he was making you a gift. Did you receive it? The only reason I know is that I overheard the children talking."

"I never received his gift."

"Oh, Miss Lydia, I'm sorry I spoke of it. Maybe it wasn't my place." She clasped her hands on her lap, sealed her lips as if to discipline them, looked down, and said no more.

"Do you know what the gift was?" I couldn't help asking.

She shook her head.

Had I missed his gift or had he decided not to give it? Either way felt a little distressing. I pressed my palms into the dough where I sank all my weary weight.

Heat and tiredness intensified as the day wore on. Everyone retired early, having planned to leave well before dawn so that the carriage might pass through town unnoticed. I drew the tall curtains closed to force night upon the room which Netty and I shared.

As I lay down, Netty whispered, "Are you frightened?"

I answered, "I have many emotions, and fear is likely one of them."

Netty shuddered. "I've never traveled so far, but my father will take care of us."

I did not voice it, but my concerns extended far beyond our travels.

Through the night, I was trapped in a fog of restless sleep. Words, which Galen had used to describe his father, played through my mind: *stubborn, hard, cruel, a liar*. This was the description of the man whom I was going to for help? Then my mind rose in Cloven's defense. He is a Trimont! He is Vala's son!

I had not resolved these inconsistencies by the time Levinia gently came into the dark room, whispering, "The time has come."

Though the days were hot, the nights were cold. I hurried to dress and donned an old cloak of Vala's which I had sought out yesterday. To be wrapped in a garment, which had partaken of her life, brought her near.

Moaning, Netty also rose.

"You can sleep in the carriage," I whispered, "for eight days."

With provisions having been loaded earlier, there was

nothing to do but say goodbye and board the carriage. Netty entered the carriage first. I stood hooded and slightly shivering before Emerson and Levinia. Levinia held her shawl around her face as she leaned to kiss my cheek. "May the words and strength be given you to break past Cloven's walls. Be safe."

I looked to Emerson for his last advice. He raised the lantern in his hand until it illuminated his face. "Fight for him," he entreated.

It was an appeal I would not forget. "I will," I answered.

He nodded and added earnestly, "We will not stop trying to reach your family and tell them where you have gone for help."

"Please know how grateful I am." I then turned and entered the carriage. Netty took my arm, shivered, and was asleep on my shoulder as we left Trimont.

In need of rest, I closed my eyes, but my soul as well as my body jostled within the carriage. Why had Cloven never returned? What kept him hidden in Dresden? Was he watched by one of Breemore's guards? Would Breemore kill him if he returned? These questions could not be answered before being thrown into the fire of an unknown and an unavoidable meeting.

Chapter Two
~ *Danek* ~

Crevilon Castle

My hand was numb from the dark hours of clutching the carved figure of Lydia which I had found in her room. It was Galen's carving of her, yet he did not know her. The wooden braid was too short, the cheeks too chiseled, and the feet shod. He had never watched a hundred times how she would remove her shoes before a shallow creek or an endless field, lifting the hem of her dress either to gracefully pass from stone to stone or run like a doe. He didn't know the way her cheeks bloomed after she had walked through a grove of golden aspen trees. He didn't know the arch of her brow and the spark of her eyes when she was playful.

I squeezed the carving harder. These haunting hours before dawn whispered dreams that had to be destroyed. I would suffocate her rulership over me! There would come a day when I would not think of her. But the heart knew a lie.

Yet I would prove my will stronger! I yanked open the library window and hurled the carving, cursing the day I first loved her.

Angrily, I turned when a guard entered my library unannounced. His sudden torchlight exposed the dark tomb of my agony. The stench of uneaten food, the stale air of enclosure, and the wretched pallor and red eyes of sleeplessness startled this novice guard.

"Have you never loved?" I chided to his uncomfortable face. "Report and leave me."

He said urgently, "A Trimont carriage is leaving the valley westward."

My heart pounding against my will at the speculation of Lydia's whereabouts, I pushed past him and ran to the bridge. The torchlight I had commanded to be lit at all entrances granted my eyes the last sight of the carriage before it disappeared into the hovering darkness.

I slapped the stone railing as the night chill whipped through my unlaced shirt. Still, my impulse yearned to woo her.

Hardening my jaw, I turned my back. I possessed no grounds to follow nor cared where she went. I possessed her family; she possessed my heart. We were equal thieves from one another.

Only then did I realize I was watched. A wagon sat in the shadows of the town edge, occupied by two people. One helped the other down, and together they advanced toward me. When I perceived it was the old gatekeeper, Emerson with his wife, I turned from them to stare into the fiery reflection of the torches in the Crimson River. They would not find favor in this direction. Though they had known me since my boyhood and had been my example of eternal love, they were a fortress around Lydia's decision to reject me.

When they were near enough, I challenged without facing them, "Where have you sent her?"

Emerson answered, "If you force us to answer, we will tell you, but if you stay true to your declaration, you have no right to know."

I turned a sharp eye on him, but spoke nothing.

"We have come to give you something," Emerson continued.

I laughed. "Your gifts could not be to my liking."

"That is only because you have yet to taste it."

"I have no stomach to taste."

"Perhaps you only need to read," Levinia said, handing me a sealed letter. "Lady Vala left this for you." Levinia also handed me a handkerchief. "Lydia knew how much you loved your mother. She wanted this returned to you."

I fisted both in my hand. As they did not leave promptly, I cut past them and returned to my library.

Folded within Lady Vala's letter I found a key. The letter read:

My Dearest Nephew,
In Trimont's top tower there is a chest of items which belonged to your mother. See them as your own. I believe you will make the connection.

I extinguished the flame and flung my cloak over my shoulders. "Ready my horse," I commanded the first guard I passed down the corridor.

A stable boy led my saddled stallion from the stables when I arrived.

As I mounted, the boy asked, "Will the Tavishes be locked up forever, sir?"

Without answer, I yanked the reins from his hand and rode to Trimont.

Dawn broke overhead, but my face remained grim as I dismounted before the castle. Trimont revealed no response to my presence. The curtains were drawn, giving the castle the appearance of a dormant face. Having been given a key and seeing the signs of abandonment, I did not knock. My steps echoed as I determinedly sought the stairs, for only the tower had beckoned me here.

Warmth rose as I ascended. I loosened my cloak and let it fall to the stairs behind me while I continued climbing unencumbered. At the top, I entered a round room. Windows encircled the walls as to capture any passing beauty and flaunt Trimont's choice land. A vein of envy shot through my eyes that partook of the view Trimont owned. Gardens, fields, rivers, forests, mountains, sky, and Lydia — Trimont possessed them all.

The few furnishings made the room seem not neglected, but it was apparent the items had not known human touch for over a decade. The ornate chair had been placed beyond the sun's reach, so its rich colors were preserved. Likewise the harp and large chest were safely situated. However, the rugged walls and faded rug had taken the daily whitewashings of the sun.

I slowly touched each precious belonging of my mother's. Kneeling before the chest, I caressed her engraved name, *Rhoswen Trimont*, and the carved roses enclosing it. The smell, as I lifted its cedar top, carried me into my mother's arms. Beautiful gowns of silk and fur lay folded on top. I buried my face in the place I knew I had been loved.

When I had drunk my fill of her scent, I dug beneath the gowns. I found nothing but a wooden box with a broken lock. Inside laid a beautiful dagger forged in Multa. The blade curved in deathly perfection, a costly pearl was inlaid in the hilt, and an inscription read: *Lord of War*.

The dagger was a thrill of suspense in my hand. But I laid it aside for a greater find, for beneath the dagger were letters written in my mother's hand.

My Own Dearest Bree,
I love you; I love you! Please come back. I'll leave them
for you. I'll follow you anywhere. I hate them now.
After what they did to you... to us. Why should we
let them separate us? Why have you left? I wait for
you every day in our circle in the woods.

Always, Your Crimson Rose

My gaze leapt to the next letter:

I've left them. I couldn't stand to be there. Not when
they hate you so. Now I'm destitute and have nowhere
to go. It looks as though it will rain tonight. I have
nothing but my cloak and the overhang of branches. I
imagine your strong arms around me and your perfect
dark eyes and black locks gazing over me. Bree, don't
you see, my only hope is that you will come back for
me. I've left them for you; don't you see how much
I love you? Even now I clasp the pearl necklace you
gave me and hold it to my heart.

The third letter read:

I'm sick. I fear I may die. Lord Simon Crevilon has
found me and offered to help me. I believe he is in love
with me. I have no choice. I must go to him or die. His
love is living while yours is dead.
You won't come back, will you? You did love Multa
more than me. I see that now. Farewell, my Bree.

I grabbed for another letter, but there was none. Did
I need more? Was not the connection Lady Vala spoke

of clear? Bree was Lord Breemore. My mother's love for him is what severed her from Trimont. Her family must have objected to the match because of his ties to Multa. For the first time I understood why my mother had married my father.

Trimont had concealed the missing knowledge of my mother that I sought all these years! Why tell me now? Of course, it was to convert me!

I took the dagger in hand as I moved to the chair where I smelled a musty waft of perfume. Lady Vala was using this to force me to consider the charges Trimont had always laid against Lord Breemore. I could not deny the proof was persuasive as well as riling. Linked to my prior knowledge of Lord Breemore having staged the death of Cloven Trimont, I had no defense for Lord Breemore except that I believed all things should be tested.

Perhaps all Lord Breemore desired was power, and now that he reigned, all was well. This box was thirty years in the past, dead and buried. However, that he had chosen Multa over my mother, demonstrated that he had an infinitely deep tie to our enemy.

So then, what did this bespeak of the Trimonts? If it had been known to them that a man so faithful to Multa was in our midst, why had he been allowed to roam free? Trimont's loyal vow was to protect against such entrances of the enemy. They distrusted Lord Breemore now, but what if, in the beginning, they had allowed him in?

Mysteries had risen from that buried box which I could not stuff back in.

Chapter Three
~ *Galen* ~

King's Castle in King's City

Alone, I stood at the edge of a high castle terrace. The towers above were lost in the misty clouds, seeming to have gone to receive counsel with the divine. A sheer cliff dropped below. Wind shook the mountain trees, heralding the fiercer rain and thunder to come.

I squinted against the mist that blew in my eyes as I sought to see the road far below. It had been announced that Lord Breemore would return today. I had quickly learned that I could do little without his intervention on my behalf.

King's City was so full and clamorous that one new face did not so much as stir a pigeon. I felt as if I had slipped into the King's Castle as a gnat—unnoticed and free to roam as I wished.

Fine dinners and gatherings were abundant, but in the company of rival lords and knights who drank themselves into more noise and absurdity, they were hard to endure when my heart longed for the dear and innocent conversational dinners with the children.

Likewise, sparring and swordplay was a constant racket clanging out of the arena, but I had neither entrance with the knights nor heart to join. The hours Meklon and I had trained together became invaluable to me. Every morning I practiced what Meklon had taught me in the solitude of the mountain trails. I read his books and the Book of Truth.

Through all of this, however, all I had gained was regret. I should have told Vala and Meklon all Lord Breemore had revealed about my father. And I should have waited to speak with Lydia. Exhaling, I straightened myself after leaning upon the railing.

I often visited this lonely terrace, gazing upon the distant beauty. The city was magnificent. Nestled much lower than the heights of the castle, the city seemed to be the castle's adorned footstool and the farther outlying villages and farms its honored servants. Just now ruler and servant were separated from one another by the heavy mist that lay between.

The trumpets blared as three carriages and several horsemen entered the gates. Already wet from the intensifying rain, I took the outer roughhewn steps down to the castle entrance which then led to the grander staircase of marble.

I converged with Captain Rhys, also descending the steps to meet Lord Breemore.

"Our mysterious castle guest," Rhys greeted. "I'm glad you found it expedient to meet His Lordship even though you do not indulge the rest of the castle's curiosity."

"I'm here for the tournament," I replied, quickening my pace to pass him.

The rain's pulse quickened. The horsemen looked alike in their dark hoods, but I perceived Breemore as he dismounted. He motioned for me to come near.

He called loudly over the rain, "The children are in the carriages, help them into the castle."

I did not know what he meant by children, but the

moment I looked back and saw Hazel looking out from behind the carriage curtain, I rushed to the carriage.

"Galen!" she cried and threw her arms around my neck. As the rain now pelted her, I didn't have time to question.

"Hand me Emmy." I reached for her from Badrick's arms. I held Hazel in one arm and Emmy in the other. Badrick and Haxel quickly exited, but Cadby sat frozen in the corner.

"It is safe, Cadby," I spoke to him. "I will make sure no one hurts you. Come walk beside me."

Tears began filling his eyes as he inched across the bench and stepped down from the carriage, nearly falling as he kept both his hands in his pockets.

Guards helped the other children out of the carriages, but instead of climbing the stairs to get out of the rain, the children huddled and shivered around me like I was their greater shelter.

"Hurry, up these steps," I directed. Together we ran.

The entry hall was flocked with gentry. Instantly, the children and I became the object of their observation and comment. The children froze as frightened animals.

Lord Breemore entered with Captain Rhys and commanded, "Light a blazing fire in the east music room for these poor children, and take them to be dried and clothed."

"Don't take me!" Hazel shrieked as a young nursemaid came to remove her from my arms.

Seeing that Hazel was truly frightened, I said to the maid, "I'll take the children if you will lead me."

The maid smiled understandingly, turned, and led the way.

"Hazel, can you tell me what happened?" I asked, my heart pounding with worry.

She looked at me and tried to speak, then shook her head and buried it on my shoulder.

"Badrick, tell me what happened."

"Breemore stole us. You never should have left."

His answer pierced me. I found I could speak no more, for my conscience readily accused me.

The maid stopped us at a closed door, gently advising me, "It may be best if you leave the children here with me so that they may be dried and clothed. When I have done so, I will bring them to the music room where you may spend the evening with them."

I stooped to set down the two girls. "Go with her, and dry yourselves. I promise I'll be waiting in the music room."

The maid kindly took the hand of Hazel and Emmy, saying to the children, "My name is Alene, and I was just as frightened as you when I first came to King's Castle. But it is only scary at first because this castle is so big. Once you know the castle, you will be whistling down the halls like this." She began a cheery tune.

"Thank you," I mouthed before I left, comforted that they were left in kind hands.

My attention was then aimed at Lord Breemore as I marched back to the entry hall to demand an explanation from him.

Though he was engaged in conversation, I brashly interrupted. "Why did you take the children from Trimont?"

Captain Rhys stared indignantly.

"Excuse me," Lord Breemore eloquently addressed his audience, "I must attend to this man's question." Breemore walked aside with me, speaking sternly. "You must learn decorum, Galen."

"I will only be civil when the injustice made against the children and Lady Vala is made right."

Breemore's face softened. "Walk with me, Galen, and I will explain. I knew this was a decision you may not agree with, but I had to think of what was best for these children just as I have always kept in mind what was best for you."

"My case is different. Duty is involved. The children's home is Trimont. They were happy, loved, and cared for. I must demand that you return them."

"Galen, don't think me heartless. You know my good intentions better than anyone else in this castle. I do understand your feelings, but you must think of the children's future. If they stayed at Trimont they would have no place in society. Lady Vala won't live forever."

"I will inherit Trimont," I stated.

"But you yourself will dwell in King's City as you will be steward king. Do not forget why you have come. Would you not rather have the children here with you than alone at Trimont? Since it is inevitable that they will make the transition eventually, I thought it best that they move during the same time as you, so that you may help one another bear the pains of change. The children will live here in the castle with every advantage of noble connection and grow to be beloved ladies and renowned knights."

"What of Lady Vala and Meklon?" I challenged. "They aren't dead yet if having the children taken didn't kill them."

"I believe in time they will forgive me, when they see the children come to no harm and you come to your rightful place. I hope you will forgive me. You do see my reasons, hmm?"

I nodded stiffly but did not look at him. "I must return to the children," I said, leaving him.

The confusion I thought I had been freed from rushed back. I could not fault Breemore's logic, yet I adamantly refused it. I knew what this place was like. It wasn't right for the children; it wasn't right for me. But how could I defend my feelings when duty and logic upheld Breemore's words?

I hurried to my room, changed from my wet clothes, and walked to the east music room.

Unexpectedly, I found Breemore alone there. He stood before a newly birthed fire.

"Galen, your words caused me regret. Perhaps I was a bit hasty. I still firmly believe the city is the place for the children as they grow. However, I now see it was abrupt of me to have taken them from Lady Vala, who has been so good to them all these years. I, therefore, want you to invite Lady Vala to King's City. She may stay at the castle for as long as she wishes, for truly it is her rightful home as much as it is yours. My only other desire is that you meet me tomorrow morning in my private dining chamber to talk of other matters."

"What of Meklon?" I asked.

Breemore winced ever so slightly. "You may invite him too."

Hearing the children approaching, Lord Breemore took his leave.

Breemore and Meklon in the same castle... I could not imagine it. Nonetheless, I would write them.

The children entered, appearing to have been calmed. Curiously, they looked around and plucked the strings of lutes and harps.

"This castle is so grand," Hollis marveled, her gaze

sweeping over the painted ceiling.

"It's still a prison," Badrick stated.

Haxel asked, "Why were we taken?"

"Didn't you listen," Hollis scolded, "It was for our good. We have to grow up sometime."

"But I was growing just fine," Haxel replied. "I believe at least six inches since I was at Trimont. I feel as if I will stop growing here."

Hazel tugged my hand. "Galen, is Breemore bad or good?"

Her eyes pled to understand. She was in the same dilemma as I. Not wanting to worry her further, I answered, "I believe he thinks differently than we do, but I do not think he means you harm. I will watch over all of you. You do not need to be afraid."

Many of the children sat on the rug spread before the fire. However, I saw that Cadby had slipped behind a curtain draped over a large window where the storm still fiercely kicked.

I sat next to him and pulled the curtain around us both.

"Cadby, this isn't your fault. I let this happen. I should have never left."

He continued to sit with so much stuffed inside him — an entire storm of feeling with no outlet.

"Did you get my note?" I asked.

His hand bulged within his pocket; I knew it indicated the note was held tight within his small fist.

I expressed, "It's true, every word."

When there was no response from him, I leaned my head against the window. Was I shaping up to be no better than my father? No, please, no.

Chapter Four
~ *Galen* ~

The restless night was a beast to my conscience. I had stuffed into the night so many conflicts about Breemore and worries concerning the children that the heaviness of my thoughts must have clouded the sun, for only a dull sunless morning slowly dawned.

Light enough to see the shadow of things, I rose, dressed, and grabbed from the desk the letter I had written last night to Vala and Meklon.

After tucking the letter in my boot, I dug through my saddlebag in search of the parchment Vala had given me before I left Trimont. Perhaps the man she had asked me to visit could reveal information about Lord Breemore and know of a safe means by which I could send my letter to Vala and Meklon.

As I dug, I carefully avoided the emerald ring—its destiny for Lydia having been shattered. It was Danek's ring that would forever rest upon her finger. I shook my head to dispel the distasteful image.

Harsher with the last items I handled, I found the small parchment and memorized its words: *Sedgwick at the Ruins of Lenrow.*

The name Sedgwick lingered in my mind from some distant conversation, but I could not remember who had spoken of him or what they had said concerning him.

At my earliest opportunity, I would seek Sedgwick. First, however, I desired to inquire after the children's first night and fulfill my obligation to speak with Lord Breemore.

The corridors at this early hour belonged to the servants who prepared the day for the gentry. Candles were being lit in dark hallways, baskets of linens were carried either downstairs to be washed or upstairs to be worn, and breakfast trays were carried to those gentry who had called for them.

The same sunless morning deadened the music room where I would wait to hear of the children. As I walked the long length of the room, I could distinguish the furnishings, but their luster and designed glory were hidden in the dull hue.

An elderly maid entered with a candlestick in hand. She saw me but, without acknowledgement, went about her work of lighting the room.

After I'd watched three or four candles being lit, I asked, "Do you know how the children fared their first night?"

Her small stature rose with dignity as she began speaking from a self-pitying mind. "Disheveling to an old woman who needs a peaceful night's rest. My, they cried! Some didn't want to be left alone, and others were afraid of everyone. That poor nursemaid, Alene! She stayed up with them all night. They are waking now, so the weariness begins all over again. Did anyone consider that our workload would be tripled by these children coming?"

Upset by the children's suffering and surprised by the strong, whiny voice that piped from the little woman, I defended, "You must understand the children have been taken from their home! I promise you they are well behaved and will do their share of the work once they have adjusted. But they are frightened."

"I suppose; I suppose," the woman huffed dryly. "But it might collapse my poor bones."

She blew out her candlestick and departed before having completed her task.

Vala would have better known what to say to sooth the old woman. I had merely blurted out my feelings and turned her away.

Observing a writing table in one corner, I wrote a note to the children.

Early this morning, I came to see you but learned you were still in bed. I thought about each of you throughout the night. I am certain so did Lady Vala and Meklon. Even at night, you are constantly remembered and protected. Duties call me away this morning, but I will return in the evening to see you. Remember to be kind to the maids.

I left the note on the rug before the hearth where the children would be sure to see it. I then made the long journey to the other wing of the castle.

"I'm here to see Lord Breemore as he requested," I conveyed to the guard who blocked any further entry.

"I shall announce your presence. Wait here."

When the guard returned, he bid, "This way. His Lordship says you may join him for breakfast."

He led me to Lord Breemore's private dining chamber from where Lord Breemore confidently greeted, "Good morning, Galen. I was not expecting you so early, but there is plenty. Please, sit and eat."

The round table where I joined Breemore perfectly filled a small curved recess of stained glass windows which the sun now shone through, sailing colors into the room.

Breemore expressed, "I tell you, I've immensely enjoyed this morning after so long an absence from home. Nonetheless, the journey was worth it, for the sun is shining, here you are, and the children are with us."

As the sun warmed my back and I ate of the moist pheasant and sweet porridge, I felt myself melting into contentment. I admitted, "I have been glad to see the children. I had missed them greatly."

Breemore gently smiled. "And now are you ready to begin your training? I did promise you the city's best trainer and that would be Sir Cantley."

"What of Meklon?" I asked.

Breemore answered, "When Meklon arrives, he may again take charge over your training."

Seeing no particular danger to begin training under Sir Cantley, I complied.

"Good," Breemore affirmed. "We need you ready for the first scrimmage, which I'm arranging during the harvest. That doesn't give you more than two fortnights."

"At times, may Badrick, Haxel, and Cadby be allowed to watch my training?"

Breemore chuckled. "Sir Cantley may grumble, but I shall heartily allow it. After we have breakfasted, I shall take you to him."

"I have a question," I began, changing the subject to one which I had pondered through the night as a means to corner Breemore. "I never grew up learning of the Book of Truth and only first heard of it when I was brought to Trimont. What are your thoughts on the Book of Truth?"

Breemore smiled, "I know the Book of Truth quite well. Unlike you, I did grow up learning it. As a boy, its teachings and history enraptured me. But then I began to see it as very narrow. To believe one source is the truth for all people began to seem unkind to me. People are so unique and special. They should be free to do and think as they please. When I began to rule, I didn't want this kingdom to become stuck in an old rut while other kingdoms surpassed us. That is why I made the decision to get rid of the Book of Truth in the kingdom. It was hard for some people, but King's City has been better for it. I think the people feel freed of a burden which had locked them down for generations. And that is why I think they fought so hard against Frederic Tavish. They saw him as a threat against my rule and a threat against their newfound peace and freedom."

I asked perhaps too quickly, "Are you against the people who do believe in it?"

"No, no, as I said, everyone has a right to what they choose to believe. I simply believe freedom should be the rule of law and not one truth. I have always acted in accordance with this rule, and the kingdom has thrived in peace for twenty-five years, which is another part of the tournament — to celebrate peace."

"What would you say if my intention was ever to restore the Book of Truth?"

Breemore blinked. "Well, Galen, it would not be according to my own judgment, but I would respect your rulership because I know you are a noble man. I might advise that you first consider all people in their uniqueness. Take into consideration that believing in one truth means the exclusion of all other ways."

As I looked at his earnest half smile and sympathetic eyes, I saw and heard from him nothing to condemn.

Breemore added, "I don't expect us to agree, and your ideas may sometimes be better than mine. I'll listen if you express your concerns and insights as you did yesterday when I saw I was wrong to have taken the children from Lady Vala.

"What I want you to know most of all is that you are heir, and it is my pleasure and duty to see to it that you are given your birthright whether we agree or not. I believe if we are both kind, understanding men, it does not so much matter about our beliefs."

I nodded as his ending words enforced what I had desired all along — that both Breemore and Trimont could be right. However, after our exchanged agreements, I wondered if I was being a traitor to my own Trimont blood which pulsed hot within me.

I set my fork down while food remained on my plate. Breemore dabbed the corners of his mouth with the linen, then rejoined, "Shall we go to the armory?"

Not able to think of an excuse to delay training for a day or two, I rose with him.

Men already in training crowded the armory. Though the ceilings were tall and the doors open, the fresh air was absorbed by heavy breathing and profuse sweating. As we cut through the dueling pairs, Lord Breemore pointed out Sir Cantley.

Instant resistance rose within me, for Sir Cantley's bearing and actions resembled a perfect mixture of Danek and my father. His accomplished refinement, stern back, unaccepting eyes, and fierce expectations brought back unpleasant memories.

Sir Cantley stood in an unflinching posture of scrutiny. He held his gloved hands behind his back as his steely eyes, like needle points, mercilessly stabbed the imperfections of his swordsmen's maneuvers.

I stepped back not wanting to entangle myself with

such a man. But Lord Breemore spoke, again drawing me near to hear him. "You will have to prove yourself to Sir Cantley, but I do not doubt that you will."

I had no intention of trying. I knew such men could not be pleased.

When the fighting match ended, Sir Cantley addressed the victim. "You delay your movements and waste your eyes by looking at your sword instead of at your opponent's. Rectify these errors."

To the gloating victor, he sharply discouraged, "You did not win on your own merit. Your opponent was a bumbler."

Sir Cantley then turning an unapproachable back upon them, coldly acknowledged our presence. "My lord, I see you bring me the stranger. What could you possibly want me to do with him?"

Lord Breemore laughed. "You claimed you would train the victor of the tournament, did you not?"

"Sir Langston will be that man."

"Perhaps, but before you decide, I want you to begin training Galen. I found him in Dresden and see great potential in him."

"As you wish, my lord," Sir Cantley assented, but merely to dismiss rather than to accept the task.

Regardless, Breemore was satisfied. "Very good. Now I shall leave you both to begin your work. Galen, I leave you in Sir Cantley's skilled hands. And, Sir Cantley, I give you a champion."

Neither of us looked at the other until Breemore departed. Then Sir Cantley's superior refinement cast its eye over my rugged, raw form. "My daughter has mentioned you," he said. "She too thinks I ought to train you for the tournament, but I see nothing in a man until he possesses complete mastery over himself and his weapon. Choose a sword."

Not expecting that I would impress him, for neither of us seemed capable of impressing the other, I walked to the sword rack. A stick leaned against the far side where the inferior swords collected and rusted. I considered choosing the stick for Meklon's sake and took hold of it, surprised that my hands formed a grip that was all too familiar. I examined the stick closer. This was Meklon's stick! I smiled and swung it around like an old friend. This had to mean that Meklon was in King's City, and placing his stick here was his secret way of telling me so. I should have known that he would come on his own accord.

Assuming Meklon waited somewhere nearby, my eyes excitedly searched over the armory for sight of him before I remembered I was being watched. I quickly returned the stick, chose a sword, and returned to Sir Cantley.

"Eldon, come here," Sir Cantley demanded of the man who had lost the prior match. "Spar with this new man." Sir Cantley gestured to me.

Not knowing their methods and distracted by watching for Meklon, the man easily pinned my throat.

"Eldon, teach him how to properly swing his sword," Sir Cantley presumed without so much as a look at me before moving on to censure another pair of swordsmen.

Having not anticipated any greater response, I followed Eldon's orders but focused on finding Meklon.

"You do not wear out easily," Eldon heavily exhaled some hours later. "Go there to the water barrel. I need a drink."

As we drank, a woman approached me. "I am Sir Cantley's daughter, Lady Laila," she informed without the warmth of smile.

"I'm Galen," I introduced, slightly bowing.

She was as tall and refined as her father, with exceptionally regal tresses of black hair. Her serious eyes were large and deep as if they looked out from a locked tower of contemplations.

Eldon warned, "Ignore her. She speaks spitefully. It's hard enough to take her father's verbal assaults; I won't begin to accept insults from a woman."

She replied, "As you can see, I am not liked among the men. They find me too dry and honest with them. But that is not what I've come to say. I've been watching you since you arrived at the castle. I want you to be the victor of the tournament. I've come to ask you to try. You are clearly not trying."

"Why do you want me to win?"

She answered without a flinch in her direct gaze, "I've watched men my entire life. Few if any impress me. However, you have astonished me. I want you to win because I believe you are worthy of the honor."

Stunned by her praise, I spoke the only answer left to my mind. "I will try."

Eldon dumped his ladle and stood. "Don't let her bewitch you, man! Back to work."

This round, I focused and triumphed over Eldon. As I continued to surpass him try after try, his eyes turned vicious and his face red. At length, he snagged my sword and declared, "That is enough for one day."

Glad to hear it, I allowed him to take my sword without objection. I glanced to where Lady Laila had been, but she had vanished. She seemed to match her father in hard scrutiny, but she searched the internal side of a man. I was humbled and honored that I had passed her scrutiny and thankful that she had offered her thoughts to encourage me.

Though now free of obligation, I took no further time to wonder about her and quickly left the armory, anxious to find Meklon.

Exiting into the fresh air of the open arena, I scanned the immense space. The ground, skimmed with a muddy slime, was bright as it reflected the sun. The place being barren, I left the arena through the outer gate and walked around its exterior.

"I'm here, Galen," Meklon called, stepping from under a bridge.

His wrinkled cheeks and whiskered chin appeared beneath the brim of his floppy hat. Though old and weary, he was yet a shield, and King's City felt a stronger place for having him within it. I hurried to him and was about to speak my gladness at seeing him when he raised his hand to prevent me.

"I know," he acknowledged, "but there is no time. Follow me."

Immediately, he passed under the bridge and beyond. I followed him into the current of busy roads and through the market crowds. I had to keep my eyes constantly on the tip of his hat, or I would have lost him. People shoved on all sides, and I had to press to pass through them. It seemed to be my lot to follow Meklon without knowing where he took me.

Gradually, we came into an area where there were fewer people. I caught up to him for he slowed, heavy of breath. He began to explain, "Vala and I came for the children. I don't know what Breemore told you, but they were forcibly taken from Trimont."

"I've seen and spoken with the children," I assured. "I

know what happened. At present the children are well and safe in the castle."

"Good, because something else demands our attention at this time. We arrived at the Ruins of Lenrow to find that Sedgwick is dying." Meklon's own words spurred him for he quickened his pace as he kept explaining in short, breathy sentences. "We should have guessed it. He is over a century old. It grieves us nonetheless. He was King Cordell's scribe. He foresaw things Vala and I did not."

Meklon stopped to take a deep breath before going on. "Sedgwick has been a part of your life more than you realize. It was he who crowned your father steward king and commissioned Lydia's father to search for King Cordell. And whether you accept it or not, his secret work these past twenty-five years will impact your future. His dying wish is to see you, and I believe you must see him. That is why we must hurry."

Pressed by the guilt that I should have gone to Sedgwick sooner, I asked anxiously, "How much further to Lenrow?"

"Up this way," he motioned, and again we quickened our pace.

The city scape changed as homes and buildings were built up on the mountain. Roads became sloped, and every next road was at a higher level. There were stairs to some places which wagons could never reach.

The higher we climbed, the less suitable living conditions became. Children became abundant in the streets and ran past us frequently. Homes became hovels. Clear roads turned into ravines. Clothes which hung on laundry lines looked spoiled and shabby. The place reminded me of a mother who'd borne so many children, she could no longer handle them and had given up and sat emotionless and blank as the world below passed her by.

"These desolate conditions did not exist when King Cordell ruled," Meklon sadly commented as we passed through.

When it seemed we had climbed entirely out of human habitation and tramped along an abandoned road which hugged the mountain on one side and dropped to a cliff on the other, we suddenly came to an open alcove of ruins where a large area of the mountain had been hewn and built into. Homes and entryways into the mountain formed a half circle and a big central courtyard extended to the edge of the cliff. Where the mountain hung over the alcove, it was braced by thick beams, which in their day would have been mighty arms of strength but now slumped under the weight.

The homes were made of wood and stone — bathed with the filth of decades. A few trees grew in the courtyard but were dull in color and stunted in growth. The vast view was of an endless forest. Faded into the stone were symbols and intricate designs — the Trimont symbol among them. I felt as if my forefathers had accomplished great feats here. Their fragrance remained because the place was untouched by intruders.

To the far side where Meklon led us, there were signs of unobtrusive living. A cow was tethered to a tree from which a child's swing hung, chickens pecked a sparse spread of grass, and a small garden struggled to grow. Clothes on the laundry line flapped. The wind never long left its home in the heights. There was a bench from where one could sit to admire the view.

Meklon informed, "The only ones who live here now

are the Hendrys: Braun, his wife Hildie, and their son Cote. The three of them take care of Sedgwick. They are trustworthy and have been told everything. You need not worry what you say around them."

We entered their home which was filled with un-mended shoes and cobbler tools. I would have taken it for a workshop except for the womanly touches of a tablecloth, curtains, vase of flowers, and the smell of freshly baked bread which sat in three loaves on the table. The hearth was unusually large and drew my attention as Meklon ducked into it, stepped beside the dying coals, and opened the back wall of warmed stone.

I should not have been surprised, but I was amazed and glad to learn King's City, too, had its secrets.

I followed him through the hidden door into a much taller and wider tunnel. I judged the tunnel to be about twelve feet tall and seven feet wide. Every twenty feet there were arches made of carved pillars. Bright lanterns hung at each pillar, illuminating that the walls, floor, and ceiling were all made of smoothed stone.

"These were not tunnels made for common passage, were they?" I questioned, trying to prompt Meklon to speak of its secrets.

"No," is all he answered.

I heard an echo and stopped.

"It is Braun." Meklon lowered his voice, "I hope we are not too late."

Braun, who had the intensity and stance of an ancient bodyguard, met us in the tunnel. I was actually intimidated by him, for he looked to be twice my strength and very stern. But he exhaled when he saw me, and his whole countenance changed. He greeted, "You are most welcome, Galen Trimont. Master Sedgwick is this way. Hurry."

He led us through a room brightened by natural light, which entered from a row of windows that gave sight to the high open mountainside. The ceiling was highly domed and painted with faded images. The stone walls were carved into shelves, each completely filled with bound parchments. A desk sat in the middle as if it were a throne to which the numerous books bowed.

We entered a small, plain room where Braun's wife and son stood at the foot of the deathbed while Vala sat at the bedside, holding the withered hand. I couldn't tell if he still lived, so I silently knelt at the bedside opposite of Vala and waited.

Blankets were bundled around him, and his head lay on a soft pillow. It was clear that he was loved and cared for. I had imagined a scene like that of finding Lydia's mother. I was relieved to find it not so. He looked peaceful and somehow not as old as I expected him to look. He was heavily wrinkled, but he still had much of his white hair which had been neatly combed.

Vala looked at me from over the quiet body which lay between us. She gently stroked the hundred year old hand, softly whispering, "My grandson is here."

Sedgwick's eyes struggled to open, but the weight of sight was too great for his waned strength.

Vala, therefore, lifted his hand and placed it upon mine. I didn't dare move as I watched and felt his ancient and ink stained fingers slowly travel across my hand. Though his eyes never lay upon me, I felt overwhelmingly known and loved. Suddenly, the slow, choppy movements of his hand stopped, and the full weight of the hand lay motionless over mine. As I heard the tears behind me, my own were formed.

I did not move the dead weight of his hand, for it had felt like a last anointing which I had no right to remove.

Suddenly, the boy hugged me. His voice buried in my shoulder, he said, "You will be the one to give the Book of Truth to the people and find King Cordell."

Engulfed in the intimacy of the circumstance, I was not startled by the eager affection and assurance of the boy and held him with my free arm.

"You are right, Cotey," his mother encouraged. "Papa Wick died smiling."

Her words lifted my gaze to his silent face. Indeed a smile had been captured upon it forever. In that moment, I gained an insatiable desire to know what he had known.

I asked, "Have you long known Sedgwick?"

The boy's mother wiped her tears with her apron as she shared, "When I was just a wee girl of eight, Sedgwick came to our well for daily water. By and by, we came to know one another, and several years later he trusted me with his secret. When Braun and I married, we made our home up here in the ruins with him. He taught the three of us to read and showed us the joyful life of the Book of Truth. We took care of his body, while he took care of our souls. He will always be our beloved and missed Papa Wick."

I confessed, "I know it is impossible, for I only knew him for a moment, but I feel the same." I then turned my eyes on Vala, who had been softly watching me. "Are you all right?" I asked.

"I feel both the sorrow of his loss and the strength of his trust. In my younger days, he helped me through the dark time after Amond died. He believed in the Book of Truth so greatly that merely his trust in it strengthened me. What I see lingering on his face even now is his same timeless trust in the Book of Truth. He once told me that to doubt it was to believe a lie."

Though beautiful, her words stung because of the sharp remembrance of my agreement with Lord Breemore that his beliefs and the Book of Truth could both be right.

I turned to Meklon, but he was no longer behind me. In the distance, he had retreated into the larger room and sat in a chair where he faced toward the windows.

"Lady Vala is right," Hildie asserted, stepping nearer the body from her husband's side. "And you need to know what an extraordinary gift Sedgwick has left to you and the kingdom."

I stepped away from the deceased body as she kissed the silenced brow and covered Sedgwick's face. She whispered, "Your countenance is captured within us."

"Come," she beckoned, leading us to the larger room. She stopped at the desk and momentarily set both her hands upon it and dropped her head. Collecting herself, she handed me the book which had lain open upon the desk.

"This was the one surviving Book of Truth left in King's City after Breemore burned them all. Protecting truth, Sedgwick spent the rest of his years at this desk writing copies of it. These shelves are all his hand written copies. There are now more volumes here than there were destroyed by Lord Breemore. I believe we must restore them to the kingdom, though they may be rejected and our lives may be at stake."

"I'll help," I sincerely volunteered. "Breemore may not be so against it as we thought."

Hildie turned, shock displaying on her face, while Braun's brows came down like boulders. "Frederic Tavish was murdered," Braun stated.

"Yes, but by a mob," I proclaimed foolishly. "I mean, I don't know for certain, but Breemore may be misunderstood simply because he does not think the same as we do. He has told me much that you do not know."

When their response did not soften, I fumbled again, "I mean... I'm finding that Breemore is accepting of everyone and intends to return the kingdom to Trimont." I ran my hand through my hair and frankly exclaimed, "All of this is not his fault. It's my father's."

Meklon stood suddenly but did not speak.

Vala asked calmly, "What has Breemore told you, Galen?"

"From what I know, he has only told me the truth," I answered limply. I pulled the letter from my boot and handed it to her. "This explains everything. Please don't read it now, but when I am gone you may read it aloud. I should be leaving; I told the children I would see them tonight."

Braun advised, "If you follow the road, it will take you to a back entrance to the castle. Though it is overgrown, it is possible you may be spotted. Be careful no one follows you."

"I will guard this place with my life," I vowed.

Braun shook my hand heartily. Hildie said, "I must be allowed to give you a loaf of bread before you leave. We will walk out with you. Cote, run ahead and fetch a loaf and butter."

The boy promptly did so.

"I thank you greatly."

I gripped Vala's hand, saying, "I'll be back in a day or two after you have had time to consider my letter."

Chapter Five
~ *Lady Vala* ~

Hildie soon returned with Cote to hear Galen's letter.

"Is Braun joining us?" I asked.

"No," Hildie answered. "He is determined to dig the grave. His grieving drives him to it. Cote and I shall convey the letter to him tonight." Wearily, she settled on the floor and leaned against the desk. Cote found a pillow for her back and then dropped next to her.

Meklon drew near to the back of my chair, resting his hands upon it.

I read:

> *"To Lady Vala and Meklon,*
> *I imagine your misery about the children; the same misery is my own. They were brought to the King's Castle to be cared for, but they are frightened. I will personally see that no harm comes to them.*
> *But I write this knowing full-well that the fault lies at my own feet. If I had never left Trimont, Breemore would not have taken the children.*
> *My hand has stilled for some time. It is difficult to put this next portion into words.*
> *The night Lord Breemore announced the tournament in Traiven's Pass, I sought to speak with him privately. My purpose was to test him… He proved himself true. And because I did not think you would believe what he told me, I left.*

Breemore openly confessed that he had staged my father's death. Late in the night, on the day that my father was crowned, my father went out on the dark mountainside alone with a woman. Thomas followed him and tried to persuade him to return. Angered by Thomas' intrusion, my father pushed his own brother down the mountain.

My father followed Thomas' helplessly rolling body, but when at last he reached Thomas, his death was unchangeable.

The woman told Breemore what had happened, and he rushed to the site she had indicated, finding my father holding his dead brother. My father commanded Breemore to stage his death and made him promise to take his place as steward king while he vowed to never return.

I know this story is true because I know my father.

Breemore sought me because he intends to return the throne to its rightful heir. He did not think I should lose my birthright because of my father's fall. Breemore believes me capable of winning the tournament. Once I do, I shall be second-in-command and then heir and then king. I can restore Trimont.

Breemore asked me to invite you to stay at the King's Castle that you may be with the children. Please come though you may be suspicious of him. This castle finds itself greatly in need of you both.

-Galen"

My eyes felt red from the onslaught of emotion the words stirred.

"I can't believe that of your son," Hildie uttered. "It has to be all a lie."

Neither Meklon nor I spoke.

"It is a lie, isn't it?" Hildie questioned quietly.

Though it took me a moment, I answered, "I've often remembered the night Cloven was crowned, for it was the last I saw of my sons. Cloven beamed with such pride. Together, he and Breemore made great swelling jests. For hours Cloven danced with a woman, neither of them long taking their eye off the other. My frail Thomas watched it all with worry building in his eyes."

"You are saying the story is true," Hildie spoke lowly.

"I need time to consider," I responded.

Meklon abruptly said, "I'm going to help Braun dig."

Chapter Six
~ *Lydia* ~

Village of Dresden

In the haze of sleep, I fought to retain the sweet dream of Galen and curled tighter against the carriage seat. But when the problems and suffering of others began to faintly return to my consciousness, I forced myself to wake and sat up, accepting instead the bumps and jerks of the carriage, the soreness of my lower back, the smothering heat, my hunger from rationing our food, and my apprehension of our near arrival.

Netty peeked out the window in dreamy expectancy. She was learning to make dreams; I was learning to let mine go.

"Oh, you are awake now," Netty said, excitedly scooting to take my arm. "I just saw a sign for Dresden."

A dash of nerves were mixed into my eagerness. I had rehearsed dozens of imaginary conversations with Cloven. In the realm where I controlled both wills, they went considerably well. But now nearer to facing him, not even my imagination could assume confidence.

There, however, was tremendous reprieve from all discomforts as I gazed beyond the carriage border to partake of Galen's homeland.

The sky was blue with magnificent sweeps of white clouds. The richest of emerald grasses found their roots in the free and reckless steeps, then ran down the slopes and rolled over hills of endless meadows of wildflowers! Cottages, skirted by their farms, dwelt amid the soft thriving slopes. Goats and sheep bleated. A child in the distance sang an old rhyme.

My instant fondness embraced Dresden. What had Father thought at his first sight of Dresden? Had he so loved and felt its significance? Had he sensed great purpose when he humbly traded his map for a brokenhearted boy's carving?

I noticed with a nervous jolt that a young man jumped on a horse and rode from cottage to cottage as if heralding our arrival. In response, families peered through the bright sun to the road and began crossing the meadow to follow our carriage.

What was I to do if they expected something of us? What was I to give as my reason for coming?

Too quickly for my scrambling thoughts, we came to the village which consisted only of a single row of tidy wooden shops, a grassy meadow, and the throng of villagers waiting for and following after us.

"They act as though we are queens," Netty marveled.

"I wrongly imagined that we would arrive unnoticed," I whispered back.

An unseen bell suddenly rang, and more people flocked over the meadows to meet us.

Hurriedly, I tried to think of an explanation for our arrival. I couldn't outright proclaim that Galen's father was truly the steward king, who was thought to be dead, nor that I had come to convince him to reclaim his throne. Yet, I needed someone to tell me where I could find Galen's father.

Auden stopped the carriage in front of the last shop

before the road led out of town again. People began questioning Auden, but he kept his attention on the horses.

Slowly, I opened the carriage door. With so many people gathered, I progressed no further than the carriage step. Questions were excitedly and curiously repeated: "Where have you come from?" "Why have you come to Dresden?" "Who are you?" "What have you brought us?"

Collectively, I sensed they were innocent in their inquiries, even if a little nosey in their manner.

Smiling to make them feel at ease, I introduced myself, "I am Lydia Tavish. This is Netty and her father, Auden. We've come from Traiven's Pass." I hoped they would forget their other questions.

But as soon as I was finished, someone asked, "Why have you come to Dresden?"

I felt my face flush as I openly stood before the village answerless. After what seemed a prolonged moment of swelling embarrassment, I suddenly shouted, "I have news of Galen!"

"He is not dead… is he?" one asked fretfully.

"No," I answered, smiling, relieved that the subject had changed. "The worst that befell Galen was a broken arm when he was thrown from his horse during a storm. Therefore, he was delayed in Traiven's Pass where I met him. He is now healed and continued on to King's City."

Cheers rose up among them!

"That's the lad for you," a large man standing in front of the carpentry shop covered in sawdust boasted, as he threw a rag over his shoulder and folded his thick arms over his heavy chest. "Is Galen showing those fancy city folks the might and dread of Dresden?"

I laughed. "I'm sure he is."

"How did you meet Galen?" a woman asked.

"He helped my family greatly in a time of need and was a friend to me."

"Will Galen come back?" a boy asked. "I've been waiting a long time for him to come home."

"I'm sure one day he will."

Confident by the common connection we now gained, I asked, "Can someone tell me where I can find Galen's father?"

As they grew quiet, I regretted I had asked so soon.

The carpenter cautioned, "If you have come all this way to see Amos, he won't accept visitors."

"I would at least like to try to see him," I treaded lightly. "I should think he would like to hear news of his son."

"It's no use," a woman lamented. "We haven't as much as seen Amos here in the village since Galen left. He goes into his disappearing spells, but never for this long. It's been over three months. Even if he is at home, which I doubt, it is best not to talk with him. He won't have much to say, if anything."

"Couldn't you at least tell me where he lives?" I dared to press.

"If you are Galen's lass, you are a friend of ours," beamed the carpenter. "Come inside, and tell us more about our Galen, eh."

"Don't you have stories to tell and trinkets to trade?" others added.

"Yes, show us what you have brought," several people adjoined.

Beseechingly, I scanned the faces for one who may yet volunteer to take me to Galen's father. An older woman made her way through the people using her basket to nudge those who did not move before she reached them.

When she stood in front of me, she unruffled herself with a little shake, exhaled a short breath, and said, "I'm Helena, and any friends of Galen are friends of mine even if you have nothing to sell us. The people are disappointed because you are not a peddler, and you shock us all by wanting to see Amos. A person asking to see Amos is rarer than tulips in autumn. So you must understand their reluctance. But I will take you to Amos' farm, though no guarantees we will find him there. Maybe you could leave him a note. We will think of something." With that she pulled herself up on the seat next to Auden. I quickly reseated myself in the carriage, and she yelled, "Drive on, good man."

Netty looked at me agape. "She certainly took charge of things."

"I am most thankful," I acknowledged, then happily mused, "I think she must have been the nursemaid Galen told me about — the closest he had to a mother."

I settled back into the cushion for the first relaxing moment during the trip, for I felt awakened and safe among Galen's people.

Gradually, the open meadows and rolling hills flattened and crowded into a forest. Pine boughs scratched against the carriage on both sides. It was either colder in the forest or growing anxiety made me shiver.

The road led to a cleared farm, though the clearing still bore the damp shade of the forest. A horse grazed in a field, all fenced except the farthest reaches where a small moutain decided its borders.

"Stop here," Helena instructed. "This is Amos' place."

Auden halted the carriage in front of the large barn, newer in its sturdiness than the grey-weathered shed and cabin which looked small and withered beside it.

"Are you nervous?" Netty whispered.

"Yes," I answered as I opened the carriage door and stepped down onto the cold, packed earth.

Netty only ventured to peek her head out. Helena climbed down from the bench, saying, "Yes, Amos is here just as I thought."

"How do you know?" I asked.

"See the freshly chopped wood and the full trough. Never listen to the village folk when it comes to Amos. They know nothing. Just because Amos doesn't choose to show himself in town doesn't mean he is not at home. They just never come by to see him. I, however, do. And I know why he will always stay nearby." She leaned in to tell her secret, "Because I bring him pies. A man can never be so hard as to not like a pie. So see, Amos has a soft spot. Don't be afraid of him. Say what you must. It will appear he will not listen, but he will, to every word. I guarantee it. And here," Helena placed the pie from her basket into my hands, "this will soften him."

Armed only with a pie and jumbled thoughts, I walked to the roughhewn cabin and knocked on its door which had been left slightly ajar.

When nothing but emptiness tumbled out of the crack, I gently pushed the door open and feebly voiced, "Hello?"

The cabin was four walls of sheltered space and not much more. Even the smell of smoke signified survival, not living. The only light that entered followed me through the door, for burlap hung over the one small window.

I admired the table and two chairs which had been well carved, though evidently neglected. I set the pie on the table while righting the tin cup which had lain empty on its side.

The hearth was badly scraped and chipped as though squirrels had long ago chosen the blackened bricks as part of their common passage.

A limp curtain hid the belongings of one corner and a bed was in the other. I was drawn to the old friendly quilt which was spread over the bed and found Galen's initials sewn at the edge. I set my hand upon the quilt. The fabric was coarse, and my hand was swallowed by an invisible layer of webs and dust. Rather than remove my hand in disgust, I let it linger to prove there was still love for the ragged patches someone had once collected and sewn together for Galen.

Unexpectedly, the light which had lain in the opened doorway was replaced by a broad shadow. If it were Helena, her voice would have accompanied her presence. This shadow was silent. As I turned, I knew I was to meet Cloven Trimont.

Startled by the blue eyes which looked so much like Galen's, I stared. His cheeks were reddened from either surprise or prior exertion. Three dead rabbits hung over his arm, and an ax was strongly gripped within his hand. His hair was grey like stone, and his face hard like stone. Yet, through his blue eyes, he searched my face as if it may have been a lost memory.

I forced the first words, "I've come from Traiven's Pass to speak with you."

His eyes froze. Abruptly, he left the cabin.

"Wait," I pleaded as I followed him. "You must hear what I've come to say."

He spurned my entreaty, leaving me his retreating back with his dead rabbits flopped upon it.

"Amos, come back here," Helena yelled. "This woman has come far and has news of Galen."

He walked on as a deaf man.

"Well, dear," she said, coming to stand beside me, "he is a difficult man. Thank goodness Galen turned out quite different. Come to my house tonight where you can rest from your travels. We can try again tomorrow."

"No," I exclaimed. "I might not get another chance. I must speak with him now."

I ran down the path he had taken into the forest. For a time, I could not find him. After a careful search off the path, I discovered him in a gully, sitting on a fallen log. The gully being steep, I half slid down, grabbing onto young trees and branches to balance my descent.

Though my arrival was clamorous, he shunned my presence in favor of skinning his rabbits. A little reassured that at least he stayed, I braced myself several feet behind him.

"My name is Lydia Tavish. My father was Frederic Tavish, whom I believe you knew."

I faltered as his knife strokes grew brutal. His sheer unwelcome manner petrified my tongue. Yet, I willed and I dared, so I spoke, "And you are Cloven Trimont."

Every muscle in his body visibly tensed. "You are mistaken," he spoke low and cold. "Cloven Trimont is dead."

Though quivering, I withstood his icy denial and enforced, "It is irrevocably known by Galen, your family, and my family that you are alive. I've been sent to ask you to return."

"Cloven Trimont will never return. Now leave." His voice was an iron bar that locked into its permanent hold.

After such a vow, the woods went silent. My own throat battled between speech and submission.

Swallowing several times and taking many deep

breaths, I began, "Then please listen to what you are subjecting *your* kingdom to—what you refuse to see—what you are allowing to happen. In your place, Lord Breemore has ruled deceitfully. He banished the Book of Truth since the beginning of his rule, and now truth is disbelieved, despised, and hostilely treated.

"My family and yours remained in the truth but have greatly suffered. My father, who spent his life searching for King Cordell, was murdered, and my mother, brother, and young sister are languishing in prison at this moment because we chose truth.

"Trimont Castle, *your home*, one of the last refuges of light and truth, is abandoned. Your mother was raising thirteen orphan children at Trimont. Breemore forcibly stole the children and took them back with him to King's City. Your mother and Meklon have placed their own lives in danger by going after the children.

"And Galen, he too is in the city under Breemore's deceiving influence. And what of King Cordell? He suffers somewhere more greatly than any other.

"I'm certain Breemore is building toward destruction. But you can thwart him by rightfully reclaiming the throne. You must dethrone Breemore. Whatever it is that keeps you here, it cannot be greater than your responsibility as a Trimont!"

I was hot and panting, having lashed passionate and painful images, but all died at his unyielding back. I sunk in the dip between two tree roots, lowering my head to my folded knees.

Though I was in a position of defeat, the battle continued in the silence, for I would not leave. Inevitably, time passed. What damage was incurred somewhere to others because of these stubborn moments? I lifted my head to speak again, but first, he spoke.

My ears latched to his hoarse whisper. "I'm not who you seek. If you seek hope, seek it in Galen."

"I do hope in Galen," I expressed ardently. "Meklon has trained him. But you can't leave Galen to bear this alone."

He harshly retorted, "He can bear it!"

"No. Only you can reveal Breemore's lie about your death and rightfully reclaim the throne."

Cloven dropped his knife. I waited, for I sensed that revealing words were at the precipice of his lips.

When at last they came, they fell from the heights of sorrow — fathomless sorrow. "Galen is enough because Breemore did no wrong. I let you say your piece and gave you your answer. Now go."

His body left, but I sat, with the weight of his broken soul in my arms. Anger I could fight against, stubbornness I could be patient with, but sorrow... I had to wonder what had so harmed and deceived him.

Once Cloven was long beyond sight, I slowly climbed out of the gully and located the path. When I entered the clearing, Auden held a lantern while the three anxiously met me, saying they were just about to go in search of me.

"Well?" Netty asked expectantly.

I shook my head.

She frowned.

"I spoke to him, but he refused. I'm determined, however, to stay until I can speak with him again. I can't leave him as he is."

"Dear," Helena comforted, "heaven knows what you are trying to accomplish with Amos, but come to my house where I will feed you and give you a place to rest."

"We would be most thankful," I answered, climbing into the carriage, scooting small and tight against the other side.

Helena gave Auden directions to her home, then settled in the carriage across from me.

"Now you must tell me," she began, then paused. Motherly perception filled her eyes. She must have known that I was not ready for questioning, for she simply patted my hand and resumed a prior conversation with Netty.

Tucked in my solitary corner, I stared out the window — consumed by Cloven's broken soul.

Chapter Seven
~ *Lydia* ~

The further away the carriage rolled from Cloven's darkened cabin, the brighter the sky and the clearer its happy aspirations shone in the gentle sunset. Back in the forest, the sky had seemed caught and tangled in all the heavily laden branches. I doubted if the sky ever reached the forest floor where Cloven and I had battled and both lost.

Now watching the glorious sky so freely reflect itself in the glowing meadows, I wished Cloven saw it too, so he might remember that there was a sky and believe the simple fact that it was beautiful and nearer than one would suppose if nothing hindered it.

Helena was saying, "I know the three of you must be famished, but I dig my heels against feeding my guests scraps. A fresh stew will be made. With all of us, it will not take long."

The carriage suddenly lurched uphill and stopped at the top. Helena opened the door and motioned for Netty and me to exit first. A peaceful wind whispered greetings, and the loveliest row of lupine softly waved.

We were high up on a knoll. I turned around to take in the miles reaching out to the world in all directions. Lantern lit cottages cheered my eyes along the expanse, and the light between sky and horizon slowly tucked the land into its nightly protective blanket. It was so quiet—so few people compared to the great mass of unknown land.

"You are now safely in Helena's Nest," she announced, "for that is what this knoll and my home upon it is called."

I smiled, thinking the name perfect. While Helena led the others to her small barn, I stood for a moment to gaze, to breathe, to listen, and to climb.

"Netty girl, here is the pail," Helena called, swiping it from beside the lupine. "The nanny goat tied on the other side of the barn will give you the least trouble. Auden, I see you found the axe yourself — good. Now there is no need to chop the entire fallen tree, just chop enough for tonight. The strapping lads who chop for me come tomorrow."

I joined them, asking, "What may I do?"

"Come with me inside the cottage. You and I will start the fire and peel the vegetables."

From the outside, her cottage looked like a steep upward slope as the roof rose much taller on the back side, like a third story might be tucked in the tight little peak. The thatched roof, still light in its straw color compared to the darkening sky, was old and tousled as if it were the nest of many birds.

We stood in the dusk of her cottage until she aptly lit two lanterns which hung in the middle of her home. Peculiar and cluttered were my instant perceptions. Peddler trinkets were scattered in every corner of available space. Many foreign objects hung from the rafters, and for a time, my eyes weaved through the elevated maze of colors and shapes. Despite how interesting all else may have been, my attention rested on a carved bird with outspread wings.

Helena disappeared into a hidden storage space beneath the steep steps which led to a loft, and beyond it was a second smaller loft. She came out with a bucket of vegetables and an empty bucket with two knives. She handed them both to me, saying, "I'll start the fire and then join you."

Finding a nearby stool, I sat and began peeling over the bucket. As the heat of the new fire began reddening my cheek, Helena pulled a second stool near. She was about to slice one of my potatoes when she exclaimed, "Dear girl, there is much weighing on you. I've never seen a potato peeled so unevenly. It tells all that is in your heart."

I looked up as she displayed one of my butchered potatoes. I laughed, though it came out rather pitiful. At that moment, I could have gushed forth my myriad of sorrows, but I simply corrected, "I'll peel the next potatoes better now that you have pointed it out."

"Peel as unevenly as you want; the pigs will love you for the extra bit of potato on the peel. But won't you tell me more? I've tried keeping my curiosity un-hatched, but it is cracking despite my care. So let's be out with it. Once an egg cracks it is good for nothing except being put to use at that moment. Do tell me why have you come all this way just to see Amos?"

My eyes swept into the cracks between the floor planks. It was still too early to tell the secret. I replied, "I hope soon I'll be able to tell you, but for many reasons, I'd rather not speak of it at this time."

"At least relieve an old woman that Amos and Galen are not in trouble."

I could only offer her heavy eyes.

She sighed, "I've always suspected there was a deeper mystery behind Amos. You don't know how earnest I am to know, but I'll wait. I will insist, however, that we are trustworthy folk here in Dresden. In time, you will trust us. You will have to, if you want help with Amos. In the meantime, I'll have to find you permanent bedding and see if your driver can stay at Grenfell's."

"We can't stay that long."

"Dear girl, now that Amos has left, he might be gone for weeks. Nobody knows where he goes."

I picked up the next potato and dug the knife into it harder than I intended.

Netty entered, holding the door open for her father whose arms carried the load of firewood.

"Very good," Helena acknowledged. "Go ahead and add a few logs to the fire. And I'll take the pail of milk."

Netty hesitantly handed the pail forward. "Girl," Helena exclaimed, "my nanny goat's got more milk than this. Tomorrow I will teach you how to milk a goat."

"I'm sorry, miss," Netty apologized. "I've been only a children's maid."

"And that's nothing to be ashamed of," Helena commended. "I'll just be adding to your already fine knowledge."

Taking the potato and knife from my hand, she insisted, "The three of you sit and rest at the table while I finish the stew. Move whatever might be in your way."

To clear the four chairs, Netty and I moved paints and fabrics to the stairs.

Auden was the last to sit as he had first stoked the fire and now stood looking at the table as if it were unnatural, for a large purple iris had been painted over the whole top. He accepted his unusual surroundings in silence as he sat. We all had to accept the unexpected surprises and setbacks that were and would continue to befall our seemingly impossible errand.

Helena served cups of milk only a fourth filled. Even

though no one complained, Netty winced at the lack. Helena then joined us. She downed her few swallows of milk while the three of us sipped slowly.

She suggested, "While the stew boils, tell me about yourselves. You don't have to tell me your secrets right away. We can start with your common life."

We were quiet as none of us possessed a common life anymore.

"Well, you must have come from a family, haven't you?"

"A beloved family," I answered, now not able to keep from speaking of them. "I grew up with Mother, Father, my two older brothers and younger sister." I then expounded of life before Father's death and the imprisonment. Little stories sprinkled upon my memory as I spoke. They were sparse at first but then came rapidly as Helena was an eager audience. "When I was twelve, I grew a beautiful patch of sunflowers which my brothers accidently burned. Together, Mother and I mourned over the singed stocks and charred ground. To console us both, Mother had said, 'If it is good that burns, the ashes will bloom.' True to her words, the next year the ashes were wiped away, and the new sunflowers which grew thereafter were stouter, yellower, and more stunning than ever before. Every summer people came to see those sunflowers."

Helena listened enthralled. "You all are very good folk," she concluded. "I can sense it. And you," she pointed to me, "are a good one for our Galen. I knew he had the good sense to fall in love well."

"He has never claimed such love for me, nor I for him. We were only friends. During the time I met Galen, I was forced into an engagement with another man." Panged in heart, but restraining myself to be outwardly light, I added, "It will most likely be such a great deal of time until I see Galen that he will be engaged himself."

"You are not engaged to such an imposter now, are you?" Helena severely pried.

"No."

Helena settled her ruffled countenance and hinted, "I saw you staring at my bird. You knew Galen carved it, didn't you?"

I nodded and looked down as if one whose heart had been caught and exposed.

"Dear girl, whether you realized it or not, love poured out of your eyes when you stared at that carving. You won't be keeping any secrets of that nature from me."

Some smiles couldn't be helped even when the mind forbids them. Such was the struggle over my lips. I wanted to hope Galen would discover that I hadn't married. But who would tell him? Vala didn't even know. As it remained, it would be wrong for him to love me, and he should quench and deaden all his feelings for me and rightly accept any new ones which might naturally occur toward another woman.

Helena stepped back to the hearth to test, then to serve the stew.

Thanks and compliments were murmured, but no one really spoke.

When all was finished, Helena recalled, "How unhospitable Amos was today. My pie is probably sitting untouched in that empty cabin of his. Tomorrow we shall fetch it; a pie must never go to waste."

Sensing our weariness, Helena took Netty to help her prepare beds in the second loft, for the first was her own. Auden would sleep in the barn tonight. I washed the dishes in the bucket of water which he had fetched from the river.

A knock pounded on the door, and my heart pounded with it. Cloven?

Helena came down the stairs crankily mumbling, "I knew this was coming," then yelled to whoever was behind her front door, "The visitors don't need any company tonight. Go home."

The man at the door sounded back, "When was the custom in Dresden for one cottage to hoard all the company? We ask *genteelly* that you let us in."

"Come back tomorrow," Helena repeated, unmoved.

The man persisted, "The visitors could be gone tomorrow for all we know. I have suspicions about these strangers. I won't go tonight until I have had a better look at them."

"Won't you," Helena huffed. She looked at us, saying, "You all look so miserably tired. I can't imagine you having to bear with all of them tonight."

"All of them?" Netty questioned.

"Oh, yes, you may hear one voice, but I assure you, there is a whole crowd on my doorstep. It's just the Dresden way whenever strangers come."

"I can understand why they might be suspicious," I ventured. "Maybe we should let them in." I looked to Auden and Netty for their say. They both consented.

Helena acquiesced, "Fine, come in Grenfell, but not too late! And no lute playing tonight!"

Triumphantly, the large carpenter entered. In his hand was a lute. Behind him tumbled in various ages and sizes of men and women. They squeezed in until I was nearly pressed into the hearth.

The carpenter introduced himself. "I am Grenfell, and if this woman has given you the wrong impression of me, I'm quite the gentleman. Taught Galen all he knows despite her claiming the same."

"Were you the one who taught Galen how to carve?" I asked.

"I surely did!" he boomed. "Do not the best pupils come from the best teachers? Have you seen his work?"

"Yes, a knight on a horse. It was a carving very precious to me."

"Well, do you have it to show us? To bring a little of Galen back to us."

"No, it was taken from me."

"Well, the rascal who did that! I'd like to see him after I'd be done with him. I don't stand for thieves. Tell us why you are here. Nobody comes to see Amos. Nobody knows Amos. Tell us, why has Galen sent you to his father?"

His personality produced quickening, and I answered forthright and assured. "I will tell you the truth, but at this time I cannot tell you everything. Galen did not send me, but my sole purpose in coming to Dresden is to talk with his father. We are not thieves and will not be a burden. We will work for our keep and follow the laws of your village. I hope you will accept us."

To my astonishment, Grenfell broke into applause. So too did everyone else. Grenfell shook our hands heartily, saying, "It will be our pleasure to get better acquainted with you during your stay here. Though you won't speak of your errand, that you speak honestly is proof enough to us that you are sincere. Welcome to Dresden!"

Through its people, I embraced Dresden all the more tightly. It was a hold I suspected not likely to ever break.

"One request I make of you," Grenfell insisted, holding forth his lute. "Do any of you know how to play?"

Not even Helena protested now but wore a relaxed complexion.

Netty shook her head and hid behind me lest he forced her to perform.

When he presented the lute to me, I tentatively accepted it. "I only know a little."

Grenfell grinned as he laid his lute in my palms. "A little is a lot more than we've gotten in a long time. Play!"

All eyes watched me expectantly as though I might be a masterful musician. I disclaimed, "Please understand that I don't play well and only know a few folk tunes and rhymes. My eldest brother Creighson is the musician you ought to hear."

"We don't have your elder brother; we've only got you. You can't be any worse than what we have plucked out of the lute ourselves. So don't apologize; play!"

I began a little rhyming tune which had been the first Creighson had taught me. Grenfell beamed like he'd struck gold and bellowed, "Let's all sing!"

They began singing a lyric of which I had never heard accompany this tune before:

There once was a bonnie lass who milked the cow, and a fine brawny fellow who worked the plough. He saw her one day which swept him away and he asked her to be his lady.

She frowned and said, 'You have straw on your head and a nose which looks like a pickle. So be on your way for my word is nay. I will not be your lady.'

He answered her no with hopes still aglow, 'My heart is gold and my hands never grow old. I will prove you are my lady.'

All summer he wooed and all fall she booed and in winter he never saw her. But he continued his song, not thinking his wait long, 'One day she will be my lady.'

Spring came along with daisy and song, and he knelt on his knee beside her. 'Bonnie lass, bonnie lass, will you marry me? I've waited this year and proven sincere. Will you now be my lady?'

She paused and then said, 'I still see the straw on your head and your nose hasn't changed, but I don't see them the same. Your words proved true. You have won me through and through. Yes, I will be your lady.'

The only notes everyone had landed on together were the ones held out in word "lady" at the end of each stanza. But with what heart they sang! Their voices enlivened the words, and their bodies animated their voices. I'd never experienced anything like it.

"Well, merry, merry!" cried Grenfell. "Let's sing it again!"

As I readily began the tune, all voices collected together and bellowed in merriment again and again. Each time, my playing gained confidence while their rhyming gained consistency until together we radiated the night with joyous song.

Chapter Eight
~ *Galen* ~

"Sir Bunny made a sword from a long thorn and prepared to meet the menace of Tiny Tubblet! However, Lady June Bunny said…" Breemore transposed his voice to a lady's, and the children laughed. My gaze wandered over the children's faces which were eagerly engaged with Breemore's animated voice and gestures.

My eyes again stalled upon Alene holding Emmy. The sight connected me so strongly to the memory of Lydia holding Emmy the day of the picnic, that I couldn't prevent being drawn to the sight. Alene suddenly turned her eyes toward me. I quickly concentrated my gaze back to Breemore.

When the storytelling was over, Breemore announced, "It is time for one of you to entertain this evening. Hollis, would you like to sing for us? The ladies were praising your progress after your lesson earlier today. They called you the young nightingale."

Hollis' cheeks filled with pleasure as she answered, "Of course."

As she situated herself beside the front chair from where Breemore beckoned her to stand, her expression mimicked the vain, superior demeanor of her new music teacher. This was the second time I'd noticed the woman's distasteful plague spread to Hollis' face. If Vala came, I was certain she would cleanse the plague and replenish Hollis' countenance with selfless beauty.

To give Vala and Meklon time to consider my letter and to mourn Sedgwick's death, I'd let a week pass without returning to Lenrow. But tonight, I was anxious to return and hear their response to my letter. I greatly hoped they would accept Breemore's invitation to stay at the castle. I had discovered nothing more in which to condemn Breemore and hoped they could come to the same conclusion. But if not, I determined to listen to their side as I promised. I would do nothing to create a rift between us again.

Emmy began bouncing on Alene's lap and desirously begged to be taken to me.

Alene hushed her and, smiling, carried the girl to me. She whispered, "Are you willing to take this leaping doe into your arms?"

I smiled and lifted Emmy to my shoulders. "You are good with the children," I whispered. "I do want you to know how thankful I am for the extra attention you have given them—especially Cadby." I looked in the direction of the bulging window curtain where his shoes peeked out at the bottom.

"Cadby reminds me of one of my brothers," she confided. "I have six of them. And three sisters. But I'm closest to my silent brother. I can speak with him easiest. He listens; the others don't. And I believe Cadby also listens. He just doesn't know what to do with all that he hears yet. One day he will, and his wisdom will astonish us all."

"I believe you are right."

We joined our applause to Breemore's enthusiastic response to Hollis' finished performance. She bowed and on her own accord began another ballad. Badrick left from where he had slumped in his chair and stood beside me, saying, "You left Trimont for this endless singing?"

Breemore, who also joined us, chimed in, "Wait until tomorrow before you make your mind up, young man. Tonight we are indulging the ladies. Remember, tomorrow you may help Galen in the arena."

"Then let me go to bed so it may come the sooner," Badrick moaned.

Breemore laughed, "You won't always think so, my lad. One day you will find that you will do anything to stay in a lady's company — even listen to her sing."

"I'll never become like that!" Badrick proclaimed. "Because I know for certain," he stomped his foot, "my lady won't sing!"

Haxel came over and claimed, "I think mine will. I like singing. It reaches inside like plain speaking does not."

As Hollis proudly landed her last note, smiling again at Breemore's applause, the other nursemaid, the older self-pitying one, sleepily stood from her chair, from where she had been dozing, to announce the children's bedtime. She began dousing candles to prove it.

"Finally," Badrick huffed. "Galen, prepare to be pinned tomorrow. Haxel and I have perfected our plan."

"I'll be ready," I lightly challenged.

Alene retook Emmy from my arms. As the other children were herded out of their various positions and corners of the music room, I went to Cadby.

Brushing aside the curtain, I knelt beside him and offered him a small block of wood from my pocket. Gently, I pulled his stiff hand from his pocket and placed the block within it.

"So you may practice," I whispered.

When I released his hand, it drew back into its pocket. I whispered again, "I always keep my knife in my pocket.

72

Do you know why? It keeps you near. I'll always have my knife in my pocket for that reason. Will you keep your knife in your pocket to keep me near?"

After a minute, he pulled out his other hand and showed he too had his knife. He also lifted his downcast eyes and offered the best he could make of his countenance.

I smiled and nodded, pouring into that pale, lonely face all the pride and acceptance I felt toward him.

His hand tucked quietly back in its pocket, clutching perhaps a bit of love with it.

I placed my hand on Cadby's shoulder and walked him to Alene, who waited for him. She held Emmy in one arm and led Cadby's shoulder with her other hand, speaking kindly to him as they went.

Breemore and I were the last to exit. He noted, "I have no doubt that you will be an excellent father."

"I don't plan to marry."

Breemore stopped and for a moment looked at me ponderingly. "Did you truly love Lydia Tavish that much?"

I turned my head from him and kept walking.

"I'm sorry," Breemore consoled. "I truly wish I could have gained her for you. However, Sir Danek also greatly loved her."

"Only selfishly," I accused. Then despite myself, I asked, "I've overheard talk about Danek coming for the tournament. Do you know if this is true?"

Breemore answered, "He did not sign for it. Being newly married, I would think not."

Regretting I had asked, I again plunged my pace ahead.

"Galen," Breemore stopped me. "I would encourage you; consider a wife."

"I can't."

"I know, and I understand. But let me explain my reasons, for I have been pondering this. If you never marry, there will be no future security for the throne, and the Trimont lineage would truly cease."

My head hung as I felt the heaviness of my obligation. I just wanted Lydia.

Breemore continued, "We both know the confusion and misunderstandings caused by lack of a direct heir. If King Cordell had married and had a son, so much harm could have been avoided."

"King Cordell never married?" I asked.

"No. In his case, want of matrimony was for a very selfless reason. His face had been severely scarred when he was a child. He didn't want to force a woman to marry him in his ugliness and no woman chose to. You are lucky to have options, Galen. Sir Cantley's daughter, Lady Laila, is an exceptional woman as I believe you have witnessed — likewise, so is Alene."

"You would not object to me marrying a servant?"

"Why should I? Marry whomever you learn to love."

"Why did you never marry?"

"Ha, you will now catch me in my own counsel. Perhaps the reason I never married is nearly the same as yours."

"So I need not heed your counsel?"

"No, but as one who went down that path… I don't advise it. I would have perhaps changed some things if I could go back." Something of a veil lifted from Breemore's countenance. Before I could explore the new reaches of his bearing, he concluded, "But I'm not in the line of the true kingship and always knew that you were the rightful heir. If I had children, I would not have been able to restore the throne to you. So that is another reason I never married. You, however, do not have that excuse, for you are the rightful king. Come, there is something I want you to see."

Following him, I dared to asked, "What do you know about Lady Laila?"

"I have heard she is in strong support of you winning the tournament."

"Yes, I was surprised. She, more than anyone, has helped inspire me in training."

"She must see your potential as do I. Indeed, she has an eye for quality and is a woman of mental strength. A beauty as well, but she keeps that to herself as she is not a flaunter."

"But she is also mysterious and a little hard," I remarked.

"That is because she has known great loss as have you. The only man she ever loved died the month before they were to marry. The two of you would certainly understand each other, hmm?"

I nodded, involuntarily feeling nearer to her than before.

Our walking stilled as all that now lay before us was the sealed doors into the throne room. Breemore pulled out a key, and raising his brow in amused intrigue, opened the doors and gestured for me to enter. I matched his look of intrigue, for everything he did was contagious, and I had wanted to see the throne room.

As I entered the darkened domain, my steps echoed across the massive floor of ornate marble of which it was too dark to see its end.

"Galen, your pain may cause you to see your future empty of happiness just as the night strips this throne room of its glory, but what lies! Your future is one that any man would envy just as this throne room has the most spectacular stained glass windows ever erected. Of course, right now, we can see neither. We stare into darkness and obscure shadows, uncertainties, doubts, and endless heartache. But if we raise light over both, we shall see the truth. And that is what I want to show you."

Breemore handed me a torch from the corridor and took another for himself. Without a word, he began walking the grand throne room aisle, lighting the mighty torches at each column. I did likewise on the other side—curious what he meant by truth.

With each dormant flame that we summoned, a sleepy circle of the throne room awoke and showed its magnitude. The giant columns held up the balconies, then extended higher to a ceiling that could barely be discerned through the torchlight. The stained glass windows, which were behind the columns, glowed like a fiery sunset from the reflection of the torches.

I hesitated at the foot of the steps which led to the throne.

"Come up, Galen," Breemore invited as he himself ascended. The throne was also made of immoveable marble. Words were inscribed which I neared to read, but Breemore, facing toward the room's immensity and grandeur, drew my attention as he began to speak. "What I want you to see, Galen, is the glorious day your father was crowned king—right where you now stand."

Instantly, I took a step down. I could admire the throne room's splendor, but I had no wish to see my father's past within it.

Taking no notice of my coldness, Breemore lifted his arms and, looking around in blessed memory, reminisced, "Imagine this throne room filled with thousands of people. Bodies circled around every column and the balconies overrun. Then add thousands more pressing into the castle entry and lining the outer stairs and streets. Every space from the city gate to this front row, people were eager, people were excited, and people were ready for their new king.

"Your father," Breemore exclaimed fondly, "in the prime of every desired attribute: young, handsome, clever, and unmatched in skill and strength, riding through King's City to the castle on his powerful stallion, girls yearning for just one glance, and boys vowing to be like him. As he walked down this aisle, among so many who loved him, this room was filled with your father's brilliance, and it filled the land with rejoicing."

Breemore trotted down the steps and flung open the double doors which led into the banquet hall. Breemore stood in the middle, holding up his torch grandly. "Here, after the coronation was pure celebrating!"

Tables extended into the dark, seeming as though there was no end to them. A stage was elevated for the minstrels. Flags adorned the upper walls while gold candlesticks were stationed along the base of the walls.

"Oh, Galen, can you hear it? The laughing that was here? The feasting! The dancing! The music! The happiness! If you could have been there, Galen, you would have seen who your father truly was. You are the son of a magnificent man."

"I wish I could have known that man," I spoke quietly.

"Galen, look at you! You are that man. I believe you will become an even greater man because you will not fail. These rooms will be filled again. You will ride through adoring crowds, walk down the royal aisle, and take your rightful place upon the throne while the kingdom rejoices over you.

"Come, there is one place more which testifies to this truth."

We came to an outer courtyard which I quickly perceived as the graveyard of the kings. It had been a rainy day, though now the air was but a breath of moisture which lay to rest its fallen droplets upon the tombs.

Breemore pointed to the largest monument. I approached and read:

Steward King Cloven Amond Trimont
First Trimont to succeed the Line of Cordell
A man greater than them all

"You and I know that your father fell, but the kingdom never knew. If one were to rise up in the likeness of Cloven Trimont, the people would welcome him. You have only to make yourself known to be loved. You possess everything your father possessed. I see it very deeply within you.

"I don't expect you to speak. But in your disappointments, Galen, know the truth of who you are, and see the truth of your future."

As I stared at my father's mock grave, Breemore's steps retreated back into the castle until I was certain that I had been left alone with the past. The visions he had painted pelted my mind. I envisioned myself in place of my father and knew the vision could be true. I was gaining a growing understanding of my strength as a Trimont. I knew I could win the tournament; it was something my blood told me. I hadn't seen it until this week, when for the first time, I had others to compare myself to since Meklon's training. I was stronger; I was faster. It all came natural to me, and I knew it. I possessed something more. Something superior. But I hadn't fully embraced and solidified the knowledge until now. But this was no guarantee of anything. My father had been a great swordsman too, yet he ended with nothing.

With my torchlight, I read more of the gravestones.

King Cygan Cordell
Never Found

Though fixed to the grave, the inscription yet reached out to me in hope. But what could I do? Every power had already been employed to find him. After twenty-five years of searching, there had not been a single clue. It suddenly struck me that a king could not vanish unless evil intent was behind it. Someone had meant ill for the kingdom. But then why had nothing more become of it? I had to remember to keep Breemore in question.

The next gravestone read:

King Aland Cordell
Ender of the Multa Wars

I did not know anything about the Multa wars, but I needed to gain knowledge of them.

First Loyal Amond Royston Trimont
Laid down his life for his friend

My grandfather. I laid my hand at the heart of his monument. The more I read, the more I feared this sacred ground. Generation after generation the lineages of Cordell and Trimont laid side by side, their beloved families surrounding them. The inscriptions powerfully overwhelmed me.

Gave himself, Gave himself, Gave himself was a repeated

phrase.

I came to the oldest date so worn I could barely make it out.

Alistair Cordell
The Man of Rags

From reading the Book of Truth, I knew Alistair had been the first king. He was chosen because of his noble and selfless character and called the man of rags because he gave so much that all that was left for himself were rags.

I exhaled heavily. If I was ever going to lie comfortably in the ground of my ancestors, my life would need to be worthy.

As I came again face to face with my father's monument, it felt like a betrayal of the sacred — a spot in unblemished ground. Meekly, at the shadowed side of the monument was a small gravestone which I hadn't noticed before. I stooped and held the flame near its inscription.

Thomas Raymond Trimont
Brother of Cloven Amond Trimont

I knelt before it, overwhelmed by the weight of my father's murdering of his innocent brother.

After a moment, to fill the silence I offered, "I rode your horse. And read your letters. Meklon spoke well of you." Then as if my father's guilt fell upon me, I set my hand on Thomas' gravestone and whispered, "I'm sorry. You shouldn't have died. That is where it all went wrong. And I can't fix it. I can only…" I sighed. "I can only win the tournament." To Thomas I admitted my deepest fears, "I don't know how to restore the Book of Truth, or find King Cordell, or marry another when I love Lydia so deeply. I promise that I will try. But if I fail, I wish not to be buried here."

I rose and set my torch in an empty bracket. Making sure no faces spied through castle windows, I disappeared behind my father's monument, left the castle grounds, and climbed the back trail to Lenrow.

Chapter Nine
~ *Galen* ~

There was something majestic in the night as I climbed. Strong air filled my lungs. My legs stepped with conquering strides. In the power of my exertion, I grew certain of my course and the power to accomplish it.

I didn't stop until I reached the alcove from whose sheer edge the starry night performed its endless art. While calming my breath, I marveled at the night sky. Strangely, I thought of my father. Somewhere, hiding beneath the dark canvas, he was alone, and I knew he would always choose to be alone.

Turning from the view and the sudden thought, I slowly walked to the Hendry's door.

Braun soon answered, cracking the door open.

"Enter quietly," he instructed. "My wife and son are sleeping."

"Are Meklon and Vala awake?" I whispered, heedfully shutting the door behind me.

"Meklon waited up in case you came," Braun answered. He stooped to pick up the lit lantern from the floor. One of Sedgwick's copies of the Book of Truth lay open beside it.

"You were reading," I commented.

"I was seeking," he returned.

Now that the lantern was nearer to his face, I saw that his eyes were red and moistened. Braun didn't have to say more for me to humbly acknowledge that I stood in the presence of a truly honorable man, and that I had stepped into the silence of his deepest heart cries. I respectfully said no more as he led me to the hearth and silently opened the secret door for me.

He handed me the lantern, for the passageway was dark.

I thanked him.

He nodded and shut the door behind me.

Nothing happened in thought or sound during my trek down the tunnel except maybe a little humbled envy toward Braun and the family and home he had. Braun's presence made me feel a little dissatisfied with myself — like there was more I could be. The thought of him with his family whispered to my heart that it might be nice to seek a wife.

When I entered the domed room, there was no light beyond the glow of my lantern, but I saw Meklon's shadow in front of the windows as he shifted to put on his hat.

"Hello, Galen," he acknowledged.

I hung the lantern on a wall bracket near Meklon then settled in the chair across from him.

"I imagine all is going well," he stated.

"Better than I expected," I answered. "I hope you and Vala have decided to accept Breemore's invitation to stay at the castle."

"Vala will join you and the children at the castle, but I will remain at Lenrow."

"Are you certain? I was hoping you would finish my training."

"I will teach you as often as you visit me."

"I shall try to come as often as I can."

"Your letter," Meklon began... "thank you. It meant a

lot to Vala as well. But while you have a right heart, you do not have a right mind."

"What do you mean by that?"

"A right heart is not enough. A right heart must also have truth. Without truth even a right heart lacks wisdom and is therefore easily deceived, manipulated, and in the end, profits nothing. But I also simply meant that I have not told you everything when I perhaps should have."

I leaned forward in great curiosity.

Meklon first established, "I know you can't stay long, so I will be brief." He then held my eyes as if there may be the chance of his losing them.

He suddenly disclosed, "Breemore was raised at Trimont by your great grandfather, Royston Trimont."

I jerked upright. "Why has no one told me until now?"

"Because a secret long past buried deep beneath the surface is difficult to rise up, especially when it has to do with the wrong of those you love and yourself. Vala asked me to tell you before, but circumstances were not dire enough to force it out of me. Now they are. If you are settled down enough to hear the rest, I will continue."

I nodded and listened.

"Have you ever heard the name Lord Marcus?" he asked.

"No."

"He was Breemore's father and was the ruler of Multa—a very vicious man whose aim was to conquer our kingdom and destroy the Book of Truth. Brutally, he forced Multa armies deeper into Calderon. Your great grandfather, Royston, fought to push Multa back to its own borders, but Lord Marcus would not be pushed back.

"Royston had no choice but to lead all of Calderon's

strength against Multa. There came to be a battle which is known as the ender of the Multa Wars. Lord Marcus was so certain of his victory that he foolishly brought his family with him to the battlefield so that they could witness Multa's glorious triumph; however, he and his wife were killed along with three fourths of his army. All of Multa was then pushed out of Calderon.

"That would have been the end of the story. However, a cry was heard through the smoke and ash of the battlefield. Royston heard the sobbing of a small boy."

"Breemore," I breathed.

Meklon nodded. "Royston pitied the orphaned child and brought him into Trimont to raise as his own alongside his two children, Amond and Rhoswen.

"From the beginning, Breemore's identity was kept a family secret because Royston did not want people to see him as an enemy, nor did he want anyone to know that he had spared Lord Marcus's son. People assumed he was an orphan from a Calderon village.

"The family was kind to Breemore, and he partook in every benefit of being a much loved son. Throughout his childhood and youth, he was taught the Book of Truth and all of Trimont's noble ways, but sadly, amid all this, there remained an angry resistance and rebellion within Breemore. Once he confided in me that he wished to return to Multa to see if they would not take him as their king. I strongly opposed him. He rarely spoke to me after that.

"The one who possessed the greatest softening power over him was Rhoswen. They were companions throughout childhood, a continuous string of flirtatious banter through youth, and the more desperately they fell in love as they grew older, the more rebellious they both turned against the family. When they expressed their desire to wed, Royston set firm conditions which first had to be met. Breemore continually ridiculed these conditions and convinced Rhoswen to run away with him. When their secret plan was discovered, Royston forbid Rhoswen from seeing Breemore and told Breemore that he was no longer welcome at Trimont.

"Breemore left without a word—not even to Rhoswen. For many years, no one saw nor heard of him. However, the family knew that Breemore had returned to Multa.

"Out of fear that Breemore would bring revenge against Trimont, I threw myself into learning sword mastery and helped Amond improve his skills. When Cloven was five, I began his training.

"One day, Breemore returned. He approached us friendly and apologetic. We were gladdened by his transformation. The past was amended, and our fears of another Multa attack subsided. He became a knight and fell in the circles of the castle and court. For a time, all was well.

"Then an attempted murder of King Cordell took place. This is when Amond, your grandfather, gave his life to save the king. I did not associate Breemore with the crime at all.

"Next, King Cordell vanished. Again, I did not suspect Breemore.

"It was not until Cloven and Thomas were announced dead that I began to wonder if Breemore was involved. I had only ever anticipated an attack of war and vengeance. It took time for me to think in terms of deceitful infiltration.

"I told Vala and Sedgwick my thoughts and learned that they shared my same suspicion. Sedgwick advised that we needed more proof. Vala and I set to finding it.

While we continued to perceive that Breemore was not filled with truth, he left no condemnable errors, neither in speech nor in deed, even when I confronted him. This is when Sedgwick sent Lydia's father to search for King Cordell.

"When Breemore convinced the city to burn the Book of Truth, we knew Calderon's fall would eventually come, with little we could do to prevent it."

Meklon sat silently, tapping his thumb on the other. Then he added, "So you see, whether what Breemore revealed about your father is true or not, your father has little to do with this."

It took me several moments to develop a response, for much had raced through my mind as he had spoken. I began by asking, "How did you come to know all this about Breemore?"

He pressed his lips together, and when they parted a moment later, he whispered, "I was there, Galen. I was there. Breemore is my brother."

Chapter Ten
~ *Galen* ~

Meklon's shocking revelation drove me to be alone. Aggressively, my mind hurled itself upon this new perception of Meklon and Breemore.

Finding a tree near the cliff of the alcove, I climbed it. The stars had been put to sleep by the clouds, so I too closed my eyes while my feelings churned.

I was a little upset that Meklon hadn't told me before. It could have prevented me from trusting Breemore. But even now, weeks later, I was aware of how much I had wanted to believe Breemore, to the point that I would have excused any persuasive speech against him.

Disappointment finally surfaced as my governing emotion. Frankly, I had to admit how high my hopes were set on the future unfolding as Breemore had described — that all I had to accomplish was winning the tournament, so the throne could be imperceptibly returned to Trimont. After which time, I would rule according to the Book of Truth, and the kingdom would be restored. But now I did not have any ground to believe Breemore's convenient, happy ending.

I could no longer question whether Meklon and Vala were misguided about Breemore. One would not be mistaken about his own brother. Meklon had every pertinent argument to condemn Breemore of treachery and deception.

Was my role as a Trimont to find King Cordell and

distribute Sedgwick's copies of the Book of Truth? In which case, I would most likely be murdered as Lydia's father had. At least I would be worthy of being buried in the graveyard with my forefathers.

I tossed a branch I had broken off. Why did Breemore seek me out? If his plan was to destroy our kingdom, why had he not yet executed it? Breemore's intentions may have reversed in these recent years. Anyone could change. The thought of my stubborn father came to mind, reminding me that some never did.

I jumped down, just able to see a sliver of pale ground in the dark. Answers were not going to come from my own mind. I would have to seek them.

In the throne room, words had been engraved in the marble above the throne. Purposeful or not, Breemore had diverted my attention from them. It compelled me to go back and read what had been written.

The dark night was a plague to my footing as I hastened down the overgrown trail. When the thicker forest of the mountain gave way to the clearing of King's City, torchlight blazed forth as if the earth was trying to warm the darkened heavens.

As I came under the castle's light, I did not dodge among the shadows, but entered the castle as if I had every right to its secrets. In the stillness, it seemed no hindrance lay between me and what I sought. The throne room's torches remained burning, although they had heavily waned from their first igniting passion—much like my vision of the future. I could no longer envision the grandeur Breemore had enticed me with. Meklon had struck a deathblow to my gullibility.

Taking a smaller torch in hand and lighting it from a larger, I hovered it before the engraved words above the throne.

> *Hope shall hereby be secured, except on the day the*
> *Line of Cordell in one accord is rejected.*

I recalled similar words in the Book of Truth. Meklon and Lydia also mentioned this portion when they reasoned that King Cordell was still alive.

I returned to my room where I flipped through the Book of Truth until I found the matching passage:

> *Not one hand may be laid to the Line of Cordell to kill*
> *him unless it be done at the hand of his own people*
> *because of a treason he has committed against his own*
> *people and the Book of Truth. In the hands of this*
> *people alone is the power to honor or destroy their*
> *king, and none other. For he who comes by stealth to*
> *kill the Line of Cordell, him be cursed and the land*
> *of his origin. Thus forth the kingdom shall never, by*
> *any means, be without a rightful king of the Line of*
> *Cordell — except on the day this people in one accord*
> *reject him.*

Several times, I read the words slowly. If Meklon's and Frederic Tavish's claims were true that Breemore had kept King Cordell in hiding all these years, it implied that Breemore believed these words and was working toward fulfilling them.

I trudged through training only half present. As my mind remained occupied with the thoughts of the day before, out of habit my body was obligated to respond to the constant onslaught of iron blades. My eyes were in pursuit of watching for Breemore; however, he never made an appearance. I departed the moment my presence was no longer bound by Sir Cantley's strict reign over the armory.

Even though I no longer excitedly engaged in training, I knew maintaining daily routine would be my safest guise to prevent Breemore from suspecting what Meklon had told me. Yet I supposed that Breemore had to know that at any time Meklon or Vala might tell me his history. Was Breemore so assured of his deception that he did not fear any of us thwarting it? I needed to speak with Meklon, for I was ready to drench him with questions.

In my room, I splashed water on my face, rubbing my cheeks in an attempt to lift my heavy and tired countenance. What form of entertainment would Breemore enchant the children with this evening? I had to admit, he never failed to suggest something to their and my liking.

I changed to evening attire and walked to the music room directly, not wanting Breemore to be with the children when I was not present.

When I entered the music room, Hazel excitedly leapt up before me. "Breemore is bringing in real musicians tonight so that we may dance!"

As I gazed down into Hazel's dancing eyes and considered the comfort and safety of so many evenings spent in this room, I soon felt the tug toward Breemore's innocence.

Alene scooted the couch to provide a larger area for dancing. I took hold of the other end to assist her.

Alene thanked me and asked, "Are you fond of dancing?"

Only able to recall Helena's insistent dance lessons when I was a boy and my one half-dance with Lydia, I was conflicted about how to answer.

Breemore suddenly gathered the room's scattered attention as he entered and presented several minstrels whom he introduced as some of King's City's best fellows.

I was unexpectedly awakened to the similar features Breemore and Meklon shared. It made me wonder which brother was older. Meklon definitely looked older, thinner, and balder, but being the older would make him the heir to Multa's throne.

I lost handle on these thoughts as Breemore and the minstrels began a compelling tune. The entire room seemed to lift on its toes and dance in response. Alene shared her smile with me as she began clapping.

"Alene and Galen, dance with us!" Hollis invited.

Alene startled me by grabbing my hand and pulling me behind her. Once I was in the middle, it was natural to begin skipping and exchange the linking of arms with the children. When Alene and I linked arms, her smile broadened. "You never answered my question. How do you like dancing?"

"It awakens a sleeping joy," I answered, now having gained an answer.

Alene looked impressed, but had no time to say more before she went off to Haxel's arm.

When the song ended, the children asked Breemore to play it again. He granted their request with hearty agreement. Alene and I were again taken into the movements with the children, laughing and exerting much energy as everyone's face grew rosy.

After a few songs, Alene opened the windows. I helped her. A fresh breeze filled the room, and the children became more exuberant, but I was tiring from lack of sleep mixed with all my bodily and mental exertion.

When I made no attempt to return to the dancing, neither did Alene.

"How do you like working at the castle?" I asked her, feeling that we had become good friends.

"It is far better than living in the slums, and it has become tremendously better since you and the children arrived. Lord Breemore is more jolly fun than folks say about him. I feel as if I have the best company of the castle every evening. You won't hear me complain."

"Does anyone complain about Lord Breemore's rule?"

"People always complain, but I have never heard a contrary word spoken against Lord Breemore. You yourself know how kind and lenient he is."

I nodded, more to indicate that I heard than that I agreed. However, she would not know the difference. Lydia was the only woman to whom I could have spoken what was really in my mind.

However, Alene did notice and asked, "Is something bothering you?"

I thought for a moment how to find a safe way to tell her something of my thoughts. I said, "I've heard talk of a man named Frederic Tavish. He thought Lord Breemore was perhaps responsible for King Cordell's disappearance. Since I am hearing differing opinions, I am curious to know more. Did you ever hear Frederic speak?"

Alene responded in a surprisingly rebuking manner. "No, but I know he was not for peace. I would not speak so freely of him, if I were you. It could put you and the children in danger if it were ever thought that you agreed with that madman."

"Who were his enemies?" I asked, now seeing how this conversation had opened a door to gain information.

"*He* was the enemy. People only reacted in defense. I suppose everyone was against Frederic Tavish. He verbally assaulted Lord Breemore, who has only ever been good and brought us peace."

Realizing how much Breemore did own the allegiance of the people, I nodded again, not knowing how to respond. I however did assure her, "I will never act in any way which would place the children in danger."

Alene smiled, her lighthearted, playful countenance returning as she bumped my shoulder. "And don't do anything which places yourself in danger. There are many of us who care for you."

I considered returning her smile when Hazel suddenly exclaimed, "Lady Vala!"

Before she could be officially announced, the children were in Lady Vala's arms.

I drew near to take part, and then remembered Alene. I turned back to invite her. "Will you come meet Lady Vala, whom you have heard the children talk so much about?"

"Of course," she answered, joining me.

I hugged my grandmother as the one who knew all that wrestled within me. "I am glad you have come," I whispered and then introduced, "This is Alene. She has taken thoughtful care of the children."

Lady Vala took Alene's hands in hers and thanked her.

There was no hesitation as next, Breemore took Lady Vala's hand and smiled winsomely. "Dear Lady Vala, welcome home. I was not sure when to expect you, but I have a room prepared for you."

"I thank you, my lord," she answered graciously. "I would like to stay near the children."

"My dear Lady Vala, you are quite free to do as you please; however, the closest rooms are servant chambers."

"I shall not mind."

"I can prepare the chamber that is next to mine," Alene offered.

"I would like that," Vala answered.

"So be it," Breemore accepted the arrangement, "for I shall never be the man who contradicts two ladies. Any accommodation you lack, I shall have brought to you immediately."

It was so strange to see Lady Vala and Breemore interact for the first time. They were so elegantly mannered to one another. Did Vala have hopes of changing Breemore?

After Breemore spoke a handful of pleasantries and asked the right amount of polite questions, he declared, "I shall disturb this happy reunion no more. I bid all of you marvelous dancers and Lady Vala a good night."

As he parted, Hazel hugged him which surprised me. She expressed, "You must be good. You brought Galen and Lady Vala to us."

Breemore smiled and patted her head. My instinct rose violently to fling his hand from her, but Vala, unshaken, gently and discreetly held out her hand to Hazel to draw her from him. Vala always seemed to know the perfect touch to give a situation. I felt starved for the same ability.

The children began telling their stories to Lady Vala all at once. Vala set their excitement in order, so that each child was able to share their story. I settled to the background so that the evening might be devoted to the children. Alene sat in a chair next to me. Silently, we watched and enjoyed listening—smiled some and laughed a little.

"Where is Cadby?" Lady Vala asked the children.

Upon her question, I instantly regretted that I had forgotten him. My mind had been too full. I looked beneath the window curtain and saw his shoes.

Lady Vala gently pulled the curtain aside. Cadby looked up at her as a snail might to a high tower.

"Cadby," she began, "I have something to show you." She rolled back the sleeve of her gown to reveal a slashed scab on her wrist. "The cut is healing, and all is well." Softly, she pulled his hand from his pocket and set it over her wound. "Your touch is very special." Then, she returned his hand to his pocket as if she were putting away the finest possession.

The older maid, who the children had come to call Groana, suddenly woke as she always did when it was time for the children to go to bed and announced, "Bedtime," in a craggy, sleepy tone.

"Lady Vala," Badrick interceded on behalf of all the children, "can't we stay up later tonight? You just arrived."

Groana swooned back into her chair ready to bemoan herself if she be overruled.

Lady Vala adhered to the bedtime. "Now that I am here, we shall have much time to spend together. Go to your beds as the woman instructed, and I shall come say goodnight to each of you."

Even with nothing to murmur about, Groana wore the look of an injured soul as she gathered the children.

I told Groana I would extinguish the candles, for I wanted a reason to linger that I might speak a brief word with Vala without the others. Vala also knew to discreetly linger, so when the others had left, it appeared natural that we had both remained.

Vala sat on the couch, motioning for me to sit beside her. "I rejoice to be among my children again, though my heart is weighed down as I imagine yours is."

I leaned forward, resting my elbows on my knees. "I cannot seem to think about anything beyond what Meklon told me about Breemore and himself." Intently, I turned to look at my grandmother as I asked, "When were you told that they were from Multa?"

"From the beginning. When I was a child, my father worked the farm next to Trimont. Amond and I were already fast friends at the time Royston returned from the battle with the young Meklon and Breemore. The very next day, Amond told me everything and especially that I must keep it a secret."

"I'm glad Meklon finally told me."

"It was a secret that never should have been kept. Meklon and I did tell the elders everything we knew about Breemore when they were discussing what ought to be done after my sons were pronounced dead. But Breemore had such a wonderful explanation for each of our concerns against him that we were overruled, and Breemore was chosen to rule. Telling of Breemore's past and origin does no good when the people are already persuaded to his side. Indeed, even Meklon and I, in our readiness to forgive Breemore, fell prey to his deception when, at first, we believed his change to have been sincere. I cannot call our hope for reconciliation foolish, though it was, but it perhaps was foolish of us to have never told Cloven of our family's history with Breemore. Ever since reading your letter, my wish has intensified that I would have told him. In his guilt, he needed to know that there was a greater evil than himself at work in the incident."

I asked, "Do you think what Breemore said about my father is true?"

"Yes," she answered heavily. "The pieces fit. Thomas

had instinctively known that Breemore had ill intentions; Cloven had become smitten by Breemore's praise. Thomas' and Cloven's differing perceptions separated the close brothers in a way that was acutely painful to Thomas. Thomas clearly saw the danger which his brother was falling into, and I know that the love which so filled Thomas' heart would have caused him to follow his brother that night. And Cloven... I can only imagine the pain and guilt he has endured because of the death of his brother. And he never gave me the chance to help him through it."

I had never hurt for my father, but an unfamiliar pain for him came to me as I watched my grandmother. I wondered if I had been as good to him as I thought I had.

"Galen," Vala said after a moment, "I've wanted to tell you that before we left Trimont, Meklon asked Emerson if he would travel to Dresden to speak with your father."

I rose suddenly to begin extinguishing the candles, while I struggled to know what my own feelings ought to be.

"He will not come," I stated as unattached to emotion as I could. "I can search for King Cordell without him."

"Can you win a war without him?"

"A war?" I questioned, turning to face her.

"Meklon has more to tell you. He asked if you would meet him and the Hendrys at the Inner Tavern in Middle Quarters tomorrow during your midday break."

Chapter Eleven
~ *Galen* ~

I braced myself on the rickety chicken wagon which I'd been assured was taking its delivery to Middle Quarters. At the devilish speed of the driver, the distressed chickens clucked and flapped against their wooden cages like a massacre was happening. Feathers overtook the meal which I was attempting to eat amid the bumps and stench. Regardless, I did appreciate the speed, for I was anxious to hear what Meklon had to say and worried about how little time I could stay to hear it.

Deteriorating and narrowing alleys increasingly jostled the wagon. I could nearly reach out and touch the blackened buildings on either side as they infringed over the jagged and often missing cobblestones. Overhead, dingy laundry lines brushed against the top chicken cages. I ducked once or twice. Only someone born and bred in these alleys would dare push their horses this fast through them.

When the road turned uphill, I recognized that the decrepit streets were the ones Meklon had led me through the first time he took me to Lenrow. At intervals, people hurriedly passed, scooting between the buildings and the moving wagon. The wagon abruptly slowed, and I heard the commotion of a crowd over the din of chickens. I stood to look over their cages to see what it was about.

A crowd so stuffed the narrow street that the wagon was now forced to completely halt.

"Out of my way!" the driver yelled to the crowd. "Do you want your chickens decayed between your toes before you get 'em! And I won't take a penny less for 'em if they are. Move!"

Like swelling water, people gravitated to any crack of space, pressing around the wagon — even climbing into it. The stench intensified as everything that emanated out of man and animal was trapped within this over-crammed street and forced into the nose.

The interest of the throng seemed to be toward the building at the corner. Heavy and brooding upper stories bore heavily upon the lower level. Its sign was faded and hung half hinged, but it read the Inner Tavern.

I jumped from the wagon into the crowd, managing to land on my own feet and not on another's. I squeezed my way into the building where I struggled to maintain a place along the back wall.

Beside me, a man grumbled to his wife, "Jist ye see, woman; the man will speak about Multa. Jackson is right. You let our boy go with him."

The woman stiffened her neck against her husband, causing her foul gaze to fall on me instead. "A stranger, are you? From Multa," she presumed.

"I'm from Dresden. What is this word about Multa?"

The woman ignored me; however, her husband pushed her out of his way so that he could stand next to me. "Ye haven't heard," he whispered. "Near two months ago, Jackson sent spies over Multa's borders. Yesterday, they returned. Their report..." he paused for effect. "Multa has built an army. An army so massive that the spies said they couldn't see it from one end to the other. Jist ye envision all those men, beasts, catapults, crossbows, and maces the size of my strapping head! We must prepare and demand that Lord Breemore build a defense. Join us, man! You look strong."

"Is Jackson the one speaking here?" I asked.

"Nay, I don't know who this man is; the runner boys called everyone here. But it must be Jackson's doing. One of his men come to tell us what to do."

Extending on my toes, I searched for either Meklon or the Hendrys, but in vain. There were too many people. I forced myself to wait, knowing they were here as Vala had informed.

A thud thundered from the front. Braun Hendry soon stood his entire height above the crowd and stomped his foot on the barrel on which he stood until every voice silenced and every eye, whether expectant or scornful, was fixed on him.

"Eh, the cobbler," the man, who had spoken to me earlier, carelessly muttered.

What I saw in Braun was more akin to a general— tall and broad with thick, calloused hands that could wrestle with iron. His gaze was firm and direct. The crowd seemed to cower, looking like humped skeletons beneath his strong, healthy form.

Under my breath, I cheered him.

"Truly, listen to me," Braun began in a voice that matched his stature. "Now that Jackson's spies have returned from Multa, the rumor is rampant that Multa is preparing an army to attack this kingdom. I believe this is true."

"Here, here!" the man beside me shouted.

"Nonetheless," Braun continued, "I am here to declare that something worse is happening."

The man beside me again raised his voice. "What is worse than war?"

"The battle for your mind," Braun answered evenly.

The man scowled at Braun, but said nothing more.

Braun spoke on with authority. "Hear this! Your fathers and grandfathers were the ones valiant in battle who defeated Multa. But their victory and strength came from a source that you know not. If you attempt to fight without the knowledge they possessed, you will fail. It was their honor for the Book of Truth and the Line of Cordell that made them victorious. They were men and women who humbled themselves enough to climb to the heights of truth, love, and sacrifice.

"But you have followed after Lord Breemore, a man who has deceived you and stripped you of your strength and understanding. Even if you build an army, you will still be defeated because you have not truth. You heard what Frederic Tavish proclaimed about Lord Breemore's deceit and the Book of Truth's promise that proves King Cordell is still alive. I declare that I believe what Frederic told us. I implore you to also consider the words you heard from him."

A stone of insecure silence seemed to have lodged in every throat, until I noticed the hot, rattling cheeks of the man beside me.

"You are not of Jackson!" he erupted. "Nor are ye friend to this city!"

My heart pounded, and I wondered if I should defend Braun. But Braun addressed the man strongly, "You can report me to the rioters who killed Frederic Tavish, or you can first listen to what I have to say. I have here hand-written copies of the Book of Truth that I am asking you to read. If you care about our kingdom and having victory over Multa, I beg you, at least read the Book of Truth."

The man beside me pushed his way through the crowd, waving his hands to draw attention to himself. "Don't listen to him! We don't need any of that trouble. Ye know the old book is forbidden and for good reason. War is coming; we must prepare to fight. Any men who want to join with Jackson, raise your hands. Yes, yes, keep raising them. You, man, in the back, who was standing next to me, why haven't ye raised your hand? Are ye a coward?"

Heads turned to look back at me. I took a deep breath and looked the man right in the eyes. "I want to know truth first."

"Then know that you and all like ye are cowards and traitors who have turned your back on this kingdom." He cut through the crowd and spit on my boot. "I've heard enough! Let these lunatics be left. All who want to join with Jackson, follow me."

He marched out of the tavern, accumulating the entire crowd in his tracks. Braun made one last appeal, "Does anyone want a copy of the Book of Truth?" But the words just seemed to make the crowd shuffle out faster. As the crowd thinned, I saw Meklon, Hildie, and young Cote near the front. I made my way toward them.

Braun stepped down from the barrel, tensely clenching his jaw and letting the rejected copies of the Book of Truth lower limply in hand. His wife and son drew near him. His face gentled as he enfolded his family in his arms. "This was our first time; it is to be expected. Don't lose heart."

"I won't, Papa," Cote consoled his father.

Longing for Lydia rose in my heart. She would have fit so well into this moment. We would have known all that the other felt without either of us speaking—like Braun and Hildie.

I harshly cast the thought from my mind and followed Meklon to an empty corner of the tavern.

"I wanted you to come so you could see what is happening for yourself," Meklon began. "I did not know until yesterday morning that Jackson's spies had returned. Their word is spreading like fire in a gale. The news has not reached the nobles yet, but it will. Within a fortnight, Jackson will petition Breemore to prepare an army for defense. This, I believe Breemore will grant in order to prevent a rebellion, but it will not spare us. Breemore has already positioned this city for defeat whether we have an army or not. We have one hope, Galen." Meklon lifted sorrowful eyes to the back of the tavern where the last stragglers left. "We must help them to understand the truth.

"It is how the curse works. In the past, when Multa has attacked, they have always been defeated because their rejection of truth weakened, blinded, and hardened them; while Calderon's acceptance of the truth made them triumphant with fortitude, wisdom, and love. But if Calderon now rejects the truth they once loved, we lose all advantage, and the battleground becomes equal. If Breemore's plan progresses to the stage that is written about in the Book of Truth, when the people with one accord reject the Line of Cordell, Multa will grind this kingdom into worthless dust. Thereafter, it will never again be known that there ever was such a pure and beautiful possession as truth."

Until now, everything in my mind had been consideration, but after this, all the forging of Meklon's words finally set into conviction. I spoke without a second thought, "I will find King Cordell. Our only chance is if the people reinstate him as their king."

"I'm glad to hear that your mind was prepared for this. You having freedom within the castle gives you a great advantage that Frederic did not have."

"When do you think Multa will attack?" I asked.

"I believe during the time of the tournament when King's City will be thrice its size and ripe for the slaughter. For now, play into Breemore's hand; win the upcoming scrimmage. This will ensure your freedom within the castle and the protection of the children and Vala. Meanwhile, the Hendrys and I will continue what was begun here today, striving for the ear of the people."

I knew it could not be evaded, but I could not help voicing my fear, "You and Braun might be murdered as Frederic was."

"So could you."

I looked down, knowing how true this was but still feeling my task the safer at this point.

Meklon added, "I concede that I feel as if we are setting a pebble, hoping it will stop an avalanche. Nonetheless, if a pebble was set right within each mind, it could contain the power to awaken the light in them.

"Do not worry. We will be wise and begin here in Middle Quarters where such talk is safer than the city at large. I only fear that our influence shall be limited, and the rest will befall your shoulders because you are the only one who can obtain a prominent voice. Once you win the scrimmage, you will have the attention of the entire city. When they see your strength and skills, you will be the man the people look to in perilous times, even possibly above Breemore. That is when you must lead them, not to battle, but to remember their rightful king and the Book of Truth. It is a dangerous line to walk, but I am entrusting you as a son of Trimont to walk it."

I humbly bowed my head, accepting my commission.

"Now," Meklon hurriedly unfolded a map and held it between us, "We must hurry, or your long absence will be noticed. Frederic Tavish left you some help in finding our king. This is a map he gave to the Hendrys before he died. In the end, Frederic firmly believed that Breemore held King Cordell hostage somewhere in the Inner Tunnels, but there is no way into them beyond Sedgwick's chamber."

"Did Breemore seal the entrances?" I asked.

Meklon looked up at me. "Royston did; he had no choice. He shared all the secrets of the Inner Tunnels with his children, including Breemore, who had a deep fascination with the tunnels and spent hours exploring them on his own. When Breemore returned to Multa, Royston feared that Breemore would use the tunnels against us in an attack. Therefore, Royston made the difficult decision to seal them."

Meklon's gaze returned to the map. "Frederic has marked here where all the Inner Tunnel entrances are, all of which remain sealed to this day. However, Frederic was convinced that Breemore must have made a new entrance into the tunnels from somewhere within the castle. Frederic, therefore, began to calculate where a new entrance could have been constructed. These lines indicate where the tunnels run throughout the mountain in connection with the castle. That is as far as Frederic progressed. Study this map; study the castle. See if you can discern possible places where a new secret entrance could have been made. We will see what comes of it."

Meklon folded the map and gave it to me. As I looked at him, he began to place his hand on my shoulder then took it back, smiling to himself. "You do not need any more weight on your shoulders just now."

I was surprised as Meklon lightly chuckled. It was the old familiar softening of his countenance that I had not seen since our training days at Trimont. To hear Meklon's old humor was a gift, and nothing could have sent me on my way better.

I shook Braun's hand on my way out.

He held my hand long enough to warn, "Beware of Captain Rhys. He will suppose himself in charge of the army and will not like a rival. I suspect he was behind the rioters who killed Frederic."

I nodded. "You be careful as well. What you did today spoke powerfully to me, if to no one else."

"We are just glad you and your father are alive," Hildie encouraged.

I ignored the harsh feelings that still arose whenever my father was mentioned and bid them a heartfelt farewell.

As I ran back, the voice of my father haunted me, "If you go, you better not fail."

I repeatedly mouthed what my answer had been, "I won't. I will not fail. I won't!"

"You will not what?"

The woman's voice startled me. I had stopped at the back arena gate to catch my breath and had not seen Lady Laila standing by the opposite pillar.

There was no obvious reason for her to be in the secluded spot except maybe for a personal stroll.

"I won't be late returning to training again. I hope your father is not angry."

I decided it was better not to ask her any questions and kept walking toward the gate.

To my surprise, she followed me, though a few paces back. She said lowly but loud enough for me to hear, "I have kept myself hidden during the time of your necessary absence. If we enter together, it may be concluded that you were on an errand, escorting me, and your secret business will be safe."

Her words stopped me. I knew my reaction gave credence to her claims. There was no way into her dark eyes, but her delicate mouth was known for honesty, so I would trust her.

I asked, "How did you know?"

"Observation and pondering what I see. I help the cases I deem worthy, of which you are one."

I offered her my arm. "Then I must thank you."

Together, we entered the arena, and no one questioned me. When we parted, I strangely felt separated from my guardian angel and desired strongly to tell her everything.

Chapter Twelve
~ *Lydia* ~

I'd come to Cloven's cabin so often that I knew the screech of the door before opening it and the cabin's forsaken smell without sniffing. Every day I hoped to find that a dish had been moved or mud prints added to the floor, but as my eyes again swept over Cloven's untouched belongings, I at last conceded that the items were permanently stilled.

The blanket of dust on the table sneered at me. The dust had clearly long known and relished its new ownership of the abandoned cabin.

With my apron, I swiped the dust from the table, blew it from the scant dishes, swatted it out of the quilt, and shook it from the curtain. Dust whirled in fury. Yet, nothing changed.

I knelt on Galen's bed to open the window. Leaning out, I gasped for the fresh air, for swaying branches, for birds in flight, and for the clouds which never abandoned the sky.

"What should I do?" I whispered.

I was only just feeling what Galen had suffered his entire life. Now I understood why he wanted to win a tournament—anything to escape from this trap: the impossibility of reaching his own father.

As the others arrived in the wagon to pick me up, I pushed myself away from the window. On my way out, I closed Cloven's door with finality.

The three of them, attuned to my discouragement, watched me climb into the wagon next to Netty. I took into my lap, just so I could stare into it, the wooden bowl of green beans which I had picked and boiled early this morning for Dresden's late summer feast that we were now heading to.

Auden prodded the horses onward while I thought very heavily of telling Helena and Grenfell about Cloven and asking for their help.

"Hello, Lydia!" a girl yelled from the back of her family's wagon as we joined the main road.

"Hello!" I waved. The child's voice pulled me back into the healing brooks of Dresden.

"Do you wish Galen were here to take you to the feast?" the girl continued chatting. "If not my brother would like—"

Her arm was suddenly tugged to the other end of the wagon by her red-faced older brother.

I inwardly laughed, and despite my mental caution, I drifted into my secret hope that one day Galen would ask for the other half of our dance which we had only just begun during the feast at Crevilon Castle.

Netty supplied cheerfully, "You will have to marry Galen since all of Dresden calls you Galen's girl. I've seen Grenfell growl at any young man who so much as looks like he is going to speak to you."

"And I'll pinch their ears," Helena trumped. "Lydia's for Galen and Galen's for Lydia. No Danek, nor Amos, nor anyone else can prevent destiny."

Over the bowl of green beans was a good place to spill my smile.

The road progressively grew crowded as the people of Dresden gathered to the village meadow for the outdoor feast. Tables, taken from homes, had been unloaded from wagons and pushed together to form a long line through the middle of the meadow. Families walked from their wagons, hauling chairs and food. Once arms were emptied, the table setting was fidgeted over by mothers while the children spread throughout the meadow like blown dandelions.

I met Grenfell at the edge of the meadow where he was meticulously overseeing the roasting boar.

"Welcome, welcome!" he greeted. "How's my Galen's lass?" His eyes twinkled with mischievous cheer.

"Happy to be among his people," I answered.

"Ah, Galen would choose a girl who would melt my heart. Don't go far, lass, because I have a surprise coming."

I joined in step with Helena as we still needed to unload our contributions. She sighed as she reminisced, "You know, there was one time Amos smiled. Of course, one faint smile amid his thousands of frowns hardly warrants mentioning. Still, I never forgot it and am remembering it especially today because it happened at a feast just like this one. His wife, beautifully radiant with child, was with him. They were the handsomest couple and stayed on each other's arm all the glorious day. I had the silly notion that he would be a different man from that point on. But the truth be told, it was the first and only glimmer of a smile I have ever seen from him. Dreary to be speaking about on such a festive day, but I knew Amos was on your mind."

"Helena," I ventured. "I have decided to tell you and Grenfell all that I know about Amos. Perhaps tonight after the feast Grenfell could come to your cottage?"

Helena burst out, "If you are ready to tell, girl, let's not wait until after the feast! We'll make time now!"

In the swiftest movements, she set her basket on the table, did the same with my green beans, took my hand, and pulled me after her, while saying, "We'll go to Grenfell's shop."

She waved her other arm to gain Grenfell's attention. When I saw Netty and Auden, I motioned for them to follow us.

Together, we all entered Grenfell's shop.

"What's this about?" Grenfell inquired.

"Bar the door, Grenfell," Helena ordered as she closed the shutters. "We don't need busybodies barging in just now."

Grenfell barred the door, and then turned with his arms folded upon his chest, demanding an answer for his obedience.

Helena whispered, "Lydia is ready to tell us about Amos."

"Why so suddenly?" Grenfell questioned, his brow brooding in stern worry.

"I didn't mean for it to be sudden."

"I did," Helena stated.

"For my part," I added, "today, I finally accepted that my waiting for Amos was madness. You both warned me it was so. I am at the end of what I can do on my own. I would like your help."

Without another word, Grenfell found a chair for everyone.

Helena smoothed the wrinkles on her lap, folded her hands together, and affirmed, "I'm ready."

Tied by the difficultly of knowing where to begin, I acutely felt the stifled, dim room and the sawdust clinging to my warm skin.

"You are safe telling us," Grenfell prompted.

"I believe you. But will you believe that Amos is not who you have always believed him to be?"

Grenfell leaned back and folded his arms skeptically while Helena scooted her chair forward, stared at me, and gave a breathy, "Yes."

"What are you saying?" Grenfell challenged Helena. "That Amos is a liar? We know his origin — the fire, him coming here, his wife dying, and Galen. How could Amos be anything but that? Now, lass, tell us about Galen. Is he in trouble?"

"She'll get to Galen later," Helena answered. "Let her speak about Amos. I've been waiting to hear this since Galen's mother died. She knew there was something greater. Go on, Lydia, tell these old ears the missing pieces they have never heard before."

The way was opened. The weight of the secret rolled from my lips into their broad view. "Amos is the rightful steward king. His name is Cloven Trimont."

Their gaze, having been committed to my face, now seemed to suspend between their eyes and mine.

"It was a shock to Galen as well. There is so much to the story. One of the discoveries was the Trimont mark behind Galen's right ear. I saw it myself."

Helena quietly confided, "I've seen it too, when Galen was just a wee thing, though I never told anyone of it. It's why Amos told Galen not to shave his head, isn't it?"

"Mark or not, I need to know more," Grenfell required, "for certainly this does not make sense!"

I continued to explain everything to them and answered their many questions.

Grenfell summed up, "Now Galen and the whole kingdom are in danger by this Breemore scoundrel. Pe'h! I knew he was a skunk! His stench won't remain in this village! Injustice won't last through the night. Something must be done!"

"Then I must ask if you would help me search for Cloven?"

"Lass, you are in Dresden; ask and it will be done. And I too want to hear Amos speak for himself."

Outside, we suddenly heard the voice of a boy proclaiming, "Amos is a king! Amos is really a king. We thought he was a grumpy hermit, but he is secretly a royal king!"

All of us jolted to the door. The boy avidly weaved throughout the crowd, repeating his overheard news. I watched helplessly while the kingdom's invaluable secret was flung aloud as if it were chicken feed. Everyone stopped what they were doing to ask the boy questions. He, in answer, pointed to me.

"Don't worry, lass," Grenfell assured. "I'll handle this." He motioned everyone to himself with his broad arms. "Come," he bellowed, "and I'll explain."

As people gathered, they threw their questions, "Is it true?"

"Tis true," Grenfell began. "I just learned it myself and hardly believed it. But our Lydia here explained to me everything. Amos is a king in hiding. You all remember when that Lord Breemore came to announce that tournament! Well, it was a trick to snatch our Galen!"

Grenfell animatedly retold the secret as if it were his to tell. He forgot nothing and spoke in rich tones which both stirred fear and devotion. Compared to my small, disordered delivery, his was masterful. His speech blew heroic winds over his audience. I felt momentarily woven into a Trimont tapestry.

Grenfell powerfully concluded, "Now the entire

kingdom is in trouble because Breemore plans to destroy it! We must help. Amos needs to reclaim his throne! Lydia came to convince him, but she can't when he is not here. Our part is to find him and make sure no one who passes into our village ever hears one word of this."

A lad of about fourteen stepped forward, saying, "If Amos is a king and Galen in trouble, I'll help in any way I can. And I swear not to tell."

I recognized him as the one who helped care for Cloven's farm.

Many others echoed the lad's pledge.

Grenfell, seeing his audience ripe for commanding, proposed, "Let us turn our feast into a search party for the sake of our kingdom, our Amos, and our Galen! Men, eat what you can in a hurry, gather weapons and lanterns, then gather into groups of five."

He then strode to the roasting spit where the boar had burned from neglect. Without a word or grimace, he sliced and distributed the meat.

I sought Netty, who I found directly behind me. She looked as though a whirlwind had blown her thoughts beyond her current reach. She breathed, "I could hardly explain what just happened, but I believe it was good."

"It has to be. Look how everyone is responding."

We joined the table where the once heaping bowls and pots were hurriedly emptied. No one seemed to notice that the food was either cold or burnt. The secret had produced such reverence and duty that complaint and idleness was wiped far from Dresden.

When I next saw Grenfell, he had a sword buckled to his waist and held four more. These swords he distributed to choice men who would lead the different search parties.

"You will allow me to go, won't you?" I asked him.

"Of course, of course, just stay close to me. Wild beasts will be lurking once the sun sets. Auden, you join our group, and I suppose Barley since he is my apprentice."

"I shall join you as well," Helena determined.

"May I come?" Netty asked nervously.

"Very well," Grenfell consented.

When ten groups had assembled, Grenfell delegated search areas for each. "If anyone sights Amos, send two men to tell the next group and so on. If found, don't let Amos out of your sight. Drag him here if need be."

As nearly fifty of us set out under a glorious sunset, I believed I had reason to hope… at least a little.

Our group of six would search the west gullies. To reach them, a walk across the fields was required, so there was time to enjoy the sunset. I discerned that Helena especially basked in the view with a joyous glow on her face. When she perceived I watched her, she freely manifested the thoughts of her heart, "I was imagining what Galen would have felt when he discovered that he was a prince."

"I wasn't there when Lady Vala and Meklon told him, but when Galen told me, his entire countenance had been elevated."

Helena linked herself to my arm, nuzzling her shoulder against mine like a young girl who was very happy.

Alongside her, my soul was dazzled by the sunset and the excitement of our quest until the deepening woods suddenly disturbed both.

We stopped to light the lanterns. Grenfell began to call, "Amos!" while the rest of us continually swept our lanterns and thoroughly scanned every inch of our moving light.

Slowly, we moved deeper into the gullies as the land

rose high above us on each side. We might as well have been swallowed by the intestines of the earth where a man could hide and never be found. I was comforted when I heard the distant voices also calling his name.

After a while, Helena suggested to Grenfell, "Why don't you stop calling Amos by that fraud name. He is King Cloven. He might better come under his respectful title."

"The last he told me, his name was Amos. I'm not going to mess with a man's wishes until he decides to change his name for himself."

We searched until it was the time of night when sleepiness was powerful and bodies moaned for bed and blanket.

"Perhaps we should start again in the morning with the light," Netty yawned, stumbling in her next step.

"Perhaps a smart man would suggest that," Grenfell answered, "but I'm a practical man, and when something needs doing, it needs doing, no matter what time it be."

"I've found him! I've found him!" Barley yelled ahead of us. We stood on the top of the ridge, and all looked to where Barley pointed as he quickly slid back down into the gully. We all rushed after him. Before we reached the edge of the descent, Barley climbed back up with a horrified expression. "He's dead."

My body responded by shaking and involuntarily stepping backward into Helena. Her lantern dropped, immediately extinguishing light. Auden removed his hat and fell to his knees.

"I'll go and see to him," Grenfell offered huskily. "Barley, show me where you found him."

By this time, the other group in our area had joined us. Before Grenfell walked down, he asked, "Does anyone have a blanket?"

An old woman removed the shawl from her shoulders. "It's not fit for a king, but it's been the source of my warmth on many a cold day and night. Let him have it."

Grenfell reverently took the offered shawl and followed Barley down the hill. We all stood looking down into the darkness into which the two men descended. My eyes stared down. Chills, pressure, restriction, heat… *guilt.* My body couldn't regulate itself.

Helena placed her arm around me.

Out of the darkness below, all of us heard, "You numbskull, Barley! The man is still alive!"

Instantly, I ran down, fumbling as I went. Auden caught my arm before I slid, then we both quickly descended together. The body looked dead, lying there curled in a ball of stillness.

"Is he really alive?" I asked.

"Yes, yes, but he doesn't want to be, by the looks of it. Nearly starved himself to death, I would guess. We've got to wake him up before he drifts too deep. Water! Does anyone have water?"

Barley lifted up a tin cup, saying, "All I gots is an empty cup."

I quickly grabbed it and followed the sounds of a nearby stream. I had a difficult time finding it in the dark, but again Auden came to my aid, like an overseeing grandfather, holding his lantern before me.

When we brought the water back, Grenfell had propped Cloven against a tree and was lightly slapping his face. "Come on old Amos, wake up. You've got explaining to do. WAKE UP!" He shook him.

A deeper breath rose from Cloven's chest. "Hurry! The water." Grenfell forced a little water into Cloven's mouth. Cloven's eyes flicked open then shut again.

"Let me die," he whispered. "It's the only answer."

"Death isn't your answer, Amos, whatever it is that ails you. Not when you have a whole village ready to help you. And we are going to help you, Amos."

But Cloven was, again, too unconscious to hear it.

Chapter Thirteen
~ *Lydia* ~

With a strenuous heave, Grenfell picked Cloven up and carried him out of the gully. I anxiously followed, stumbling, because I refused to take my eyes from Cloven as if my gaze had the power to keep him alive. Cloven's beard, hair, and nails were all grown and frayed. His lips bled. His cheeks were sunken like empty bowls. As Grenfell carried him, his head and limbs drooped down like fragmented pieces of discarded cargo.

Once we reached the top, only Helena and Netty remained. The group who had joined us must have dispersed to tell the other searchers that Cloven had been found.

Grenfell breathlessly commanded Barley to share the weight of carrying the body. Barley took Cloven's legs, and Grenfell plunged on.

"Where are you taking him?" Helena questioned, as she and Netty hurriedly made pace with us.

"Cloven's cabin," I answered without thinking, for not long ago I had detected the top outline of the small mountain which shadowed Cloven's farm.

"Aye, lass, lead the way," Grenfell panted.

Auden handed me Barley's lantern. I led in the straightest path that I perceived, hoping that my eyes had not deceived me.

When I began to distinguish the familiar landmarks, which I had noted during my daily rambles about

Cloven's woods, I quickened the pace. Soon the farm clearing was evident as the moonlight pooled in the open space.

I ran ahead to open the door and prepare Galen's bed. Cloven's bed, I knew, was not fit for anything since its musty straw mat had worn thin and was often damp from leaks.

Once Grenfell and Barley had laid Cloven down, Grenfell collapsed in the only chair, breathing too heavily for speech.

"Quickly, we need water for both of them!" Helena exclaimed.

Auden promptly responded.

"Cloven also needs food," Helena called after him. "There are some berry bushes along the back of the barn."

"And perhaps some eggs in the hen house," Netty added as she followed at her father's heels. Barley too grabbed a lantern and dashed to help.

He must not have realized that the lantern he took was the cabin's last light, as the cabin was suddenly submerged into utter darkness. I tried to feel my way to the window shutter when a flame thankfully rose in the hearth.

Helena climbed up from her knees, mumbling to herself, "Well, Barley, be glad I already had a match in my hand."

"Does he still live?" Grenfell asked anxiously.

The firelight was not yet bright enough to tell. I tentatively set my hand on Cloven's forehead. Human warmth still resided. "He lives," I answered, removing my hand, for it felt very foreign upon his leathery brow.

Auden supplied the bucket of water, then silently positioned himself out of the way. Grenfell loudly drank his fill while Helena filled the tin cup for Cloven.

Like a grandmother nursing a sickly child, she gently raised Cloven's head, softly encouraging, "Drink, Cloven."

There was no response from him as the water dribbled from his useless lips.

Netty and Barley interrupted her effort, rushing in and pouring a handful of berries and two eggs on the table. "Sorry it took so long," Netty apologized. "We discovered a fox has been sneaking into the hen house. Many hens are missing, and a lot of ruffled feathers are about. As for the berries, the birds have eaten the best of them. We gathered what we could."

"It will be enough, I'm sure," I answered for Helena, who frightened me by her failing efforts to wake Cloven. She was now at the point of jostling Cloven's head and splashing water upon his dormant features.

Suddenly, his eyes cracked, and his forehead furrowed from the light.

"That's it, Cloven," Helena coaxed, quickly giving him the water while she could.

Hurriedly, I cooked the eggs and mushed the berries. Once I gave the plate to Helena, I fetched the wool blanket from Cloven's straw mat behind the curtain, so we could more comfortably prop him up that he might eat.

I took comfort that his lips numbly received the small bites pressed to them. However, even as he pitifully swallowed, his eyes despondently stared at the beams above him.

When the plate was empty and the fork no longer rose, Cloven's eyes closed, and the room seemed greatly hushed. Helena quietly set the empty plate on the table as we realized all the others had fallen asleep — Grenfell in his chair, the others on the floor.

"Sleep, dear girl," Helena whispered as she betook

herself to the rug before the hearth and curled there to sleep.

In the absolute stillness of night, I cast a last look at Cloven and found his eyes open and staring at me. Something passed between us as if our vulnerabilities clung to each other, revealing our inner most need for the other's help.

As soon as the bond came, it passed like a wind not likely to venture down the same path again, for Cloven turned his head as if I did not exist.

I retreated to the straw mat as it was the only place left to sleep. Its shabbiness engulfed me, but I would not succumb to so meager a discomfort. Still, I could not calm my body's tense shivering from the worry.

Having not slept soundly, I was among the first creatures to awaken. Pale light and songbirds were my first conscious companions. I slowly sat up, bravely lifting my mind to face the heavy load that swarmed it.

I watched Cloven until I saw his chest sufficiently rising as he slept. I then crept around the others until I stood outside where I inhaled of the morning and tried to exhale out all the worry and tension.

As I drew water from the well, I noticed Auden in the field tending to one of Cloven's horses. Repeatedly, Auden looked at me and then away, as if he was trying to make up his mind about whether to speak to me or not.

I set the bucket aside, intending to go to him; however, he took the first and concluding steps toward me.

"Miss Lydia?" he appealed.

"Yes," I eagerly answered, for he never went out of his way to speak.

"I don't imagine myself wise, but I've known Master Cloven since he was a boy. I've seen him like this before. It was his way as a child to hide himself when he knew he had done wrong. I see it all the same now. He has done something which he is ashamed of. He holds guilt and shame so tight."

"You think guilt has made him as he is?"

"I have no advice—only a story to tell which proves my words. Long ago Master Cloven disappeared from Trimont. For two days, none of us could find him. On the third day, his father and I found him in the woods, hiding in a hollow log. Right there, Amond set his son on his knee and questioned him until he perceived the boy's wrong. Amond then led his son away from his error and cleansed his conscience by bestowing forgiveness. Cloven beamed with new life and was ever after devoted to his father."

"You believe there is hope for him, then?"

"I wish you to believe there is hope for him." Auden bowed his head and walked on with the horse to the barn.

I pondered what he disclosed very seriously until I heard Grenfell waking the cabin. As Grenfell opened the door, I approached its threshold.

"Morning, lass. We have a tough day to live, haven't we, but we'll manage."

"Is Cloven awake?" I asked.

"I've made sure of it."

"I would like to speak with him."

Grenfell made way and set the chair at the bedside for me.

I sat, though unwelcomed.

"What is troubling you?" I probed. When Cloven made no response, I asked a different question. "Why do you want to die?" I paused after every question to see if it provoked any response from him. "Is there something which you regret? Why did you leave the throne when you were still alive? Do you know that your mother never believed you were dead?"

I was surprised when, below a whisper, he said, "Mother knew he was dead."

"Who?"

For a long while he did not answer. I thought he might have fallen asleep, but then he spoke a name—"Thomas."

"Your younger brother? Please tell me what happened," I coaxed, leaning nearer to hear his reluctant voice.

Another silence followed in which I and the others in the room patiently waited. At last he warned, "If I did, you would regret that you ever asked me to re-claim the throne. Don't waste your time on me."

"I will judge what I have wasted or not. All I ask is that you would speak to me plainly."

He scoffed in evident bitterness, "You want a good and noble Trimont on the throne to save your family, to save the orphans, to find King Cordell, to venerate your father's death, and to bring back the Book of Truth. You want a good man. You want a selfless man. That man is not me. I killed Thomas; I murdered my brother. I left to spare the kingdom of having to announce its first condemned ruler."

Hardly able to believe it, I asked, "How did Thomas die?"

"I told you; I killed him!"

The brutality of his voice shot a tremor through the cabin.

"How?" I persisted.

"You wish to torture me?"

"I need to understand more clearly. Please just tell me."

"I'll tell you, but my words will not ease you, nor is there any answer in them. On the night I was crowned, I fell in love," his voice was hard, biting, and self-hating. "She was all I saw and all I wanted. I had been encouraged to marry quickly as I was the last known heir to the throne. I therefore instantly set my intentions to make Gaynor my bride.

"In this I asked no advice nor did I listen to any, for indeed Thomas tried to stop me, and I silenced him forever. He knew that I was being led astray.

"I met Gaynor late that night on the moonlit mountainside. Thomas had the presumption to follow. Presumption is what I called it then; now I would be a fool to call it anything but love.

"He was sickly, and the festivities had taken their toll upon him. He had run up the mountain after us. His heart pumped so fast that his breath consumed him. Still, he besought me to return with him.

"I knew that he was on the verge of collapse. I knew I should have carried him back to the castle. But I ignored him; I turned my back on my brother. He set his hand on my arm to persist, and I flung it from me. Because of it, he collapsed, and his limp body fell down the steep mountainside.

"I went after him, instantly blind to everything, except an eternal horror. You will never know those first hours of agony I held his body, begging death to take me.

"Thus, Breemore found me. Now here lies the answer to the secret. It was I who commanded Breemore to stage my death and take my place as king. It was by my command! You wish me to save what I myself established? If Breemore is your enemy, then so am I."

I could hear no more. Weakly, I rose and left the cabin.

Becoming lost within the field, I entered the greatest despair I had ever known. Cloven—a Trimont—was to blame, not Breemore.

Something of anger churned at the corners of my heart as I thought of all my family and the kingdom had suffered because of Cloven's cowardice and selfishness! The man who should have thought of others first—who should have protected his kingdom from the very man he gave it to—who should have... But as my thoughts rose to condemn him, I knew this direction of my mind to be unhelpful.

Think. I told myself. But my little body had become enfolded within the tattered wings of injury and injustice. I felt wronged. I felt deceived. I felt the loss of hope which I had stored in him for so long. I had waited, fought, and believed in him in vain. Why couldn't he have told me this at our first meeting? Then I could have returned to my family and been of use to them.

"Ahh," I chided myself. Purposefully, I changed the course of my mind away from self-pity and accusation to much needed consideration.

What was to be done with Cloven? This question, my mind circled around as if it were larger than it truly was, for after thinking down the crevices and branches of all the circumstances, I should have concluded from the first that despite anything else, Cloven himself had to be saved.

Intruding back into his cabin would be to endure the presence of a grave from which a dying man had no wish to resurrect, but that cabin had long become my battleground.

A wind began to howl and with it, the scent of rain.

Clouds drew over the sun. Thunder rumbled in the distance. Tossing the stick I had been fidgeting with, I trudged to the cabin once more.

Grenfell and Barley were carrying supplies in from the wagon.

"I had not realized you had left," I voiced.

"You were afar off thinking, lass. I, like you, wished to be alone to sort through what Amos confessed about himself. While doing so, I brought back supplies and told the villagers the news. It was a bit more of a disheartening story to tell. I suppose it is fitting that a storm is fast approaching. Amos will have us for company until it passes whether he likes it or not. You hurry inside now."

As the first raindrops fell, I spoke to Auden, who unhitched the horses. "Did you hear?"

He nodded.

"Since you knew both Cloven and Thomas, do you have any more advice to help me?"

He looked as though the topic was very raw on his emotions. "Master Cloven won't be capable of forgiving himself. They were the most devoted brothers. It is a tragedy more than I realized. Forgive me. I can find nothing more to say."

Inside, I found Cloven shaved and better settled in the bed, with the quilt neatly folded at his chin. He slumbered, yet his facial muscles were fixed in disgust.

"I've done my best with him," Helena offered, gazing up from sorting through the new supplies.

Barley and Grenfell entered, and though they only looked toward Cloven, Helena quickly spread her wings over her chick, saying, "Let him rest while we eat. Nourishment will help us all."

The extra chairs Grenfell brought crowded the room.

Once we settled around the table, it did not matter, for there was not much reason to rise once seated. We ate bread, cheese, and leftover stew from yesterday's feast, which seemed so long forgotten. The storm unleashed during our quiet meal, making us even quieter beneath its tantrum.

After eating, Helena attended to Cloven's meal. Grenfell settled himself by the hearth to whittle. Barley and Netty played a game of wooden pegs. I cleaned what little I could. While we were all about our occupations, it was obvious that our minds were keenly aware of Cloven. The moment Helena helped lay him back down, he turned on his side to face the wall away from us.

Not knowing what good it would do, but knowing my task was not finished, I scooted my chair to his bedside.

"I understand now," I began, but I knew the rain had spoken louder. Though it felt foreign to place more force behind my speech, I repeated stronger, "I understand now."

"Then leave me be—all of you."

Before his depressed words could find a lodging place in the mood of the cabin, I dismissed them and spoke what I knew to be life giving. "I understand that your brother loved you and that he would have forgiven you. He wouldn't have wanted this separation and punishment for your life. He would have wanted you to confess your wrong, and then rightfully rule as steward king."

A wordless moment crept by as I had nothing else preplanned. "Your brother thought that you were worth risking his life for. It seems to me that he gave his life as much as you took it. He followed after you to save you without regard to himself. His death still calls you to return. Love Thomas. Return for his sake. Change for his sake. Don't let his death be in vain. Thomas was willing to die for you. What are you willing to do for him?"

"Enough!" he shouted, turning and rising on his elbow. "Tell me one unselfish reason why you wish me to return."

Stunned, I silently considered his accusation.

Upon my silence, he lashed, "Everyone is selfish. The Book of Truth is only an unnecessary ideal to burden men. If Breemore has rid the land of it, I applaud him. I would do the same."

All my faculties burned from those words, and as a sulfur match strikes flint to ignite, his dark soul had whipped across mine and lit a passion.

I stood, proclaiming, "No. Those are not the words of Cloven Trimont but of Lord Breemore. Cloven Trimont knows the promises of the Book of Truth. He knows who he is. He has a tapestry begun in the Hall of the First Loyals to the king. He has a mother who desperately loves him. And a son who has fought for him his entire life. And a king who faithfully waits to be found by him."

I fell to my knees at his bedside, begging, "I know who you are. I won't let you be anything else. You must listen. Not for my sake, but for your own, I beg you. There is hope for you. There is love for you. There is life for you."

His chin quivered. "I know better than anyone what I could have been. I failed! I made pledges, and I meant my vows with all my heart. I still broke them. I broke them all." Sobs cracked his aged exterior, and he confessed as a shattered man, "I cannot change what I am."

Now both our souls were exposed, and I too wept. "No, you are believing a lie. You are looking to yourself and not to the truth. You can still fulfill your pledges. You can stand on your father's achievements. Trimont blood runs through you. The Book of Truth speaks of new life that is rooted in love, forgiveness, and peace. I have lost my father and my home. My family is in prison, and I don't know if I'll ever see them again. Yet I have found life and hope. That is why I am desperate for you to find truth. Please, allow yourself to find it."

Cloven lay, turned to the wall, and spoke no more, but his shoulders shuddered from emotion. I then realized just how heavily I was breathing.

"That is it, lass!" Grenfell surged as if he could no longer fit in his own silence. "You eased the burning words on my tongue and spoke them better than I would have myself. Indeed, keep speaking. Speech from the heart such as this is powerful music to my ears."

Helena nodded, "Yes, keep speaking, Lydia. I want to hear more about the Book of Truth."

With my tears still damp on my cheeks, I retook my seat and spoke freely from the treasuries which had been built in my heart since Father's death. Not mere circumstances, but the deeper things of my soul which I had learned and clung to which fortified me. I was surprised how beautifully the lessons came out compared to how bitterly they had gone in.

They asked questions, pulling everything out of me that was within me concerning King Cordell and the Book of Truth. Never before had I spoken so freely those things for which my heart burned. I was enlivened. Nevertheless, I was always conscious of the unmoving body which lay facing away from us, wondering… hoping that he was listening.

When night fell and we all rested on the blankets Grenfell had brought for us, I felt peace residing in the cabin. No grudges were held, and forgiveness to Cloven had been offered by all but himself.

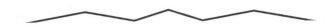

I wakened by a touch on my shoulder. "Wake, Lydia."

Helena knelt before me, clutching Galen's quilt. Behind her, the bed was stripped of everything but its old grey sheet.

"Where's Cloven?"

"Gone." Her word was empty, but her face was full. "Auden said that Cloven took a horse in the twilight hours. Grenfell is following the tracks. If they lead to the north, our steward king is returning."

Admiration and tears filled her eyes. She ran her hand down my cheek. "I believe he heard every word you poured forth. You may have given a man back his life, dear girl."

Chapter Fourteen
~ *Lydia* ~

"Goodbye, Lydia," the little girl sobbed, clinging to my hug.

I held her, equally breaking within. How I would miss these people. In the two days since Grenfell confirmed that Cloven had indeed traveled North, I'd been blown through by every emotional wind, both high and low.

The girl pulled away after the gentle urging of her mother, and I went on receiving the many hugs offered me one after the other. To Netty and Auden also were hugs given and received.

Repeatedly, I was made to promise that I would write them, for they were eager to be included in the coming events which they anticipated would unfold in King's City.

Helena stood by me all the while, we having already spoken our farewells at her home. Grenfell came last, and in earnest, handed me a folded parchment.

"If you remember, lass, the day of the feast I mentioned I had a surprise. I've concealed it until the fitting time. What you hold is a letter from Galen."

My heart, never suspecting, leapt.

"I haven't yet read it myself, though I've been aching to. Will you read it to us before you go—as a parting gift to you and all of us?"

With a smile rising from my heart to my face, I unfolded the letter and read aloud.

"Dearest Dresden,

After a few setbacks, I'm well settled in King's City. As Breemore promised, I have room and board in the King's Castle and the attention of the city's best sword master. I like to think I'm under way of making you all proud. Soon, there shall be a scrimmage where all I have learned will be tested. I will fight my best, remembering you all. People around here don't think much of Dresden, but they don't know that in Dresden is found the best pies, the happiest feasts, kindest neighbors, and most persistent lute seekers.

To answer the lads' questions to which they sent me to discover: There are more knights than there are people in Dresden. If you stand in the meadow and try to count all the wildflowers, it may match how many knights are in the army. To the second question, there are dyes and fabrics of every color sold daily in the markets. There are so many choices that one's apparel is never the same as their neighbor's. The third question is my favorite to answer because I've been inside the tallest tower. It rises from the castle far above King's City. Only the mountain and sky may boast above it. Think of Helena's Nest thirty times taller.

I continue to carve and am teaching a young orphan boy named Cadby. I must say, I have come to feel toward Cadby as if he were my own brother. There are many people whom I have met that have become dear to me. Every evening, I spend with thirteen orphan children, Lady Vala—"

"Oh, they are safe!" Netty exclaimed, and then clasped her hands over her mouth to help contain her joy. But I felt the same joy and expressed it in eagerly reading on.

> *"Every evening, I spend with thirteen orphan children, Lady Vala Trimont, who one day I will tell you more about — "*

"We already know; she is your grandmother!" someone shouted.

I nodded affirmatively.

> *"and Alene, a kind and fun nursemaid to the children."*

Who was Alene?

> *"These, along with a wise gardener named Meklon, a family of noble character named the Hendrys, and Lady Laila, a confidante and support in my training for the tournament, are the friends I've come to trust and love in King's City."*

Who was Lady Laila?

> *"I've also learned there are people who cannot be trusted.*
> *You shall be jealous to learn that I hear the lute played often in the castle. I wish I could capture the music and release it in your ears. Every time — "*

"Stop, stop, stop. Let me see that letter," Grenfell asked quite disgruntled, reaching for it.

I handed it to him. His eyes skimmed it over. "P'eh, I

don't like it. It hits me sour. Your name isn't in it while all these other ladies' are. For instance, do you know who this Lady Laila is?"

I shook my head.

"You need to be leaving now, lass. You have got to let Galen know you never married that rascal. You promise me that you will go to Galen."

"I have to see about my family first."

"Aye, I can't deny you that. But as soon as you can, you go to Galen, and you tell him that you will marry him.

"Don't give me that uncertain look, lass. You must promise me. I'm left here in Dresden, knowing the wolf is still about in the kingdom. I need assurance that the kingdom will be in the proper hands. This isn't about love; it's about our kingdom. That's why you can be bold. No lady is half as good as you for our Galen because you loved his father, you love his people, and you love the truth. If he may be a king one day, he needs a lass like you by his side. You promise me that you will go to him."

I tried to explain that it wasn't that simple. "I was never his girl. I can't force him to marry me. His heart has all this time been free to go to another. I can accept that."

"You are a selfless girl, lass, and can bear much self-denying, but I'm giving you permission to claim Galen as your own. You are as disheartened as I am. I could hear it in your change of voice as you read on in the letter, so don't let him go without a fight. Fight for him just as you did his father where you proved that you are of dauntless Dresden stock. Now will you give me assurance that you won't be passive about these other women stealing Galen's heart?"

He held my shoulders until I made an affirmative response.

Finally, I nodded and not without a hint of a smile.

Grenfell didn't hesitate to engulf me within his large arms. "Now I'll do something for you, lass. I listened to every word you spoke about the Book of Truth and our missing King Cordell. After you are gone, I'll be repeating it to all of Dresden and every stranger. I've got an excellent memory. I'll remember it right."

There was a little choke in his voice as he added, "Be safe."

Chapter Fifteen
~ *Danek* ~

Faye's knock persisted. I slammed the book shut, causing its loose and ancient latches to clang upon my desk. Returning the book to my drawer, I answered irritably, "Come in, if you must, Faye."

Faye entered, as she often did, with a candlestick in hand, always attempting to bring cheer and light into my darkened library where the sun was forbidden.

"I've heard talk," she began. "Lydia's mother is dying."

"I know this," I rebuked, standing abruptly. "She has requested to speak with me."

"I know you will go to her, and ease her if you can."

"Yes, though I wish to avoid it. Guilt, Faye, is now one of my faults. I would only speak of it to you."

"Don't blame yourself!" her voice slightly shrieked. "You are suffering too much as it is. I know your good heart. It was you who was wounded most. You freely offered Lydia all the devotion of your love and property. It was her choice. You are free in the matter. And her mother was already sickly. You must not blame yourself or your heart may fail!"

No longer able to indulge in her foolish sympathies, I ignored her and left my library. Faye did not know what I had discovered in my mother's trunk which pointed to Breemore's connection with Multa. Nor did she know the irritation I had gained by my readings and prying into Trimont and Multa affairs.

I winced as I entered the windowed corridor, where the sun sprayed me with its forgotten brilliance. I forced my eyes open and let them contend in their discomfort.

Once I stepped outside, my senses were further assaulted with heat. The day had selfishly shut off its breeze and offered nothing new to the world. However, as I descended to the prison underground, cold air exuded from the moist walls, and the gloom allowed my eyes respite. Here, my soul fit rightly.

I held a stern countenance as I followed the guard to the Tavish cell and maintained it while I waited for him to unlock the door. When I entered, I would not yield my exterior's indifference.

Ophelia was a near corpse bundled in many blankets, yet shivered. Garret rubbed her hand and breathed upon it in an attempt to bestow warmth. The little girl, Rose, dropped her doll and hid behind her brother. Her hair, mingled with straw, spiked out behind him as she peeked at me fearfully.

In the corner of the cell were surprisingly elaborate structures made of straw, chips of stone, and pieces of wood. A ball made of string lay in the middle of the cell.

Garret took his sister's hand and stood. He requested simply, "My mother wishes to speak with you alone."

I nodded my consent.

The guard escorted Garret and the girl away.

While Ophelia's eyes were open, she made no movement toward speaking. I coldly looked at the straw structures as I stated, "You requested to speak with me."

Her voice reached out weakly, "My request is for the release of my children. I would not ask if I were not dying."

Having prepared myself for the question, I now gave

my verdict quickly. "So be it."

"How will you provide for them?"

"Faye shall raise the girl, and Garret may return to rebuild your farm."

"Lydia must care for Rose," she insisted in a whisper, for her voice had dwindled to such.

"Lydia is not my concern."

"Then don't allow thoughts of her to rule your life."

"I shall think as I please."

"Your cheeks are pale and sunken. Your eyes are vacant. I fear you have imprisoned yourself just as much as you have imprisoned us."

"Whatever you think, I am a free man who rules himself well."

"Then this may have no value to you now, but I want to give you my freedom. I forgive you and offer you all the light of my soul. There is no darkness in it. Believing the truth has set it free. Remember this gift when I am gone."

Then her lip quivered. "Allow Garret and Rose to leave with you. I don't want them to have the memory of watching me die. Let me say goodbye, and then take good care of them."

I left the cell and motioned for Garret to return with Rose. As Garret passed, I informed him, "At your mother's wish and my authority, you shall say your goodbyes. Then you and your sister shall depart with me."

With great sorrow, he swept his eyes to his mother and painfully led Rose to her.

When Ophelia saw her daughter, her remaining strength produced a smile. "You will see the sun today, Rose. In a letter, write and tell me about it. Write and tell me everything." Gathering tears then married with her voice. "Never stop writing me. I will love every letter.

Rose, there is something I want you to memorize. Listen carefully then repeat what I say. Love is not selfish."

"Love is not selfish," Rose repeated barely audible.

"Anytime you are tempted to act selfishly, remember those words. If you follow them, they will make you beautiful."

Rose, frightened and confused, glanced at me. She then scrambled beneath one arm of her mother, wrapping its limp safety about her. Ophelia cradled her daughter as much as she could, then slowly raised her other arm to her son, who rushed to her weak beckoning.

"Oh, Mother!" he tragically exclaimed. "Let me stay with you."

"Don't let your heart be troubled, Garret. You shall rebuild our home. Do so for your father and me. We shall be proud of you. Go and raise a happy family there, and provide for Lydia when she has come back. You have the letters I left for her and Creighson?"

He took two letters from his pocket and held them for her to see.

She nodded. "Now take your sister, and go with Sir Danek."

Rose seemed too stunned to know what was happening and allowed herself to be lifted by her brother.

"I'll come back," Garret promised, carrying Rose out of the cell.

"I will send for the doctor along with Emerson and Levinia," I assured stiffly before I followed them out.

"I thank you," she replied, her eyes already closed. She would never know, but as her life faded away, her soul rose and smote me.

The doctor, Emerson, and Levinia were summoned. Rose was deposited to a happy Faye. Garret was free to go to his family's land.

I returned to my desk where I fell into a languid stare until a guard came that evening and reported, "Ophelia Tavish has died."

Chapter Sixteen
~ *Lord Breemore* ~

The tunnels were dark and cold as I waited for the distant torch in Remus' hand to draw near. The larger his firelight grew, it cast fearsome shadows on the tunnel walls. Upon them, neither to the left nor to the right, did my eyes stray. They narrowed precisely down the center of the tunnel from where Remus at last arrived with King Cordell.

I had forgotten how tall his stature was as he stood, blindfolded and bound at the wrists. It was the first time I had laid eyes on him in twenty-six years. I greatly disliked that his straight posture and confidence were among the first attributes which caught my notice.

This was not what I had expected. A man alone in captivity, for as long as he, should not have the air of confidence. Yes, his legs were as thin as lances, but his ankles did not waver. His skin upon his face was like a wrinkled cloth, but the muscles beneath were serene and patient.

His lips were cracked and white, but they did not beg to know who his captors were nor plead for freedom. The deplorable sight of him mixed with calm assurance almost compelled me to slap him, but I refrained. For all his body's deterioration, he was not conquered.

If all men reached this inner strength, I would be thwarted indeed, but few… very few ever did. Truth was powerful, but only when followed. The will to follow was present in few men… very few.

I adjusted my fur robe—a luxury which the shivering king was sure never to possess. I motioned for Remus to continue on his task. He yanked the rope which held together the king's bare wrists, and again the torchlight slowly diminished. In the end, it would not matter the greatness of the king if his people did not see it, and they wouldn't. I would send further instructions later. It was perhaps a little early to move the king, but Galen was seeking entrance into the tunnels, and I preferred for the old king to be discovered by different means.

I returned to my bed though my eyes remained wide.

Absolute thought and focus was required at this stage of the plan. People acted so haphazardly, I had to be prepared to redirect any of their willful actions, such as Captain Rhys' jealousy. While his hate for the old ways would accomplish my goals whenever needed, his jealousy against Galen would, I predicted, rise out of hand. I, however, would risk allowing him to make his mess and clean it after.

As for Galen's recent prying and distrust, I knew what it stemmed from. By the way Galen studied my features when he thought I was not looking, I knew that Meklon had told him that he and I were brothers. It was the only information shocking enough to completely convince Galen against me. But I had taken this into account; it was of little consequence. I did not require Galen's allegiance to position him for my use.

The scare of Multa's army had been effective, and I was pleased to grant the people whatever protection they petitioned, for in doing so was nothing contrary to my own goal of fueling a desire within the people for a mighty warrior king, whom they would discover for themselves tomorrow at the scrimmage.

Meklon and Galen had no choice but to play into my hand. It was like chess, cornering them at two angles. There would be no way out. That is why I would not fail. They would be trapped into doing just what I wanted them to do.

At the first light of dawn, my servant knocked to wake me.

"I am awake, my good man!" I called cheerily.

Chapter Seventeen
~ *Galen* ~

Wind howled through the arena like a trapped beast. Flags and garments snapped like whips, and the autumn leaves were spewed to the north. The clouds sped by, blinking shadow and sun over the arena. I inhaled, hoping for the fragrance of rain. Instead, it smelled of sharpened metal and blacksmith fires like it had for weeks since King's City began preparing a defense.

I quickly crossed the arena to meet Lady Laila, who had sent word early this morning that she wished to speak with me before the scrimmage began.

When I reached her, she requested, "Will you escort me to my father's observation balcony?"

I offered her my arm and walked on the side that most blocked the wind from her.

She began in a low tone, "Last night Captain Rhys followed you."

My steps hesitated as I looked down at my new boots which I had picked up from Braun last night at the market square.

She pointedly drew my eyes into hers, as she warned, "If you win the scrimmage today, I suspect that Rhys will try to kill you. By following you, he is already seeking a way to do so. Jealousy is in his blood. Do not win this scrimmage if you hope to be a future help to this kingdom."

While our eyes were thus intertwined, I felt a shudder

escape her. "I must never lose you," she whispered.

In the moment that lingered, I did not know what I felt, except that my heart beat faster. Before I knew how to respond, she parted from my arm and ascended the stairs to her father's balcony.

Strangely overcome with the urge to assure her that I would give the victory to another, I took a step to follow her, but I had to think beyond my responsive impulse. I drew my step back.

Meklon had told me to win the scrimmage. I could not allow the threat of Captain Rhys or Lady Laila's worry to deter my commission. I would just have to be more cautious around Captain Rhys.

I looked up at Lady Laila. She was draped in maroon velvet and crowned with her midnight hair, which was twisted through with silk and gems. When her dark eyes finally lowered into mine, I mouthed, "I will be careful."

She assented stiffly before resuming her straight gaze away from me, but I knew she would be watching.

On my return to the armory side of the arena, I eyed Captain Rhys standing on the royal balcony.

"Galen!" Badrick yelled as he was the first of the children to rush to the edge of their balcony and find me in the crowd of other men.

I moved toward him and waved as all the excited children joined him. Alene smiled as she held Emmy and pointed me out to her.

When the trumpets suddenly sounded, Emmy burrowed her head beneath Alene's chin. Alene tucked her away from all the noise. I smiled, as I often couldn't help when I watched Alene with the children.

The trumpets had announced Lord Breemore's entrance onto the royal balcony. Lady Vala entered with him and

147

was seated at his side as she had accepted Breemore's invitation to join him as his guest of honor. She looked regal. I was proud to see my grandmother in her rightful place as the true queen. She had more legal right to be there than Lord Breemore. Soon the entire kingdom would know it, for I felt I was close to getting into the Inner Tunnels and finding King Cordell.

All I needed was an opportunity to search Breemore's study. By countlessly walking throughout the castle with Frederic's map and noting the unusual location of the room which Breemore had chosen for his study, I'd concluded that, if indeed there had been a new entrance made, the opening was within Breemore's guarded study.

My hopes were high and so were the Hendrys from the brief note Meklon had left in my boot. The Hendrys had been well received among the ill and bedridden to daily read from the Book of Truth. Family members of the sick also quietly overheard their readings.

I began warm-up maneuvers, gaining energy from my thoughts and the crowd, which I observed had filled the large tiered seating and lined the walls.

Lord Breemore's colorful garments flapped in the wind, and his jolly eyes squinted against the gusts as he announced, "Let it be known to all that this is a scrimmage, and its establishment is for the practice and recognition of our city's finest men. I trust it shall bring forth strong and skilled warriors, and brave men who will lead our kingdom forever toward peace! Multa's threats will not last against a city of valor such as ours.

"I also introduce to you, my guest of honor, Lady Vala Trimont, mother of our late steward king, Cloven Trimont, who was a warrior above all. Today, may a man among us rise to be like him! Let the scrimmage begin!"

As the trumpets were blown again, I lowered my gaze to my task at hand. The first twelve names were called as six matches would take place simultaneously. Knights and commoners both took their place in the rings as Breemore had opened the scrimmage to all men. To keep my mind sharp and undistracted, I watched, perceiving errors and envisioning the corrected maneuvers. I also maintained Captain Rhys in my view.

My first opponent was a big, burly commoner fellow — too rosy in the face to look threatening. I felt sorry for the man, for he was already out of breath.

"Are you all right?" I asked him.

"Eh, just have a sweetheart watch'en." He wiped the sweat from his brow with hands that were already saturated. "I know I can't beat one like ye, but I wunt to put on a good show for her."

I remained silent as the trumpet blew. I fought noncommittedly for this man's and his sweetheart's sake. It was not a fair match, and I could not be cruel. The man's determination proved to have some power and truly from the eye of a bystander, would have looked impressive. But as his lungs weren't as exercised as mine, he grew tired and eventually dropped his sword.

Yet, his face beamed as he went running to his sweetheart. However, mid-way, he paused and ran back. "Thank ye! I'm pleased as calves' knees to have strove so long and don't wunt to suffer thut excitement again, for I'm but a butcher and wield a knife better thun a sword. I know a strong man such as yourn-self could have ended me sooner. For yourn kindness, ye come to me for all the meat ye wunt. Ye aren't fashioned after the other knights."

He offered his hand; I accepted it heartily.

149

My next opponent was Eldon. We knew each other well since from the first day we had been paired together in training.

"They could have at least given me a chance!" he said angrily when he perceived I was his first opponent.

He attempted to spring on me unexpectedly before the match was signaled. I was forced to block his mad onslaughts until his elimination was called.

The next man I faced was a real fight. I fumbled twice, nonetheless, emerged victor. I felt a little thrill of success, and if no one else cheered, the children and Alene did.

I won the next five matches and realized that my name was carried on the voice of the crowd. Pleasure tugged at my countenance. Briefly I bowed, before taking a break in the shade.

When I was called to my next match, I dumped the rest of my water from the flask around my neck and took my place. My opponent did not appear at first. Then I suspected he was the man who sauntered this way from the other side of the arena, having been among the spectators. Sir Cray he had been called.

When I saw his features, I was shaken. Instantly, his blue eyes sent me to think of Lydia's. His hair also shared her color.

He leaned into his fighting stance before me, but my mind, now racing in other directions, desired to talk. I gave a noncommittal blow, commenting, "You look like someone I know."

"I do not have a twin. Unless, I daresay, my mother hid that from me." He laughed.

"Perhaps not a twin but a sister?"

"Oh, the imposter in question is a woman!" He lunged into a light blow, not to strike but to whisper, "I do have a sister; indeed, I have two."

"Might they be Lydia and Rose?" I asked earnestly.

"How could this stranger know my sweetest of sisters?"

"I helped them while they were servants of Crevilon Castle when your mother nearly died."

"My mother," he whispered fondly. "They are all well now, as I hear. And Lydia has finally married Danek." An odd little smile joined his following words. "It was destined to be."

I shoved his sword from me.

He kept talking as we circled around the ring. "I'm glad they weren't imprisoned. Nasty little place. I was imprisoned in King's City for a while, but since my sister's marriage, I've been knighted and given property. Perhaps soon I'll have a wife of my own." He looked back to where he had come from in the crowd.

I struck at him. He parried. I struck again to the same result. I kept swinging, but it felt I was now fighting against my own rising feelings.

He, looking as though he sensed my irritation, inquired shrewdly while we were in a clashed standstill, "What was your relation to my sister?"

My heart welling up against my will, I pushed away from his sword. "Nothing," I spat.

I stepped away, to regain myself. After which, I lunged into an onslaught of attacks until I held his throat at sword point. "Have you seen them?" I demanded.

"No," he answered, carefully hovering his chin above my blade. "All that matters is that they are safe. Would you not agree?"

I lowered my sword and let him go. He returned to the spectators with an air of imposed dignity.

Restlessly, I waited for my next opponent. However,

by the time he came, I had refocused on the unchanging fact that Lydia had made her choice, and honoring her preference, I *would* move on.

Each following match equaled victory for me and excitement for the onlookers. Cheers resounded.

It was now evident that Sir Langston would be my final rival. Langston was younger than I and very agile. I doubted my abilities against his. While Sir Cantley had shown me some respect and attention, his efforts had maintained focus on Langston, whom he had trained since Langston's childhood.

Our names were called with much fanfare as we positioned ourselves in the middle of the arena for the final fight. Sir Langston stood self-assured, yet stoic of any other emotion. We had never spoken beyond stiff greeting, and he did not offer comment now.

Our blows and parries sprung intensely. My every muscle and thought was focused second by second, move by move.

He attempted the trick hold, as Danek had done. This surprised me since it was widely known among the knights that such a maneuver could never overpower me. With my free hand, I secured his sword while I sharply spun free.

Our strikes continued even and consistent until I realized that we had fallen into routine patterns of practice. As this went on, I perceived that Langston did not want this victory and was waiting for me to take it.

This realization shot a tremor of fear and doubt, so I continued a little longer in the rhythm of routine passes. But Meklon had given me my orders. I needed to gain a respected voice so that when I found King Cordell, the people would listen to me. Other men's fears could not change my course. My life may hereafter be hunted by Captain Rhys; Lord Breemore may have devious plans for me beyond any reasoning, and I may have to lead a kingdom into war. Nonetheless, I was a Trimont. The protection of this kingdom was my responsibility. It was time for me to claim it.

Powerfully, I swung my sword in one quickening blow against Langston's. The brutal impact, at last, freed Langston's sword from his hand. His sword landed on the ground from where it sealed my fate.

Chants of my name submerged my ears as I was elevated as King's City champion. Langston bent to pick up his sword, and said as he departed, "I do not envy your future."

Chapter Eighteen
~ *Galen* ~

I dropped my hand from the sword, thudded my head back against the wall, and flicked my boot into the linens which hung upon my bed. Scuffed and dust beaten from the scrimmage, I needed to clean up, but I was too exhausted and restless.

Bigger things should have been on my mind, but it was Lydia who pervaded my thoughts. Seeing her brother threw me off my course more than I realized. Now that I was alone, she was all I could think of.

I tightly re-gripped the hilt of my great grandfather's sword. This was my future—to end war with Multa once and for all.

What might my future have been if Royston had never allowed Meklon and Breemore into the kingdom? My entire life would have been altered as well as countless other lives.

Lydia would have never lost her father, for King Cordell never would have been taken. I would have grown up at Trimont alongside my father, grandfather, and Thomas. Likely, Lydia and I would have married. Instead of facing death threats and war, perhaps I would have been near to becoming the father of our first child.

It made me consider pity because, ultimately, it was Royston's pity which had allowed evil to enter into our kingdom. But how could pity not have been bestowed? Breemore had been but a child. Yet the consequences had been so deadly.

Footsteps in the corridor jerked me back to my more present concerns.

My hand steadied on the hilt as I listened. Light, timid steps stopped at my door and then quickly retreated. Silently, I rose to open and look out the door. Down the corridor, the last of candlelight and a small shadow turned the corner. My boot stepped on a small hard object. In the dark, I stooped to feel what it was—a carving of a sword. *Cadby*

Re-entering my room and softly closing the door, I lit a candle so I could examine Cadby's craftsmanship. As I turned the piece over in my hand, I smiled. It was just as grand as the king's sword depicted in the tapestry which hung in the music room. Now I knew why Cadby had gazed at the tapestry so often.

I blew out the candle and lay upon my bed. Having exchanged Royston's sword for Cadby's, I felt infinitely more at peace. I fell asleep cradling the carving within my hand.

I awoke suddenly. My heart raced; my sweaty hand clung around Cadby's carving. The distant shouting was real. I placed Cadby's carving into my pocket as I hurriedly made my way through the dark room to the window.

An unearthly dawn rose from an incalculable number of torches thrashed about by a mob. The castle front was mayhem. The streets were run through by men, causing confusion and terror. Old men in night caps and robes, widows with their howling dogs, and mothers with their children, all fled into the castle for safety. Guards tried to contain both the angry and the fearful, but only voices rose over voices and muscle pushed over muscle. No one was in a state to be controlled.

In nervous haste, I belted Royston's sword around my waist and exited my room. Running down the hall, I collided with a guard, hastening in the opposite direction.

"You," he insinuated harshly. "You are wanted in the throne room immediately."

I had barely stopped to hear his words, for I already knew this had something to do with me.

In the throne room, fuller and noisier than I had ever seen it, Breemore delegated knights and assured frightened commoners who had come to the castle for refuge.

"Galen," Breemore called authoritatively. "Have you publicly spoken anything about believing in the old ways?"

"No," I answered, only recalling the time in the Inner Tavern where I had said that I wanted to know the truth.

"Very well. We must stop this lie."

I followed him. "What lie?"

"The lie that you are like Frederic Tavish. The rioters have been stirred against you and have thrown the city into terror. People are confused. They don't know if Multa has attacked, or you are trying to murder me and usurp power."

I stood for a moment as Breemore walked on.

"Is this Captain Rhys' doing?" I demanded.

Breemore finally stopped and answered me directly. "He has betrayed us both. He foresees you rising to power instead of himself. Stay in the castle. I am trying to silence the rioters, clear your name, and find Captain Rhys as soon as possible. Also, many of the guards have sided with him against you. Be careful even within the castle."

I watched Breemore, who continued declaring orders concerning the riot. I wondered what to do with myself when I overheard the word, "Lenrow" among Breemore's commands.

I demanded of him, "What is happening at Lenrow?"

"A fire."

I began to run from the throne room.

"Galen!" Breemore yelled. "I demand of you to let others fight this battle."

But my feet and heart had surged to panic, and I could not prevent myself. Safety for Meklon and the Hendrys was all I could think of.

I did not stop even when the steep incline up to Lenrow nearly took all my breath and stripped away the strength of my legs. When I reached the landing, my heart was staggered by the sight. Flames, smoke, and ash spewed over the whole alcove as if it were the open mouth of a fiery beast.

Rioters were still there extending the flame, but neither the Hendrys nor Meklon were in sight.

I crawled beneath the smoke to reach the well where I dowsed myself with water. Ducking as I ran, I dashed toward the Hendry's home.

As I was about to enter, Meklon crawled out, gasping for air. His hat was missing; his shirt singed to a rag. Beneath the skeletal fabric, his skin was blistering.

I quickly bent down to wrap my wet shirt around his arms, asking, "What about the others?"

From Meklon's eyes, hollow and red, the answer was passed from his pain into mine. I fell back. Eternal sickness seized my body. I struggled to keep aware of my surroundings for Meklon's sake, for the rioters had taken notice of me and were advancing.

"There is the traitorous champion. Kill him too!"

I went for my sword, but before my grip was strong on the hilt, I was dragged near the edge of the cliff and pummeled by men's fists. I cowed my arms around me in meager protection, finding that I possessed no strength to fight back.

The assaults suddenly stopped. I looked up to see Meklon's body hovering over me in protection.

"Run!" he demanded.

I rolled out from under the men, but when I saw Meklon crumble beneath their beatings, I became possessed by a vengeance. Gripping the men by their necks, I yanked them away from Meklon.

I firmly stood my ground in front of Meklon, unsheathing my sword. The weaponless ones backed away; however, two others advanced with swords. The flames spewed and hissed around us. The smoke made it hazy and difficult to breath.

They came at me unreservedly. I'd never used a sword to fight two men at once. I knew I could not win. Flames and men blurred together. I lost sense of the fight and fell. I still blocked from the ground and kicked them away hard. My defense could only last so long. In the distance, between their strikes, I saw a third man—Captain Rhys. His satisfaction was sure and so was my end.

"The beam is falling!" Meklon cried out. The fire had eaten through, and the beam wavered with thunderous cracks. My attackers scattered.

I hurried to Meklon's side, heaving him over my shoulders and rushed from the alcove as the glorious ruins collapsed. Not able to go any further, I cut from the road into thick shrubbery for cover, trying to quiet my heavy breathing as to not give us away.

Meklon did not speak. I dropped my head to his chest to check his heartbeat.

"I'm alive, Galen. But at this moment, I would not mind being left as dead."

I pulled away and rolled upon my back, exposed to the raining ash. My eyes were dry and burning from the smoke. I stared up, waiting to be buried beneath it all.

Breemore's guards came, but I didn't go to them. What could they do? The Hendrys were dead, and the rioters had fled. The guards took some pains to put out the fire, and then they left.

A dark quiet rested over me like a cold blanket. I drifted in and out of tears and sleep.

Into this dead silence, Meklon at last spoke, his voice thin and raspy, but the sound of it raised me to the world again. "There is a chance Braun got them out in time. But if not, I wish that Royston never had spared Breemore and me. I wish we had died that day. I would have given up my life at Trimont if it would have spared this kingdom from my brother. How many worthy men would still be alive today if my brother and I had not been foolishly spared?"

I was silent, for it was true. But I could not wish Meklon away for anything, and he could not dare attempt to take the blame for the Hendrys death.

"This is my fault," I asserted. "I knew Rhys followed me last night and was warned that he sought to kill me. I should have thought that he would have also followed Braun and discovered what they were doing in Middle Quarters. I could have prevented this if I would have come to warn you. I failed the Hendrys and you. How does one live with the guilt?"

Meklon was silent for a long time, so I closed my eyes, sinking under the tightening straps of guilt and loss.

Meklon answered, "Not as your father did. We do not have Vala to correct us, so let us speak no more folly."

I followed his gaze which led me to see past the thickets to the rising sun. The sky was still dark except for an infant light so soft, so pure, and so assured of its rising that it took its time and did not worry about the clouds passing over it.

I stared for the whole of its rising until the light suddenly blinded my eyes, and I had to look away.

For the first time, I observed Meklon. He lay tensely as if enduring much pain. I sat up immediately. "You need help. Other than your burns, are you hurt?"

"Bruised or broken ribs."

In way of gratitude, I attempted to console. "I cannot say that I am worth much, but I am alive because of you."

"Galen, you are worth this pain and more. Help me up. There is a nurse in Middle Quarters who can help me if you can bear half my weight to get me there."

I helped Meklon up and pulled his arm around my shoulders. He grunted but walked as much without my help as he could. I kept a gentle hold around his ribs.

When we came to the clearing of the road, we both instinctively paused and looked back at Lenrow. It was unrecognizable. Trees which had grown on the mountain above the alcove had fallen and now lay half burnt and sideways as a solemn guard over the once beloved home and invaluable store of Sedgewick's copies of the Book of Truth.

The tears fell for both of us.

Silently, we turned away. We followed the old road down, then turned onto a shortcut which was too steep for Meklon's condition, but he insisted.

The day was well on its way by the time I knocked on the shadowed alley door which Meklon wearily indicated. When there was no answer, Meklon told me to knock until there was. Repeatedly, I pounded on the door.

Finally, a woman peeked out at us.

I could not understand her sudden scowl when she saw Meklon, yet she helped him inside and laid him down on a long wooden bench.

She began rubbing salve into his burns. "Here." She handed me a cloth and the box of salve. "Rub it into his other arm. The sooner this soaks into his skin the better."

I could not do it so abrasively and quickly as she when I saw the painful contortion on Meklon's face that she was causing.

"Move aside if you are not man enough," she huffed, ripping the salve from my hand and pushed me out of her way.

She then sighed and yelled, "Come out, all of you. You are safe from this lot."

From out of a closet came the Hendrys, all three of them alive and well.

I watched Meklon's face visibly revive, before his eyes closed again in pain and exhaustion.

Cote ran into my legs in his desperate attempt to embrace me. I lowered to my knees glad to return his hold, shedding tears of relief.

Hildie gasped over seeing Meklon's condition. "Oh, but he made it out," she breathed and fell against her husband, seemingly still shocked from all that had happened.

"How did you escape?" I questioned over Cote's

shoulder.

Braun answered, "There is a dangerously steep path down the other side of the alcove. I was awake and saw the men coming."

"Like lightening he got us out." Hildie looked up at Braun. "And then the thunder of the collapse, I can still hear its terrible fall in my ears."

Braun held her close and kissed her head as if he had come to the cliffs of losing her, but by great mercy had her safe in his arms. Cote scrambled to them and wrapped his mother's loose arm around him and kissed it too. There was a bandage on her arm and scrapes down her face as if there had been a close encounter to losing her.

The woman suddenly sniped at Braun, "If you loved your wife so much, you would give up your ways of reading people the Book of Truth."

"No!" Hildie cried. "He mustn't. We cannot stop now."

The woman could stand her passion no longer. She stormed, "You all speak of continuing in what you think to be a noble cause, but tonight proved that it will only bring more destruction and death. My job is to keep people alive. I cannot approve of your work any longer." Marching to her cupboard, she brought out one of Sedgwick's copies of the Book of Truth and looking right at Braun challenged, "If you will not care enough for your family, I will." And she threw it in the fire.

Braun stood like a man of character neither lashing back nor tainting his countenance with offense.

But I was angered at her unjust insult. I defended him, "Braun saved his family. He is one of the best fathers and husbands in this kingdom because he reads the Book of Truth. His work of sharing the Book of Truth would make for peace if people would but listen and believe it.

Your words are completely unfounded."

She eyed me sharply. "Who are you?"

"My name is Galen."

"The Galen the rioters seek to kill? The Galen who started all this traitorous work? Get out of my house! I'll take care of the old man, but you are not welcome. I have people in my care that I have to protect. Never again try to convince these people of what in the end will kill them."

When I realized I had caused an uncomfortable scene for the Hendrys, I tossed into the fire the rag which I had unconsciously been clinging to since dressing Meklon's burns and left the house.

Chapter Nineteen
~ *Lord Breemore* ~

"Galen has returned, my lord."

"Is he well?" I asked.

"He can walk. I saw no signs of bleeding, though he was coated in ash and smelled like a furnace. He went straight to his chamber, acknowledging no one. Do you wish to speak with him, my lord?"

"No, no. Let him rest. Ensure that he is not disturbed for the remainder of the day. Instead, send for Captain Rhys. I am ready to speak with him."

As the squire left, I drew the letter from my drawer from where it had lain for some weeks, waiting to be played.

Captain Rhys entered. He was washed and groomed as if all that had happened during the night had been far beneath him.

"My lord," he said, bowing. "I have acted no evil against you. Galen Lukemar is the one who betrays you. While you have welcomed him and bequeathed all you have for his comfort and use, he, behind your back, spent his nights plotting against you with a traitorous family of the old ways. He is indeed as Frederic Tavish, believing King Cordell still lives and that you are an imposter. I have only acted on your behalf, my lord."

"I heartily thank you, Captain. I commend you for having silenced any contrary voices. Harmony must be our goal, especially when threat of war with Multa looms.

However, I must speak on Galen's behalf. He is not at all like Frederic Tavish and the others as you presume. Frederic was unmovable and crazy—a real threat; we both agree. Galen is moldable and reasonable. He may have some influence from the old ways, but he is not dedicated to the cause as was Frederic. I believe Galen is more dedicated to goodness, not to truth. In which case, he may be persuaded to anything that is kind and reasonable. That is how you must work with him if he is to be your second-in-command. You will find he will give you no resistance."

"*My* second-in-command?" Rhys questioned.

"Yes. In the tournament, did I not myself state that the winner be awarded second-in-command. Does that not raise you up to first-in-command, hmm? Because I am raising Galen up does not mean I am bringing you down. I have plans of my own for Galen that you need not worry about. Your position is secure, Captain. You have faithfully stood by my side all these years."

Rhys was one who could not temper his expressions; therefore, his pleasure smeared across his countenance. "You are saying, my lord, that if Galen wins the tournament, he will be second-in-command under me?"

"Of course! Galen is young and does not possess your experience and knowledge of the kingdom. There is so much you could teach him."

"I believe you are quite right, my lord."

"As we both know," I began, turning the conversation toward my letter, "Frederic Tavish was a true threat. You once warned me of his daughter, Lydia Tavish. I have received news of her, which I now fully entrust to your judgment." I extended the letter to him.

After Rhys read the report, he dropped it back to the

desk. "I knew Sir Danek could not be trusted! This report is not even from his own hand."

"No," I confirmed. "Sir Danek gave no report of her incompliance. I was surprised by this, as well as to read that Sir Danek had set her free."

"His heart made him weak," Rhys accused. "I will not allow that Tavish girl to get away with such insolence. She knew the consequences. You may expect my absence for the next fortnight, my lord. I have unfinished business in Traiven's Pass."

"Of course, Captain. I leave the details to your hands completely."

As he left, it was the last time I intended to see him. After he dealt with Lydia, I had no more use for the brute. Galen was the all-important piece now.

Chapter Twenty
~ *Lady Vala* ~

Alene wrung her hands as she paced my room. "Why didn't Galen come to us this evening? Do you think he is injured worse than Lord Breemore is telling us? I can't stand it. I need to tell someone. I love him. And I can't stand not knowing how he is. Oh, help me." Tears welled in her eyes.

I took the young woman in my arms and as it was late, led her to my bed and made her to lie down. "Sleep here tonight. I'll sit in the chair by your side."

As she looked up at me from the pillow, she asked, "Do you think Galen loves me?"

"I think Galen cares for you greatly. May I advise you for his sake?"

"I'll do anything for his sake."

"Let your love be patient and unassertive toward Galen. Continue as the friend you have been. I perceive he is not yet ready for love." I ran my hand down her cheek, "Even a love as precious as yours."

"Will he ever be?"

I explained, "Before Galen came to the city, he grew fond of a woman and her family. However, she was forced to marry another. Galen is still hurting."

She closed her eyes as a fresh flow of tears pressed through her eyes, and she said no more.

Perhaps one day this sweet woman, who was like Lydia in many ways, would become more to him, but both

Galen and I knew she was not the lost piece of Galen's heart even though he was in hers.

"Be brave," I whispered to her as I ran my hand across her hair which looked like an embroidered sun on the pillow in the dim candlelight.

I loved her so and felt her pain as much as Galen's, whose heart I saw would become pulled by both Alene and Lady Laila when the memories of Lydia at last released him. Each would be required to honorably uphold their own heart to survive the entanglement wherever it led.

When Alene's face at length relaxed into the unconscious peace of an angel, I quietly stepped outside the door and, leaning against it, released my own heart. Meklon had sent word explaining all that had happened as a result of the riot—of Lenrow's merciless destruction, the loss of Sedgwick's copies of the Book of Truth, the distrust of the few followers which had been gained in Middle Quarters, and the attempted murder of the Hendrys and my grandson—my Galen—my very heart. That danger would henceforth attach itself to him was hard to bear.

My heart ached for the many losses and suffering hearts—the pains of the past and the coming ones. I desired to uphold each tender heart, especially the heart of my grandson upon whom all the weight would befall.

Chapter Twenty-one
~ *Galen* ~

Hunger at last drew me out of the bed. No heroic motive. That had been completely drained from me. Weakly, I walked to the table where a tray of food had been left for me last night. My hunger did not prevent the food from turning sour in my stomach, yet I ate and drank every crumb that was my lot.

I sat, gazing out the window, realizing for the first time that it was raining. The water ran down the windowpane in a blur of small rivulets. I listened to the rain, staring at the confused waterways seeking their course down amid a massive castle of endless surface and sudden cliffs. No inspiration was found in the blur or the drizzle. It just mirrored my own mind.

I shook my head from the daze and reached beneath my bed for the Book of Truth. Much through the night, I had envisioned the memory of Braun down on his knees, pouring over its words and remembering what he had said, "I am seeking."

Lowering to my knees, I whispered, "I want to know the strength and the comfort which Vala, Braun, and Lydia found. I want to be like them, not like my father."

I read and re-read. The words poured into my soul as I drank them in.

When next I looked up, perhaps an hour or two later, the window was clear. All the blurred water courses had fallen to their place. I saw the sky. I understood that the truth was not just for ruling a kingdom, but for the stability and rule of my own heart. And if every heart was born into this great truth, the kingdom would stand undefeatable. If the people could just grasp this! It was this light — people finding truth — that Breemore was snuffing out so that his darkness could overcome. It was not that we were simply being overtaken by our enemy, but we were becoming the same as our enemy; we were merging with them. We were giving up more than we realized in letting the truth go.

I ran my hand over the boots which Braun, Hildie, and Cote had together fashioned for me. I owed them so much.

A knock came to my door. Although not ready to face the world, I stood to answer it. When I saw that it was my grandmother, I regretted I had not gone to her sooner.

"I'm sorry," I confessed. "I should have come to you first." I could not look her in the eyes as I added, "Have you heard about Lenrow?"

She nodded.

Glancing up, I acknowledged, "I needed time."

"As did I," she returned, able to look me fully in the face.

Feeling I ought to have been stronger, I promised, "I will still search for our king and find a way to regain Sedgwick's copies."

Then I noticed the letter in her hand which she held out to me.

"It arrived this morning… from Danek."

Unfolding the parchment rapidly, I read:

To: Lady Vala Trimont,
By right of lordship, I hereby inform you that Trimont
Estate has been taken into custody until your return.

In your absence, I have reason to believe that Multa scouts have made use of its vacancy by depleting its harvest and lodging within Trimont Castle. Guards, henceforth, shall be posted along Trimont borders.

Fears arose as I read.

By right of relation, I shall also inform you that Lydia refused me in marriage.

My heart stopped. I read the words over. She refused him. In an attempt to subdue an irrepressible smile, I bit my lower lip. However, neither embarrassment nor willpower could prevent the most sincere smile from overtaking my countenance. The news had unlocked a wellspring of joy.

Suppressed memories and feelings flooded through me: shared looks, her words which had both chastened and inspired me, the touch of her hand as I led her through Crevilon's secret passageways, her wounded eyes when I told her that her mother was dying, and her strength when she showed me King's View. My entire soul filled with Lydia. There was a place for her in every portion of my being.

But I had to let my mind catch up with my heart. Did this mean that Lydia and her family were imprisoned? I read on.

I have relinquished my hold on the Tavish family. Ophelia Tavish, however, has passed on.
*   -Sir Danek Crevilon*

Vala watched me. I looked into my grandmother's face

hardly knowing what my own expression displayed.

"Must bad news accompany the good?" I spoke. "Their freedom will be greatly shadowed by the loss of their mother. Could I dare hope that I could go and be a comfort to them?"

"Galen, I believe that you would be the best of balms to the Tavish family in the midst of their sorrow."

"Do you agree that I should leave for Traiven's Pass this very hour? I will also learn what I can about the Multa scouts at Trimont. I may be gone as long as a fortnight, but I'll try not to be away longer."

I retrieved my saddlebags and began packing them when I paused. "Do you think Lydia will be pleased to see me?"

Vala smiled amusingly. "Yes, Galen, very pleased. From the beginning, I saw that you and Lydia have what Amond and I had — a call, as well as love. Go to her and her family, and know that I rejoice over you all."

My heart brimming, I released my hold on the saddlebag to embrace my grandmother who had just spoken the words of my deepest desire. I was glad she had been with me when I received the news, for she understood.

When I pulled back, I remembered to ask, "Do you know what has happened with the rioters?"

"The riot has completely abated. Breemore imprisoned many and proclaimed your innocence."

"Whatever Breemore's purpose, I am relieved that for now he is playing on our side. How did Breemore handle Captain Rhys?"

"I have not yet heard," Vala answered.

I stepped into my boots. "I need to tell Cadby before I go. I cannot leave him without explanation."

"I'll send Cadby to your room. Bring him back on your

way. Be safe, Galen. Tell Danek that I grant him lordship over Trimont for whatever purposes he deems necessary."

"You trust him?" I asked surprised.

"Yes."

"I cannot," I uttered grudgingly, "but Trimont is yours, and I'll honor your message to him."

"Thank you. Farewell."

"You and the children will be safe, here, won't you?"

"For now."

As she left, I gathered my belongings and began stuffing my two saddlebags. Soon I heard Cadby's small knock.

I drew him in, so I could close the door. When he saw my filled saddlebags, he tucked his chin down and squeezed his arms against his body.

Quickly, I knelt at his level to set my earnest care before his eyes. "Don't fear, Cadby. I wanted you to come, so I could explain why I must leave for a time. It is not because of you. You have done nothing wrong. I would never want to leave you. I have to leave because Lady Vala and I have heard news about Lydia. I must go help her and her family. I'll return as soon as I can. This is a secret though. Do you understand?"

Cadby nodded.

Then, with a smile, I pulled his carving from my pocket. Cadby nervously shifted. But he surprisingly eased as I praised him, "This is an excellent carving, Cadby. I keep it with me because it has become my favorite sword."

Tears filling his eyes, Cadby flung his hands from his pockets and clasped them around my neck. "I want you to be my pap."

After all his silence, these were his first words. I held him tight. "Then I shall be your pap, Cadby."

"I'll talk more if you want me to."

"I'd love to hear anything you would like to say."

"Will you bring Lydia back?" he asked.

"I don't know yet. That is what I have to find out."

"I won't tell your secret," he affirmed.

"I have complete confidence in you, Cadby. Come, I've finished packing. I'll walk with you back to Lady Vala."

He held my hand as we went, as if my hand was his new pocket. I could not help smiling; my heart was full. When we neared the courtyard where the other children were playing, I again knelt to his level. "I'm sorry to leave you, but I'll return soon. Keep a look out for anything suspicious. When I return, we will finish searching for King Cordell."

Cadby nodded as if accepting a solemn duty.

It was difficult to part from him, especially as he stood, a grave little statue, watching me go. I waved to him before I turned out of sight. That Vala would be with him was my consolation.

Destiny neighed and stomped from within her stall as I entered the stable.

"Shhhh, Chess." Her original name came back suddenly. "Good girl, Chess," I repeated as I patted her neck. "Let's both admit, I think you have missed that name as much as I have."

After I saddled her and mounted, I drew the hood of my cloak over my head to conceal myself through the city. I briefly hesitated when I noticed that Captain Rhys' horse was missing.

Chapter Twenty-two
~ *Lydia* ~

Though my face was cold and though I saw nothing beyond the fleeting shadows which Auden's two lanterns cast along the dark roadside, I pressed my cheek against the glass of the carriage window, wishing there was something I could do to hasten the wearied horses, for the nearer we came to home, the more I yearned to learn news of my family.

The wind clawed at the carriage as if all its forces were trying to prevent the carriage from going any further, but I was determined that it should — that it must.

In her sleep, Netty's head fell onto my shoulder. I relinquished my vigil as to not disturb her. I let the curtain fall and closed my eyes, listening for the tap on the side of the carriage which Auden promised to give when the view of the valley could be seen.

Auden's tap soon came.

"Netty," I whispered. "We are near."

She lifted her head as I lifted the curtain.

I was surprised by how lit the valley was with torchlight. Usually the valley was left to the natural night. Even the more remote farms were spots of light. There was no time to scrutinize as the horses pulled on and trees again hid the view.

We held onto the seat to prevent ourselves from sliding while the carriage was swayed by the wind and the precarious descent into the valley. Once upon straight road again, I lifted the curtain, surprised to see that our carriage was being stopped by a watchman. I dropped the curtain instantly.

Netty fearfully grabbed my arm when we heard a man's loud demanding voice, "Where do you come from, and who is with you?"

I could not hear what Auden's quiet voice spoke over the wind before the watchman swung open the carriage door and shown his lantern directly at my face.

He gasped. "The missing Tavish girl!"

We stared at each other, both seemingly startled into silence.

Then he took a step back, shaking his head and lowering the light from my squinting eyes. "I'm sorry. You are one of our own. Where do you wish to go?"

I was surprised to hear him speak so. "Trimont Castle," I answered.

"Again, I am sorry, but I cannot permit you to go to Trimont. It has been under guard ever since Multa scouts were sighted in the Trimont fields. No one is allowed to enter without Sir Danek's permission."

A surge of worry rising, I asked, "Multa is advancing into our kingdom?"

"Have you not heard?" he said gently. "Multa has built an army; it is only a matter of time before an attack."

"Certainly, I did not know," I voiced heavily.

"There, there now, I do have a fragment of better news for you. Your brother has been rebuilding your home. I'm sure there is room enough for all three of you in the small portion he has finished."

"Garret—he is free? And my mother and sister?" I asked eagerly.

When the watchman looked down, a sickening feeling

instructed me as a youth, and befriended me as a woman. There was never a time in my life that I could recount when Mother had not availed herself for me. No one on earth knew Mother like I had.

At last my body lay still, but I did not sleep. I stared numbly at the golden leaves that fell around the lantern and the vast darkness beyond, which was blindly subjected to the wild beatings of the wind. My ears ached from the buffeting wind, but I made no move to cover them. I was so weak, my bones seemed to have dissolved within me.

The lantern died out, and my eyes dwelt in the dark allotment until dawn crept like a whisper. Only shadows at first, but as I watched the rising, a golden glow overtook the grove. The power of its loveliness drew me up and into it. The air was as light as a caress. I passed among the trees as if I was within the delight of light.

I whispered the ending line of Father's poem about King's View, "Golden throughout—Mother, you were golden throughout. Father was golden throughout. I am…" I hesitated, for it seemed prideful to say. Was I golden throughout? To shy away from saying that I was, meant that I would be in some way cleaving to darkness. I would not ever cling to darkness, so I proclaimed, "I am golden throughout, for I believe the truth, and I shall cleave unto no darkness. I will keep walking, Mother and Father, whatever my future must be."

In the midst of these thoughts, I saw Garret, leaving the cottage. I hurried after him.

When he saw me, he changed his course from the road to meet my pursuit. He enfolded me in brotherly arms. "Liddy, you made it home."

I began to cry as I could not help thinking that Mother

had not. I tried to calm my swells of sorrow as Garret kept speaking.

"Auden and Netty told me that you may have convinced Cloven Trimont to reclaim his throne. I'm overwhelmed."

"Garret, I do not know for certain that he will. He made no such claim. Cloven was… different than I expected. His course is out of my hands."

"But you did what you could. And how could he not?"

"Garret, did Mother know any freedom before…"

Garret sadly shook his head. "Rose and I are only free because she was brave enough to beseech Danek for our freedom. She didn't allow us to be with her when she died. Emerson and Levinia were with her. She also ensured that you would have full custody of Rose when you returned. I was now going to Faye's to bring Rose home to you."

"Please allow me to come with you."

"Are you sure that you do not need to rest?"

I shook my head, and we began to walk down our lane together.

Garret asked, "Did you read what Danek wrote on Mother's tombstone?"

"No, what does it say?"

"*Ophelia Tavish – Unjustly Sentenced*. He is different, Liddy. I cannot explain how. But I think he regrets what he has done."

I nodded but did not reply.

Garret led us through the woods for which I was glad, for I wished to see no one. I found that I could only walk slowly, and Garret dropped his pace to mine. "Are you sure you are strong enough for this? It is a long walk, and you are still weak with grief. I could not do anything for days after she died."

"I need to see Rose," I replied, trudging on.

Garret placed his arm around me to help bear some of my limp weight.

"How is Rose?" I asked.

"She is withdrawn inside herself. I cannot imagine what terrors are in her head. She has endured much worse than we ever did as children. I do what I can, and Faye is never dissuaded from attempting to cheer her, but I think you will be best for her. You will stay and raise her, won't you? No more gallivanting around the kingdom. Let the men fight the battles now. Travel is becoming too dangerous."

I nodded. "I shall stay with you and Rose." I knew as I agreed that I was giving up Grenfell's wish that I pursue Galen, but this is where Mother wanted me and where I was most needed — my family.

Garret shared, "I've sent word, trying to hear of Creighson, but there has been nothing returned. It is hard not knowing."

I nodded, having learned the extremity of those words while I had been away.

When we came near Faye's cottage, I instantly beheld Rose. Her brown hair hung down in tangles as if she had just risen out of bed. Motionless, she sat in the sun while Faye brushed her hair and graced the atmosphere with song.

Quickening my pace, I was soon beyond Garret's side. "Rose," I mouthed at first and then louder. "Rose."

Rose looked.

Like a startled doe, she stood from her chair. She had grown taller and thinner. Except for the sun's morning work of splattering her nose and cheeks red, she was as pale as aspen bark. I was afraid she would not come to me as she stared, frozen in movement. Then she rushed to me and clung.

We embraced one another with a strength and determination never to be parted again. Her head and arms locked over my shoulder as I lifted her up and rocked her. All my strength returned for Rose.

Faye silently disappeared into her cottage. I was not sure how she felt toward me since I had refused Danek.

I walked with Rose under the boughs of loaded apple trees, through the gate, and around the evergreens, silently knitting our sorrow together and beginning to revive the chords of home.

When I began to set Rose down due to my waning strength, her arms tightened around my neck.

"Rose," I whispered, renewing my hold, "I will not leave you. From now on, we will be together."

I could not say it without crying, for what did I know of what the future held.

I rested on a low drooping branch so that we did not have to part. Rose's body molded and rested against mine. She kept not one muscle for herself and was a ragdoll in my arms. I felt as if this was the first true rest she had since Mother's death, and now that she felt safe, she was exhausted.

When I saw Garret speaking with Faye, I returned with Rose.

Garret lifted Rose from my arms as Faye took my hands in greeting. Her touch was light and quick like a brush of wings. She remained fairylike, though her countenance was dimmed. A great deal of her welcome was forced.

"Please go to Danek," were the first words Faye uttered.

I was surprised and answered, "I do not think he would wish to see me."

"He does," Faye interjected quickly. "He needs to see you." Faye added imploringly, "I don't want him to die."

"Is he sick?"

Faye shook her head. "I cannot recall Danek ever being sick. It is that he has no will to care for himself. Please, please try to help him. Forgive him… if you can."

Faye brushed away a small burst of tears, lifting her face higher and smiling brighter. "I remain at your service. I shall come and dress and do your hair whenever you like. I still have some nice gowns for you and Rose. My orchard and garden are open to you. I shall be lonely without Rose, though she was a languid creature. Perhaps you can cheer her. Garret has the bag I have packed for her."

"Thank you for caring for Rose and for all that you have offered us. We shall visit often. You are likewise open to all that we have."

As we left, I turned back and hugged Faye, promising, "I will speak with him."

Upon returning home, I noticed that Rose's gaze longed after Mother's grave. Before we were swept into the continuance of life, I took Rose's hand and together we walked to Mother's grave. Along the way, I searched for a sharp rock which could be used to write upon the gravestone. When I found one, I scratched onto the stone, *"home"* like Father had tenderly inscribed on every map, because it marked where his heart had always been.

I handed the rock to Rose.

Rose looked at me uncertainly. "Mother asked me to write and tell her about the sun."

"That is a good idea," I assured.

Rose looked up into the sky, squinted, and followed its rays down to the earth. Rose wrote:

Dear Mother, The sun is touching me, you, and Lydia.

Chapter Twenty-three
~ *Lydia* ~

A golden leaf graced Rose's lap. She took it into her hand and looked up where many more leaves rained down. Taken by the beauty, I could bear the bitter wind that sent them, but Rose shivered.

I glanced over my shoulder at the cottage. Smoke ascended from the chimney, then immediately was swept into the invisible reaches of the sky like a soul being born to the world only to be carried away by life.

Returning my gaze to Rose, I spoke softly, "Come, there is warmth awaiting us inside."

Together we stood from kneeling at Mother's grave. Having lost both Mother and Father, we had been born through fire, and like the wind, life would take us where it would: be it stagnant air, a soft breeze, or a violent gale.

Rose's hand within mine was like a cold marble. My hands were no warmer as I brought both to the aid of hers.

Garret, who had been hammering all this time, stopped his work when he saw us and met us at the door — though Auden's continued hammering could be heard in slower less frequent thuds.

"I hope you will rest now," Garret stressed as we entered.

Warmth cuddled around us, gently unloosening the grip of the cold. I brought Rose to the fire as Garret pulled off his coat.

I stared at the low flames careful not to think of anything which could have the power to undo me, for tears seemed forever pressed behind my eyes, and the slightest remembrance of Mother was the near key that unleashed them. I had to be strong for the sake of Rose and for Netty, who anxiously stood by. There must be cooking or some useful work I could do.

Yet I could not help my knowledge that this had once been our home, and noticing the likeness with which Garret had rebuilt it, and remembering what home had once been and all the times Mother…

My lids closed over the watery pools of my eyes, my body being the frail encasement of heavy sorrow.

I could not prevent the memories now… all the times Mother's presence had been near as we had fallen asleep as children, her quilts which had been daily spread on each of our beds and the extras stored in the chest that she had brought to us whenever we had complained of the cold, the numerous bouquets of flowers she had adorned the table with during the warmer months and the evergreens she had used in the winter, the barrel full of Father's maps which she had opened every evening to figure where he might have been that night, Mother and Father's canopy bed that I had always been so proud of as a girl, having many times traced my little fingers through the intricate designs in the wood, Creighson's lute which he had often played for Mother, the pots and dishes we had used every day since before my birth — the ones I had known all the dents and cracks of, the rugs that had bunched and slid from their proper places with the shuffling of four pairs of children's feet that Mother and I had constantly straightened, and Mother's favorite herbs which had made the cottage smell of basil and rosemary — thus she had named Rose.

I opened my eyes and blinked away the blur. Rose gazed about her; I wondered if she shared similar remembrances.

"I have endeavored to rebuild our home as it was," Garret explained. "I will add the loft and the second room. Danek sent masons to help with the hearth. If not for the help, our home would not be this far along."

"You have done well, Garret." I truly meant it, but my voice bore the compliment weakly, for my heart just now felt more the loss of the old than the gain of the new.

"But it will never be the same. I know," Garret acknowledged. "I am sorry I could not have done more. You and Rose will do a better job of making this a home again."

What I had kept vague in my vision before, I now bravely observed as my new home. It was a large, tall, empty rectangle that smelled of fallen trees and earthen stone. There was only plain coarse furniture enough for one, bare cooking necessities, and a barrel of wheat.

It was enough to continue life for Mother's sake. I made my first task to pour Rose a cup of water, for she had coughed several times. But a bucket was heavier than I remembered. I dropped it and spilt the water. Bitterly, it proved, against my will, how incapable I was of the smallest duty in the midst of my grief.

"Liddy," Garret exclaimed, taking the bucket from me, "you must rest."

I happened to meet Netty's eyes which brimmed with the level of her anguish for me. Her hands were clasped at her heart as if at a loss to know what to do to help me. I stood quickly, trying to smile over my mistake. Garret's hands gripped my shoulders from behind and gently but sternly led me to the bed.

Still I moved reluctantly, for I knew the moment in which I succumbed, I would not be able to rise.

"Liddy, rest, please. You look as though a falling leaf could crumple you."

As he gently nudged me forward, I refused to step. I turned to look at him with the last strength that was in me. "I cannot until Emerson and Levinia know we have returned safely."

He came around to face me. "Liddy, I will see to that. You have done your part; leave the rest to me. I will take your load, even of caring for Rose, so you can rest and grieve."

He hugged me, and I conceded to his kindness. Though it was only late morning, I lay on the bed, Rose following me, and after I had wept for a time, finally slept.

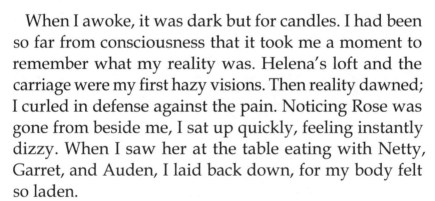

When I awoke, it was dark but for candles. I had been so far from consciousness that it took me a moment to remember what my reality was. Helena's loft and the carriage were my first hazy visions. Then reality dawned; I curled in defense against the pain. Noticing Rose was gone from beside me, I sat up quickly, feeling instantly dizzy. When I saw her at the table eating with Netty, Garret, and Auden, I laid back down, for my body felt so laden.

A warm cloth was set over my forehead which smelled of lavender. I looked to the other side of the bed and saw Levinia ministering over me. Emerson stood behind her, his hands on her shoulders. They smiled at me. Looking up into their faces was a sweet haven.

"You made it back to us," Levinia said.

I whispered, "I did all that you asked."

Levinia kissed my hand, "I know, my dear." Her tears wet my hand. "And more. I do not doubt that time will prove what you have done for Cloven Trimont and our kingdom."

"Mother... I will never get to tell her..."

Levinia grasped my hand strongly as if to keep me above the depths of bottomless sorrow. "Your mother was pleased to know where you had gone. She believed you would succeed, and that knowledge gave her the final peace she needed to be able to leave her children. Ophelia so touched my heart with her hope. Oh, Lydia," Levinia again brought my hand to her warm moistened cheek, "there was no darkness about her. She held my hand to the end, and now I bring her touch to you."

I squeezed Levinia's hand. Through her words, I had seen Mother and cleaved to the image.

"I've also carefully preserved your mother's shawl for you and for Rose." Levinia laid the worn fabric against my cheek.

Mother's familiar scent filled me with comfort. I rubbed my cheek against it, finding her life in the lingering scent.

Rose had heard that the shawl was for her too and came to see. I unfolded the shawl and wrapped it around her. It hung on her like a blanket, reaching below her knees.

Garret lifted Rose up high, proclaiming, "Now you are dressed like a queen."

When this made Rose smile, I smiled faintly.

"Now go finish eating," Garret instructed, setting Rose down and following her back to the table.

Netty timidly came to stand at the end of my bed. "Will you be all right?" she asked in a thin voice.

I replied, "After a while, I shall be myself again. I am

sorry I left you last night."

"Oh no, Miss Lydia, do not think of me. I wished all night I could help you, but I felt most ignorant as to know what I ought to do."

"Would you like to bring a small bowl of porridge for Lydia?" Levinia asked.

Netty gladly did so. I was not hungry, but I accepted what Levinia thought best, and before she was about to use her own delicate strength to help me, I sat up to spare her.

After handing the bowl to Levinia, Netty sat on the floor by the bedside. Levinia lifted a small spoonful to let the porridge cool before bringing it to my lips.

Rose crawled onto the bed, maintaining her grip on Mother's shawl like wings she held tightly about her.

A hard knock came to the door. My heart raced; by the startled look of everyone else, so did theirs. Garret and Emerson together rose to answer. A man concealed within a hooded cloak, as black as the night behind him, stepped in without invitation. Garret staunchly positioned himself between the intruder and where the man's hidden gaze seemed fixed, which I felt with a great shiver was me.

"Who are you?" Garret asked.

The man gave no response either in movement or voice. If anything, he lifted his chin to see me better over Garret's shoulder.

I felt so exposed as the candle burned so near my face. Where the man stood, there was no candle, and his face was so shrouded within the hood, I could discern nothing. I stared with curious fear at the ghost-like figure. Possibilities of who he was raced through my mind.

Garret demanded, "Say who you are!"

The man raised his hand to his hood and dropped it over his shoulders. It was Danek.

If I had imagined he had watched me from beneath his hood, there was no such indication of it now. His direct gaze from the moment the hood fell was on Garret and ventured nowhere else.

Garret jerked his head down. "Forgive me, Sir Danek. You are welcome here."

I stared as long as I felt it was unnoticed, for I was startled by how Danek's appearance had altered and was trying to see whether the severe change was due to the weak light or whether his face had truly sunken to bone and marrow. Either way, there was no health in his face. It hurt me to look at him.

Danek addressed Auden, who stood respectfully from where he had been silently sitting at the table bench. "I was told you wished to return to Trimont."

As Danek spoke for the first time, I was stirred to defiance, for through his leanness he yet spoke in his usual cold superior tone which only reminded me of the separation which he had inflicted upon my family. He had not changed. He had only dwindled lower into self-pity.

But Auden humbly bowed.

Danek continued, "I grant you entrance; return to Trimont when you wish. But my guards shall remain posted at the castle, though they shall be forbidden to enter."

Only now did Danek pretend to look at me for the first time, his eyes partially squinting and his lips a thin strip of steel. I sat up without the help of the back pillow, preparing for the worst that he could lash upon me. I did not want to be a meek mouse before him.

Danek taunted, "If you are well enough to rise yourself in such defiance, certainly you are well enough to tell me what you know of Cloven Trimont."

I looked at Levinia as if to inquire how he knew.

Levinia spoke softly, "We judged it right to tell him all."

Emerson also implied that my telling was safe by gently nodding.

I replied, "Then I shall follow your lead and answer him what he asks." I forced myself to look directly at Danek as I related only the facts. "Cloven Trimont ran from his responsibility as steward king after he caused his brother's death. Breemore was the first voice influencing him after the tragedy, and, therefore, Cloven asked Breemore to stage his death, whereupon Cloven promised he would disappear and never return. Thus, I found him a very hard and deadened man who would not listen. Only after I had appealed to him for the sake of his brother, Thomas, to reclaim the throne, did Cloven take a horse and journey northward. That is the first and last that I know."

"He is a bigger fool than I if he does not reclaim the throne," Danek commented.

"How have you conducted yourself any better than Cloven?" I challenged.

Suddenly, at their full strength, his eyes shot back at me. "Clearly, I have not. Nonetheless, I have come to tell you what I have done for you in restitution for what I have taken from you. I have written to Lady Vala and told her of our severed relation. Do not doubt that I know better than you that she will tell her grandson—your precious Galen Trimont, who will come for you like your true gallant and noble knight. Even in this, I know that not even love can make up for the loss of a mother. But he is all that is within my power to return to you of all that I have taken."

I sat outwardly whipped by his tone, but inwardly I had been deeply tamed by his words. I meekly asked, "What has changed you?"

He laughed one cold inflexible syllable. "Humiliation, guilt, incessant pain, leanness, emptiness, everything low and despised. And, yes, your precious Book of Truth; it condemned me. I've conveyed what I have come to say; I shall leave you now and hereafter."

He opened the door. The wind billowed his cloak and scattered my hair as I stood to go after him. "Wait," I sent my voice farther than my hand could reach before it was too late. I did not know if he heard me. But a pace out the door, he stopped and stood still.

When I reached the doorway and braced myself between its posts, I did not know what my next words would be, but he had offered amends after years of betrayal. I somehow had to make known to him what that meant to me. The wind blowing into my throat did not help. I was surprised how long he waited.

He did not allow me to see his face during this time, for which I was glad. Finally, I began, "I looked up to you when I was a young girl." I paused as it was harder to say, "I believe that now I can look up to you once again."

After an uneasy moment with no indication of his thoughts, he pulled something from inside his cloak. "Not for my sake but for your own, take my mother's necklace and wear it in the days of the Multa invasion. It may protect you, for it is a royal Multan pendant." Dropping the necklace into my hand, he departed.

As I watched him disappear into the night, I felt peace for the first time in many years after having been in his presence.

I looked down at the necklace in my open palm. Levinia, without a word, took it and fastened it around my neck.

Chapter Twenty-four
~ *Lydia* ~

Several nights later, the necklace remained around my neck where Levinia had fastened it. The pearl was warm from my handling of it through another long silent night. Danek's visit had left me with such unexpected feelings that the shock of them lingered through days of lying mostly numb and mute.

The others repeated his words often. I listened and stored up the words, but did not yet have the strength to do anything more with them except hope and dream a little of what, in particular, was spoken about Galen.

Rose whimpered in her sleep. Careful not to jostle her, I turned on my other side to face her and, stroking her hair, whispered barely above the voice of breath, "It is all right." Then I added even quieter for my sake more than hers, "Galen will come."

My heart and body cradled her until her shoulders softened, and her breath evened once more. Each night she had some form of frightful dreams which I had held her through, and during the times she had heard me cry in the night, she had petted me and wrapped Mother's shawl over my shoulders. How difficult it would be to leave her in the morning when I returned with Netty and Auden to Trimont for a few days to help Netty settle in.

When I sensed dawn, I rose quietly and stepped outside. There was no wind—not even a dewy breath. The morning was strangely still as if the air had removed its forces from the earth — as if having foreseen events, the wind had withdrawn its hands from taking any part.

I almost went back inside and into the bed next to Rose, but I calmed myself upon seeing Mother's grave and wandered through the aspen grove, touching the white bark of each trunk within my reach, trying to reunite with life again.

As I did so, the twilight seemed to softly roll into its celestial closet while the sun spread wide its canopy. There remained no movement either in leaves already fallen or leaves yet suspended; however, the earth was remembered by the sun even if the air had fled.

Auden came out after a while and began to prepare the carriage and horses. I returned inside to help prepare for the return to Trimont.

Rose met me at the open door in Mother's shawl. "Take me with you," Rose beseeched again. "I promise I will help and not be selfish."

"I know you wouldn't be, Rose, but it is not for those reasons that you must not come. It is an unknown circumstance that we are returning to. We need to discover how everything is set in order at Trimont first. Once we know, I will take you with me to visit Trimont every time."

Rose's anxious eyes pleaded along with her words. "But every time you leave, you don't come back."

I instantly dropped to my knees before her. "No, Rose, I will come back. Just as much as you want to go, I do not wish to leave you. But for your safety, Garret and I are having you stay here with him. The plan is that I shall only be gone two days."

Unfastening the necklace from around my neck, I bound it around hers. "Wear this for me. Danek said it could help protect us."

I stood while Rose dropped her chin to see the necklace. Garret, on his way to take a load to the carriage, reproached me quietly. "You should have kept it for yourself, Liddy. Rose will be safe with me, but you are going where Multa scouts have been sighted."

"There are guards at Trimont, Garret. I am sure all will be fine. We both now believe that Danek would not have sanctioned it otherwise."

I returned to the chest what little belongings I had used and added into it some wheat before Auden and Garret carried it out to the carriage.

Netty was quiet and solemn as she too prepared to leave. I knew her heart quaked at having to return to Trimont without Lady Vala and the children being there. For my sake, I knew she had folded her anxieties out of sight. As a result of her devoted thoughtfulness, she had grown more womanly and gracious, though I doubted she was aware of how she was thus crowned or that Garret took notice.

They came in together from the carriage — Garret to scoop up Rose and Netty to humbly tell me that it was time.

Briefly, I took Netty's hand so she knew she was not a burden but a sister.

When I entered the carriage, I was startled to see through the window a horseman coming a few paces down our lane. But as soon as I noticed, he stopped, turned out, and continued on the main road toward Trimont.

Galen?

"What is it?" Netty asked as she settled next to me, following my gaze out the window.

"I saw a horseman. I just wonder who it might have

been."

"You mean, Galen?" Netty exclaimed. "Oh, I hope it is, for your sake. You deserve such happiness."

I let her praise pass by without taking hold of it; however, I did secretly urge the carriage onward.

Once on the main road, I sought to see the horseman again. He was nowhere in sight. This made me uneasy, and I limited my gaze back within the carriage. The sun followed my withdrawal, brushed my shoulder, and coaxed me to look out again.

Instead of seeing what was not, this time, I saw what was: a blue sky without any blemish of cloud, a sun stooping low to comfort a valley that had been tightly bundled and shivering for days, trees at peace, not forced to drop their leaves, and a river (my own gleaming Crimson River) that we had followed all the way to Dresden and back.

While there was no bellowing or joyous singing like there would have been in Dresden on such a day, I perceived that people were becoming aware of such a gift and were calling others out into it.

People also seemed to notice the carriage. I shrunk my face within it when I felt that people were beginning to recognize me.

Netty suddenly blew her nose. She could not turn her face from me before I saw that she had been crying.

"Nothing is the matter," she sputtered. "I told myself not to cry. It is just when the two days pass, I'll be miserable to part with you. I am afraid of living at Trimont alone, but I am willing to do it for however long need be. I am just thankful you were there that stormy wedding night. I might have lost my wits if you had not come. With all the other servants having left to their own homes and other work, and Father not sure how to help me, I was all alone in a state of mind I could not manage. I don't know why I'm thinking back so. I think I can bear things better now, but I'm infinitely relieved that you are going to be with me at first. I have to express my gratitude that you were willing to come with us even when it hurt you to leave Rose. I am sorry. Truly, I am."

"Netty, you know you are just as much my sister as Rose. And while I cannot deny these next weeks will feel a burden, I do not think this arrangement of separation will last forever." I smiled as I spoke, thinking that one day, she and Garret may marry. "And like you said, you are stronger now. I have seen it. I could not have done without you."

Netty's eyes swam again. She rested her head on my shoulder. Soon my shoulder was damp with her tears. I treasured her devotion. In no way did I want to disrupt the pure contents spilling from her heart.

I did not cry; I wondered if it was because I had been either hardened from loss or fortified through it. As my heart still throbbed and thought of others, I knew my solemn strength had grown even while lying dormant in grief.

Could it ever be that the entire world could throw its woes upon me and that, standing on the truth, I would not break? It was a deep contemplation which gently prodded my mind up new mental stairs. These thoughts led me to King Cordell. He would have gone through the most grievously stricken life of anyone. What was he thinking right now, in this moment? His had to be lovely, strong, faithful, and wise thoughts. Discouraged or mad were not words that befit a king of truth. But he would have had a choice like all of us. What if he had failed like

Cloven had? What if he had succumbed to fear, rage, or despair? Everything lost its power if he did not hold true.

Nonetheless, just because I now had Cloven's failure jarred into my conscience, it did not have to lower my hope in others, especially in our king. Though I did not know the extent of Danek's change, he had changed, and it was a marvel. The prospect of what Cloven may yet become was a beacon in the dark future. If these two men, who had been so removed from the truth, were now gaining it within their souls, anyone could be awakened. And if Vala, Mother, and Father had never faltered despite great difficulty, I believed that neither had King Cordell.

Netty lifted her head. "We are nearly there. At least we know Lady Vala and the children are safe. And when Galen comes, he will tell us all. That is, he will tell you, and you will tell me, and I'll tell a whole flock of birds or whoever will listen."

The carriage turned off the main road. Without interference, the guard at Trimont Bridge allowed us across into Trimont's hushed lands. Our first encounter was cold shade as we passed through the avenue of motionless evergreens. Although a narrow entrance, it led to the open fields where the sun whispered kindness upon the stubble remains of the wheat harvest which Emerson had told us Multa had stolen.

In the sun, the fields were a charm rather than a scar, and the remaining blond blades blended well with the browning knolls behind. I detected the one where the picnic had been held that first day I had met Galen. His eyes had been as blue as the sky which rose endlessly over the distant autumn draped mountains. Though it was beautiful, it did not lift my heart as it would have to have seen any of the children bursting forth from Trimont's front doors, for Trimont Castle now seemed no more than one stone on top of another. It was the people I yearned for.

Netty tugged my arm. "Oh, it is so beautiful and frightening at once! I don't know how I feel."

When Auden stopped the carriage between the stables and the kitchen door, Netty climbed out quickly, but I slowly — marking every movement and listening to every sparse sound. I was pricked again with the eerie feeling of the air being far removed. The crimson leaves over my head did not rustle, yet the fallen ones cracked beneath my shoes as I stepped down from the carriage. I took a deep breath and followed the path which had been raked to the kitchen door.

Roguish red ivy spread wide and tall like a wild flush on the castle's grey cheek. The window was hidden within the ivy. The door also would have been hidden, except that the vines had been neatly cleared away.

A horse, beyond the two attached to the carriage, neighed. I turned to see a horseman come from around the stables and dismount a few paces from me. He bowed humbly. "I hope you are well, my lady."

"Thank you, sir," I returned, recognizing him as the grey whiskered watchman who had told me about Mother.

He continued, "Forgive me for having not introduced myself when we met before, though I took the liberty of telling you the most intimate news. I am Alfred. Sir Danek has stationed me as head guard over Trimont. Since knowing you would be returning here, Sir Danek handpicked which guards were sent. You are surrounded by allies. Yet neither I, nor my men shall disturb you; nevertheless, you may approach me or any of my men for the smallest necessity or concern. All is safe within the castle. We have scoured it for any sign of invasion and found none. Only the harvest has been compromised." He put his head down. I thought when he lifted it, he would say more but hesitantly he bowed and departed.

Netty joined me the moment he left. I voiced, "That man, Alfred, just brought me great comfort, Netty. I believe you will be safe here."

"I'm glad to hear that."

Together we followed the raked path until, at the door, I set the key in the lock. When we entered the kitchen, it smelled as though it had lost its purpose — dust instead of bread and mice instead of children.

Netty shooed a mouse off the table, suggesting, "Do you think we could get a pussycat? It would bring fear to the mice and comfort to me."

As I was about to agree, a light knock came to the open door, and Alfred stood in the open frame. "Pardon my second intrusion, but there is something else I judge it right to tell you. My lady, will you follow me outside?"

I followed him to the well.

His eyes, naturally hooded, squinted in the sun so that there was not much of his eyes showing. But even from the small slits, so much kind concern poured out. He began, "I had been careful to spare you worry, but I believe it was wrong of me because I think there could be danger. You should know that a bandit was caught here last night. He was taken to Crevilon for questioning. We are awaiting Sir Danek's further orders. Also, evening last, a knight from King's City arrived, demanding reports and asking many questions, some pertaining to you. On my honor, I relayed as little concerning you as I could. I am far from knowing what it all means, possibly nothing, but let this be a precautious warning between us. Do not venture far. Sir Danek should send word sometime this morning on any further action we are to take."

I nodded, accepting the words heavily. Then I asked suddenly, "Did the man from the city make any inquiry of Rose or Garret?"

"No," Alfred answered softly, "they were not sought after."

I was greatly relieved, but still gravely pondering as I acknowledged before I left, "I thank you for your warning. I shall be on my guard."

He stopped me for one moment more as he uttered, "You have been brave enough to express truth; so must I. It is I and others in this valley who must thank you. I did not understand most of my life. I went along with the criticisms of your family and the old ways because it was all I had heard, but when I listened to you speak at the wedding, my eyes were opened. I understood your words, and I followed where they led—to the Book of Truth and believing that King Cordell was still alive. I want you to know that I am with you." He looked around before adding in a confidential tone, "I've shared private talks with Sir Danek. He no longer trusts Lord Breemore. He has told me that he believes Lord Breemore is in league with Multa."

Alfred's words were of such a hopeful force upon me. I offered him a deeply heartfelt smile which he warmly returned. He then gestured back to the kitchen door. "The other woman is waiting for you."

When I returned inside, Netty had begun to dust the kitchen with a rag. "Am I allowed to know what he told you?" she asked.

"Of course," I answered. "There is so much to what he

said. First he gave warning that a bandit was caught—"

I cut off speech when I heard a horseman storming up and yelling. With apprehension, I swiftly shut and bolted the door. The room severely dimmed.

Netty stared in fright. "Lydia, what is it?"

"It may only be Danek, but we have need to be careful. A bandit was sighted and taken into custody to Crevilon Castle last night, and a knight from King's City is seeking me."

I drew near to the vine covered window, trying to find a gap to see through.

To my relief, it was Danek. His features were intense as he spoke with Alfred. Alfred responded with such haste to the stables that I began to fear. I opened the door as Danek was now coming toward us.

He yanked his stallion quickly behind him. I met him halfway.

"You must leave now," he commanded, not looking me in the eye—only handing me the warm, leather reins to his black sweating beast. "Call the maid who is with you, and ride straight to Crevilon. Garret, Rose, and Auden are taken care of."

"What about you?" I implored.

He turned on me angrily. "Captain Rhys is encamped just behind that mountain, and he has rallied bandits against you and Trimont. They know you are here; they will attack at any moment. Do not speak another word to me. Go!"

"Netty." My voice shook and would not project louder than a frightened child, but Netty was attuned and came running to my side as soon as I spoke her name.

No movement was swift enough for Danek. He helped boost me into the saddle and lifted Netty up behind me.

Then came the confirmation of all warnings. The sound of a hundred crashes wailed forth from the other side of the castle, piercing through the valley and through my heart. There was a pause of horror before, without warning, Danek so slapped his stallion that the beast reared and charged.

Netty screamed and clung to me, neither of us fully realizing that her fingers dug into my ribs. I clung to the horse for both our lives, struggling to breathe and see through the resistant air as we fled.

We had not yet reached Trimont Bridge when suddenly we were sharply jarred forward as the horse tripped. An arrow had been shot into his upper leg. Panic swiped through me. I urged the horse onward, but another arrow struck him, and he fell. I was forcibly thrown.

When I landed, pain seized my entire body, and my eyes opened fully into the sun, causing my vision to blacken. My heart beat violently, but I could not move; I could not see.

"Netty! Netty!!!" I screamed.

Instead of her reply, I was picked up and slung over the boney shoulder of a man with a foul stench. I fought and yelled as I could, but my gut was bounced in agony as he ran. In blurry pieces, my sight returned, but, as my head hung upside down, I became dizzy and faint.

But as stride by stride I was re-plunged into the attack against Trimont Castle, I remained acutely conscious despite my body. I wanted to cry out against what was happening to Trimont, but my throat was barely hanging on to breath.

Trimont Castle, thrown apart in every heinous way, blurred across my vision as my captor darted past broken glass, ground fires, and heaps of plunder. When I saw bandits flaunting tapestries from the Hall of First Loyals as robes, thoughtlessly dragging them on the ground near the fires, tears stung my eyes. Trimont's love and sacrifice treated common and criminal! I began to beat my fists against the back of the man who carried me and kick him until he suddenly released me onto the ground.

Scrambling toward the river to get away, my ankle was stomped on with vengeance. I dropped in pain.

"Let me have a good look at her first," muttered a man, stooping near me to take hold of my chin and force my face toward him.

After I saw it was Captain Rhys, I tried to jerk my head away, but his hand locked my neck in his evil direction. I closed my eyes as my only way of escape from him.

He sneered, "For this pathetic face, Danek fell."

My eyes shot open; my heart beat violently.

Captain Rhys threw my chin from his grasp, and instead grabbed my arm and yanked me to my feet.

"You there, hand me that torch," he commanded.

In the exchange of hands, the torch was purposefully brushed near my skin. I knew then that by this torch, I was going to die. My pain abated while a worse stricken panic took its place — Rose. I had to live for Rose. I began to fight against him harshly and to scream, tears of wild desperation bursting forth.

But his body was a bulwark against my thin arms. He pulled me toward Trimont, a chaos of flames and bandits.

I pulled, flailed, and screamed only to have Captain Rhys turn on me sharply and ridicule, "You live by your truth, yet you are afraid to die by it?"

I did not listen to him but kept screaming and fighting against him. My heart was thinking too greatly of those for whom I had to live.

"Your father went much more peacefully than you. Is it not your dream to be like him? You hypocrite; you only want to be like him in life but not in death?"

I knew both Father and Mother would want me to fight for my life, so with renewed force, I tried to pull away from his grasp. But all of my strength did nothing to him.

He dragged me into the kitchen which was hazy with smoke as it was scattered with little fires in the curtains and in the shelves. "Netty," I whimpered, hoping she was safe.

Captain Rhys then backed me into a dark pantry, and with his torchlight demonizing his face, he said, "Here is your tomb."

His words seized me with terror. I threw myself around him so he could not leave except to take me with him, but he flung me harshly against the back stone wall. Before I could move, with big sweeps of his arm, he thrashed all the flasks of oil and flour from the shelves onto the ground, and then tossed his torch into the spilt pile which surged into an impassable flame between us. He left, shutting and locking the pantry door behind him. It was completely black except for the horrifying flames.

With tears that could not stop spilling, I forced myself to think of Mother and Father. I remembered the words, "Those who believe in the truth will not be put to shame." Alfred's words also returned to me like a stream of water within. And Cloven. And Galen. And Danek if he were still alive. They would all continue for the truth. I would die with this assurance that the truth was greater than I and would sustain all those left to fight for it. I whispered Rose's words written upon Mother's grave, "The sun is touching me." Though I could not see it, I knew the sun was penetrating all this vile destruction and that the light could fashion good out of the devastation. I felt a kind of sorrowful peace, but still I could not give up.

With the short time remaining, I found a pot and banged it against the stone wall, though even I could barely hear the clanging above the whipping flames and clogging smoke.

Coughing uncontrollably, I dropped lower where the smoke was thinner. And though intense heat began to smother any movement, still I banged the pot against the wall. "Please, someone help."

Suddenly, there was another eruption of flame. Smoke gushed into my lungs, heat clawed beneath my very skin, and I screamed for Mother!

Chapter Twenty-five
~ *Danek* ~

With unrelenting pressure from my heels, I demanded speed from the old horse who was unfamiliar to a demanding rider. I cut through the fields to reach the road to meet my guards, who were coming, and to make sure Lydia made it through.

A large black mass lying on the ground caught my eye. I sharply turned course and charged toward it, all the time knowing that it was my stallion. My teeth ground viciously against one another. The taste of gall and death sloshed in my throat.

With abrupt force, I yanked the reins, dismounting before the profusely panting horse could stop.

"Lydia!" I demanded of nature.

A voice, crazed and frightened, called to me.

I jerked round to see the maid, who had been with Lydia, step from behind a nearby fir tree. Anxiety alone allowed her to stand. Sense was vacant from her sodden red eyes as they flinched from everything they darted toward.

"Where is Lydia?" I demanded.

"You don't know either?" she gasped, despair welling to every feature of her stricken face.

I lunged for the reins and remounted. "Stay hidden!" I instructed before riding straight into the heart of the attack. As soon as arrows began to whiz past me, I knew I would be struck. In an instant, my shoulder roared in agony. I fell from the horse, rolling. At last coming upright, I yanked the arrow out and angrily yelled, "One of you tell Captain Rhys to come face me."

One man obeyed while several others remained to keep watch on me.

Captain Rhys rode from around the castle with two other guards. I stood erect, paying no attention to the loss of blood spilling from my shoulder.

"Where is Lydia Tavish?" I demanded.

"Rightfully dead with her father," he answered without qualm.

"You fool!" I seethed!

Captain Rhys relaxed in his saddle as he smugly looked around him unperturbed. "No, not I. You are the one who chose to play the fool when you broke our agreement. As I am sure you well remember, you agreed that if Lydia Tavish refused to marry you, she was to be imprisoned. I am tempted to think that you are as much a traitor as she." His hand signaled the bowmen. "But I will first listen if you have a defense."

I met Captain Rhys' eyes evenly. "If you kill me, kill me for this." I raised my voice. "Let it be known that I have turned against Lord Breemore. He is of Multa blood, and his plan is to give us over into Multa's hands."

Rhys cried out, "Blasphemous traitor!" He dismounted and, unsheathing his sword, walked toward me. When close enough, he pricked his sword to my heart. "You would thank me for killing you, would you not?"

"I would," I answered, my heart growing so fierce that it rose into his sword's point.

Rhys harshly drew his sword away. "Since I am a man who believes in inflicting the greater punishment, I shall leave your death to your wound, for your face grows paler by the moment. I never liked you, but I never thought you would stoop to lunacy and treason for the lowly sake of a woman."

"I never stooped for her! I held my ideals to the utmost while trying to force her to stoop before me. Do you not yet see what a venomous snake I was? But if I am this, you are worse. You stoop to murder; I have since accepted the truth — let us be judged."

From loss of blood, I suddenly trembled and staggered.

Rhys commanded, "Move him against that tree, out of the way. Let wild dogs come lick his blood."

Two men dragged and leaned me against a tree. Rapidly I grew weaker as their rough handling increased the stream of blood dripping from my arm. Rhys and his men disappeared behind the other side of the castle. I despondently stared at the scenes around me in wretched pain of body and heart. My mind was my only strength which kept me from fainting prostrate. But I had died long ago; this feeling was not unknown.

The thunderous collapsing of Trimont's inner timbers and upper floor caused bandits to scatter like rats from the lower levels. My guards arrived at the perfect time to capture them.

When Alfred saw me, he rushed to aid my wound, ripping my cloak to make a bandage from it. When there was no more he could do, and I offered him no words, he reluctantly left to attend to the urgent demands around him.

If I died here, I died here. I inhaled the smoky air, lifted my eyes to the sparks above me, and left my legs exposed to the low fires slithering near.

My guards quickly overcame the bandits and bound them as prisoners. Rows of them were prodded toward the road, swearing and complaining. Over the hill, I caught glances of villagers who, drawn by the smoke, came to see its source. As soon as they saw it, they turned back to spread their report.

Beneath din and motion, I sensed a deep quiet into which I sank, like a tranquil grave. While I thus lay with eyes closed, pounding upon the ground roused them open. A horseman charged toward Trimont. Who was this intruder when the earth was just calming for the dead? Yet, all nature, of what was still lovely and of what was now vile, spread way for him, and I saw that it was Galen Trimont.

My eyes closed again as I whispered, "I do not envy your future, Cousin."

Chapter Twenty-six
~ *Galen* ~

The intensity bursting from my heart vented so loudly through my breath that Chess's thundering hoofs were lost to my ears. The faster I rode to Trimont, the more horrors flashed through my sight. Possessions of Vala's and the children lay butchered and strewn. Their home, my home, was in the mouth of a nightmare. Flames ascended like towers of evil, gnawing and clawing with all their strength to rip apart any timbers. Breakings and crashes never ceased screeching from the castle's burning bowels. Smoke vanquished all connection between Trimont and light. Black smoke and hideous orange were the only colors my eyes could now detect.

I jumped off Chess, quickly pulling the old horse, Gregoreo, from a closing circle of ground fire. "Is anyone here?" I yelled!

Yanking off my cloak, I relentlessly slapped out the flames from a tapestry half burned. Heat and soot leapt into my face, but I kept vigorously swinging as hot tears also streamed down my face. My efforts were only ridiculed by the enormity of the disaster. I wasn't saving anything! All was already lost.

I hid my head in my hands as animosity and incomprehension built up and erupted into another bout of slapping out the fire and shouting, "How did this happen?"

When next I looked up, a crowd rushed its way down

a knoll and began to help. "What happened here?" I beseeched of the first man who joined me.

"It is not yet clear enough in my own mind to say, but the road is clogged with a horde of bandits that guards have taken captive."

My heart hammered as I asked my next question. "Was anyone within Trimont?"

The man looked at Trimont solemnly. "Only guards were on the grounds that I know of, but there was a rumor that makes me concerned."

A guard suddenly rode past us. We both watched as he went straight to a tree where a man was lying wounded. The guard helped him up. I also intended to help when I heard a small female voice behind me. "Master Galen?"

I recognized the woman as one of the children's maids. She looked so parched, I brought her my canteen. She shook her head, insisting, "Where is Lydia?"

If my heart had been clenched in affliction, it now dropped in violent agony. "Tell me now when you last saw her."

The woman answered, incapable of fluency, "We were followed... our horse shot. We fell over there." She pointed vaguely with a feeble arm toward the road. "I searched everywhere for her. I don't know where they took her. Please, please find her."

I looked frantically in the castle windows which were either curtained in flame, or burned out blank hollows. "Can't you tell me anything else?"

"I don't know," she wailed. "I never should have been so selfish in wanting her to return with me to Trimont."

"It was Captain Rhys," interjected a stern voice.

I turned to see Danek, standing by the aid of his guard whose face was deeply grieved.

"Where is she?" I implored, having a horrific remembrance of Lenrow and the Hendrys. I also recalled Rhys' missing horse in the stall the morning I left from the city. Rhys must have likewise learned that Lydia had not married Danek! He would kill her!

I grabbed Danek's shoulders, demanding, "Where is she?"

Danek stared at me from eyes as dark and dwindled as coal set within a face as pale and thin as plaster. He answered, "She loved you; let that knowledge be enough."

Dizziness pervaded my head. I stepped away. It couldn't be. It couldn't be. I looked at the castle. Knowing how Rhys had attempted to murder the Hendrys, she had to be within it.

I ran toward the castle despite Danek's demanding me to stay. With my sword, I smashed through shards of glass to climb through a window.

Instantly, my sight and ease of breath were taken from me as smoke charged into my throat. I dropped to my knees, trying to cough out the vast irritation. Then covering my mouth with my tunic and keeping my eyes squinted, I crawled forward.

"Lydia!" I yelled. "Lydia! Lydia!" Desperation as my only guide, I searched for any glimpse of her and listened for the faintest cry, while her name was constantly begged for from my lips.

I burnt my hand several times as I kept pressing forward. Every moment became more painful to my skin, lungs, and eyes. But imagining Lydia enduring this was my greatest torture.

A hand grabbed my heel. Irrational hope surged as I looked behind me. Danek's body, so nearly claimed by death, lay on the ground except for his hand reaching toward me. "Get out," he gasped.

"I am willing to die even if there is only a slight chance of saving her," I stubbornly shot back.

"You do not have the freedom to die in vain! You are a Trimont! Your kingdom comes before your feelings!"

His words sobered me. Meklon had been willing to give his life to save me in the Lenrow fire and now Danek. Better Lydia saved than me. I set my face to continue.

"You fail everything she lived for if you die uselessly," Danek growled.

Facing Danek again, this time it truly hit me that it was useless, and he would die if I did not save him. With a deep groan, I heaved him over my shoulder and followed the way I had come.

I was hit full in the face with a bucket of water as Danek's guard flung one bucket after another to extinguish the flames for our exit. When he saw us, he dropped his bucket to help pull Danek through the window.

After I had climbed out, I staggered to the line of people who had gathered from the river to the castle to douse the fire. I joined them in passing bucket after bucket—anything to keep me from thinking.

I was startled when a voice shouted, "Hear me!" Captain Rhys sat atop his horse with two mounted knights on either side of him as he addressed the gathered crowd.

My eyes narrowed; my teeth set. I stepped away from those around me and re-drew my sword.

"This was not an attack," Captain Rhys declared. "This occurrence is justice befalling Lydia Tavish and others who chose to rebel with her. She was fairly warned, and so was Sir Danek. This is warning that no act of treason or sympathy toward it shall go unpunished. Anyone here would do well to bring forward any such traitorous persons of whom they are aware. We are on the brink of war with Multa and can have no divisions among our own kingdom. Above all else, we must be strong and united to defeat Multa once and for all. Therefore, return to your homes now that you have been warned. If you..."

His speech ceased when he saw me advancing toward him. Unmistakably, his face displayed, first, shock and then evil glee.

"You are a murderer!" I shouted.

"Arrest him!" Rhys ordered.

But his men did not dare dismount. They *saw me* – my smoke and tear burnt eyes, my grief-stricken countenance, my scorched clothing, my sword strong in my hand, and my determined gait aimed toward them. They knew I had won the scrimmage, and they also knew Lord Breemore would not respond kindly to a report of my death.

Again I declared, "Captain Rhys is a murderer and has caused destruction both here and in King's City from where I have just come. I witnessed his attempted murder of an innocent family – husband, wife, and child! He will kill countless others if we do not prevent him. Help me stop him; he must be captured and tried."

Man after man came forward, with a face and fist ready to pull the offender from his horse and carry him to true justice.

Captain Rhys spurred his horse away. I whistled for Chess. Mounting, I yelled, "Any with a horse, help me catch him!"

I chased Rhys never looking back to see if any followed. At the end of Trimont's lane, he turned to the east, out of the valley. Chess, with the determination to outrun every horse, began to gain on him.

Through the blur of the speed, I watched Rhys

unsheathe his sword. I braced for anything he might do. Suddenly, he turned sharply and swiped his blade toward my head.

I escaped by sheer reflex. Recovering, I turned Chess to face him, and this time met his sword with mine. After several strikes, I pulled back, jumped off Chess, and on foot desperately ran at Rhys in an attempt to gain control of his mount. With all of my momentum, I cut through both reins beneath the horse's muzzle. Rhys angrily threw at me the useless portion of his reins while I grabbed the newly shortened reins hanging from the bit.

His sword strikes flew all the more. I struggled to block them over my head while I staunchly restrained his horse. I finally struck his hand, and he involuntarily dropped his sword.

I kicked his sword behind me and demanded, "Dismount!"

"Remember who your superior is," he spat.

"No murderer is a superior."

Rhys narrowed his eyes at me. "Prove to me the difference between us. Who is ever to say that one man's opinion and actions are better than any other? It is merely the strongest will that wins in every generation, thus the dominant force is ever changing. Long ago it was Multa, then Cordell and Trimont. In your young generation, it has been our Lord Breemore. And now once again the powers rise to fight for dominance. It is a vicious succession. You and I are nothing new. We are offspring of our sides, neither better than the other."

"You are wrong," I defended. "Those who believe the Book of Truth follow a higher way because they do not trust their own wills and opinions, but obey a source that is pure, selfless, sacrificial, and faithful beyond anything I've ever seen! I follow them who follow the Book of Truth, not to prove anything nor gain advantage or control, but because I desire to become like them and to manifest what a man can be."

"A children's nurse and a king's pet, you mean."

"Dismount," I commanded again.

Though he slowly obeyed, his eyes held their pallor of doom and distain. I pointed my sword toward him, for he was not subdued.

Suddenly he slapped his horse so that it ripped the reins from my hand and knocked me off balance. Amid my disorder, Rhys kicked my legs out from under me, and I fell to my back. He mercilessly pressed and ground his boot into my wrist. Though I held onto my sword desperately, he ripped it from my hand.

Then, holding my own sword at my throat, he declared, "You are a deceiver and a thief. I do not doubt for a moment that you would have stolen the throne in the name of your truth. You may have deceived Lord Breemore, but you never deceived me. Justly, you die at my hand."

As he applied strength to the blade, I grabbed it and pulled enough that his thrust sunk into my shoulder instead of my throat.

Pain paralyzed my body, but with my will, a force of its own, I frantically groped for Rhys' sword which lay on the ground above me. As Rhys pulled my sword out of my shoulder to strike again, my hand found his fallen sword and with gritted strength, I defended myself against his next strike until men arrived and held him back. I collapsed in frozen agony.

After Rhys had been bound, the men helped me up. One poured ale over my wound. I would have thanked them on a normal day, but the only words retained in my throat were for Captain Rhys before they took him.

I set myself before him and asked, "Where is her body?"

Rhys' face turned smug. My question had revealed to him that he had yet inflicted the greater fatal blow. He forged his answer as gruesomely as he possibly could have. "Her corpse lays smoldering upon the castle's pantry floor."

My entire body felt sick. Without another word, I mounted Chess and rode back to Trimont. Where the kitchen once was, I found an insurmountable mound of smoking rubble. There was no door to allow me in and no wall to keep me out.

I descended to the ground; all my limbs squeezed toward my tormented heart.

I lay until all was silent; I lay until all was dark.

Chapter Twenty-seven
~ *Galen* ~

The sun awoke, but I did not. Though my eyes began to see the shadows of destruction, it did not move me. Though the sounds of hissing and collapsing continued, my ears had long ceased hearing. My existence knew only one desire — that I might have given my life to have saved Lydia's. If my body could not be given for that purpose, I would never rise again.

However, the brighter the light grew, the more sensations returned to me. I loathed the sun for stirring them. I was dead! Do not make me feel!

But already I was aware that a tapestry had been laid over me as a blanket, and curiosity raised my head to consider the mystery. "Lydia?" I foolishly questioned.

Dawn's lips were sealed.

I threw the tapestry aside, feeling sudden intensity from my forgotten wound. I dropped back in pain and severe stiffness. As I lay on my back, a broken body full of pains and thoughts it could neither heal nor forget, tears began to slip from the sides of my eyes and dampen my ears with rivers of sorrow.

Slowly, it dawned upon me that, in the distance, a male voice repeatedly called my name. When it grew nearer, I answered hoarsely, "I am over here," as my second attempt to rise failed.

Emerson and Garret came. Emerson instantly stooped to help me sit up. "Oh, my dear boy," he breathed, looking at me. "Come back with us."

"How can I leave her?"

Emerson's eyes were of the palest blue, like color had been flushed out of them. He attempted no words, yet heaved his entire strength into helping me stand. Garret helped, although his countenance was lost within the rubble.

"I'm sorry," I whispered, knowing he, as her brother, had a closer claim to her than I. He did not acknowledge my condolence as he walked away.

"Does Rose know?" I asked Emerson heavily.

Emerson nodded. "Netty and my Livy are with her."

Suddenly we heard stones being thrown and looked to see Garret madly digging through the rubble.

Emerson sadly turned his head and gently led me on toward the wagon. I craned my neck to see him, for I felt jealous. Why could I not exert all my strength to lift every stone in search of a last hope of Lydia still being with us?

"Both he and Netty unjustly blame themselves," Emerson explained solemnly. "Something you must not do."

My very nerves retracted from Emerson's care, for of course I was to blame! No one could justify self-blame more than I. If I had not slept as much on my journey, if I not spent extra time to dig through my satchel for Vala's ring, and if I had never left for King's City in the first place, I would have been here to save her!

Emerson reasoned quietly, "Lydia would not want any of you to feel this way. Love her, mourn her, but do not ruin yourself over her loss. In time, build yourself up for her sake."

My feet continued to plod alongside his, but my gaze pulled back toward Trimont, longing to see Lydia come from behind any corner. My eyes strained on the one chance I somehow just hadn't seen her. Without Emerson steering my body up into the wagon, I would have fled back.

I was startled by how peaceful the ruins looked with the day's new light playing about it like a young child, peeking in and out of the newly formed crevices. But it was merely one nice fleeting thought amid a thousand horrific fixed ones.

Garret soon despondently slumped beside me with his head in his hands, which were black with ash. Our journey was an utter desolate one.

When the carriage wheels could take us no further, we shifted to the use of our own leaden feet down the slope overtaken by wild growth. The frazzled and finished fragments of summer crunched beneath our feet. I stepped without pity upon the bent necks of yellowed and browned vines.

The door was open to the home beneath the bridge, and the moment I stepped inside, I found myself in a den full of excruciating feelings. I envisioned Lydia at her mother's bedside, heard her gently singing, and felt her touch through the secret tunnels. I stood like stone, defending against the pummeling memories.

Soon, I felt frail arms around me. Levinia spoke nothing, but when I continued to stand as stone, she released me. Sadly refraining from attempting any more comforting touch, she beckoned me to sit in a chair by the open door. I obeyed.

The home was dark except for what morning light first made it beneath the bridge and then through the door. The hearth was dead. Dead—just as it should be—though it was cold and Levinia bore many shawls upon her shoulders. Her hands felt like winter as they tended my wound. I realized that it must have been for our benefit that there was no sight of flame. I was thankful and looked at Levinia in a repentant, softened gaze.

There was a dim corner in which Netty and Rose lay. Their bodies scrunched in tight balls, buried above and beneath many blankets.

Garret sat on the floor next to Rose. He stared at his sister with the most pitiful expression as if he had no muscles within his face.

Emerson stood by silently and fetched anything he anticipated Levinia may need and held her cold hand whenever it paused.

"I have no desire to rise," Netty broke the silence. The continued silence was enough to know that her words echoed from each of us. She bemoaned again, "I could never tell those in Dresden. They loved her so."

My head deliberately lifted toward Emerson. What Netty shared triggered the remembrance of Vala's forewarning that they had asked Emerson to send someone to my father. There was no way Emerson could have been so thoughtless as to send Lydia! "Someone tell me. How is Lydia known in Dresden?"

"Oh," Netty startled, sitting up, "I did not know you were here."

Her eyes anxiously besought Levinia, who appeared grim about the timing but acknowledged gently, "You may answer him freely, Netty."

"Tell, please," I stressed, "how was she known to them?"

Netty's voice shook as she explained, "Lydia, my father, and I journeyed to Dresden and have only recently returned. We went to convince your father to reclaim the throne for the kingdom's sake."

When my head fell into my hands, and I harshly squeezed them over it, she ceased speaking. I did not care, for I did not desire to hear anymore. The knowledge could only grow in distaste to me whatever the outcome may have been. My father would not make a good king even if he did return. That Lydia had spent her last days in the presence of a hateful and broken man like my father was unthinkable! A precious life like hers should not have been wasted on him! Someone else could have gone to my father at the very most, but not my Lydia. I did not want her near him!

Whether Levinia's tending to my arm was finished or not, Levinia had retracted her fingers from my shoulder, so I stood and left the house in favor of a rock on the riverbank. How could the water keep flowing! How could the birds keep singing! Didn't they know the world would never return to commonplace? Why was the sky blue? Why was the day perfect for her to be sitting here beside me? I rose and left for a more dismal place near dying thorn bushes.

Why instead hadn't she come to King's City — to me? She never would have been murdered if she had come, for I would have protected her with my life. But instead she went to my father!

Perhaps she never had loved me. Perhaps she loved her heroism more than she had loved me and Danek both. If my father had not been alive, she would have come to me and would have been safe — in my arms as my wife! It was his fault!

Suddenly, I realized that Garret was watching me. The presence of a person made me conscious of the angry heat which had risen in my face. I lowered to my knees to wash my face in the frigid river.

"Sir Danek has summoned you," he informed me.

I glanced up and nodded, expecting him to then leave. Instead, he asked, "Have you heard anything of my brother, Creighson?"

"I saw him once, during the scrimmage. He believes you all to be well and troubles himself no more about it. I know nothing more."

Garret looked stung by the report. "If you see him again, will you tell him all that has befallen us?"

"I will," I answered and then asked, "What will you do now?"

"I will offer to marry Netty, and if she accepts, we will raise Rose together the best we can."

Though it came with a pang of emptiness, his decision struck me as one which Lydia would fully approve. We each nodded and parted ways.

Once alone, the terrible thoughts came snapping back. I knew they were wrong, but blame against my father was so strong that I could not control it.

"I cannot allow these feelings!" I yelled. "I will not allow them!"

I tore away to Crevilon's entrance and was led to Danek's upper story bedchamber. The chamber was like entering an ancient tomb, for there were no windows, and candlesticks were only lit along the far perimeter. In the middle was a curtained bed, completely sealed except for a crack at the foot where I was led to stand. The guard remained beside me, holding his candle near to light my face. I saw the covered form of Danek's feet by the same light. The rest of Danek's body was shrouded in complete darkness and silence. I wondered if he were dying.

In a voice drained of health but not of will, Danek began, "I saved your life. I want assurance that my efforts were not in vain. Can you give it?"

I turned my head, immediately wanting to escape these bonds of responsibility, so I too could lie down and die. However, I threw out a harsh, "Yes," because it was the proper answer.

"So if I die," Danek reiterated, "I may know with complete assurance that you will do all within your power to find King Cordell, expose Lord Breemore's tie to Multa, and not waste a day wallowing in pity? I will only accept your yes if that is what you mean by it. Now say your yes again."

Tears stupidly came, and I stepped outside the circle of candlelight.

"Don't you dare be that selfish!" Danek scolded. "Choose now to rise above yourself, and for the first time become truly worthy of the name Trimont which you bear to the world."

I shot my eyes into his which now glowed in the back of the bed cave. "How do you know all this, and why do you refuse me my grief? Don't you know how much I loved her!"

"Of course! Don't you understand what I am telling you? Do not become as I—a wasted, useless skeleton. Grief and guilt have the power to eat away a man's very bones. It is your greatest enemy now. I would spare you of it."

My father's face, red with rage and hard as crust, flashed before my mind's eye. I felt the tight contortion of my face mirroring it. For the first time since these events, Cadby returned to my mind. He was as my own son now. What if Cadby had seen me?

Visibly, my hands trembled. I forcibly shook them as I walked to the other side of the room. Had it been this hard for Vala when she lost her husband and sons? Hadn't her heart been torn from her very soul? Yet even so, she had more love and strength within her than anyone I knew. And I knew better than to make the excuse that she had been born with such a heart. No, it was because in moments like these, she chose love and truth over her feelings, and thus she reached the heights where few ever ascend. Lydia had followed closely behind her.

Lydia – I held her name on my silent tongue. *How could I have judged it wrong of you to have gone to my father when you had been so selfless to go? I am so ashamed.*

I returned to the foot of Danek's bed. "This time I answer you a truer, yes. I will faithfully serve my kingdom."

"Alfred is witness," Danek confirmed.

Alfred, with watery eyes, set his hand on my shoulder, saying, "When the time comes, the knights of this castle will be your ally."

I acknowledged his words with a respectful bow, then asked Danek again, "How is it that you know about Breemore's ties to Multa and that I am a Trimont?"

"Lady Vala did not forget me, her coldhearted nephew. She gave me letters written by my mother to Breemore. I did not rest until I knew all."

Deciding my own course of action, I responded, "Lady Vala was wise when she told me to entrust Trimont to you. Do with the land and ruins whatever you wish. I will return to King's City before this day's end."

"You should know that Captain Rhys is dead," Danek remarked.

"I am grateful for your swift sentence."

"I do not believe you understand me. This morning Rhys was found in his dungeon cell with an arrow through his back."

"Murdered?" I exclaimed. "Is it known by whom?"

"Every guard has sworn against it and has claimed that the night watch was so alert that there was no possibility of someone breaking through."

I asked, "Do I have your permission to go to the dungeons?"

"Alfred will take you to the corpse."

My eyes, now adjusted, could make out the outline of Danek's face. He nodded. "Farewell, Cousin."

I bowed in return, bidding, "If you expect this commitment from me, I expect you to live to see it. Farewell."

Alfred offered sad condolences as we walked, and I kept my thoughts as present as I could.

In the dungeons, riotous uproar burst from behind each cell door. Bandits banged, stomped, and yelled for their freedom. Several guards were posted at each door and knocked with clubs the vicious hands that clawed from the barred window. "We only obeyed orders! Give us justice!" one man clearly yelled out above the inarticulate mayhem of the others.

I stopped. "What did Captain Rhys tell you?" I asked.

The man's dirty face pressed through the small space of bars. "He promised reward and assured no punishment. Rhys said that to vanquish Trimont was Lord Breemore's will. And this is how we are tricked? You are all liars, crooks, and cruel to people lower than yourselves. We hope you all die at Multa's hand! We will never help you fight against them." He spat on my cheek.

I wiped it away and walked on, pondering. If Lord Breemore had sent Rhys, Lord Breemore must have also secretly sanctioned the Hendrys death. But why did he defend and promote me publicly? What I did not understand is why did Breemore not kill me? Wasn't I his greatest threat?

"What will be done with the bandits?" I asked Alfred.

"Whatever Sir Danek judges."

Alfred unlocked a heavily oaken cell door. We both stepped in. Captain Rhys' body lay stiff on his side with an arrow through his back. As the blood had already dried, it was something that had happened in the dead of night.

Alfred explained as he pointed, "The only possibility is that the arrow was shot through that window slit twenty feet up. For one arrow to have so perfectly struck him through such a narrow space, it had to have been made by a trained assassin. I know of no one in these parts who could have made that shot."

"He must be an ally of ours if he used his skill to kill a man such as Rhys," I noted.

"Perhaps or perhaps not."

Alfred's response made me feel as though I needed to think, but my mind struggled to return to its normal capacity. I asked, "I see what you are possibly saying, but can you explain?"

"I'm only reminded that once Frederic Tavish warned that the ultimate goal of the enemy was not to kill us but to use us to destroy truth."

My eyes began to burn with a type of fire as I listened to him repeat the words of Lydia's father. From an inner zeal, I spoke, "That is why I will use my body and soul to protect the Book of Truth."

Chapter Twenty-eight
~ *Phelia* ~

Warmed and comforted on all sides, my body heavily lay as though eternally put to rest. I was perplexed when light and dark shadows began blinking over my closed eyelids. I tossed my head one way and then the other to avoid the discomfort. When the reality struck me that I was alive, my eyes sprung open.

Branches arched as a low roof over me. A thick layer of pine needles filled in the gaps, so thoughtfully, that not one stream of sunlight or draft reached me except by the opening at the top of my head from where sunlight and cool air glided over my awakened senses. The space so richly smelled of earthy pine that my nose was filled with the scent without effort.

I turned my head to see out the small opening. A low cracking campfire was in partial view. I did not like how frightfully my body recoiled from the innocent flames, for at the sight, I was filled with all the horrors I had experienced within the darkened pantry.

I was safe, I assured myself and forced my mind to more practical rather than irrational thoughts.

Straining to remember how I had come to be here, I had a vague consciousness of being carried and recalled dreaming of Galen, which brought the thrilling sensation of him being my rescuer. With such an overwhelming desire to see him, I spoke his name. A sense of foolishness came over me when I heard no reply.

I slowly turned myself around that I might crawl out of my burrow. These first movements revealed that I had not escaped the fire unscathed. My entire body felt bruised. Up both my arms, bandages wound thickly. Pain unleashed everywhere, though I coddled my wounds tenderly. Nevertheless, determined to know who rescued me and what had happened at Trimont, I moved forward.

As soon as I nudged my head out, I was startled and progressed no further. I saw Cloven. He sat at the campfire, tanning a rabbit hide while the meat roasted on a spit.

Despite being stunned, I rejoiced at seeing him, for I had feared he would never be seen again. It calmed the many doubts I had stored toward him. If he had traveled this far, surely he intended to reclaim the throne. However, I noted simultaneously that his cold unapproachable manner was unchanged. He did not look up.

Beginning to shiver, first from his cold manner and second from an increased breeze, I crawled the rest of the way to the fire. Instinctively, I knew I would have to speak first if any words were to be used at all.

"I am grateful you saved me. How did you manage it?" As I spoke, question followed question. "What about the others? And Trimont? Was Captain Rhys stopped?"

When his eyes only drifted further away, my heart hammered for explanations, for where were any of the others? Why hadn't I been taken to them?

"Tell me," I pled.

He faced me. I was surprised to find the thinnest fall of tears in his eyes. But the blue which looked out was so cold that the moisture looked like ice.

"Everyone else survived," he answered. "But you are dead."

"I cannot understand what you mean when you have clearly saved me," I said after I had first tried to make sense of his words.

He turned the spit. "The valley believes you are dead; it is best you remain so."

Perceiving his intent by this time, I restated it candidly, "What you mean is to make everyone believe that I am dead as you have made everyone believe about yourself."

"Yes," he answered unashamed. "Since you were saved by a dead man, how can you be shown alive without giving me away?"

"The point *is* to make you known," I asserted. "We cannot hide if we are going to do any good. My father never hid."

Cloven perfectly honed the point of his gaze toward me as he purposely jabbed, "And you told me that he was killed."

I fell silent.

Abruptly, Cloven stood. "Can you travel?"

Looking up earnestly, I implored, "To my home. That is the only place I will go."

"It would not be safe," he muttered as he limped toward the shelter and began pulling it apart.

I stood to follow him, for I had to change his course of intention. I would rather be dead than to let my family believe I was dead when I was not. It burned my heart to know how they must be suffering!

"You will take me to my home," I demanded.

When he ignored me, taking in hand big piles of the pine needles and scattering them around the foot of different pine trees, I again followed him, begging, "Please. I cannot let them needlessly suffer. They have suffered enough."

He merely passed me to retrieve another armful.

"Please!" I beseeched. "Where else could you possibly take me?"

He dropped his pile and sharply answered, "You will travel with me to King's City as my daughter. I will allow you to choose what name you shall be called by."

My hands flew down at my sides as I perceived what he was doing, forcing my life into a cowardly lie like his. "I will not hide like you! I will not make my family suffer. Do you know what you did to your mother when you did not return, when you let her think you were dead? Do you? It was a sorrow she bore every moment. I refuse to inflict my sister, brother, and my friends in such a way. If you choose to remain hidden behind that false name, Amos, that is your choice, but I will not give up my name as Lydia Tavish."

Only in a flash did he show his face. But it was enough for me to take a step back. He held his jaw stronger than a boulder. Snatching the furs from the ground, he stuffed them into his saddlebag.

I hobbled back to the fire, my ankle inflamed and swollen. In a purposeful glance, I saw his eyes; he was thinking. So I rested my ankle and patiently waited—a trait he had ingrained into me very well.

After it could no longer be detected that there had ever been a shelter, Cloven stooped down to turn the spit. My ears perked in earnest at the new tone in which he began, "I believe, in the end, you would find me crueler, if any harm came to you or to the ones you love. If Breemore wants you dead, he will ensure your death. And if you are among your family, there are more chances of their harm. Whereas, if you are thought to be dead, you will be forgotten, therefore, spared and able to be of more use. I shall reveal myself in time, but not carelessly. It would not be wise."

These words of his were the sanest, most thoughtful words I'd ever heard uttered from Cloven's lips. I felt bound to listen.

He placed the cooked meat on a plate and handed it to me. "There will be no more food until morning."

I took a reluctant bite, for my appetite would not exert itself. Suddenly, at the thought of a solution, I set the plate down. "I understand your reasons," I readily agreed, "but my family and friends can keep the secret. They already know of you. There can be no harm in assuring them I am alive before I travel with you to King's City."

"It is best no one knows," Cloven maintained solemnly as he poured water over the last of the fire and began disassembling the stones around it.

Resistance flushed through me at his unreasonableness when I had offered perfect reason. Did Cloven really have this strict right over me? I began to note the thick woods that surrounded us, but could not discern our location. I could not even hear the river, whose sound was the compass for all who lived in the valley.

"Where are we?" I asked.

He ignored my question as he continued packing.

"What became of the bandits and Captain Rhys?"

"They were taken to Crevilon Castle as prisoners. No harm shall come to your family by way of them again."

"Then why do you refuse to take me to my home?"

Cloven looked at me. "It is you who stepped into the crossfire of kings. One as wise as you does not imagine that position to be one of safety, *ever*, do you? Now eat. After you are finished, we shall leave."

"Then I am finished being in the crossfires," I said,

overcome. Pertinent tears mingled with the words at hand. "We just lost Mother. Netty and Garret will blame themselves for what they believed happened to me. And I promised Rose that I would return to her." Here I raised my voice, "I have no bigger ambition than to raise my sister. I could no longer be a threat to Lord Breemore. I'm done fighting; just let me go home." I dropped my head toward my lap.

When next I looked up, Cloven had taken the neglected meat from the plate and wrapped it in a fur. He placed the bundle inside the saddlebag on the second horse — a grey speckled mare which I knew was destined for me to ride.

He then mounted his own horse, doubtlessly waiting for me to do the same on the prepared horse beside him. The camp was now completely deserted, as if no one had ever set foot there. Having no choice, I mounted in slow, careful movements.

"Keep your hood up and never pass beyond my horse," he instructed as he moved onward. I followed him, for I could not run away. I had no idea where I was, and my body was in such a condition that I could not long care for myself in the forest. So I lifted Vala's hood over my head and fell into a dull weary trance behind Cloven's horse.

When at length we emerged from the woods, I realized that we had traveled back into the valley toward my home. Afar off, I saw the backside of our cottage. Cloven had brought me home! I sat straighter and leaned forward on my horse, straining to see ahead as we continued to move toward it.

A large crowd was gathered around the aspen grove. Immediately, I knew the reason — my funeral. I was stunned and touched by how many showed their respect.

Without realizing it, I had prodded my horse ahead of Cloven. "No further," he commanded harshly.

"For what purpose then did you bring me here?" I questioned bitterly.

He replied, "To say goodbye."

I dismounted — an act of great restraint. Catching hold of the nearest tree, I leaned beyond it as far as my bandaged arms allowed.

My eyes pushed through the crowd until I located Garret and Netty close beside him. Her head rested on his shoulder. The unanticipated tenderness between them comforted my sore heart as I knew that Garret would provide for both Netty and her father.

Rose, whom I sought harder to see, I could not. I supposed her slight body stood between Netty and Levinia. But not seeing Rose was a strong case to my desperate mind to make myself known, regardless of Cloven's demands. For I could; I could run to them this very moment.

A man, however, who looked much like Galen, parted from the gathering and arrested my attention. My eyes traced over the solitary figure until I confirmed all of Galen's features and manners blessedly known to me. I let go of the tree and took a step forward, my eyes not once leaving him — an outward expression of my heart. This simple knowledge that he had come back to Traiven's Pass was instant health to my entire body. I could not expel the notion of running into his arms, looking into his eyes, and telling him I was alive. Grenfell had told me not to let anything prevent me from going to Galen.

But my better thoughts did, and Cloven's warnings did. Grenfell had not known that my life was hunted and could bring danger to those I loved, especially to Galen. I stepped back, beginning to feel that if I came too near them, I would cast a dangerous shadow over their future peace. Because of my love for them, I could not relieve their sorrow... nor mine.

At last I saw the back of Rose's low bent head as Garret picked her up and carried her toward the cottage. Netty and Auden walked with him. While my maternal heart could not let Rose go, I perceived that between the four of them, a beautiful family would be forged. And within such a knowing, came the sense that all would be well with them.

With Galen it was different. No matter how long I watched him, as he stood like stone, I could not gain peace regarding him. And I had to rip myself away, not knowing what would become of him.

Remounting, I spoke in a voice that was to my own ears quaking, "I shall go by the name Ophelia, my mother's name."

"Just Phelia," Cloven allowed, showing no signs of sympathy or gratitude.

He turned his horse and led the way back into the forest. In that moment, I was filled with absolute resolve to help hasten the day in which Cloven reclaimed the throne — when this curse would be broken. Phelia, as he would have me, would be his relentless daughter compelling her so called father to his duty. Thus, I encouraged myself that this severance from my name and family would not last forever.

Chapter Twenty-nine
~ *Galen* ~

"Master Galen?"

Numbly, I turned toward the voice.

"Your horse," Auden offered, bringing the reins to my hand. I clutched the leather straps, desperate to grasp anything.

I had neither asked nor expected the task of him, though I had planned to leave after the funeral. Nor did I know him well, only that he had been Trimont's stable master.

Finding my voice, for it had been a long while since I had spoken, I requested, "Please do not call me your master. From my negligence and rashness, Trimont was destroyed, and I could not prevent the most worthy woman in the world from…" my eye wandered toward the distant aspen grove where they had placed a stone in memory of Lydia. I bit my lower lip, fighting against the eruption of the harsh, dead, and painful words which I could have spat out. Not able to bear the sight of the golden-leafed trees, I whipped my gaze far from the grove, shuddered, and curbed my words into kinder ones. "Forgive me. Forgive that I have failed all of you who once made Trimont Castle your home and all who loved Lydia."

I leaned my face into Chess' neck; it was a hiding place. The scent of sweet hay, which I heavily inhaled, made me yearn for the endless possession of Lydia's scent—to keep her alive and near—something I could hold.

My hand rushed to the emerald ring within my pocket. But what good was it without her hand! I released the ring and grasped Chess, knotting my fingers within her mane.

Auden had left, but I understood what a great service he had rendered to me, for I would not have moved from that stone place of remembering, mourning, and loathing, had he not come to break me from it and send me on my way. His simple act, implying so much trust and generational faithfulness to the Trimont family, stirred me—at least enough to move.

To Chess, I murmured, "I think only you knew just how high my hopes were—just how much I loved her... still love her. How during our journey here, every glance she had ever bestowed upon me had freely become the jewels of my mind."

Clutching the reins harder, I used the inner pain to lift myself into the saddle. Already, I knew my intention was to go to King's View, though to do so was against my first reasoning. I would risk anything for a scrap of comfort. My emptiness far outweighed my fear of piling upon myself more severe pain from treading so near potent memories. I knew now, more than ever, that before I left, I needed to feel as if I had somehow embraced her and taken her back with me to King's City. King's View was my only hope of gaining anything near my desire. I propelled Chess over the harvested fields toward the southern mountains where I sought the hidden trail Lydia had shown me.

Chess grazed while I climbed up the mountain. I tried to remember the words which Lydia had taught me of her father's. Instead, my mind tenderly pictured her, waiting at the top for me.

What I actually saw when I reached the lookout was exactly what I had left — the swing, my gift to her. Desolate, it quivered over the barren branch. *Wretched sight!* The tree from which it hung was stripped of its leaves, exposing its old grey craggy skin, and its branches now laid bare were proven to have grown askew.

Just as the world was proven to have crookedly grown when it was exposed! Unfair! Unreasonable! Uncontrollable! I gripped both ropes of the swing, my body becoming limp over my soul. She was meant to be here.

Breathing came quick and my throat tightened. I closed my eyes, reminding myself to breathe calmly.

At length my eyes opened over the swing and read the words which I had carved into the wooden seat:

> *In honor of Frederic Tavish, who climbed and saw above.*

I fell to my knees and crawled to the edge, where I looked out into the view for help. The sky sagged wearily in its endless monotony, the brown fields were used and tired, and the mountains bared their rock teeth through the thinned leaves. What help was there in that? Where was her face? Where was her voice? Where were her words which had so inspired me before?

Regathering myself, I took my knife and, lifting the swing, I held it against the trunk of the tree while I added to my inscription:

> *and Ophelia, his wife, and Lydia, his daughter.*

When I had finished, I let the swing go. It softly rocked

to a stop.

The utter emptiness of the moment provoked me to cling to the ring in my pocket and set the green emeralds before my sight. Bravely, I considered a deeper meaning for this symbol of Trimont matrimony. Lydia and I may not have been one in marriage, but I knew we had been one in heart after I had begun to walk in the ways of truth. If I continued walking thus, would this not keep us one?

Tighter and higher, I held the ring. These were the thoughts I needed; the ones which would help prevent me from slipping down the path my father had taken, for I indeed felt the pull to give up, to run away, and the dourness building on my face came so easily.

I tried to soften my face; my effort felt like such a sham. I was not trying to pretend happiness but to defy hate.

I envied Vala's perpetual expression of wise calm, but how foolish to covet wisdom and peace when they were free attributes for my partaking as she had partaken of them in her most grievous losses. That was the way of the Book of Truth—it offered so much goodness if one took its words into the fabric and construction of their thinking.

"All right then," I whispered. "I'll throw away my thoughts of abandonment and hate. Again and again and again, I will draw my life from the truth. I will to be one with Lydia in heart and purpose."

It felt awkward when I suspected that all nature scooted in to listen to me, but to conclude my heart, one action more I had to take. Drawing near the swing, I caressed Lydia's name on the seat, and spoke directly to her, "When I thought you had married Danek, you were not mine to think of, but now I think of you every moment and carry you in my entire being. I came here not to say goodbye, but to take you with me."

Before my vision threatened to wash away her name from before my eyes, I looked away first. The barren tree seemed glad to have my notice. Its trunk stood broad and boasting. I supposed it took all the brunt of the wind, for it stood out amongst the other trees like a mother or captain who willingly took the fits of the elements for all of its kindred. I supposed the tree was like a symbol of the Tavish family's sacrifice for their kingdom.

Ignited with a sudden passion to carry on what the family had begun, I began the descent. The rest of the kingdom needed to be told of King's View. Not a physical view, not warm emotions, but the strength of the perspective of truth and of love.

I could maintain a soft, tender, and caring mindset even when surrounded by the sorrows, evils, and impossibilities to which I must return.

The trail ahead was covered by obtrusive arms of autumn trees which I marched through until I stepped out of the woods and into the valley which had forged such a one as Lydia. I, therefore, loved the valley and found its fading foliage lovely. Traiven's Pass was truly changed because of her. The testimonies shared at her funeral today were rightful glories to her.

It hadn't struck me then, but now that I had refocused on truth, my mind had opened to more positive thoughts which an hour ago, I would not have allowed into my torturous brooding.

When I reached Chess, I patted her neck. "One good result I can say for all that has happened: I'm not as rash as I once was in the midst of suffering. Your name shall remain Chess."

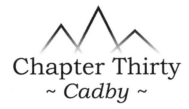

Chapter Thirty
~ *Cadby* ~

Hearing that the other children were gathering for a game, I drew my feet tighter beneath the curtain and pressed my cheek against the cold window, keeping my eyes searching through all the travelers who passed across the bridge toward the castle.

"Cadby." Hazel knocked on my curtain.

I opened a crack for her to come in.

She entered, standing in her pretty red dress. "Galen won't come back today, you know, Cadby," she said. "Lady Vala told us it would be at least a fortnight. It has only been half a fortnight since Galen left to check on Trimont. Come and play with us. It will make you happier."

She shivered. "And it's so cold behind the curtains now with the autumn drafts."

Alene suddenly swooshed the curtain away from us both. "Cadby," she exclaimed, "What did I tell you last night? Stay away from these drafty windows. You will catch a cold, and what will Galen think of my care for you if you became sick while he is away?" Alene tugged on my arm.

Groana dryly appealed on my behalf, "Leave him be. You are the one who has made it too hot in here with that blazing fire. You are going to roast us all out the windows with your "care" as you suppose such actions to be. I, however, perceive your recent behavior as overbearing insecurity."

Alene dropped my arm and the curtain, leaving it to fall around Hazel and me once again. Soon we heard the handle of a tin pail of water and then a sharp hiss from the fire.

"Are you pleased now?" we heard Alene ask.

"Until my bones start complaining of the cold," answered Groana.

Instead of leaving, Hazel sat next to me. She sighed. "Maybe I don't want to play a game. You are a boy, so you probably do not know, but Alene likes Galen. Hollis told me. I wish Alene didn't like him because Galen is going to marry Lydia. Remember, we put them together in our tapestry. If I had the chance, I would have asked Galen to bring our tapestry back with him. I wish we could have all gone back with Galen to check on Trimont. I miss being home at Trimont."

As I watched her speaking, I knew she would be glad if Galen brought Lydia back with him. No one knew but Lady Vala and me about Galen helping Lydia.

Hazel shivered again. "I must leave you now, Cadby, for I am much too cold here."

I watched her until all there was to look at was the swaying curtain. I wished I could have made it warm for her.

With a little longing that she had stayed, I resumed my watch. Men lit the torches to take the place of the sleepy sun slowly closing its eyes. There was a rush of people on the bridge and then fewer and fewer until only one crossed every so often.

I sat alert when a man slowly walked across the bridge, pulling behind him the reins of a horse that looked like Chess. The saddlebags were also like the ones Galen had packed the day he left.

The man looked up right into this window. It was Galen!

Hurrying to Lady Vala, I brought her to see. She held my hand as we peered out the window together. Her reflection in the glass looked worried. But, in the next moment, she looked at me, gently smiled, and squeezed my hand. "You are right, Cadby. Wait here; I think I must greet him first."

She departed. I watched Galen until the last sight of him, and then I made a crack in the curtain from where I could see the door where I expected Lady Vala would bring Galen soon.

But I waited, and no one came.

"Bedtime," Groana announced.

The children lined up at the door. I shuffled slowly to the end of the line, always looking back to watch for Lady Vala and Galen. When Alene saw me lagging behind, she came beside me. "I didn't mean to fuss at you, Cadby. It is just… I know you miss him, but I miss him too, more than anyone knows. But you see there is nothing I can do about it. For me, it is a desire of despair because there are many hindrances between Galen and me. You cannot understand. No one can."

What I didn't understand was why Lady Vala and Galen hadn't come. I kept looking behind me until Alene scooted me into the bedchamber with all the other boys.

I curled on my bed, weary with disappointment and shivering. Lady Vala had looked worried when she thought I wasn't watching. Something wasn't right, and my whole body felt it.

When the candles were blown out and the other boys had stopped talking, I crawled out of the bed and sat at the closed door, listening for when Lady Vala would return to her room.

I sat, in a tight ball under the blanket for a very long time, and she didn't come. My body shivered; I couldn't make it stop even when I put my head beneath the blanket.

Once I heard her footsteps and her door open and close, I felt a little better and, so tired, returned to my bed.

In the morning, I dressed and waited at the door again for Alene and Lady Vala to bring us to the dining hall. Alene came but not Lady Vala.

At breakfast, I did not eat, but watched the door which Galen might come through.

"Cadby, you aren't sick, are you?" Alene asked. "I knew I was right to no longer allow you to sit behind those curtains."

Then Lady Vala entered and Galen behind her.

"Galen!" voices exclaimed all at once.

"Dear children," Lady Vala said gravely, "I have something that I must tell you. Please, silently follow me to the music room."

Startled and wide-eyed, we all obeyed. My hands sank into my pockets.

"Wait, Cadby," Galen said, coming to stand beside me. We stood together until everyone had left. Then he led me to a corner of the dining room and sat down, drawing me before him. His face looked different, deeper and sadder. And his eyes looked desperate as he asked, "How are you, Cadby?"

I didn't say anything because I didn't want him to know that I was scared.

He began again, "I haven't forgotten about being your pap. I do not know how to make an adoption legal, but I'll learn. Only, it could take a while. But do not worry. I will see it through because I truly want you to be my son."

I pulled my hands from my pockets and hugged him. If he was still going to be my pap there was nothing else to be afraid of.

He held me tightly, like I really was his son, and I heard him crying. He pulled back, saying, "But you mustn't cling to me more than to the truth, Cadby. What if something happens to me? I still want you to be strong and good and full of hope. It is a lesson I am having to learn." He bit his lower lip, which was redder and drier than it usually was. And it quivered. "Cadby, what Lady Vala is now telling the others is that... Trimont has been destroyed."

"Can't we mend it?"

Galen slightly smiled and dropped his head for a moment. When he raised it, he said, "Perhaps, you are right. Perhaps, one day you and I will rebuild Trimont."

"Is Lydia coming to live here, to be with you, like in the tapestry?" I asked.

Something fell over Galen's face which I did not like. He dropped his hands from my shoulders, saying so lowly I could barely hear his voice, "Lydia was harmed when Trimont was destroyed. She will not be coming. But do not worry; we will make her very happy once we have found King Cordell for her."

Galen's eyes wandered away, and he didn't speak for a while. I sat on his lap and leaned my head on his shoulder. He drew me in, and I fell asleep.

Chapter Thirty-one
~ *Galen* ~

My burdens were many, but this one burden which peacefully slept in my arms was light and eased the weight of the other burdens much larger than himself and enabled me to rest. Securing Cadby's body, so that he would not slide from my lap, I leaned my head back against the chair, closing my eyes. For these moments, Cadby was all in all.

My mind, loosened by sleepiness, wandered within dreams until I felt a potent sense of Lydia entering the room. I awoke with a start.

The room, having no windows and the candles having been extinguished, was lit only by the natural light which crept in from the corridor, a light flat and grey, but bright enough to see the four corners of the room, the round table in the center, and the yellow and green flags which hung from the high ceiling. With the dishes cleared and the high-backed chairs tucked in, all was in order for the hardships of my life to continue. I comforted myself in Cadby's sleeping presence curled against me and did not dare move, preferring his comfort over my own.

The sound of a chair softly scooting from the other side of the room startled me. Alene slowly rose from the table and made her way to us. How could I have missed her sitting there? Her face was sweetly moist with thoughtful tears as she whispered, "I was sent to retrieve Cadby if you are finished speaking with him."

I answered, "Please leave him. He is a comfort to me as much as I am to him. I want to be here for him when he awakes."

Alene smiled. "I'm glad of your answer. You and Cadby make such a peaceful picture. After hearing such heartbreaking news about Trimont and the children's friend, Lydia, it eased my heart to gaze at the two of you peacefully slumbering."

"The other children," I asked, "how did they respond?"

"Lady Vala is still with them, of course. I fancy that for a few days their routine will be broken. They are devastated. It pains me because I know how much they and you loved Trimont. You all talked about Trimont so much that it became one of my dreams to return there with you all one day. Now that will never be." She paused, then forced a smile and went on, "Some of the children were quiet. Others could not stop speaking of all they remembered and loved of their home and friend. Hazel's tragic expression broke my heart. I believe that she is one who, when her heart holds something, cannot let go. Hollis buried her face in a cushion, not caring what became of her hair. Badrick, you know him; he goes on about wanting to stop the offenders."

I could envision every word of Alene's description and could feel the unique pain of each child.

"Badrick blames Lord Breemore vehemently," Alene added. "But it couldn't have been Breemore to do such a cruel act when he has bestowed nothing but kindness. Captain Rhys must have completely turned against him."

My heart struck out bitterly before my brain took hold. "It was Breemore," I spat.

She stared at me. "Please don't say such a thing. You must not mean it. The only reason that the news of

Trimont being destroyed can be bearable to the children is because you came back alive. If you hadn't, it could not have been borne." Her desperate eyes pressed her deep care.

I did not know how I ought to return her look, so I lowered my gaze to Cadby's smooth cheek which was flushed with healthy slumber.

"At least think of Cadby," Alene whispered before she departed.

I regretted that I had unthinkingly insisted upon Breemore's deceit when Alene had no proper understanding of his past. I could not expect her to agree until she had been told. Perhaps she should be. Perhaps the entire kingdom should be told! Breemore deceiving innocent people, as kind and good as Alene, was most distressing.

Already, I had decided that when Breemore attempted to explain to me this last offense, I would trap his vile mind into exposing itself! He had to have a weakness within his speech, and with these recent crimes of Captain Rhys, I possessed leverage to push and pry him. And as a last resort, I could confront him with the secrets which Meklon had confided in me of their past. Vala had not objected to me doing so when she and I had discussed it last night. I was beyond hiding what I knew.

Unexpectedly, Alene rushed back, quietly exclaiming, "Lord Breemore's guard is urgently seeking for you. You aren't in trouble, are you?"

I assured her, speaking more mindfully, "I have never spoken publicly against him."

Cadby slid from my lap to his feet as he had naturally awakened. Pouring all my attention into his blinking and sleepy eyes, I explained, "All is well. I have only been summoned to speak with Lord Breemore. Alene will take you to Lady Vala."

With those words, I tarried not a moment more, for my mind was already fueled for an encounter with Breemore.

When I came to his study door, I was promptly allowed in by the guard. Behind me the heavy door immediately latched. This gave me the feeling of being lured into a trap, but the penitent face of Breemore, who in earnest lifted his eyes to mine as he slowly stood from behind his desk, seemed to be the one humbly posing as the victim.

Neither of us spoke.

Then Breemore with both his hands on the desk and his head hanging down, admitted, "I know all that you have encountered in Traiven's Pass, Galen, and there is no easy way to break into the subject." He raised his eyes again to mine, but I added no sympathy into them. He went on, explaining, "A bandit, who escaped the Crevilon guards, told me everything just yesterday. I feared all night what it meant for you. Lady Vala told me that you had gone to Trimont. You do not know how relieved I was this morning to receive word that you had returned alive and well."

Refusing his counterfeit kindness, I demanded, "Why did you not restrain Captain Rhys after he burned Lenrow and attempted to murder me and an innocent family? His actions during the riot were enough to prove his intentions."

"I reproved him," Breemore answered carefully, "but I cannot control him. I was obligated to give him another chance. He was, after all, my second-in-command and had proven himself worthy for years. I could not sentence him for one unruly charge inspired by his jealousy of you. But of course, I now see what a blunder I have made. I am sorry, Galen, though I know nothing shall be sufficient. I know that the worst of it was losing Lydia."

I turned away for only one moment before I plunged back hard, "How did Captain Rhys know that Lydia did not marry Sir Danek?"

Breemore sat down. "Here I am at fault again. I fear you will never forgive me. I have known for some time that Lydia refused Sir Danek."

"You told Rhys but not me?" I challenged.

"Yes, but, Galen, listen. I wanted separation between him and you. I sent him to Traiven's Pass purely to investigate the status between Sir Danek and the Tavish family, *never* supposing that he would take his rage to the extremes that he did. For I thought his feud was solely against you. In destroying Trimont and taking Lydia's life, he acted completely of his own accord. I am as horrified at his behavior as you are. I assure you that he shall be tried for his actions."

"He is already dead," I dryly informed him.

"Not at your hand, I hope," Breemore questioned.

I answered, "Captain Rhys was mysteriously murdered while a prisoner at Crevilon Castle — most likely committed by one of the uncaptured bandits. But you have not yet answered me fully. Why did you not tell me of Lydia?"

"You and Lady Laila have a unique attachment, do you not?"

Promptly, I corrected, "I respect Lady Laila immensely, but my heart binds to no woman but Lydia."

"Your heart is noble, Galen, but hear me finish, for in all my considerations in making my decision, your and Lydia's best welfare was utmost. Your future is heir to this throne; therefore, whomever you choose as your future wife will be queen. If you had chosen Lydia Tavish, the known daughter of a man who is widely viewed as a traitor, there truly would have been an uproar, and one that I could not have quenched so easily as the last. In marrying Lydia you would have been securing and publicly announcing your loyalty to the old ways. Both you and she would have been endangered. Surely you must see the validity of my words after what happened at Lenrow. Drawing Lydia to yourself would only have been to draw her to yet more danger. The outcome may have been the same or worse."

"But I would have protected her!" I nearly yelled as my heart panted after what could have been.

"You are not all powerful, Galen," Breemore grieved. "Can you see why I did my best to protect the naturally forming bond between you and Lady Laila? Lady Laila would be accepted by the people, if a little feared for her directness, but it would not cause any unrest. She is your best choice."

I turned away from Breemore toward the back wall in an attempt to think past his words.

"Galen, believe me that this is not the outcome I would have wished."

Facing him deliberately so I might watch his eyes, I laid my deeper accusation. "Then why are you preparing Multa's army for war?"

Breemore's eyes did not flinch nor darken. Nor did he have to linger before he answered, "You are right to question me with the knowledge I supposed you have gained about my past. Meklon has told you of our Multan heritage, hasn't he?"

I nodded.

"You may not believe me when I say it now, but I am

not behind Multa's army, though I am just as Meklon says — every bit his brother, and together we are the sons of Lord Marcus, late ruler of Multa."

Breemore came from around his desk and gestured to the velvet upholstered chair behind me. I sat, though remained guarded against his silver tongue. He took the chair beside me. "I humbly maintain that I have been honest with you from the first. At the same time, it may also rightly be confessed that some of my words have been veiled and that my plan until now has only been disclosed to you in part. I must go back in time in order to properly answer your question and to explain my exact and pure intentions, so that there are no misunderstandings between us."

Breemore spoke with such sincerity and kindly features that I looked down as he spoke on, so that his bearing could have no influence over me.

"I am sure Meklon told you of our life as boys growing up at Trimont. I trust him to have portrayed it accurately, even my bad temperament, for I was every bit that terrible at times. But there are points after I left Trimont of which my brother knows nothing.

"As suspected, I did return to Multa as a foolish, proud, and angry young man with vain imaginations of how I should be received back into my father's kingdom as Multa's rightful ruler. However, my expectations were wrong. I was accepted as no such king, and nor did I want to be after I experienced the offence of Multa's poverty and disorder.

You see, when I first arrived in Multa, up to that point in my life, I had only known the charming beauty and goodness of Trimont. Throughout my boyhood, from Trimont's safe haven, I romanticized of how much more excellent and powerful my own kingdom would be when I returned to rule. I was, therefore, shocked when the only welcome I received was the abhorrent stench of poverty. The kingdom was in such a low state, Galen, you cannot imagine.

"After the war, when my father died and his two sons were thought to be dead, Multa had no ruler, no heir, and had lost many of its finest men. Land and resources were also lost since Multa was pushed back to its original borders. There were few men left to hunt and sail. Many widowed mothers and wives had only scant gardens for their food supplies. Food in the market squares was so expensive that it was beyond the reach of the majority.

"With no ruler, the kingdom was subject to group after group rising to power only to be brought low by the next. Constant conflict and destruction came with this fight for position. Daily, people were dying in the streets of hunger, disease, or executed by insurgents. For years there was only deterioration on many fronts.

"About the time I had come to Multa, a man named Seeris had risen to power. He was older, wise, and pledged to build Multa back up on the principle of revenge and the plunder of its enemy, Calderon. The people unanimously hailed him, and Seeris' rule was established.

"I revealed my identity to Seeris, and while he gave me no position, for he claimed I was too young, he allowed me into his close company. I was very much surprised to discover that while Multa spoke of revenge, I felt homesick for Trimont and the Kingdom of Calderon. Trimont had been my home, and I did not want to see the beautiful kingdom devastated by war nor its good people harmed.

"I began to ponder some way to subdue Multa's desire for revenge, which compelled me to consider the ultimate possibility of having the two kingdoms merge. I pursued this idea and gradually presented it to Seeris.

"I clearly remember that he first laughed before he had sworn, 'If you can rid that land of its ingrained Book of Truth and King Cordell, I shall relent and join such a sensible people.'

"And so, Galen, I returned to Calderon in hopes of preserving both kingdoms in peace by having them unite."

"Then you did abduct King Cordell," I spouted suddenly.

"Yes, but you understand it was for the kingdom's own peace."

Full of tension, I stood, making it as far as Breemore's desk before my fist heavily thudded upon it. Years of ridicule, unfair treatment, pointless searching, innocent death, and then... to me the answer was simply given. "Is he alive?" I asked.

"Yes."

"Where is he?"

"King Cordell is unharmed and safely hidden. He only had to be removed for a time so that the people would be unattached from him and loosened from the Book of Truth in order that they would become open to other ways of rulership. At the time of the tournament, King Cordell shall be safely returned at which time the people will have to choose whether or not to receive him back as their king."

"And you wish the people to refuse him?"

"I wish the people to choose you, Galen. My plan is for you to be the next king, for you are rightfully next in line and one whom all the people will accept, love, and one who is both of the old ways and the new. Between now and the tournament, I want to exalt you so that you will be everyone's choice. Because, if the people choose King Cordell, there would be no stopping the war. Multa would attack with all their strength, and even I could not prevent it.

"But if the people choose you, I would then be endowed with the authority granted by Seeris to peacefully unite the two kingdoms. Seeris would rule as sovereign while I governed Multa and you governed Calderon. I would ensure that this castle would remain your home and that Trimont shall be rebuilt."

Harshly, I questioned, "But I could not govern according to the Book of Truth?"

"No, nevertheless, you may still rule as I have in goodness and peace. I would advise you to talk it over with Meklon and Lady Vala. I have always wanted them to understand; however, I fear they will not. May I ask, do you understand?"

"I think what you mean is… do I agree?"

Breemore smiled. "You are perceptive, Galen."

"Then you must also know that I cannot answer you at this time," I said, then left the room.

Chapter Thirty-two
~ *Galen* ~

No one guarded the door into Breemore's study except the moonlight, and it could only tell eternity what I was about. Leaving the shadows of the corridor, I approached the door, assuming its lock would yet prevent me from entering unbidden. However, the cold iron handle bowed in secret submission to my endeavor. I opened the door wide enough to squeeze through, then quickly closed it behind me.

Again, only the moonlight was present; pale and limited to the three narrow windows fixed high above, it was not enough light to search by. I lit my lantern and set it on Breemore's desk. The ruddy light shot to the room's full perimeter like an excited boy rushing to search everywhere at once. Neither did I hesitate to begin my search by lifting aside the first rug in hunt of the possible entrance into the Inner Tunnels. This morning, after hearing Breemore say that King Cordell was indeed alive, I had every hope of finding him this very night.

I lifted every rug. They hid nothing but the unsightly chipped and cracked old grey stone. Mindfully, I laid the rugs back before exhaustively examining the fireplace behind Breemore's desk. I felt along every seam and pressed against every stone without the slightest encouragement of there being a secret door. Discouraged, I rose from my knees, wiping on my tunic the thick layer of soot from my hands.

I began to re-observe the circular room. It was the first time I had a prolonged look at it without having to be engaged in conversation.

Doubtless, the room was the base of either an unfinished or ruinous tower of which the stairs and floors above had either never existed or had at some point been destroyed. The walls rose far above before they were capped by the inner pinnacle of the tower's roof. The high placement of the windows proved that they each should have belonged to three additional upper floors. As they were now, their vantage point was useless to anyone in the room. Though Breemore had furnished the room most comfortably, it was still such an unlikely location to have been chosen for his study.

Taking the lantern, I studied and felt along the walls as I slowly made my way around the room, moving much furniture out of my way and returning it just as it had been. All the stones of the tower appeared to be sealed in thick mortar.

Next, even though it seemed impractical, I stood on a chair in order to reach the heights of the portraits and tapestries to look behind each. Again, the walls continued thick in mortar.

The only varying object was a hidden portrait behind the last tapestry. Like all the others, it was the face of a stranger. I studied the face, wondering why it was hidden. The young man portrayed in the painting was not unpleasing, although the lower portion of his face was scarred. Suddenly startled, I realized that this was the face of my king.

His silent eyes, which in a painting I could look into unhindered, evoked within me strong emotion. These were the steadfast eyes which showed the world how to see from King's View. More than duty began to pull me toward finding him; this painting compelled my heart. He did not deserve to be used as a pawn in Breemore's hand, but should be free to rule as he ought.

Unhooking the portrait from the wall, I climbed down from the chair. Resolutely, I laid the king's portrait across Breemore's desk like a reinstatement of the truth.

As I proceeded to search around Breemore's desk, I caught sight of another rug beneath Breemore's chair. I pulled the chair away, and when I tried to slide the rug with my boot, it was pinned tightly in place.

Reaching down, I tugged on the rug's edge. A heavy board began to lift. With both hands, I heaved opened the trapdoor I sought. Crude steps led down into the blackest midnight.

I stared down, wondering why I'd been given this moment when it had been the dream and pursuit of so many others. They had given their lives for this discovery when I hadn't. They deserved this honor more than I did.

Nevertheless, it was an honor I boldly accepted so that their sacrifices might be made known.

Swiftly, I hid the portrait beneath the couch, made a quick sweep with my eyes to make sure all was as it had been, grabbed the lantern, and cautiously descended the steps beneath the desk, closing the trap door behind me.

My feet felt their way down the uneven steps while my eyes guided me around the jagged walls and the low ceiling which at times grazed the top of my head. Before long, the primitive passage broke through into the high, broad glories of the Inner Tunnels just as at Lenrow.

In excited triumph, I held the lantern before me, but the light only manifested the strong aggression of the ceaselessly confined darkness. I'd been in utter darkness before, but this pricked the back of my neck with trepidation. It was unknown darkness which forced strong evils into the imagination. And my light made me an instant target to any meditated harm. What if Multa guards were kept within the tunnels? What if Breemore himself loomed around any corner? What if this was a trap? That would explain why the study door had been left unattended and unlocked.

From out of the silence came a sound. I froze except to move my hand to the hilt of my sword. Footsteps came down the passage I had just descended.

Instantly, I blew out my lantern and quietly unsheathed my sword, backing against the side wall, waiting in the complete darkness for the follower to reveal himself.

Light of a small candle appeared from within the stair passage. A moment more revealed that the possessor of the candle was Lady Laila.

Bewildered, I watched her, wondering if she was in league with Breemore. She looked one way down the tunnel and then the other. Her fawn colored riding cloak tilted on her shoulders, and her black hair freely flowed in tempest waves as if she had not been prepared to come. She held her candle close to the wall and ran her fingers down the smooth stone as if this was her first discovery of them. Slowly, she moved along, nearing where I stood.

When I was illuminated by her light, she startled in the slightest of jolts, then stared as if I owed the greater explanation.

Nevertheless, I inquired first. "How is it that you have come to be here?"

She answered, "I often remain awake into the late hours. This night there was much in particular to ponder, and in the moonlight I saw you crossing the lower balcony beneath my sitting room. I followed you from there."

"But the trap door," I questioned.

"I saw you descend within it. You were so absorbed with the portrait that you did not notice when I cracked the door and watched."

I exhaled, sheathing my sword. "What you must think of me for trespassing as I have."

Her brow rose in a dominant arc. "As here we stand in secret tunnels, evidently, you are no fool. If this is a traitorous expedition to find King Cordell as it appears to be, I would tend to believe you possess good reason to do so."

"Understand," I swiftly clarified, "that I am not publicly speaking against Lord Breemore. I simply want to follow the clues I have been given and see where they lead. I suspend my judgment on Lord Breemore until I find King Cordell. I think the true king should be the one who passes or excuses Breemore. I certainly cannot. He is too much a mixture of good and bad; I do not know what to make of him."

"A fault of his appears to be over-trusting of you," she supplied. "Is it true that Captain Rhys is dead? And that before his death he burned Trimont and murdered Frederic Tavish's daughter for refusing to marry Sir Danek Crevilon?"

Anguish welling in my heart, I nodded. "Every word of it is truth. Did Breemore announce this?"

"Yes, at dinner. He makes you out to be quite the noble victim as he did likewise after the riot, but I also know that Breemore is no fool. Does he know you meddle behind his back?"

I answered honestly, for Lady Laila had a way of making a straight way for the facts to come forth. "Since this

263

morning, Breemore knows my misgivings toward him. In exchange, he told me of his future plans of trying to peacefully merge Calderon and Multa into one kingdom. He wants to use me in this endeavor. That is why he defends me publicly. Before I give him my answer, I want to do all I can to find King Cordell, for I believe the choice should be in his hands — not mine."

"Then do not let me prevent you from your purpose. Only allow me to witness with you whatever is to be discovered within these tunnels."

Her request unearthed an inner revolt. It would be giving to Lady Laila what ought to have been Lydia's place! However, I saw the necessity to squelch the painful surge and reasonably discourage her from coming further. "It is not safe. You should not entangle yourself in my brazen actions. I could be caught. Please return."

Her eyes had fallen a shade distant as she replied, "I would relent for your sake, except that I esteem seeing a thing for myself above every other argument under the sun." Her features strictly displayed her resolution.

Biting my lower lip, I lifted my lantern to her, stiffly requesting, "If you will relight my lantern with your candle, we'll move on. I do not believe Breemore would keep the king far from here."

Despite being displeased with the idea of her taking Lydia's place, I fell into observing her as she lowered her head in concentration of lighting my lantern. When the brighter light ignited, I shied my gaze away from her and extended the light before our way and moved forward, noticing that we each left a large gap between us. I strongly sensed that she was aware of my detachment from her and felt ashamed, for I knew that we had indeed bonded to one another before I had known about Lydia. I was sure Laila was hurt by my coldness. But there could be no remedy.

I constantly swung the lantern back and forth to make sure I did not miss any doors or opened ways. The tunnel continued straight for a long while with a gradual slope upward.

When we came to a fork, I surveyed the entrance of each passage. They looked similar except one's torch bracket had remnants of more recent use. I silently took this most likely way, and Lady Laila followed at her continued distance.

We walked only a little farther when the tunnel wall on the right side gave way to a wide archway into a large room. There was an illusion through the darkness of it being furnished, but not until I risked lighting a torch did the room glow with orange light and exhibit itself something like an ancient royal sitting room, yet shamefully used and unkempt. Dinner bones lay upon the table, scattered goblets, coal piles, clothes and cloths draped and piled throughout, barrels of oats stacked in a corner, and a stench which matched the sight.

I made one round about the room to ensure no one was lurking and noting details that I may need to recall to mind later. The couch on closer observation looked as if it was used as a bed, for the cushions were worn down very low and lumpy. I could not imagine such an open location would be used for the king's confinement or that King Cordell would live so disorderly. This was evidence that certainly others lived within these tunnels. I settled my hand upon my sword's hilt, prepared to press on until hindered.

Making my way back, I took the torch from the bracket for its more significant light and offered Lady Laila the use of the lantern instead of her candle. She accepted it, but spoke nothing. I began to wonder what was in her thoughts.

We resumed our trek down the unknown tunnel, which to my fascination led into a room of greater magnificence than I could have imagined to be crafted underground. I quickened my pace around what appeared to be a great feasting hall in an attempt to take it all in. Giant columns upheld the elaborate vaulted ceiling. Orderly rows of tables with their benches waited in obscurity until men returned to them. Fastened to each column were two torches. When lit, this room would be as bright as day. Where my attention stalled the longest was the underground spring which had been forced to flow halfway around the room in a great stone cistern.

I scooped some of the freshly flowing water within my hand to taste. It was as good and clear as the fresh brooks of Dresden. "An army could survive down here," I marveled.

I glanced at Lady Laila whose gaze was uplifted in thorough observation.

Roaming further, we found ourselves in a kitchen of mass proportions. There were several large hearths where whole game could be roasted and a harvest of bread baked. Venting shafts ascended into the ceiling as if they were the giant lungs of the mountain. I had never considered how ingeniously these tunnels had been engineered for survival.

It was unfortunate that the ancient magnificence was stained by slobbery. Uncleaned pots of crusted porridge hung within the hearths. Chicken feathers and bones mingled amid the mess of coal which tumbled down from a larger pile and coated much of the floor. Stacks of dirty dishes were piled on the large wooden center table, along with buckets of water and buckets of oats.

Rather than returning to the feast hall, I pressed on into the unexplored passage on the other side of the kitchen, thinking that the king would not be kept far from the source of nourishment.

Noticing a narrow shaft, I dared an eerie step within it and discovered perhaps what I sought. At the end of the shaft was a solid door secured by a bar.

My heart beating a little faster, I stepped toward the door, then stopped. I would wait for Lady Laila because finding the king was for all. I knew Lydia would agree. And by Lady Laila not imposing herself, I had come to accept and value her company.

When Laila joined me, I pointed to the door, whispering, "It may be nothing, but we will go in together."

With trepidation, I advanced. There was a flap in the door's lower half through which food could be passed. It signified complete loneliness and seclusion on the other side. This convinced me further that only this door kept us from King Cordell.

I lifted the heavy bar and tried to open the door, but it remained tight in place as if the mountain held the door as a part of its own immoveable structure. I had to apply my body's weight before the door swung open. The paralyzed hinges shrieked, moaned, and then fell deathly silent. The crackling of the torch and my own breath pounded within my ears.

"Hello?" I ventured, stepping within.

There was no response and nothing to be seen, so I pressed the light further in. The expansive space was intriguingly cave-like, for the walls were irregular in shape, and the floor and ceiling rose high and dipped as they liked. There were low ledges and higher ledges and a trickling waterfall which pooled in an area large enough for bathing.

When our light had revealed the limits of the lower portion of the cave, I searched for a way to climb to the upper ledges. I found my way prepared by narrow steep steps.

As I climbed, the higher walls came out of the darkness into the light, and a magnificent awe came over me, for the walls were coved with every variety of art and writing. It was overwhelming to know where to begin looking or reading.

At the far left side of the ledge was a straw stuffed mat and a blanket neatly folded at the foot. I walked to it. There were also several candlesticks and two sharp etching stones. On the wall above were rows and rows of counting marks. At the top was written:

The Days of King Cygan Cordell's Captivity.

"Laila! Laila!" I called only to realize she was already at my side, her eyes mesmerized by the wall.

To see the magnitude of the number of marks and knowing that they extended beyond the expanse of my own life, the reality of what he suffered staggered me.

"Where is he?" I demanded, swinging the torch around. However, my eyes soon returned their fixation upon the wall.

My heart melted as I read the king's repeated declaration:

I will not lose heart. I will not lose heart. I will not lose heart —

These words were written over and over again. Tears came unbidden. I wiped them away, but I knew Lady Laila's perceptive eyes saw. What I did not expect was to find tears within her own eyes.

In silence, we gazed at the wall. There were words and pictures to pierce every part of the heart. Endearing etches of scenery, people, and families were each remembered and marked by name. Passages from the Book of Truth also continued across the vast breadth of the underground stone.

At the center of the etchings was the King's Castle and a crowned man with the words written above him:

My Steward King — Cloven Amond Trimont, keep the people safe in the knowledge of the truth.

Once I'd read it, I could not help falling to my knees. Laila took notice. I felt her gaze linger upon me.

I tried to explain the turmoil of my feelings. "It is just… we have failed him. He remembered us, and we, his own kingdom — his First Loyals, completely turned our backs on him and left him to suffer in this isolation for a lifetime. We loved the ease of lies over truth, and he suffered while we pleased ourselves, pretending his existence away."

Lady Laila solemnly returned her gaze to the wall and a moment later shared her thoughts. "I once read the Book of Truth."

I looked at her in surprise.

"It was after Kelston died. He was the man I was going to marry. Unlike many others, Kelston was interested in the forbidden Book of Truth, though he never gained possession of one. For his sake, I traded a jewel necklace with a peddler for the Book of Truth, and I read it — every word. At the time, its words meant little to me, but I've since wondered what the world will be like when its last pen strokes are erased from among us. And now I find myself wondering what we have missed while not having this man," she lowered her gaze upon his humble bed, "as our king."

"What cost do you think it is worth paying for their restoration?" I asked her.

"Our lives," she replied simply, then turned and walked toward the steps.

"Are you sure?" I questioned. "What if the entire city were to be destroyed and many innocent lives taken? I would give up my own life, certainly, but can I give up the lives of others that I know it would cost? If I cannot find King Cordell, that is the choice I have to make."

"There is a reason fate has chosen you to answer such a question," she echoed the confidence I had often heard her place in me. Then she descended the steps.

I followed her. "Why do you have such faith in me? You always have."

"You will not like my answer."

"Please tell me, for I do not have such faith in myself."

"Love," she abruptly answered. "Through the ages has it not been suggested that love believes all things and hopes all things?"

There was an awkward silence between us. I did not know what to say.

"You do not need to reciprocate my sentiments; I know you do not love me, and I do not ask you to."

Tripping over myself, feeling I had to say something to ease her, I did not think as I said, "Laila, if things were different. Maybe in time. But my heart has bled dry. Before I ever met you, I loved Lydia Tavish with all my heart. She is the true reason I suddenly departed to Traiven's Pass. But she…"

"Died in the fire," Laila finished.

"I am sorry," I ended lamely.

"I could always see it in your eyes," Laila remarked and walked on ahead of me out of the cell.

I regretted a little for having told her, for what if I could come to love Lady Laila as I had loved Lydia, and I had just pushed her away?

I followed her out of the room, for it was evident that King Cordell was not here.

Without speaking, we both seemed to know that it was time to retrace our steps, for though I wished to explore every tunnel, the longer we lingered the higher chance we risked of being caught.

As we walked, my mind alternated between King Cordell and Lady Laila.

When we reached the unkempt sitting room, I extinguished the torch in a nearby bucket of water and returned it to its bracket. As Lady Laila handed me the lantern, she intentionally pulled my eyes into hers as she expressed, "I am twin to your agony. Earlier, I failed to offer you my understanding which I do so now, freely and without expectation. You belong to Lydia; I belong to Kelston. Let us be friends."

Her words slipped into my heart so perfectly that I could not think of any reply which equaled her thoughtfulness. However, as gratitude and respect toward her speedily welled up into my countenance, I allowed my genuine expression to speak for me.

As we walked on together, I shared with her my plans, "Tomorrow night I shall renew my search. The only explanation I can think of is that the king was moved somewhere else within the tunnels. It would be too risky for Breemore to bring him out. But perhaps it is best if I continue looking alone."

She bowed in queenly submission.

"As soon as possible, I shall form a meeting with other allies to speak over our findings and disclose Breemore's purpose which he has spoken to me plainly. I wish you to be there."

"Then I shall," she whispered.

With that, our words ceased. I first passed through the narrow stair passage, and once I had cautiously raised myself into Breemore's study, I offered her my hand to help her out of the trap door.

After I hung the portrait back behind the tapestry, Lady Laila and I parted ways in the moonlight.

Chapter Thirty-three
~ *Phelia* ~

"Remember, you shall only refer to me as Amos or your father," Cloven sternly reiterated as we entered the city gates.

I replied, "I shall be mindful of your wish."

Already we each had raised the hoods of our cloaks, entering as simple and rugged sojourners. Of what architecture I could see from beneath my hood, I relished and matched with the vivid descriptions which Father had layered upon my young ears in answer to my repeated begging. Father had described King's City so well that as its enormity engulfed me, it felt more familiar than overwhelming. A crisp breeze ruffled my hood. I savored its fleeting passage and felt proud to take part in King's City at last, though our entry was shadowed by sorrowful and unknown circumstances.

We blended into the busy streets among other horsemen, wagons, carriages, and the less fortunate on foot, who had to eat the dust of every commotion. Yet the higher air lost its advantage as we approached the blacksmith's shop from whence dense black smoke profusely panted from the forge into the street.

Coughing, I turned away and saw the looming clock tower. Father told me he had often spoken to people from its base. I imagined him standing tall, reaching out his arms and voice to anyone who would listen. But then a very grave thought entered my mind. What if it were here that Father had been murdered? I stared at the cobblestones uncomfortably. The description of the man, who had brought Father's body home, came to mind, "They beat him, miss, with anything they could get their hands on: stones, wood, pitchforks." A pitchfork was in a nearby cart of hay. A man just then came out, taking the fork in hand and began tossing the hay into the nearby stables.

"What are you staring at, girl? Should I come set you to work?" the man threatened with irritation.

I hurriedly turned my horse away, finding, to my great relief that Cloven had waited for me.

The busy market square lay before us with little room to accommodate our passing through. Shops lined the perimeter while peddlers, farm produce, and fish carts filled the center. Minstrels played their music and raised their voices to the throng nearly in vain, except for the children grasping the edge of the stage with their little fingers as they listened with all their hearts.

Smiling, I lifted my eyes upward, again catching sight of the majestic castle with its breathtaking mountain. I had studied its grandeur on our way up to the city gates until the surrounding structures stole it from my sight. I was glad to regain it within my vision. The sun brought forth the blush of the fading autumn trees which covered the mountainside and cast a glorious glow upon the castle towers.

Cloven abruptly stopped and dismounted. He quickly pressed into my hand a small purse. "Go in this shop and buy what you need."

It was a dressmaker's shop. I was surprised by Cloven's attentiveness to my need, for I did only have the one dress and cloak which were badly rent and singed.

I thanked him, dismounted, and entered the shop. I purchased what necessities I would need, and what I had spared, I returned to him.

"Keep it," he said, bequeathing it to me.

As we gradually progressed out of the market, the crowds were not so distracting as the overhead arches, alleyways, brass gates, and stairs leading to the upper floors of the city — places which emanated mystery and extracted curiosity. In rare corners, the sun seemed playful with the cold autumn stone, but most often the buildings were impenetrable and always casting shadows which kept a person from even thinking of the sun, when its desire was to continually lower itself to the reach of the people.

On the next street we turned down, the stone buildings closed in on either side and provided little variation.

The air began to smell of confinement. Slowly, everything was becoming dingier. Stone structures gave way to wooden ones, fine carriages ceased to be a part of the thoroughfare, and my horse now occasionally stumbled over missing or protruding cobblestones.

Cloven took notice of nothing, nor did he have need to ask for directions. He just seemed to know where to go.

"Is it how you remember?" I asked.

When I realized how dangerously grim his face looked, I did not expect an answer. But on the chance he looked at me, I was prepared to offer a sympathetic expression, for I could only imagine how difficult this return must be for him.

He had not told me of his plans. All Cloven had disclosed to me was that we would lodge within King's City, that I was to be called Phelia, and that he was to be called Amos until the time he chose to reveal himself to his kingdom.

Nonetheless, I was confident that during our journey here, I had established in Cloven's thoughts my repeated plea that he reconcile with his mother and son as soon as possible — the great reconciliation of which I could never picture without tears gently pressing behind my eyes. Cloven had no excuse preventing him from taking that first step, which would heal the heartache of the long severed Trimont family in so many ways.

Thus, as the grand and intriguing wonders of King's City steadily declined into old slumping three-story abodes, I stashed away my hopes of what one day would be, and prepared for what was now at hand.

I met the stench without wincing, thought of names for the pigs lumbering down the road beside us, and smiled at any stranger who happened to meet my observing gaze which constantly lifted and lowered across the decaying buildings which were mended and re-mended and aided to stand by very creative means.

Cloven dismounted in front of Crankford's Lodging. It looked to be a dwelling a little more distinguished than many of the others. Though like all the others, the lower half was black with mud which wagons heavily spewed every time it rained.

Cloven tied our reins to a post. "It is best if you come inside."

I dismounted and followed him, surprised that he trusted our horses and saddlebags to the streets.

The front room we entered was more like an ale house, but very docile at the moment, with one man sleeping on a bench and another middle-aged man behind the counter poring over a map.

"Are you Crankford?" Cloven asked the man behind

the counter.

"Crankford the Third," the man proudly declared, standing up to his full height.

"I require a room large enough for my daughter and me," Cloven stated, setting a handful of coins on the counter. "The amount is ample for a fortnight. I will pay you no more."

The man dug through the coins. "Eh, fair enough if ye tell me how old ye be? I keen't quite tell, for your hair is grey, yet your face is too strong to be very old. Either way, it doesn't matter if you still have fight left in ye. We are building an army to defend against Multa. Join us, man! For Multa has built a strong army, and they aim to come against us. We suspect in the spring."

"Do you have a stable to lodge our horses?" Cloven asked, ignoring all the man proposed.

Annoyed to be thus snubbed, Crankford withdrew back into his chair, and yelled, "Corsey!"

A boy of about fourteen came into the room. He suspiciously regarded Cloven and me as he passed us, and then slammed the door as he went out to the street.

Through the window, I watched him take the reins of our horses and pull them away. Our eyes met once. He narrowed his at me before continuing his task.

My attention jerked back to Crankford as he yelled again. "Cranka! Pet name for my wife, ye understand. It suits her better than her own."

A woman with a pinched nose appeared. She was small, lean, and perhaps had the possibility of looking comely if she ever were to smile. But she seemed too full of annoyance for a smile to fit onto her face.

"This way," she prompted.

We followed her down a hall as she informed us, "The

washroom is down the opposite way. Breakfast is at dawn. Dinner at dusk. And if you're fool enough to attend those riffraff war meetings of my husband's, they are after dinner into all hours of the night. But you seem a mindful gentleman beyond that sort. Keep your head aloof among the bunch of buffoons! Maybe you can talk some sense into my eldest son, and my youngest for that matter."

She opened a door and after we had entered, left us. The sight of the room was enough to discourage anyone. It was overly aged wood from floor boards to rafters, in some places rotten, in some places boarded over, no rug, a little hearth which would have to warm us through the bitter winter, a crude table, short bench, and one small bed very near to the floor. The one spot of cheerful possibilities was a small four-paned window. But even through that, no sunlight shone.

There was one other door slightly ajar which I peeked around. It was a small dark adjoining space with only a bed, which was obliged to tilt with the floor beneath it.

"That will be your portion," Cloven stated.

Inwardly, I shrank from the prisonlike space, but I rose and accepted it gratefully. The arrangement was reasonable, for it granted me more privacy and made Cloven guard of the door.

I returned to the window. It offered a view of the street from where we had just come. I was glad of its shutters, for people could come right up to the window, peek in, and tap on it if they wished.

I remembered now that Father had called this impoverished portion of the city, Middle Quarters. He had said he felt most at home with these people. This thought helped me. I wondered who of the people had known him.

Peering out the window, I tried to capture the soul of the people. Many passed with cold indifference. Some were young women eager to fill their baskets. Barefoot boys ran the streets with their dogs. I felt that somewhere within each person there was a warmth that I hoped to reach. And growing to know them, I clung to as my sunshine.

Still, I shivered as our accommodations were cold. As the hearth would be the only source of our warmth, I went to see its fitness for the task. There was no wood.

Suddenly, the door burst open, and the boy, who had taken our horses, entered with his arms full of our heavy saddlebags and Cloven's furs. These he dumped on the table.

"Thank you," I offered, and then asked, "Do you have any wood for the hearth?"

"We don't do fires," the boy shot back, his face turning dour.

Cloven walked to the boy and sternly countered, "Go fetch the wood."

The boy breathed like a bull but went, leaving the door wide open behind him.

"That is the way to handle him," the innkeeper's wife bellowed, as she passed by the door. "Yell at him as you see fit. He has been a weakling when it comes to fires since the flames which burned down the ruins of Lenrow. He would surely have us all freeze before starting a fire. A foolish family is supposed to have died there, for no one has seen them since. My youngest boy got too attached to the family. Foolishness, and more foolishness," she mumbled herself out of hearing.

My heart instantly understood all that Corsey felt. Since

Mother's death and my own close encounter with death by flame, I had gained a constant inner quake which had never been there before.

When Corsey returned with an armful of wood, I confided to him, "Your mother explained why you do not like fires. I am not fond of fires either." I showed him my arms and unwrapped one of the bandages.

"You were in a fire and got out?" he asked with interest.

Cloven watched me with suspicious eyes, but I was breaking no agreements.

I went on to explain, "I was trapped in a burning room, but he saved me." I indicated toward Cloven. I could not bring myself to call him Father.

"No one saved the Hendrys," the boy accused as his countenance hardened.

"They were the family at Lenrow?"

Corsey nodded.

"How did the fire start?"

"A riot. But the Hendrys didn't do nothing wrong! Neither did the champion. They were just jealous because he won the scrimmage, and they were spreading lies about him, saying he was a traitor."

"Who is the champion?"

"Galen Lukemar!" Corsey's eyes grew animated as did mine, for I latched onto every word spoken about Galen. "He won the scrimmage," Corsey continued. "He is the best of them all. If anyone could beat Multa, it is him. My father wants him for his civilian army. But nobody from these parts seems able to get near him. He is always in the castle with a beautiful lady they say."

I abruptly lost heart to ask any more questions. I tried to smile, but failed. I knew the difference between my true smile and the one strained with heartache.

"Go on now," Cloven said to the boy.

Corsey left, evidently not fond of Cloven.

I began to sort through the saddlebags in an attempt to set some order and comfort to the room. I split the furs between the two beds. When I moved the saddlebags, I noticed a pile of handwritten parchments bound together by a leather band which had not been there before. It was a copy of the Book of Truth. My mind jumped first to Cloven as the secret possessor, but then most certainly to Corsey.

With the parchments in hand, I dashed into the hallway to catch him. I found him not far away, sitting on the bottom step of the staircase, peeking out into the hall when he heard me coming.

"Where did you get this?" I questioned.

He stood up defiantly. "I did nothing wrong! And neither did the Hendrys."

"The Hendrys of Lenrow," I repeated to get it right, "The ones who died in the fire? They gave this to you?"

He stood stiffly, so I reassured him, "You have done nothing wrong. You have done something wonderful. I am a follower of the Book of Truth. I ask because I agree with you. How many of these do you have?"

"Only that one," he answered.

I asked, "Why did you give it to me?"

"You looked like someone who could read."

"I can. Would you like me to read it to you?"

"To an old woman. Come with me." He grabbed my hand.

"Wait," I restrained him. "Let me first tell… my father."

I returned to the room, but Cloven was gone. Corsey stood in the doorway. "I never tell my pop where I go. That would take half my day. Look at how much time was just wasted. Come on."

"How far does she live?" I questioned.

"Jist down the street to old Lammy's place. Be warned, she is a grouch. I am think'n cuz she is half blind, and her son left her. But you can read to her. It seems to cast a soften'n spell over her. Plus she likes a bit of excitement to fuss over. She says walls don't get vexed enough for her liken and are a boring bone to pick with."

He led us through the bustling and warm kitchen into a small farmyard overrun with chickens and an overgrown garden which had finished producing.

Corsey raised his arms like he had wings. "Shoo, you old hens!"

We passed through a rickety old gate and up a steep dirt road. I marveled unexpectedly to see the mountain. We climbed toward what were the last structures of the city's boundary, for behind them, it was as if the mountain proclaimed, "this far and no further."

"Can you see the castle from up here?" I asked Corsey.

"Nah," he answered. "We are too far west."

At the top, the road curved into a pleasant lane. The mountain towered on one side and on the other, a row of humble cottages. Here, I partook many lungfuls of crisp autumn air, glad to have discovered this pocket of endless supply and to be so near the mountain.

Without knocking, Corsey opened the door to one of the cottages. "This one be Lammy's."

My first impression was of the low ceiling which also sank a bit in the center. The floor was pitted cobblestone with a shabby little rug before a four-posted bed lacking the drapes around it. There were several shelves of dishes and a looking glass on the wall. My attention was soon directed to the back of the single room where a woman with thick, grey hair was wringing her clothes in a bucket of dirty water, splashing it in every direction.

"Eh, Corsey, hurry shut the door. It be cold outside, and I have no more firewood till the morrow. I don't want to freeze in my sleep. Eh, who's the fancy woman? I don't want her here. Get her out!" She rose to point, but tripped and fell back down into her wooden chair.

I introduced, "I am L… Phelia. I am here to be your friend if you will accept me. May I wash laundry with you?"

"Eh, two people ought not share the same grime. What do you want?"

"She already told you, Lammy," Corsey reminded her. "Let her help you. I've tested her, and she's good. She is going to be teach'n me to read, ain't you? And I brought her to read to you. So stop your fussin and listen."

The old woman complied. Corsey got me a stool and set himself to lean against a wall, nodding for me to begin reading.

After a moment of me reading, she rose up an inch or two and interrupted, "The Book of Truth! That's what you be reading. You one of the Hendrys?"

"I never knew them, but I'm sure I am like them if they knew the Book of Truth."

"Ye might know them yet. I ain't convinced they're dead. That husband of the missis was too burly of a man to be so overcome. You know, the wife made good bread and cream she brought me once. Do you bring cream?"

"I have none. But if I did, I would certainly gift you with some."

She looked at me sourly, then rose and closed her curtains tighter and barred her door. Seemingly over her disappointment, she straightened her own collar, resumed her seat, and prompted, "Continue."

I smiled and did so with pleasure, for she wanted to hear.

In a pause for breath, for I was not accustomed to speaking so long, she asked, "Who are you?"

"I've recently come from Dresden."

"Dresden? That be the same place that champion's from—that Lukemar fellow. Do you know him?"

Realizing I had made a blunder, I slowly answered, "I do."

She eyed me with her half blind eyes, "And you say, you just came here? You sweet on him? Came to make sure no city gal gets him. Eh, you may be pretty enough, but too poor no doubt to attract him now."

"No, I'm not here for him like that," I assured. "May I continue reading?"

The woman nodded and let me read until again she interrupted, "Your heart shall be broken."

"Why do you keep going on about this?" I asked.

"Because I know who he is sweet on—my niece, Alene! She has private talks with him every evening. They have danced together."

My countenance changed. I could not help it after hearing those last words. To silence her on the subject and to silence my own heart, I assured, "I wish them happiness and no ill will. I am not seeking to marry. I have to care for my father."

I was content with myself for saying what I had, and my heart grew around my purpose of being here for Cloven and for the kingdom.

Lammy announced, "I've had enough of you today. Nonetheless, you may read to me every afternoon, but don't go think'n I like ye."

I assured her, "Your honesty and the opportunity are fair enough. I shall return tomorrow."

Corsey followed me out and returned the short distance with me. He encouraged me, saying, "You handled her real good."

I thanked him, but my heart was heavy with sorrow to hear that Galen had attached his heart to another. I should no longer allow myself to think of the past with him, nor dare to dream of a future alongside him.

"Now that you know the way to her, you can help take care of her. She will be sour to you for days, and then suddenly when the wolf strikes, she will up and defend you like you was her own chick. She did that for me once."

Dusk was descending, and the moment we re-entered the kitchen, Corsey's mother yelled at him and proceeded to load his arms with plates.

I continued to our poor lodgings now darker than ever, as I possessed no candle. Cloven remained absent, and I suspected that was the way it would often be.

The noise throughout the place could be heard: steps thudded in the room overhead, bursts of yelling shot down the halls, and continuous clamor came from the front gathering room where dinner was being served.

I could have gone to eat, but my body ached from the long days of riding which had been painful to bear upon my yet unhealed body. I lay upon my bed resting, trying not to fear that every moment Cloven delayed to reveal himself, left a moment for the love toward another woman to grow within Galen's heart. I gripped the blanket and closed my eyes tightly.

Chapter Thirty-four
~ *Phelia* ~

My eyes opened to the same darkness which had pervaded throughout the long night, except now, morning fuss echoed throughout the lodge. Wearily, I turned on my side. A thin strip of daybreak alighted beneath my door. Its gentle invitation stirred my hopes for the day. Perhaps Corsey would show me around and Lammy continue to listen as I read to her the words of the Book of Truth. I dressed, feeling my way without light as had been my custom while a servant at Crevilon Castle.

Unsure whether Cloven was in the next room, I knocked. As there was no response, I entered. The room was aglow with morning, for the sun leapt through the window, landing on the table if only for a brief passing once a day.

Cloven was there, full in the middle of the brightness, yet the cheer was lost to him, shut out by his dull grey countenance which cloaked him. He stood, staring into the barren hearth.

I did not know whether I should converse with him or quietly continue to breakfast. Deciding not to disturb him, I was about to take hold of the latch when Cloven spoke up, "Tell the boy that his friends, the Hendrys, are alive. They are temporarily living with a relative in the farmlands. When a safe way is made possible for them, they will return."

"Truly?" I exclaimed. "How did you discover this wonderful news?"

"I will answer you this one question, but do not ask any more where I go or how I learn the things I do. The less you know the safer. I went to Lenrow, the location of the fire. A man was there digging through the rubble. He told me his name was Braun Hendry and explained to me how they survived."

Cloven then preceded me to the door. "I'll be back by dinner. Wherever you venture, keep the boy with you."

He departed to his secrets, and I continued on to breakfast, hoping to catch sight of Corsey. The dining room was scattered with several male breakfasters, all staring and grumbling about the howling baby. Feeling most comfortable by a family, I chose a seat next to the embarrassed couple, who in vain, tried to hush their unhappy child.

"Where is your father?" Cranka inquired as she set a bowl of porridge before me.

"He has early work," I answered. "He will be back in time for dinner."

"So he has left you to yourself with no escort, has he? Well, I don't believe in young women roaming about by themselves. Can you scrub a floor?"

"Yes," I answered, inwardly cringing at how the work would increase the pain of my burns, which partially covered my hand. But if she asked me to help, I would consent.

"After breakfast come into my kitchen. The stairs need a good swob'n. It will be better I'm sure than any other mischief you could get yourself into."

She moved on, yelling, "Can't you get that baby hushed!"

The young couple bashfully finished their meal and hastily whisked their wailing baby out of hearing.

287

Left with only men in the room, I ate quickly and carried my dishes into the kitchen where Cranka washed with scowling vigor. "The bucket's been waiting for you. Get to it."

Corsey came in from the farmyard. When he spotted me lifting the bucket, he pleaded with his mother, "Don't make her do it, Mum. She has burns."

"Then you help her. It's got to be done."

Corsey sighed as he led me to the top of the stairs.

"I'll change the water and move the bucket if you wipe the stairs and take the brunt of the suds," I suggested.

He knelt, dipping his hands for the soapy rag. "Fair enough."

"Corsey," I said quietly, "do you think we would be overheard here?"

"Not likely. You got a good secret for me?"

"Your friends, the Hendry's, are alive. They are living in the countryside until they can find a way to return."

His face brightened. "Let's go tell Lammy!"

"We ought to finish first."

He frowned as he returned the dripping rag to the step. With my left hand, I added my share of scrubbing. Corsey responded well to my example, and soon we were finished. Eagerly, we mounted the hill to Lammy's cottage.

"You dared to come back," she greeted me. "And without any cream."

Today Lammy was in her bed buried beneath blankets tucked to her chin.

Corsey jumped up and sat on the side of her bed. "You were right, Lammy. The Hendrys are alive. They moved down to the countryside until they can find another place to live."

"Eh, finally someone who believes me. Well, good for them, but their future can't be too hopeful. Hurry up en fetch the Book of Truth under my pillow and read, so I can set my mind on something besides my pains. Corsey, sit at my feet, for they are cold."

I gently retrieved the parchments, sat on the other side of her, and began to read. I read until it looked as if both she and Corsey had fallen asleep. When I stopped, Lammy's eyes shot wide open. She spouted, "I've got enough decency not to sleep when other folks are speaking to me. Why don't you have enough thought for an old woman to keep reading until she tells ye to stop?"

So I read on, allowing myself to be trained to her liking.

The door suddenly flung open, letting in a cold breeze, a ray of light, and a woman.

"Alene, knock afore ye be enter'n," Lammy grumbled.

"Why, when it is only you and Corsey, Auntie, but I'll try to remember." When she noticed me, she startled and exclaimed, "Who is she?"

Lammy answered, "Your competition."

"In what?"

Lammy began to perk up in her bed. "For the champion."

While Alene appraised me, I tried to look friendly without any airs of rivalry.

"I am not surprised," she said lightly. "All women are in that competition, especially Lady Laila. What claims do you believe that you hold on him?"

"None," I answered.

Lammy stressed, "But Phelia is *from* Dresden. She *knows* Galen."

"Were you sweethearts?" Alene asked.

"We were friends," I answered. "He helped my family during difficult circumstances."

"Do you plan to see him?"

"No."

Happy with my answers, she jumped on the bed beside me. Taking my hand, she implored, "Then, if you have no stakes in the affair, please tell me something that will help me win his heart."

I struggled to say something. This was not a position I wished to become entangled within. But the woman's soft eager blue eyes pleaded as she went on, "Please. There are so many reasons Galen and I are perfect for one another. We have the same cheerful temperament, willing to work hard for our goals, and we have the same genuine care for all the Trimont children. Lady Laila cares nothing for the children. Honestly, I have never seen her do anything worthwhile. She does nothing more than watch Galen practice swordplay and raise her tall head above everyone like she is wisest in the world. No one could or ever will love Galen as much as I do. I know it."

I bore her speech meekly, having predetermined to not let my heart sway me either toward jealousy or despair. But, truly, all I could think to offer in answer to her plea was, "He likes chess."

She looked thoughtful for a moment before exclaiming, "Oh, what a delightful idea you have given me! I'll ask him to teach me. The children will enjoy that too."

Her words sharply reminded me of what I had given away without thinking—a treasure piece of mine and Galen's first day together when the children had gathered round to watch us play. Grenfell would be displeased with me for my lack of fight for Galen, but if he knew the circumstances he might support my decision.

Alene hugged me. "Thank you for being a friend."

She pulled a jar from her bag. "I have yet to pay a visit

home, but I stopped to bring you this cream, Auntie, from the castle's own cows just this morning. I'll help you sit up so you can drink it." Alene began whistling as she did so.

After several large and hurried gulps of the milk, Lammy said admiringly of her niece, "Just look at ye. All grown up and beautiful, working in the castle like you always intended and now winning the heart of the champion. Let me kiss you afore you be a going. Your brothers have been missen ye."

As I watched Alene go, I envied her position working in the castle alongside Galen, the children, and Lady Vala.

"Phelia... Phelia." Lammy sounded cross.

"Yes?" I responded.

"I said you could continue reading."

"Forgive me, of course." As I read, I shook myself from the wrong course of thought. Instead, I rejoiced that I was reading to an open soul the words of the Book of Truth.

"Now read the part about the prophecy again," Lammy interrupted.

"There will always be one from the Line of Cordell to rule until the day the people in one accord reject him."

"Do you think that day has already passed?" she asked.

"No," I answered excitedly. "I do not think so. That is why King Cordell must be found."

"Do you believe the same as that Tavish man? That Lord Breemore hid the king away?"

I smiled, for I liked hearing my father referenced. "Yes."

"Well, he was murdered, so there probably was something to his words," she concluded.

A little jingled knock came at the door and Lammy piped up, "Come in, Riggan."

A tall dark-headed man, with an arm full of wood,

stooped to enter. His forehead was lost beneath wild hair, which looked as though a black cat had been shorn, its fur reaped, and thrown upon his head. His face was shaved except for a thin mustache above his lip. All his features were thin, including his build, although he stood strong and self-confident like he dared the world to knock him down.

"Lambs," he exclaimed as he set the wood in the hearth and started a fire, "something smells different in here. Ah, it's the pretty woman sitting on the bed, isn't it?" He walked over to the bed and bent down to kiss the old woman's cheek. "While I do love you, I was speaking about this gentle dove of a woman whom I have never seen before. Is the beauty taken?" he questioned, glancing at me with a charming smile. Then he asked me directly, "Are you taken?"

Not able to prevent my cheeks from blushing, I yet answered very clearly, "I am in no way seeking to marry."

"Well then, the first rule in winning a fair lady's heart, listen to what her lips convey. So I will stop flirting and see you as my sister from this day forth. At least shake my hand."

"I will do so gladly," I smiled, accepting his hearty shake.

"Besides, I'll tell you a secret. It is the niece I've been after, but she won't speak to me. I just passed her in the street, and she barely acknowledged my existence. So I'm quite at a loss for a lady companion. If you find yourself ever in need of an escort, you only need ask, and I will guide you there and back safely. I see you were reading. Not many people know how in my circles. This will be a treat." He placed a chair near the bed and sat down. "Read on."

I did so in perfect ease, for his manner produced instant familiarity.

During a brief pause, he mused, "That is very peculiar what you are reading. Am I right to surmise that it is a life's guidebook from very ancient history?"

"Partially, but a much more grand description would serve it better—like the foundation and hope of all people."

"Well then, do not take my ignorance as an offense," he amended. "I do find it very interesting."

Lammy tiredly sputtered, "Now that warmth is in my bones and cream beneath my skin, I can sleep after a night of shivering. Go, go, all three of you. I don't want people watch'en me sleep."

Corsey rolled over, seeming to have just wakened from his nap. He hopped up quickly when he saw Riggan and followed us out.

I reveled in the freshness, gazing up the mountain as the fading leaves were waving their days of last farewell. Perhaps Corsey knew of a trail which wound about the mountain. I intended to ask; however, Riggan stepped before me with an idea of his own. "Might you accompany me to the market square? There are some remarkable falconers parading their best hawks. It is a sight not to miss. I had planned on going alone, but your company would grant me ever so much more enjoyment."

Intrigued by the offer, for I also wished to see more of the city, I answered, "If Corsey is also invited."

"I wouldn't have it any other way." Riggan smiled, offering his arm.

"You are better than the sister I always wanted," Corsey praised me as he took his place as my second guard.

I felt spoiled between my two new friends and

293

protectors which resulted in my long suppressed carefree spirit springing forth. In some ways, not being Lydia Tavish felt like a great burden had been lifted. And I perceived that Riggan had such an effect on people.

Riggan cautioned, "It will be a bit of a walk. Are you capable, milady?"

"Yes," I answered spritely. "I find great pleasure in long walks."

As we walked on, they both acquainted me with stories of the places and people we passed. Some stories were morbid but more often humorous, which had the three of us laughing. A smile was very nearly stained on our faces by the time we reached the outskirts of the market square.

Riggan pointed up. "Look, there is one of the hawks overhead." He grabbed my hand so I grabbed Corsey's as Riggan sped us through the crowd to the front where the hawks were displayed. Some were in cages, others freely flying, and the rest loosely tied to the beam they were perched upon. Corsey moved ahead to look at the wilder hawks in cages.

Riggan placed a special glove onto his hand and coaxed one of the most enchanting hawks onto it. "And now, milady, allow me to present to you, Princess."

She was a beautiful bird with deep black eyes, creamy brown feathers flecked with pure white, and soot sprinkled wings.

Her eye seemed keen on me until something beyond me lengthened the bird's gaze. I looked to see what the attraction might be. There was much bustle as a new carriage had just arrived. An exquisite lady with long black hair, perfectly pulled back from her face stepped out, and for a moment, froze aloft on the carriage step, scanning the scene around her.

Our eyes met, for she noticed me observing her. I would have quickly averted my gaze, but her eyes were so unashamedly direct that I was drawn to meet her on equal ground. Soon, however, she severed the connection between us as she stepped down onto the street.

Riggan leaned in. "That is Lady Laila. Most people suspect she will be the champion's pick for his bride, for her father is his sword master. She watches his every fighting match, and it is rumored that they are great confidants."

I should have guessed after witnessing how compelling a woman she was. I watched her ascend to a balcony. Though striking, she flaunted no airs and seemed more bent on seeing rather than being seen. From all first appearances, she displayed herself as a lady of quality. But this did not ease my heart; it made it sorer because I knew it was no rumor that they were confidants. Galen's own letter to Dresden confirmed that he was indeed close and perhaps in love with this woman.

The coming of the falconer to reclaim his bird was a thankful diversion. "This is Bone Claw, Riggan. Don't go renaming my hunting hawks."

Riggan maintained his possession of the hawk, boasting, "I stake my word that I can attract more attention by calling this beauty *Princess*, than by calling her that dry name, *Bone Claw*." Riggan raised his voice as he uplifted the hawk perched on his hand. "Attention all! I introduce to you the best hunter in the region, this here beauty called Princess. She will raise your hunts to that of royalty."

I listened to his sales speech until I became distracted by someone calling my name, my real name. I began to look around, although I was certain the caller could not be referring to me. Nevertheless, my heart did quicken.

I noticed that the name had attracted the attention of the Lady Laila.

When I heard, "Liddy!" I could not doubt any more. It was my beloved eldest brother, Creighson, parting the throng to reach me. I did not know what to do. So I put my finger to my lips in hopes that it would silence him.

He looked confused for a moment but stopped his shouting as he continued to make his way toward me. Thankfully the near crowd was concentrated on Riggan.

"It is... you, isn't it?" he stammered. "I believed you to be dead."

"Yes," I whispered, purposefully evading him. "Pretend that you do not know me. At a better time I will explain all."

He requested in a low voice, "Meet me here tomorrow afternoon, if you can. I will bring you to my home."

"I will try," I mouthed.

Before he departed, he bowed. "Pardon me, milady, for mistaking you for someone else."

I hated that the situation required me to send Creighson away when I so desperately wanted to see him. But I could wait calmly until tomorrow.

Cautiously, I glanced at Lady Laila, who made no pretense of watching me. I hoped she would make nothing of the scene. She had no proof to verify who I was, but to help me feel a little more comfortable, I pressed my way behind a tall man, so she could no longer study me.

I found Corsey nearby who eagerly showed me his favorite hawks. When Riggan rejoined us, it was with a triumphant smile. "My marketing prospered! Someone purchased Princess, paying a pretty penny." He jingled his pockets. "I was granted a bit of the profit. But let's get you back, for you look tired, dear one, come lean on my arm."

No one talked much on the return journey, for which I was glad since I had much to ponder. It was just after dusk when we reached the lodge. In the dark, it had been transfigured into a beacon of light. Lanterns brilliantly shone across the front, and from the open door, the light of many more interior lanterns flooded into the street, beckoning the way for the men crowding in. Crankford's booming voice could be heard greeting each who entered.

Riggan bowed his farewell.

"Aren't you coming to Father's war meeting?" Corsey asked. "Looks like he has something special planned. I've never seen so many lanterns lit at once."

"Not tonight, Corsey. I've got some money to spend. I'll be around now and again. But since the meeting has already begun, I suggest that you take our lady through the kitchen to get her some dinner from your mother. I am sure our Phelia is quite famished."

"Not more than I am," Corsey complained. "Come," he added, leading round to the back of the building. "After my mother fusses a bit, she won't deny starving bellies. Hurry, I want to overhear what's going on in the meeting."

It was much darker around the back side of the lodge. Even the kitchen light was limited to a few candles. "Why is it so dark back here and so bright in front, Mum?"

Cranka turned from the wash basin with a huff. "Because of a foolish notion your father got in his head for his precious war meetings. He insisted on using every lantern in the place, as well as borrowed ones, claiming that the extra light will draw more men and make them feel more secure to join his army. Narrow-minded thinking. With his head so full of his own thoughts, he doesn't consider that it leaves me to cook and do dishes in the dark!"

"Shall I help you?" I offered.

"Collect the dirty dishes in the dining room, if you dare. I won't step foot in there until the buffoons have cleared out!"

I accepted her commission rather gladly because I wanted to listen to what was being discussed. As Corsey was devouring scraps left out on the table from dinner, I went ahead of him.

Every bench was filled and each chair taken by both old and young men. The bright light revealed ruddy complexions fixed upon Crankford, who stood in front of his men dressed in a ridiculously grand army suit with a sword in his hand.

"See here my father's army garb and sword from the last battle with Multa, a battle we won! I'm sure ye all have fathers, grandfathers, and great grandfathers who fought and have heirlooms to be used again. Let's see what ye all have brought."

The room rattled with the clashes of metal and roaring boasts as weapons were brought into view. Men no longer sat still, but the entire room went astir. I backed to the side, prevented for a time from my duty. Weapons of all kinds: swords, maces, crossbows, and spears were raised about.

Crankford remarked kindly to all the weapons shown him. But before long, he drew the room back to attention by yelling out, "I'm going to be offering a reward!" When the room was listening, he went on to what he had to say. "Now what I have to propose tonight is bold. Seeing as now we have weapons, we need a teacher, and what better teacher than the champion? I vow that no one is like him. It is said by Jackson that the champion has both character and strength. Like all of us, he began with nothing, but with hard work, he raised himself to the top in every scrimmage. This is why I want him to lead us. And why I'm offer'en a reward of silver to anyone who can bring the champion to me."

Having seen Cloven earlier in the back corner, I glanced to discern his reaction, hoping to find in his face some sign of approval toward his son. There was nothing more than his usual unreadable hard countenance.

Disappointed, I loaded my arms with dirty dishes and returned to the kitchen where I discovered that Cranka had set a plate of fish and bread on the table for me. "There is your dinner. No need to wait any longer."

"What is your real name?" I asked her, setting the dishes in the basin.

She seemed startled by the question. "Wynnfrith," she spoke in a near whisper like a wish upon her tongue. However, despite her initial tone, she continued roughly as usual, "My mother told me it means joy and peace. Both of which I've had very little of. But you don't need to be lecturing me. I already know if one gets rid of goodness you get rid of happiness. I know it's my own fault. That Tavish man's words stuck—though I threw him out of my doors enough. Fool fickleness playing on my conscience! It is all because you remind me of that Tavish man. You work without complaint, offer to help when it's not required, and you startled my tender side by asking my name. I don't know what to make of you."

She forcibly committed her hands into the basin. "You

aren't needed anymore tonight. You may take your dinner, and go to your room."

I took my plate. Through her words, I had received enough substance that I could have borne the day all over again and many more to come.

Chapter Thirty-five
~ *Phelia* ~

My excitement to see my brother roused me long before dawn. I could not cease rejoicing that it had been Creighson who had seen me, for if it had been I who had seen him, I could not have gone to him, but fate forced me, this once, into a happy avenue.

I met the morning normally, knowing that I did not need to slip away until the afternoon. Conveniently, I found the day ripe for solitude. Cloven had yet to be seen, Corsey was occupied with a day full of chores in the stables which his mother had loaded upon him for missing his duties yesterday, and Cranka herself was heard all the morning in heavy debate with Crankford over the absurdity of his lanterns.

With my freedom, I did what kitchen chores I could and read to Lammy. All the while my thoughts were stimulated with eager anticipation to see my brother. When the approach of the afternoon pulled heavy on my heart, I dared to pause in my reading to see if Lammy would demand me to continue or hopefully shoo me out for her nap.

After waiting a moment in silence, I heard a thick swallow, a sigh, and then her hand rose to wave me off. Setting a cup of water by her bed and ensuring her hearth would produce heat for the coming hours, I quietly left her in the peaceful cradle of her slumber.

The moment the door closed behind me, the wide

awake wind whisked my cloak ahead of me. I tried to keep pace with it, but eventually had to slow after a significant amount of time retracing yesterday's steps to the city square. I mostly remembered the way Riggan had taken us, but here, where I was uncertain, I followed a group of women carrying baskets.

When the screech of a hawk pierced through the sky overhead, I regained my bearings and, strengthening myself beyond the crowd, pushed and squeezed my way through to the place where Creighson had seen me yesterday. From here, I immediately began searching for him.

During my sweep through the crowd, my eyes ascended to the balcony where Lady Laila had yesterday stood. From where her intelligent eyes had mindfully watched, now several maidens had replaced her. Their gazes did not possess half as much depth as hers, as these women were clearly more occupied with employing their eyes to flaunt rather than to perceive. I would have liked the opportunity to study Lady Laila again, although to have seen her once had been enough to know that she was a woman who could possibly capture Galen's admiration.

I lowered my gaze to a candle cart, allowing my eyes to wander through the dangling rows of tapers as I tried to ward off the difficult thought of Lady Laila and Galen being often in one another's company.

A hand tapped my shoulder. "Pardon, milady, your carriage awaits." Creighson's familiar voice won all my attention.

I bowed, acting as commonplace as he, and silently followed him. Once within his carriage, with the curtains drawn, we burst into happiness and embraced one another. He squeezed and rocked me like the ragdoll a younger sister is to her elder brother. The embrace intensified the longing for my family.

He held me back to look into my eyes. "Tell me all. I've only heard snippets over dinner-table conversations and of so much variety. I do not know what to trust. I was first led to believe that you had married Danek, with the family being grandly cared for. Then I so recently heard that you hadn't married him and because of it, Captain Rhys murdered you. I was thrown into a frenzy. But here you are, and I'm even more confounded. Pray tell me everything from the beginning. First, are the others with you: Mother, Garret, and little Rose Bud?"

When I did not answer right away, he began to gently shake me. "Is it Mother?"

I nodded, the tears pooling in my eyes.

Turning away, his hands fell from my shoulders. He exhaled heavily. "Did she suffer?"

"I was not with her. Garret informed me that she wrote you a letter when she knew her end was near, but it is in his possession. He and Rose remain in Traiven's Pass."

"I would almost ride all day and night to fetch it. Mother and Father gone, I would never have thought it. Tell me how it all took place? If I hear it from you, I know I can believe it."

Dismally, the first remembrance of our sufferings parted my lips, "It began with the wagon." The horrible events which had followed spilled forth without restraint, for Creighson understood. His eyes watched me with attention, earnestness, and questioning as we were each irrevocably tied to this history. He was part of our cause from the beginning, only having been separated at the end. My pains were his pains; my hopes were his hopes.

"Galen Lukemar is really a Trimont, and you now have

his father with you here in the city?" he questioned, his face stretched out to its extremities of amazement.

"Yes."

"So your happy ending is," Creighson heightened his playful smile, "Cloven reclaims the throne, you marry Galen, and become a princess. In all your younger daydreaming, not even you could have planned a better outcome than that."

I too smiled, yet corrected, "Creighson, I do not think so dreamily anymore. Do not stir me back into unrealistic hopes."

"But you cannot deny the escape of your inner smile at my prediction," he goaded.

"I grant I would like that outcome more than you know. But it does no good to pine for it, or to make my own happiness my goal. I am here for the brilliancy of truth to be known."

"You are as noble and brave as Father and Mother would have hoped." His face saddened with his next words, "Yet, you have suffered incessantly. I hate the thought, especially when I think that perhaps it could have been prevented."

"We were willing to bear it for the sake of truth. Now tell me of yourself."

He looked down only to bring his face back up with a newly gained half guilty, half smiling expression. "My story is quick and not as grievous. I almost feel a little ashamed going into it after what you have told me. But perhaps my good fortune will at last be of aid to you.

"After they killed father, I was taken prisoner for quite some time, but then I was told that you married Danek which warranted my freedom. I would have come home, but I was assured you were each in the best of circumstances, and in the meantime, I was offered a fine estate. However, to be honest, it was something more which kept me here." He shyly smiled. "I fell in love and married."

"How wonderful, Creighson! Mother and Father would have been so pleased. I know I am. The news strikes me as an unexpected delight. And look how happy you are. She must be remarkable."

His eyes shining, he asked, "Would you like to meet her?"

"Certainly, however, I do not know if it would be wise. No one is to know that I am alive. You are the only one who should know besides Cloven."

"If that is your only qualm then you have none, for I have already told her of my sighting you. Your secret will be safe with her. Please come." He peeked out the carriage curtain. "In fact, we are nearly to my estate now."

I eagerly leaned forward to also gain a peek out the window, but he prevented me. "The best view is not yet. Trust that I have a particular reason for desiring you to see its best vantage point."

The carriage rolled to a halt. Creighson's hand quickly went to the door's latch. "Now close your eyes. I will lead you down the carriage steps and then up a grand staircase which ascends to the place I wish to take you."

Happily, I humored his fancy, handing him the rule of my hands and eyes. My fumbling steps in the dark carried back all the mischief and fun of our long past child's play. Creighson had never been one to lose his imagination and dreams. I was truly glad to find him so well and to experience the rise of my own spirits because of him.

Self-consciousness heated my face when a female laugh

made me aware of a third person. Creighson secretly whispered something to the woman, who I assumed was his wife.

"You are climbing the stairs quite superbly without your sight," Creighson teasingly assured as a strangely familiar scent wafted before my nose — a scent instantly distasteful to me even though it boasted to be of costly perfume. I worked hard to remember the scent's association. However, too soon it weakened in potency as we stepped out into fresh air which whisked away anything of an ill flavor and filled my lungs with autumn freedom.

Creighson let go of my hand, announcing, "Open your eyes! Welcome to your own private balcony and view… That is, I hope you will choose to abide here with us from now on."

My eyes opened to the most miraculous view of the King's Castle. I briefly turned to Creighson with a radiant smile; however, I did not see his wife with him. "How did you know I'd been aching for such a view?"

"Well, I do know my own sister. Now, linger in its beauty, for I want it to compel you to stay."

I could not deny that it would be a dream to stand at this view every morning and learn of the castle's endurance. Nothing obstructed my eyes from the castle's majesty. It was near; it was strong; it felt as an old friend. Though I quivered when I thought of how much I had revered Trimont and how it now lay in ruins. I was sadly wise enough to assent that the same could happen here, but for now, the view and the comfort of Creighson's welcoming invitation overruled.

Freely I gazed, imagining the stalwart castle towers teaching of their own stoutness to the countless evergreens behind. Together, both evergreens and towers pointed toward the pure realm of the sky, just now perfectly white in grand puffs of cloud.

It suddenly struck me in a powerful way that, in this moment, the landscape was so posed as to produce around the castle the same colors as our kingdom's flag: green, white, and gold — the gold coming from the quivering aspen leaves amidst the evergreens and the radiant white clouds in their magnificent shapes throughout the sky. What a picture of triumph.

Creighson regained my attention by announcing, "And now that you are delighted by your first surprise, here is your second and best surprise. Lydia, I present my wife."

As I had turned in great readiness to meet my sister-in-law, my face froze with shock, for it was Destra who stood at my brother's side. It was her perfume I had smelled. So caught off guard, I did not have the time to compose my facial reaction. A delayed smile hurried to remedy my initial lack of greeting.

Destra smoothly spoke, wonderfully prepared, "How I have been waiting to see you, my dearest sister. What a wonderful surprise to learn of your mysterious survival after hearing of your tragic death. You shall have to entertain our many inquiries."

"Lydia, isn't it wonderful? Aren't you surprised that I was able to catch the heart of such an exquisite woman?"

"I... am very much surprised. I did not know there to be any attachment between the two of you."

"You never knew, Liddy," Creighson explained, taking Destra's hand, "but I always loved her. And when she chose me, it made me the happiest of men."

Destra lightly explained from her point of view, "You stole Danek, so I stole your brother. I believe I am better off for it as you can see."

As she ran her seductive fingers down my brother's arm, she smiled cunningly.

I forced a smile as I said, "You could not have chosen a better man than my brother. I know he will always be good to you as Father was good to our Mother."

However, my misgivings must have shown because Creighson gently led me back indoors. "Lydia, what is wrong? You seem unpleased."

"She is the last person I ever imagined…" I carefully paused to consider how to voice my concern. "I am happy for your sake and accept her, but Creighson, she was always so against the truth and our family. Has she changed?"

"Why was there need for her to change when she was already perfect? I admit that she may be a sharply witty tease, but there is no harm in it. And she has made me so happy."

"But I don't understand. Do you mean that you never viewed her as despising our family and the truth?"

He answered, "I know there were differences between her and our family in the past, but that doesn't matter now. Please say that you are happy for me and that you will accept Destra as your sister."

When I realized the change in the conversation, I began to understand that Creighson was the one who had changed.

I whispered what I had begun to fear, "Has all this grandness bought you out? Has Destra so blinded you by her charms that you no longer stand for truth?"

"Lydia, I loved Father. I love all of you, but our beliefs were ridiculous, and I'm prepared to prove it. There is no enemy, Lydia. That is what I am desperate to convince you of. It may not feel good to hear it, but I believe your suffering was in vain. Our villain was imaginary. I met Breemore, and he was not a monster. I am sorry, but it is the truth. I wish you would believe for the sake of your own happiness, freedom, and safety. There is an entire new world for you out there of freedom with no shame and no fear. I have found freedom and have loved it. After living as we did with a bad reputation as lunatics and rebels, I cannot tell you how relieving it has been to have laid that burden down and be one with the majority. They are not evil.

"I am being harsh with you for your own sake. I cannot stand by while seeing my dear sister needlessly suffer anymore. I do not like the idea of you living in Middle Quarters. That is why Destra and I want you to live here, and I'll send for Garret and Rose. But the ravings against Lord Breemore would need to end."

My voice was gone for longer than I wished. I found it harder to refute him more than any other person. Nearly, I fell prey to tears but prevented myself. Several times, I attempted to speak before I finally followed through with my heart. "I am not of the same mind. I wish the true circumstances allowed me to be. But I cannot stay here. I am sorry." After expressing this, my strength left me. I fled down the stairs and hid myself in the carriage.

My disappointment was vast. I knew Creighson had always carried discontentment about our family's reputation, but to have completely partaken of Breemore's side and to have married Destra! Only strong deception on one side and an unstable heart on the other could have produced such a dreadful change.

Before more thoughts were sorted out, Creighson entered into the carriage as it jerked into motion. He began gravely, "We have until this carriage reaches Middle Quarters to work this out between us. Will you let me explain what I have learned since living in King's City?"

I nodded, but I sadly knew it could not be settled between us with his new belief in Breemore's innocence.

"Please listen carefully, Lydia."

I looked at him with all my attention.

He exhaled and began, "I firmly believe that we would come to the same conclusion if you had witnessed the same events as I. You haven't been exposed to what I have since being in the city. I've actually met Lord Breemore and not just heard about him from mistaken opinions passed down from person to person."

"There is proof against Breemore, Creighson. We aren't blind fools, trying to create problems for no reason."

"You are just like Father," he mused, "perhaps harsher. But you know how Father always told us to give honor where honor was due. Well, Breemore has treated me beyond fair. I could not call myself a reasonable man if I did not acknowledge with what abounding kindness Lord Breemore has bestowed both freedom and prosperity upon me. He apologized for Father's death, explaining that his only concern was peace and that if I maintained it, he offered that I take this estate for recompense for the loss of my father. He begged me, with empathy, Lydia. I had been speaking against him and did not deserve such an offer. Humbled, I accepted and have not once regretted it.

"I am often invited to dinner parties at the castle. I see Lord Breemore with my own judgment at a close perspective. I assure you nothing is amiss. He is understanding, jolly, wise, and gracious. Nothing like we had been told. I simply ask you to open your mind to consider him in a different light. I should like to see the uncertainties settled between you and him."

"I have met Breemore," I clarified, standing up for the truth the best I could. "He also pleasantly explained everything to me. But that does not excuse his removal of the Book of Truth, Father's murder, the heartless theft of the orphans, and Trimont's burning. That makes him even more deceptive."

"Breemore was not behind murdering Father," he defended. "That was Captain Rhys. Was Rhys not also the one responsible for the destruction of Trimont Castle? Rhys began deviating into rebellion apart from Lord Breemore. Before he went to Traiven's Pass, Captain Rhys stirred a riot against Galen, and who do you think strongly defended Galen? Lord Breemore did. Captain Rhys, I believe was our real enemy. But thankfully he is no more, and you are safe. You do not need to suffer another day. Believe me that there is really no danger, no threat. I don't want you to miss your chance at marrying whom you love just because of a wrong belief and fear of hiding from an empty shadow. I want you to live and be happy as I am. Lydia, you do not have to go on as you are."

As he had spoken, more of my thoughts had sorted out, and I was able to answer assuredly, "There is a side of the suffering which I think you have not yet grasped. It has not been so very bad as you think, for much goodness has come out of the hardships. The people of Traiven's Pass have seen the light. They no longer believe our family was crazy. They have come to revere us and have turned repentant for their former conduct. Danek has changed. Cloven coming back is of more magnitude than I believe you can fathom. I know I have grown stronger. Garret is more steadfast. I love the poor people of Middle Quarters. They are my friends. And the people of Dresden, I will never forget. So much worth has come that I cannot regret what has happened, though it has torn my life into fragments. My life is full of joy, but of a different essence. I will not leave where I have been placed. I hope you understand."

His posture seemed to have slipped lower against the carriage bench. I left my eyes on him until he answered.

At last he said, "I cannot grudge you such heartened words. Perhaps more than anything, I really wish that you would not despise me for having married Destra."

"I could never despise you. But I do confess that I fear of her influence over you. Also, I've seen how spiteful she can be. I just worry she may bring harm to you."

"She is my wife, Lydia. I will defend her honor." His tone was injured and of high offence.

I humbly bowed my head. "You are right to correct me. As she is your wife, it is best that you love her well, whatever she proves to be. And I shall love her for your sake."

Creighson promptly turned away to look out the other window opposite of me, clearly to avoid showing some feeling he was experiencing. I could not judge of what nature. But the gulf between us remained wide, as the carriage somehow managed to roll on, carrying us in the same direction.

"Hang it!" Creighson finally exclaimed, turning back to face me. "Forget everything I said. I do not want this rift between us. But do remember this, for I know it is true beyond any doubt. Galen loves you."

Startled, I looked at him.

"I was in a sword scrimmage with Galen once. He recognized that I was from our family, and when I mentioned your having married Danek, he completely lost his focus. He was a man of much agony of heart. If he is anything like me, his heart will prevent him from marrying any other. You may have your happy ending yet, little Liddy. And I promise to never tell Destra, or any other, anything more of what you have told me nor of where you are staying. Continue your quest. Avail upon me if you have need of any aid."

My head slipped onto Creighson's shoulder, more than one tear falling down my cheeks. "Thank you," I whispered.

Chapter Thirty-six
~ *Lord Breemore* ~

"Galen Lukemar is missing out on another fine dinner, my lord," one of my dinner guests remarked. "Galen cannot be so shy if he hopes to take your place, especially now that Captain Rhys is dead. I believe you should really insist upon him joining us."

I answered to the general consensus of the dinner party, "Galen is at the place in his life where training consumes his time. And this dedication of his is for the benefit of us all if complications with Multa arise. When he is on so noble a course, I do not wish to force him into another. After the tournament, I am sure he will turn his efforts toward diplomacy. Indeed, I have every expectation that he will excel in every quality of leadership." I raised my goblet. "A toast to so hopeful a leader for our kingdom."

"Here, here!"

I drank, smiling. Galen may continue searching the Inner Tunnels and test my word to its limit; he will find me infallibly trustworthy and be chosen by the people.

The plates were taken, and the party moved toward the gallery.

A favorite of mine approached. Her devilish green eyes, which I gladly accepted fully into mine, held information worth hearing. But her husband was at her heels, pulling her back, saying, "I've ordered the carriage, love. Let us go nearer the door to wait for its arrival."

I rushed to delay his hurried departure, "But to leave

so soon before the minstrels have even begun their nightingale melodies?"

Destra added, with an irresistible eye to her husband, "Let's stay just through the first song. The carriage can wait."

He kissed her hand tenderly. "If you will behave yourself." His eyes lifted to her beseechingly.

"Come," I ushered them into the gallery.

"Will you find us seats nearest the players?" Destra asked of her husband. The moment he stepped away, she leaned to whisper, "Lydia Tavish is alive and in King's City. I've seen her."

Having succeeded in her mission, she followed Creighson Tavish whom she had just betrayed.

I sat in my chair as the peaceful streams of flutes ensued. The melody complimented my thoughts, for what Destra had told me struck a surprisingly good chord.

No matter how much Galen wanted to remain true to King Cordell, the stakes to do so would be too high, especially with Lydia still in play. The possibilities of how I could wield her were endless. Remus could have her found in no time.

I closed my eyes in complete peace.

Chapter Thirty-seven
~ *Galen* ~

Wearily, I entered the music room with headache, muscle ache, and heartache. The solemnity of one beyond my years was day by day becoming more fixed into my countenance. My face could not smile as readily, but with my will, I sincerely brought forth a smile for my grandmother and Cadby, who noted my entrance.

They, along with the other children, were gathered around a large table which had been brought to accommodate the remaking of the children's tapestry. The children's hands and eyes were red from both focus and sadness, as if the colorful fabrics, threads, and needles which slowly passed through their fingers gave only a miserable promise of a new beginning.

Cadby left the others to take my hand, and when I sat on the couch, Cadby sat beside me.

"I need to rest," I kindly explained to him.

He silently nodded. Knowing that he now viewed my hand as secure as his pocket, I gently squeezed his hand while I rested.

However, my mind had been plunged into too many perplexities, sorrows, and fears to allow me to fall asleep easily despite utter exhaustion from training throughout the days and searching the Inner Tunnels at night.

I must have shivered in my weariness because Cadby rose, placed a blanket over me, and returned to my side. Eased, I moved my arm around him and tried to sleep because tonight would be another sleepless night as the meeting with Vala, Meklon, the Hendrys, and Lady Laila had been arranged, during which time I would present the facts that faced us and plead they advise me on what to do.

"It is not coming out right!" Hazel sharply complained. "I want it to be just like the first tapestry we sewed."

I opened my eyes to see Hazel drop her needle and push the fabric away from her. She stood from her chair, her body a fragile basin of tears.

Lady Vala softly moved into Hazel's chair, offering her arms as a safe haven. Hazel crawled into Vala's lap, burrowed her head, and cried, whimpering, "Why?"

Haxel also stepped away from the table discouraged. "My feet grew at Trimont, but they have not since coming here. I will never grow now that Trimont Castle is gone."

"You are tall enough," Badrick grumbled. "Whoever is taller than me is taller than they ought to be."

"Hazel, I'll help you finish," Hollis offered, taking the rejected needle in hand and silencing the boys with a sharp look.

With more weight added to my heavy heart, I was about to close my eyes once again when Alene's cheerful whistle entered the room. She approached the table, holding a richly polished wooden box. She peered over Hollis' shoulder, asking, "Is that me you are stitching next to Galen?"

I stood to my feet in defense of Lydia, but it was Hazel's voice which angrily exploded in answer. "No! That is Lydia. It will never be you!"

Except for Hazel's intensified sobs, the room stilled with uncomfortable shock at such an outburst. With her hair pulled up, Alene's tensing neck and short breath was plainly visible. She determinedly closed her mouth, yet in the next moment opened it in soft reply. "I am sorry Hazel. Of course it is Lydia. I am sure you all miss her very much. I would never try to replace her."

"Children," Lady Vala wisely called. "Set the sewing down, and let us gather around the fire. I wish to speak with you."

As the children sheepishly transitioned from the table to sitting on the rug before the fire, Alene also tentatively approached me. "You will forgive me for that heedless comment, won't you?"

"Of course, and I am certain Hazel likes you very much."

A smile easily returned to Alene's face. "I know. It will get better in time. But I truly do want you to know how sorry I am for your loss. It is because of my sympathy that I have brought something to try to cheer you." She lifted the box in her hands. "Can you guess what it is?"

I replied, "I am sure I do not know."

"It is something of which my education was sadly deprived of. But I believe I have found a teacher of the very best caliber." She raised the box's lid to reveal exquisitely carved chess pieces. "Will you teach me to play? I am a most earnest learner and quick to turn equal opponent for the benefit of your greater enjoyment."

While I was indeed impressed by the quality of the set and her willingness to learn, I could not match her hopeful smile. The game reminded me too much of Lydia and the first day we had spent together.

When I did not immediately answer, Alene further invited bravely, "I thought it could be something special you and I could do together."

When again I did not answer, her face turned bright red, and she added, "With the children of course."

It was obvious she had hoped for a readier response from me, and obvious to my heart that I could not give it. I answered, "I cannot; I am sorry. Certainly, there are better persons within the castle who could teach you. Perhaps once you have learned, I'll be better able to play."

I only found relief once I had walked over to Cadby, who was solemnly listening to Vala's words. I was proud of him for doing so. He strengthened my heart when just now mine beat very lowly after enduring all the reminders of Lydia. I stood behind him, setting my hand on his shoulder.

When I looked back to see what had become of Alene, she was nowhere to be seen. I became concerned that I had hurt her. I was sorry if I had. But what could be done? If she could just give me time, I would act normal again and bear the mention of Lydia better. Just now, the mere mention or thought of her was like a dagger slowly dragging through every feeling known to my soul.

Following Cadby's lead, I set my attention on Vala's words, for I knew they flowed from one who had suffered and overcome. I became attuned as she was saying, "With the loss of our beloved Trimont and our dearest friend, Lydia, you may feel things which unsettle you, such as despair, confusion, or doubt. These are feelings which can turn very unkind to you and to others. Therefore, you cannot let them rule you. It is important to remember to remain good, kind, and brave children of Trimont, thinking of others before yourself. Now off to bed, for sleep is also given to aid in our sorrowing."

The children meekly obeyed, walking to their rooms in reproved silence. When Vala and I were left alone, I mused, "I know you love these children as your own and have already borne much today. Are you ready for our meeting?"

"Yes, I am eager to hear of what you have been anxious to tell us."

Together, we began walking.

"There is a matter of which we must discuss before we reach Lady Laila," Vala began.

"Of what nature?" I asked, growing alarmed.

"Lady Laila," Vala answered. "Ever since you mentioned her joining this meeting, I have felt uneasy and have concluded that it is best she not come."

I promptly advocated, "She is waiting for us even now. I cannot go back on my invitation to her. I assure you, I have every reason to include her and add her aid to our side."

Vala asked, "Have you formed an attachment to her?"

Her question rattled me. How could Vala conceive it possible that I might have considered another woman so soon? I answered, "I cannot easily bear the mention, let alone, the thought of such a betrayal to my heart. I simply hold that Lady Laila is my friend and has proven herself trustworthy. However, this should not matter. Aside from any attachment or not, we need all the aid we can gain. She is one of us."

Vala earnestly replied, "I think you could be very well right about her. I perceive excellent qualities in Lady Laila and would like to know her more, yet to trust her completely at this time remains a risk. I think it is wiser to not include her in such a significant meeting. No one will be free to speak with her presence there. Galen, we need to be able to speak openly or the meeting will have been in vain."

I relinquished with an exhale. "I understand, and I believe Lady Laila shall as well. I should have spoken with you before inviting her. She will be waiting in the gallery. I will go ahead and inform her that she shall not be joining us."

I did not prefer that I had to take back what I had offered, but I was consoled by my confidence that Laila would understand when once explained. Her emotion and reasoning were reliable.

Upon entering the gallery, my eyes found Lady Laila directly, though she moved as little as the statues and portraits surrounding her. Her face indeed was like one of them—a mystery held fast in a stilled and timeless depiction.

"I believe I read a mystery in your face," I greeted.

"Perhaps," she gave some credence to my suspicion and then remarked, "I read disappointment upon yours."

"That is because I have come to confess that I have judged wrongly and find myself in a position where I must break my invitation to you. Lady Vala and the others do not know you well enough to feel comfortable speaking freely in your presence. I am sorry that I must exclude you so rudely."

She smiled, which was a rare sweet gift from her face. "They are wise. Their caution and boldness makes me respect them more. Do not mourn for me; I have other games afoot." Her face turned downward in a bow, and before she lifted her head again, she had turned in departure.

"Thank you for understanding," I called after her.

She nodded acknowledgement without looking back at me.

I returned to my grandmother, offered her my arm, and led her to the carriage which awaited us at the forsaken graveyard lane.

The night hit us brutally, using both of its weapons: darkness and cold. Not risking a torch, I led us carefully around the tombstones.

"Is it difficult for you to pass through the graves?" I asked her.

"Have I never told you that I have visited them often since coming to the castle? This is my favorite quiet sanctuary."

Aware of her eyes lingering upon the looming shadow of my father's deceptive monument, I whispered, "You believe that he will return, don't you?"

"I know it is difficult for us both to speak of her, but ever since you told me that Lydia had been the one sent to Cloven, I have often wept with gratitude. Knowing that the truth thrived within her, I am assured that my son had the door of escape opened to him. I yearn that he takes it."

"I maintain that he will not come," I replied more heartless than I actually felt.

I opened the gate to the old road where the carriage awaited. Within was a comfortable darkness suited for sleep at last.

Lydia and I stood on a magnificent mountain peak, nothing blocking our view of earth and sky. The air was the essence of purity. Taking one another's hand, we ran and dove off the cliff side. The air became mingled with stench, the clear sky clouded, the light dimmed, and then blackened. I could no longer feel Lydia's hand within mine as I landed in a deserted field at night. But I stood up strongly, possessing the overwhelming knowledge of being one with her in heart and purpose though we were separated.

I awoke from a loud clamor, my neck stiff and sore.

Lantern light moved around the outside of the

motionless carriage.

"Did I sleep all the way?"

Vala nodded.

I stretched my neck and jumped out of the carriage. Braun, holding a lantern, gave instructions to the driver.

Briskly, I circled the carriage, attempting to shake the potent emotions the dream had excited. Yet I could not deem them as necessarily harmful, for with their longing, the dream had also brought peace.

When Vala and Braun entered the barn, I followed in search of Meklon, who I found likewise in pursuit of me. It was good to see him standing as his normal self after he had taken that beating for me at Lenrow.

Upon reaching one another, we embraced. Tears in his old eyes, he pulled back to look into mine. "Trimont Castle I can lose as long as you stand fast. Galen Thomas Trimont, are you standing despite all that has befallen?"

With tears suddenly in my eyes, I nodded, thankful that I was able to do so in agreement with my conscience.

He gripped my shoulder. "Then we can bear this. Let us join the others in the room, and you may tell us what you have learned."

I asked, "Have you told the Hendrys that you and Breemore are brothers and from Multa?"

"Yes, they have been told all that I have shared with you."

We entered an interior room which smelled saturated with old leather, yet had been converted into the Hendry's temporary living space.

Cote eagerly rushed to me, holding up a smashed pail and charred tool. "Father found my milk pail and one of his cobbler tools back at Lenrow in the rubble. Soon, I know he will reach the secret entrance into the tunnel and save the copies of the Book of Truth!"

"That is good news," I encouraged.

Happy to see that I was pleased, Cote returned to his bed of hay, ready to listen to what I had come to tell them.

Hildie offered me a chair which I thanked her for, but I preferred not to sit. I stood behind it, bracing my hands on the back.

As everyone situated, I thought of how best to begin. When they all silently attended their gaze toward me, I chose Meklon's face to set my focus upon as I stated, "I have found the way, and these last few nights, I have been within the Inner Tunnels."

Meklon's expression did not disappoint. Leaning forward, he pressed, "And King Cordell?"

"I am certain he lives and is of a sound mind; however, the prison cell where he has been kept all these years has recently been vacated."

Hildie leaned forward in earnest. "Please tell us what you found in the Inner Tunnels."

I could not help speaking soberly and reverently of the sacred place. "Our king has not forgotten us," I began. "Nor has he forgotten the truth. These facts are proven in the very walls of his prison cell where he spent the years covering them with carved depictions of his people and writing large portions of the Book of Truth. I cannot even express what feelings moved through me, as I partook of his heart poured forth onto stone. I can only now say with certainty that I truly believe he is every good attribute you ever told me he was."

Silence followed as each felt the significance of this knowledge.

"Breemore must have known you were getting close to finding King Cordell and, therefore, moved him,"

Meklon deliberated.

"No doubt," I responded, "for Breemore confessed to me that King Cordell is indeed alive, and also confessed to having been the one responsible for the king's disappearance."

"What trickery is my brother playing by confessing what we already know? Do not trust him."

I hesitated to begin the decline into the worsening news. Gripping the chair tightly, I spoke on. "Breemore revealed to me that his ultimate plan is to peacefully merge Multa and Calderon together. He claims that he had to persuade the people against King Cordell and the Book of Truth in order for Multa to agree to such a union. Breemore has laid a proposal before me, where we must choose to either side with this merger or accept war. He explained that he wants me to win the tournament so that I am in the position of heir to the throne as well as a favorite among the people. Then King Cordell shall be revealed and the choice set before the people of who they wish to be their next king—me or King Cordell. If the people reestablish Cordell as their king, Multa will attack. But if the people renounce King Cordell in favor of me as their next king, then Breemore will see that the two kingdoms unite peacefully. A man named Seeris, who currently rules Multa, would rule sovereign while Breemore governed Multa and I Calderon."

Meklon's face was now hidden beneath the rim of his hat as he stared downward in thought. "Would you accept such a position?" he asked, lifting his head gravely.

"Never!" I answered vehemently. "I know it is not my place to ever set myself up as king. I do not desire to be chosen. However, if the alternative is war, I... do not know. From all accounts, Multa's army is very extensive, and revenge beats very strongly within them. Overtaking our kingdom has been their aim all these years. Within our army, loyalties are split. While some knights will wish to fight with us, some will join the Multa cause, desiring the way of the peaceful merger. I know that as a Trimont, it is my duty to lead our army to protect our kingdom and King Cordell, which I am willing to do, but if enough people will not fight with us… is there really any hope?"

Meklon looked at me decidedly, "Everything my brother told you about peace is rubbish. Breemore's talk of a peaceful merger is just a ploy to deceive us into yielding our freedoms to their rulership. From the beginning of the Multa Wars, Multa has wanted to take away our reliance on the Book of Truth because they knew it was the source of our undefeatable strength and unity. That is why Breemore has spent tireless years removing our king, our history, and the Book of Truth — not to save us, but to weaken us for the slaughter. I have heard of this man Seeris — of stories of his cruelty and tyrannical lordship. No, Galen, we cannot allow the merge without a fight."

Meklon paced. "Galen, I believe that you must win the tournament. This will gain you the ability to hold the people's ear. Once you have it, tell them the truth of who you are, who Breemore is, and what he has done. Then plead with the people to choose their rightful king, promising them that you will in like manner be a true Trimont, leading our kingdom once again into victory against Multa."

"But how can I promise victory? The kingdom could end in ruins. Many innocent people will die. I have never led an army. Are you certain Breemore's goal is not peace?"

"Yes, Galen, I know my brother. I know Multa. If I was not entirely certain of their vengeful, power-seizing intentions, I would do all in my power to prevent war for the sake of both sides. Breemore thinks he has trapped you into surrendering to his plan—into leading our people to merge for their peace and safety. I am declaring that we must fight against his deception—fight for truth, and fight for the freedom of our people."

Braun said gravely, "I agree, but we would be acting in high risk. Breemore's influence over the people is strong. Even with all we may say, the people still may not choose King Cordell. They may even want to merge with Multa. What then?"

Meklon sighed, "That is a large possibility, and at that point, there will be nothing we can do. The merger will then take place, and our kingdom, the beacon of truth and light will be swallowed up in the union with its enemy, becoming one and the same.

"And from my experience, I do not doubt that once a merger has taken place that it will be a merger of savage slavery. Farms will be taken, houses invaded, and families split apart. This will not be a reasonable compromise but a complete takeover.

"It can be difficult when the power lies in the choice of the people, yet it is the proper place for the power to lie. Therefore, at the very least, we must give the people another voice to hear besides Breemore's before they forever forfeit their freedom."

Hildie nudged her husband's elbow with a smile. "Give him the note." Her smile was vastly out of place for such conversation and made me curious as Braun pulled from his pocket a small folded parchment and handed it to me.

"I was entrusted to give this note to you," Braun explained.

It read: *Come to the Inner Tavern tomorrow after dusk.*

Immediately, I both knew and denied who this note had come from, for the tone of command and the handwriting were familiar to my childhood.

The note lowered in my hand.

"Will you let us hear it?" Hildie asked.

"All it says is come to the Inner Tavern tomorrow night," I answered flatly, handing her the note as I walked to the door.

I saw that Vala had risen and taken the note in hand. Her fingers, shaking with possibility, touched the words. "Was it my son who gave this to you?"

Again, Hildie looked at Braun with her eyes glowing as Braun spoke, saying, "Hildie and I know little about the matter. Nonetheless, I am of a firm suspicion that the man who gave me that note is Cloven Trimont, though he has not claimed so with his lips."

"Did the man limp?" I sharply questioned.

Braun's strong nod affirmed everything.

A growl swept through my heart against my father. I set my hand on the door latch to leave; however, not before I had seen my grandmother's jubilant countenance. My hand dropped heavily at my side, and my head hung, bearing the conflict of my own negative feelings against listening to the joyous and thankful comments of the others. But they did not know him as I did. Even if my father had returned, he was not the man they wanted. My father running into the arms of his mother—he would never. He might speak with her, but he would stand aloof and, even worse, turn his back on her at a selfish whim.

"Galen, do you agree?" Meklon asked.

Slowly, I turned my face back toward the room. "I am sorry; I did not hear."

"Braun has informed us that the Inner Tavern is where Crankford is now holding his war meetings. We are planning to all attend tomorrow night in the hope of finding your father there. What do you say of this plan?"

I looked at them, but my eyes somehow could not perceive as phantom tears seemed to harden my sight. Out of the blindness of the moment, I answered bitterly, "Have I not followed every command of my father all my life? Did it ever please him?"

Before my emotions broke further, I left the room, marching through the barn doors into the barren soul of the night where I yet marched further—the chilling arrows of the wind immediately melting against my hot skin. They did not know that I had already tried everything a loving son could do to get my father to change. If he came back, his purpose was to rule the kingdom with a rod of cold iron.

"Galen! Galen!" Meklon sternly called after me.

I stopped while Meklon hurried onward to reach me, proclaiming as he came, "It is me you ought to be cross with, not your father. I am the one who did not teach him right. I should have warned him against Breemore. I deserve all your anger, not him. If I would have warned him and not pumped him up with so much pride, you would have had the most tender father in all the earth. I may not have known him all the years you did, but you did not know him all the years I did. He loved his brother as his own flesh, his father as his lord, and his mother as royalty. You must believe me. If he has returned to the truth, he will become the best man you have ever known. Give him that chance. As your friend, I beg it of you."

I had long since turned from Meklon, staring into the night as his words shot like hooks inside my ears. I could not speak.

"Galen, if we have any chance at all of preserving our kingdom, it will be because we follow the Book of Truth and truth alone. Therefore, its principles, including forgiveness and love, must be within our head, our heart, and our hands. Such reconciliation between your father, you, Vala, and the kingdom—" Meklon's voice cracked. "It could hold the power to defeat all deception and every evil thing which has made its stand against the truth."

"It will not prevent war," I spoke the imminent defeat which I felt.

"It will prepare us for it," Meklon bolstered his point back up. "Think of this, if your father reclaims the throne, which not even Breemore could deny him, he would have charge of all of Calderon's army and would have the power to tell the kingdom of my brother's treachery. We need him."

After a moment of silence, Meklon said, "I've stated my mind; I'll leave you to find yours."

My heart having been pulled the entire time Meklon had spoken, and knowing that time would be of no aid in this decision, I quickly asserted before he was out of hearing, "I will do what you tell me."

Meklon came near once again. His body was mostly a darker shadow against the thick night. The shape of his staff and hat were most prominent, making his appearance simply like the humble gardener that he had chosen to be in the Kingdom of Truth rather than to be a ruler in the enemy's kingdom. I realized then that he had not lied when he had said that he was a man of no secrets because he had forsaken his old identity, never having used it for his own gain and never would. I felt honored as he set his right hand on my shoulder.

"And I..." he began, then paused — "Galen, just know that I will lay my life down for you and your father if ever need be."

"You know," I said only slightly smiling for the weight of the possibility, "I am never going to take you up on that offer."

"I know," Meklon replied, showing in the dark shadow of his body that he had lowered his hat over his eyes, "but it is the easiest way to say how... fond and proud I am of you."

Chapter Thirty-eight
~ *Lady Vala* ~

"Our son has returned, Amond," I whispered, resting my hand upon my beloved's gravestone. "I cannot tell you what it has done to my heart. My entire mind, body, and soul are alight with the knowledge. I shall meet him tonight for the both of us. I tremble and yearn nearly more than my frail body can bear."

"My lady," a maiden servant called. "Lord Breemore has requested a word with you. He awaits you on the east balcony."

"Thank you. Please lead the way."

When I arrived at the east balcony, Breemore stood, looking off into the view of a fading autumn and dull hazy sky from the field fires far below. He spoke without turning, "I have received complaints regarding your discipline of the children. Maids of the castle seem to think that you are too quick to confront their frustrations and anger. I am not reprimanding you, but I am informing you that I am bringing in a choice tutor for the children. He shall arrive within the fortnight."

"From where does this tutor come?" I asked.

"He is from Multa," Breemore answered, now facing me. "He is an excellent man and a great promoter of peace. Judge him for yourself once he arrives. He is a splendid chap. He is young and enthusiastic with hopes as high as mine for the peace of our two kingdoms. He will teach the children of the world and prepare them for a bright future. Please, do not judge him until you have met him. Let us make for peace, Lady Vala. It is my honorable aim."

With calm dignity, I gave my answer. "My own son learned from you long ago, yet peace was not the result. The soundness of a philosophy is in the outcome of the lived-out life of the one who believes in it, not in the mere words of the philosopher. You have ruined enough lives, including my son's. You shall not ruin any more of my children with your lies and deception."

Breemore's countenance did not flinch, yet a familiar hatred burned from deep within his eyes. He mocked, "You are an old, homeless, widowed, and childless woman. Are you sure that you wish to pick this fight?"

"Yes," I answered. "It is time."

Chapter Thirty-nine
~ *Galen* ~

Cote swung his legs excitedly against the carriage bench, happily holding the hands of his parents who sat at each side of him. There was not a father I knew who I esteemed higher than Braun. I was thankful that Cote would never have to endure what apprehension I now felt at the thought of encountering my father tonight at the Inner Tavern.

When I turned to look at Meklon seated beside me, his eyes were closed. I then looked at Vala on my other side. Her brown eyes were tensely focused in thought.

"What troubles you?" I asked.

She answered, "I fear Breemore has begun the fight sooner and nearer than we foresaw — with the children."

I straightened and faced her fully, keenly concerned.

"I do not know the severity of it yet," she continued, "but he told me this very afternoon that he is placing the children under the sole charge of a young tutor from Multa. Because there is now every reason to fear that I may soon be prohibited from seeing them, I consider it time for the children and me to leave King's City. Danek, I believe, will receive us at Crevilon Castle."

My last consolation would be taken with their departure, but what else could be done if Breemore was targeting the children for his purposes? Their safety had to be of higher priority than the comfort of having them near.

"I agree," Meklon enforced, clearly having been

consciously awake the entire time. "If Breemore wishes to substitute another teacher to replace you, it is more proof of his treachery."

"What is more," Vala began again, "is that I believe we shall have to depart in uttermost secrecy. Breemore will hinder us if he detects our plan. I think we will no longer find him as kind as he has thus outwardly been."

Braun leaned forward upon his thick arms and spoke in a tone as if telling a terrible tale, "Today, I also witnessed a sight which signals how speedily our danger encroaches. A Multa peddler was allowed into the city. He made himself accepted through compelling words of peace and the enticement of his valuable pearls. Large crowds assembled around him. He mingled his sales with stirring messages of Calderon and Multa coming together peaceably. After seeing this and hearing of the tutor, I believe Breemore to be purposefully bringing in people from Multa to propagate his deception of peace so that by the time of the tournament, Calderon will readily give up their fight in favor of merging with Multa. Breemore is no fool. We must expect him to wisely counter us at every attempt we make to dismantle him."

Braun's words took heavy hold of my thoughts. Could Breemore's deception go so far as to entirely make himself and Multa sound as if they were the promoters of peace while making us appear to be the advocates of war?

My thoughts were so consuming, I concluded aloud, "Breemore will make us sound like the enemy and our message one of dishonor and hate. He will trap us into sounding like the ones who are seeking war when all we desire is to protect all people. How are we going to overcome this?"

Meklon answered calmly, "Breemore will no doubt

blacken our message beneath the sound of many lying voices, but if our conduct and motive are pure and noble, in the end, our message shall not be tainted nor go void though it be cast into the fire. Because like gold, whatever is pure is not destroyed but comes out more radiant than before it was tried.

"The vital part, Galen, is that we remain pure, never allowing our hearts to drift from the words of the Book of Truth. If your father has finally grasped this, as you have, we shall have a chance."

Again, the uncomfortable dread of meeting my father draped over me. I was tempted to inwardly mock Meklon's assumption of my father and me becoming likeminded. However, I resolved to pass no judgment against my father until I saw him as I had promised Meklon.

Though it had been steadily darkening within the carriage, due to the setting sun, it strangely began to grow brighter. Cote leaned over his father's lap to be the first one to report what was to be seen out the window.

"Lanterns!" he cried. "More than I have ever seen! And lots of men gathering into the place of the lanterns. Is that where we are going?"

"Yes," Braun answered animatedly, opening the carriage door as it came to a halt. "We are to guard your mother and Lady Vala who will remain within the carriage while Meklon and Galen attend the meeting. You will have a good view from the driver's bench. Climb up."

As Cote excitedly joined the driver, and Meklon exited the carriage, I gently grasped my grandmother's hand and looked to her, for I knew it was our hearts that were most engaged and vulnerable in this venture of meeting with my father.

She squeezed my hand and smiled. "Let's welcome your father home."

I stepped down onto the craggy cobblestones and became one among the many men gathering for the meeting within the Inner Tavern.

The upper gables of the old tavern trembled as boys could be seen through the broken windows scrambling up to its old floors, taking advantage of the extravagant light to explore the building without fear.

I remembered quite well that even at midday the building had been one of shadowed mystery. However, now illuminated from the inside and out, it was revealed to be nothing more than an old worn down hag of a building, shuddering with all the tumult suddenly pouncing within it. Yet as the skin was year by year sagging away, its thick ancient oak bones and stone foundation kept the tavern enduring.

Crankford, like the energy at the center of a wheel, making everything spin toward the goal, stood elevated in the center of the main room with his arms gesturing as he spoke. "Cranka's fussing finally led us to some good! It drove me to move our meetings here. Even if the roof leaks, we yet have our light and additional room to recruit more men. Just look how many new faces have joined us. Yes, keep coming! There is space behind me yet to be filled. My apologies for not enough chairs or benches, but let it be training for your legs. For in war you must stand! You must march! You must climb!"

Something hard fell onto my shoulder. I looked up just in time to see a young boy through a crack in the second floor rise from his knees and dash away. Smiling to myself at their antics, I began the necessary search to find my father whether I felt ready or not to meet him.

A man suddenly rushed to my side, exclaiming, "It's he! It's he!" He raised my arm as he continued proclaiming, "I have the champion. I've brought the champion. The reward is mine!"

Confused and alarmed, I pulled my arm back as a rush of attention encircled me. Crankford stopped short amid his exhortations, pushing his way until he stood before me.

It was not the first time we had stood beside one another in the Inner Tavern, and one good gulp of scrutiny was enough for him to recognize me as the man who had refused to follow him when he had stolen the people's attention away from Braun's warnings about the importance of the Book of Truth.

"The traitorous coward," Crankford hailed in disgust. "I do not believe it. You cannot be the champion. Who has made up this wives' fable? This man has already refused to join us in favor of the old ways. He is of no use to us. I ordered for the real champion. I will not give a shilling for this man. Now, who else dares to verify that this is the man who won the scrimmage? Did anyone among ye see the champion up close that day?"

Several men soberly affirmed, "It is he."

Crankford scowled. "Well then," he stretched himself beyond his full height, "I'll ask you a second time. Have ye found your courage to join us? Not to fight for show and praise but for our kingdom in true battle? I don't want a pompous gentry or fool-brained weakling who has to rely on a book because he cannot think for himself."

I answered cautiously, "I will help in any way I can."

"That is weak talk," he scorned. "I've never been so disappointed. One as un-compelling as you could not lead us. Ye don't commit yourself. I've asked ye twice now and you have side-stepped me. No. Away with ye!"

Meklon abruptly planted his stick before Crankford. "Give Galen a chance to speak to you and to all the men. Hear what is inside of him and then decide if you still wish to dismiss him."

Crankford looked delighted at the challenge. "Speak!" he declared. "Convince us to follow you."

I met Meklon's gaze with great apprehension. I wasn't prepared for this; I didn't know what to say.

Meklon, however, held my uneasy gaze without wavering the strength of his own as he instructed, "In the strongest words and voice you possess, commit yourself to these men."

I understood and accepted emphatically that I had to do this. Without hesitation I found the nearest wooden bench and stood upon it. My greatest fear was that I knew my father would be watching me from some unseen corner of the tavern. I could not worry what he thought, nor of the thoughts of Crankford, who stood with his arms skeptically folded, because I stood not in defense of myself but in defense of this kingdom.

The easiest words which first came to my lips were, "My name is Galen." Then my mind ceased to aid my cause. I swallowed thickly. I grasped for the right thought to lead my words on. "I have heard that Multa is going to feign peace to lure us to lower our defenses. But it is a trap that you and I must not fall prey to. The nobles may, the knights may, but we must not for the sake of saving this kingdom. Because this kingdom is worth…" I paused as I thought of the castle graveyard. With all my spirit rising to the cause, I restated strongly, "Because this great kingdom founded upon truth, freedom, and unfailing love was deemed so worthy that some of the greatest men gave their lives for its protection and preservation. Not because they were promoters of dominance, but because they were great defenders of peace and freedom. These noble men were our fathers, grandfathers, and great grandfathers — men of honor, men of sacrifice, and men of courage. It is because of them that we have lived in peace for so long. Let it be said that it was because of us that the next generations are free and founded on goodness and truth. Forbid that we would ever fight for the glory of war or dominance. But let it be declared that we will valiantly defend our homes, our families, and all that is good, noble, and just in the world. So, yes, I will defend our kingdom with you. I will serve in your cause because I would be ashamed if I did not give as much as my forefathers freely gave. I will not let their sacrifices have been made in vain."

Hollers of agreement burst forth so exuberantly that the old tavern shook. Through all the raised fists, I sought to know Meklon's response. My heart thudded with this success when I found his entire countenance radiate with pride. In the moment, I was so encouraged that I scanned the crowd in hopes that I might find my father similarly affected.

Such an imagined face never appeared. However, Crankford, like Meklon, beamed as he unfolded his arms, now waving them to hush the crowd so that he could speak. "Now this is the leader I was seeking! What are ye waiting for, men? I haven't trained you to be cowards. Pledge your alliance to the champion. Swear that whatever he says, you will follow. I'll vow it first." Crankford made a big ceremony of his pledge and then proclaimed, "Galen, you have yourself an army! What will you have your men do first?"

Having their allegiance, I boldly answered exactly what was necessary. "It cannot be denied that throughout the Multa Wars our army highly revered the Book of Truth. Its applied principles were a large part of our kingdom's victory because truth trains the heart of an army which is just as important as training the body. I, therefore, propose classes to be set up for the learning of both the Book of Truth and for combat."

Crankford spat, "No, no, we will not waste time on old fools' learning."

I assured, "It is a tried and proven way."

Not deeming my advice worth further comment, he jumped up on the bench alongside me to direct his own orders, proclaiming, "The champion will teach us combat and defense."

Their plans were pointless, even helpful to our enemy, if they would not let the truth be taught. They were not following me at all—not until they heeded the truth. "You must listen!" I beseeched. "Or do you deem your own forefathers as fools for having bestowed their trust in the Book of Truth?"

They roared back, "Teach us to fight!"

As their voices became too much a force to speak through, I sadly whispered, "Then start with a stick."

I was about to step down from the bench in defeat, when I saw my father. Curious, I remained in my elevated position to watch him. His face was as unreadable as stone while he walked through the men, nearing with every step to where Crankford and I stood. Not once did he lift his eyes; however, once he stood directly before Crankford, his gaze lifted to him, and his voice commanded, "Quiet your men; I wish to speak."

"Quiet, quiet!" Crankford demanded and gestured with

his hands. When there was a reasonable quiet, Crankford looked down upon my father from his elevated height. "Is that to your satisfaction?"

My father nodded and then raised his voice, "In one night, I am witness to your honorable vows to follow Galen until your dying breath, and then I witnessed you turn and disregard his proposal to heed the Book of Truth. Are you unstable doubleminded men? Do you make meaningless vows as an example to your kingdom? It is because you desire to be noble men that I keep you accountable. And it is because I desire for you to live in peace that I plead with you to listen to whom you have wisely pledged yourselves to, for you were right to deem Galen worthy. For I know that he will serve you. I know that he will fight for you. I know that he will place you before himself. So again I plead, listen to Galen if you want a chance at saving your kingdom and your families from Multa's brutality. It is your choice what sort of army you will be."

When my father ended, he raised eyes of respect to me. I was so humbled that I could scarcely hold mine up to meet his.

"Did I say that I would not follow him?" Crankford replied indignantly. "Of course I will honor my vow. I was merely advising. Not commanding. Do not confuse the two. I will not be misrepresented. Classes shall be arranged, I assure—" Crankford paused as his eyes shrewdly moved from my father to me. "The two of you look strangely alike."

My father replied immovably, "He is my son. Hear him."

This time my father's proud claim caused my eyes and my heart to rise to him.

I found myself also affirming, "He is my father." But as the act of speaking proved the sudden unsteadiness of my emotions, I stepped down from the bench, pushed my way through the men, and left the tavern.

A steep alleyway provided a place away from public view. Quickly, I jogged up the hill. I told myself I would gain just enough fresh air to strengthen my demeanor before I returned to face my father.

At the top, the alley turned into a flat dirt lane, hugging the mountain on one side and collecting a few peasant cottages on the other. I was vaguely aware of the moonlit charm of the place, but it held no arresting power over what I had just witnessed of my father—the strong, commanding man who had proudly claimed me as his son. His look of respect and his words repeated in my mind. While I tried to think beyond them, even doubt them, I could not. I could only think of my father and how he had defended me.

Ahead in the dark, another lone figure walked this way. I dropped my head low, but as we neared, curiosity caused me to glance up. The person was a woman. However, when she saw me, so immediately did she turn and flee back toward the cottages that I did not gain a good sight of her.

Her sudden change of course was baffling. I hoped I had not frightened her. To not alarm her further, I made sure not to look in the way she had gone; nonetheless, the incident clung to me. Again and again, I tried to conjure what the woman looked like. Perhaps a braid or perhaps the hair had been loose and fell free on one side. It was unfortunate that the moonlight had favored me and left her ambiguous, because what was most curious was that she had not run away until after she had seen my face.

"Galen," my father called out.

Realizing that he must have followed me, I inhaled deeply through my thickening throat and bravely turned back to meet him. We both slowly closed the distance between us until we faced one another.

Neither of us spoke. However, it was evident that we were each heavily weighed down with a load of unspoken words.

Feeling my own guilt for having left him at the tavern, I acknowledged, "I am sorry I left so abruptly. You… did me a great kindness."

"Do not apologize, Galen!" he replied intensely. "It is I who has wronged you since before you were born and every day after."

Emotion tempted to fail me again, and I turned away.

"Lydia," I whispered shakenly, trying to change the subject until I could manage it better. "She came to you?"

"Yes."

"Have you heard…" my voice failed. I tried again. "Have you heard that she was murdered?"

"I have not," he stated without emotion.

I was frustrated at his lack of sympathy toward her loss. "Are you that indifferent to her?" I questioned.

"No," he responded. "If you wish to know what I thought of her, I will tell you plainly that she was the one who shone truth back into my life which had been missing for so long. My debt to her is insurmountable."

"Then she was the reason you left Dresden?" I asked.

"Yes, but you were the reason that I did not turn back."

I stared at him, forcibly blinking away all that I was feeling to ensure that I was equally meeting his composure.

"What has Breemore told you of me?" he hard-pressed.

My eyes stung with shame at the thought of saying my

father's offenses aloud. I shook my head, preferring to leave his wrongdoings behind us rather than to speak of them to his face.

He provoked, "Tell me! No matter how vile."

Reluctantly, I gave answer. "Breemore told me that you... so fell in love with a woman that you lost yourself, and when your brother came after you, you were so angry that you pushed him to his death. And when Breemore found —"

My father interrupted, "I vow I did not push Thomas. I flung away his touch, but I never, in all my life, laid one of my hands against my brother. It was by not heeding his poor health condition and not listening to him that I caused his death. When I saw him fall, I gave the substance of all my being trying to save him."

As I listened, I found myself believing my father without hesitation and softening toward him with every word that he spoke.

"Now," he continued, "finish saying what Breemore told you. I want everything to be known to you just as it happened."

Curious to know whether this next part was true, I carried on, "When Breemore found you, you commanded him to stage your death and promised that you would never return."

My father straightened. "That is not wholly true either. Breemore did find me, and I did indeed want to die, but I had no thought of running away until Breemore placed the thought within me. Once he did, my guilt swallowed the idea whole, and I sold myself to Breemore's poisonous suggestion that turned my life into a failure. I am before you now because I began to worry that the same might happen to you."

His eyes had been dry up to this point, but now the waves of his heart swelled over. "Galen, I see that you have not failed as I have. Listen to me." His voice was tense and gripping. I listened with every portion of my being that could absorb my father's voice. "For generations, it has been said from Trimont father to Trimont son, 'Follow me as I follow the truth.' But I say to you, Galen Thomas Trimont, I shall follow you as you follow the truth." My father humbly bowed his head before me.

Stunned and so completely powerless to any longer control the store of my heart, tears and words rushed forth together. "I now see that I could have no greater honor than being called your son."

My father set his hands upon my shoulders and affirmed, "You are my son, and you are a true son of Trimont."

For the first time, we embraced. The moment was fuller than ever I imagined as one of the deepest treasures of my heart was obtained—my father.

After a moment, we each held ourselves back at arms' length before letting the other go. Our tears dried into lighter countenances. I realized we had a lifetime of topics and experiences to talk about. There were endless questions I could ask about sword fighting and of my mother...

"You must see your mother," I exclaimed. "She waits to see you in the carriage."

His face clouded. "It has been over twenty-five years, Galen, and each day that I chose to never return, I wounded her. I made her mourn for me instead of bringing her comfort. I brought her shame instead of honor. I abandoned her instead of supporting her. I lied instead of confessed. I mocked everything she taught me. I have done her more wrong than ever any son did to his mother. How do I face that, and yet I must. Indeed, I must!"

He briskly began to descend down the alley. I promptly matched his pace and walked back with him.

As the carriage came into sight, severe distress plagued my father's face. He markedly slowed when he saw Meklon, Braun, and Hildie standing just outside the carriage door as Vala stepped down from the carriage step. Braun and Hildie reverently bowed to my father, but he gave heed only to the face of his mother. The rest of the world in that moment was lost to him.

She took tender steps toward him, but he backed away, pronouncing, "Do not come any nearer. I am not worthy to be called your son."

My grandmother simply smiled and continued to approach him. With beautiful tears streaming down her cheeks, she took his rough, hardened face within her hands and joyfully claimed, "You were dead, but now you are alive. You were lost, and now you are found. Yet most of all, you are my son, whom I love."

His face softened like a child as he lowered his face into the basin of her hands and allowed himself to be washed in the pureness of her touch.

I looked up to the heavens, inwardly thanking Lydia for this measureless gift which she had sacrificed to give to us all. "I wish you were here," I whispered.

Meklon came to my side. "We have not failed, Galen. We have not failed."

Chapter Forty
~ *Phelia* ~

We have not failed, I repeated in my heart as I wiped away my blurring tears so that I would not miss any part of this perfect moment of reconciliation. Though I carefully kept myself hidden, I had secretly witnessed every part since the startling moment I had seen Galen on the mountain lane. I felt I had been blessed with the role of an angel.

When Galen raised his eyes to the heavens for a second time, I lifted mine with his. If our hands could not touch, our hearts already had, for even separately, our hearts had become one toward the truth.

I would trust Cloven to reveal that I was alive when the proper time had come.

THE JOURNEY CONTINUES…

Trimont Trilogy

~ book three ~

In progress…

A Note from the Author

Hearing from my readers is immensely encouraging. I would love to hear from you and personally connect. Feel free to reach me at:

JessicaMarinos.com

Facebook.com/TraivensPass

Many thanks!
Jessica Marinos